RILEY

With a harsh childhood behind him, Riley left school with little in the way of knowledge but brimful of optimism, and secure in the knowledge that one of his teachers, Fred Beardsley, had faith in him. Fred and his wife Louise ran into Riley while they were on their honeymoon in Paris. Riley said he'd been offered a 'position' at The Little Palace Theatre in Fellburn which Fred and Louise suspected was that of a dogsbody, but it later became clear to them that Riley had actually been appointed assistant stage-manager. And then he surprised them by forming a close friendship with the leading lady, Nyrene Forbes-Mason. Over the subsequent years, Fred and Louise observed with amazement the rise to fame and fortune of this remarkable lad. As for his relationship with Nyrene, that did indeed change; although the manner in which it progressed was not quite as Riley had planned.

RILEY

Catherine Cookson

CHIVERS PRESS
BATH

First published 1998
by
Bantam Press
This Large Print edition published by
Chivers Press
by arrangement with
Transworld Publishers Ltd
2000

ISBN 0 7540 2235 8

British Library Cataloguing in Publication Data available

Printed and bound in Great Britain by
REDWOOD BOOKS, Trowbridge, Wiltshire

PROLOGUE

CHAPTER ONE

Miss Louise Barrington locked the last drawer of her desk, smoothed the clean sheet of blotting paper into the large pad, straightened the letter rack, placed the pencil holder across the corner of the desk, then sat back in the leather swivel chair and let out a long slow breath.

She had come into this room in January as a temporary science teacher at Giles Mentor School. The only female teacher in the science block, she was responsible for the discipline of the girls, whereas Mr Beardsley, the senior science man, was responsible for the boys, both being answerable to the headmaster. Before dabbling in industry she had taught chemistry in an all-girls' school, which secured her this position, although not without some comments from the permanent staff; and as such positions went it was an excellent one. Yet here she was contemplating another move because, as she kept telling herself, anything would be better than putting up with the type of child that now attended this school. Until the change to a comprehensive it had been a boys' grammar school, the children now attending being mostly from the lower end of the town. But then, she knew that her outlook was jaundiced.

There was a strange quiet about the room, about the whole place now, for today they had broken up for the summer holidays. 'Have a good holiday,' she had been wished by an associate here and there, others adding 'down south' as though down south were as distant as Hong Kong.

Well, she had now said all her goodbyes, except to Mr Beardsley. Oh . . . Mr Beardsley.

She turned to look towards the open window for she could hear that man's unmistakable voice.

She rose and went to the side of the window and from her first-floor position looked down to where the iron railings guarded the cellar steps to the boilerhouse; and there she saw Mr Beardsley and the Riley boy. Their conversation floated up to her on the still afternoon air.

'You've seen the Head, then?'

'Yes, Mr Beardsley.'

'Well, I trust you took in all his advice.'

'No, Mr Beardsley. As you always say, it never gets far enough into one ear to come out the other.'

'Watch it! Watch it! Riley; you're not out of the gates yet. You know something, Riley? I've always wanted to say this to you: I've never come to terms with the fact that you're not a Catholic. With a name like Riley and your dad and your ma as Irish as they come, you're *still* not a Catholic. Oh, if only you had been you could have gone to St Joseph's. But then, Riley, why should I have it in for the nuns? They've never done me any harm, and had you been there you would've had their habits off them in a flash. Ah, ah! Not the way you think, Riley. And get that grin off your face! But they would've given up their vocation just to be free of you. And yet, you know, I've heard they're a tough lot. Anyway, Riley, this is the parting of the ways; and you know something? It is a desire of my life, a really deep desire, that I never set eyes on you again, not in this world or the next. On the other hand, your mother seems to be a sensible and

4

caring woman, at least so it seemed the day I took your pants down and scudded your arse.'

Miss Louise Barrington winced.

'You didn't play any more tricks on me after that, did you? But you went home and cried to your dad, and he came, all five-foot three-inches of him, and said he meant to knock the bloody daylights out of me. Your mother followed, hard on his heels, and after practically beating him up with her tongue she thanked me ... yes, she did, yes, she did, to take your pants down whenever I felt so inclined and to wallop you until you couldn't sit.'

'Me ma's daft; she's up the pole half the time.'

'But she comes down to tend to you and your dad, doesn't she? And the other three brats she's trying to bring up. I don't know why she does it. Myself, I'd wallop the lot of you.'

'Well, she tries her hand at that at times. You know nowt about her, really. But you, you're a funny man, Mr Beardsley.'

'Funny, am I?'

'Aye, me da says you could be Irish yourself and a Catholic.'

'Oh, isn't it a pity I'm not either. The things I could have done if I'd been Irish and a Catholic, whereas all I do now is try to teach you and your like to be civilised and not to beat up lads half your size.'

'I don't. I don't pick 'em half me size.'

'You did when you first came here.'

'I did a lot of things when I first came here, Mr Beardsley, that I didn't do afore I came here; I learnt them here.'

There was such a long pause that Miss Louise Barrington edged nearer the curtain and more to the side. Yes, they were still there but were now just staring at each other.

'Ah! Now that was a straight answer. That was from the part that I know is there in your napper, and if you had any sense you would have taken advantage of it all these past years, because I know and you know that you're no fool, Riley. Your main aim in life seems to be to make people laugh, not at your expense, but at theirs. Now I'm going to tell you something. You have the gift of a sense of humour, but with you it's misdirected. You've become a practical joker; and you know the only one who gets any fun out of a practical joke is the practical joker. The receiver has to grin and bear it, has to laugh or smile because a practical joker demands an audience and there's always an audience for him. Now, Riley, if you take my advice you could become something big in the funny business. Try turning that sense of humour on yourself. Try belittling yourself in describing an incident that might have happened to you, make it funny because it's happening against you, not against the other fella. That will make them laugh. Think of the comedians who've risen to the top. They're not the ones who blow their own horns; they always come onto the stage looking forlorn, asking for your pity because they're simple or daft or things have happened to them that wouldn't happen to those looking on. You can always enjoy somebody else's pain, especially if it's done through somebody making it funny, and it can be funny, pain, you know.'

Miss Louise Barrington was now standing with her back to the curtain, not looking down but with her head cocked. He had that boy weighed up all right; he was indeed a practical joker, and there were children who were afraid of him. Her head jerked slightly again as she heard Mr Beardsley saying:

'Think on it, Riley: it would be a better life being a comedian on the stage, wouldn't it, than getting nicked for pinching cars or radios out of cars? How you got out of that last car business God alone knows, and He won't split on you; and your dad wouldn't split on you, nor his cronies, nor the patrons of the Bull and Spear, not even your mother would do so this time. But you did do it, *you did it* and the police know you did it: you were seen there and there were witnesses and the car went up in flames, but they couldn't lay it on you, could they?'

'No, Mr Beardsley, 'cos they haven't got me fingerprints.'

'Oh, my hands itch to reach out to your lugs, Riley. Every so often I have this awful itch in the palms: they're crying out to make contact with your ears now. Anyway, as I said, we won't be meeting again. At least make it your business that we don't meet, eh?'

'I'll try, Mr Beardsley; and mind I'm not saying this off me own bat. What I'm gonna say me ma says I have to say, and that's ... ta. But as I see it I'm saying ta for havin' me bloody ears boxed, havin' me face pushed into the wet grass 'cos you think you see a foul, havin' me stay behind and you sit lookin' at me without uttering a word for almost half an hour, driving me up the wall; and lastly, for losing your toes in my backside so often. What've I got to say ta for? But anyway ... well, she said I had to say ta.'

7

In the ensuing silence Miss Louise Barrington edged her face slowly round the curtain again and saw, to her amazement, the two figures shaking hands; and then the boy running from the teacher, jumping into the air and punching at it. She watched until he had disappeared through the iron gates before returning to her chair and sitting down.

Really! Really! He was the most strange man. So far there had been little contact between them except in the Head's office, or at a parents' meeting, at which times he became a different person, one whose actions and speech being those of a gentleman. It was as if he had come from some quality stock. However, this was not apparent when he was dealing with the pupils, for his bawling alone could frighten some of them. But what a strange conversation he'd had with that boy; at moments you could imagine him being as rough as the culprit.

Well, she would go round her laboratory and see that everything was in order before she left the building to the caretakers, and she could only hope that she didn't return after the holidays and find half the place had been ransacked or the school burnt down, something that happened all the time.

After closing the window she took a light dustcoat from the back of the door before opening it, only to step into the arms of the man she had been musing about.

'Oh. Oh, I was just about to knock on your door,' he said.

'You want something, Mr Beardsley?'

'No, I just thought I would wish you a happy holiday.'

'Oh, thank you.' She smiled now as she added, 'I'm glad you didn't add "down south".'

'Oh, have you had a lot of that today?'

'Quite a bit.'

'The great divide still remains unfortunately.'

They were walking down the corridor when she remarked, 'Isn't it pleasant . . . the quiet?'

'You like that?' He was glancing sideways at her.

'Yes, don't you?'

'No: I'm afraid of this kind of quiet. In a school, I like the hullabaloo.' She now caught his glance and from the look in his eye she was waiting for him to say, If quietness is what you were after you're in the wrong job, but what he said was, 'At the meeting the other night I was sitting behind you. You were talking to Florrie . . . Miss Quail, and you mentioned that you were interested in an amusing book about a man who rode on a bicycle out into the country every weekend to see, I suppose, his girlfriend, but you said you had forgotten the author's name and couldn't recall it. And Miss Quail, although she seems to have read everything from Horace to the *Hotspur* during her long active life, couldn't put her finger on it either. Well, I thought then, it might be Cooper.'

'Oh.' She turned to him, her face bright. 'Yes, that's him. Yes, that's him, and he wrote a sequel to it. I don't actually remember what either of the novels was about, only that I was very amused by them at the time of reading. But it's many years ago and age may have altered my taste.'

He nodded towards her as he said, 'Oh, yes, your extreme age could have altered your taste all right.'

He was being gallant. This was the charming side she had earlier been warned about by Miss Elder

9

and Miss Turner, who had seen them exchanging a few words about her syllabus. They had laughingly implied that he was immune to all female wiles, even admitting that they themselves had tried it on, but to no avail. She had never enquired into his past as it was of no interest to her, but she was given to understand that he had been married and then divorced, all within a short time.

'Would you like to come and pick it up?'

'What?'

'I said would you like to come and pick the book up, it's in my room?'

'Oh. Oh yes, thank you.'

She was ushered into a space not much larger than a cupboard, with books tumbling from the shelves, others heaped on the floor in the corner. She was gazing around her in amazement when he said, 'Oh, I can see you've never been in here before; this is my cubby hole ... *sanctum sanctorum*. It was the storeroom, and I confiscated it some years ago. Sit down for a minute.' He pulled a chair away from a small battered-looking school desk and slowly she sat down, only needing to turn her head slightly to be on a level with a row of books, all dealing with mathematics.

She turned to him and said, 'Why so many maths books?'

'Oh, I read mathematical physics for finals. It was a toss-up which way I went.'

Then he surprised her by asking, 'How old are you? Thirty-seven, is it?'

She took in a short breath before replying, 'Thirty-five.'

'Thirty-five. That makes the division between us greater still, I'm forty-eight. By the way, I hate

10

drinking alone. I have a number of unleashed vices, I know, but this one I've kept at bay: I don't drink unless I'm in company, otherwise I'd be an alcoholic by now.'

He had been sitting on the top of small library steps. He now stepped down and, lifting the lid of the little desk, he took out a bottle, a glass, and a cup and saucer, and arrayed them along the flat top of the desk. Then dropping down the lid, he held the bottle towards her as he said, 'Illegal, and not allowed on the premises. But I break the law twice a year: at summer-holiday time and at Christmas. Do you like port?' Then without waiting for her answer, he poured out a glassful and handed it to her.

She hesitated for a moment before accepting it. She could hear her mother's voice like the twanging of a thin violin string as she warned, 'When you go into company, Louise, never never choose port; it's the common woman's drink, port. It's as much as I can bear to hear Mrs Saunders talking about her previous night's doings and always bringing in her port and lemon. Never ask for port. Anyway it isn't a lady's drink at all, it's what gentlemen have after dinner.' Well, her mother should have known what gentlemen had after dinner if anybody should, because in order to keep up with his wife her dear papa had played the gentleman so much that he was bankrupt before she herself was ten years old.

'You know the best pick-me-up for the dumps, the blues, or when you go looking for a bridge high enough to jump off?'

'No.'

'Brandy and port mixed. Yes, brandy and port

11

mixed. Of course, only in moderate quantities, and generally to be taken last thing at night. For medicinal purposes, you know.'

And she smiled as she agreed, 'Oh yes, for medicinal purposes.'

He had a deep thundery-sounding laugh; and now he was holding his cup out towards her, and as she touched it with her glass he said, 'To a most refreshing holiday.'

She did not offer any reply, only inclined her head and sipped at the port. It had a pleasant taste, almost like a liqueur. Fancy! She was thirty-five and had never before tasted port.

'Where are you going? Home?' he asked.

'Not exactly. I no longer have a home as such. My parents are dead and I've only one sister. I make my home with her and her husband and three children when I need to, and more often than not we spend our holidays together, but we haven't decided yet where we are going this year.' She took another sip from the port, then asked, 'Do you go home?'

'No, there's no central point left. But where does your sister live?'

'In Rye.'

'Oh Rye. I know that well. Years ago I had two or three holidays there boating from the harbour. Nice little town Rye, very interesting. Then there's Winchelsea and Hastings. I don't see why you would want to go further for a holiday.'

'Nor do I at times, but they want a change and the children do too.'

Here he was, bending over her with a bottle in his hand now. 'Let me put a drop more in that glass.'

She pulled the glass towards her saying, 'Oh no. Oh no.'

'Come on, come on. Look, if you can't stand I'll help you out of the car and leave you on the doorstep of your flat.'

'Oh really! But . . . but I'm not used to drinking port.' She did not add, or any other form of alcohol.

'What are you used to?' He was now topping up his cup; then he sat down on the steps again, repeating, 'I said, what are you used to?'

'Well, maybe a glass of sherry now and again.'

'Just now and again?'

'Yes,' she emphasised, 'just now and again, Mr Beardsley.'

'OK, Miss Barrington.' He had assumed her tone; then he laughed and went on, 'You know, I often wonder why I'm not a secret drinker because my father was, and many other things as well; High Church man, too.'

'Really?' She was smiling at his frankness. She felt relaxed, rather warm inside. Of course it was a warm day.

'Do you mean you're surprised at him being a High Church man and a potential alcoholic?'

This was the sort of argumentative question adopted by some people to get you going and at the moment she didn't feel up to answering him one way or the other, and so she said simply, 'I wasn't differentiating.'

'Oh.' He was laughing again, and at her; and he now took almost a gulp from the cup and wiped the beads of sweat from his forehead before he said, 'My father, you know, was a man who always said there should be moderation in all things. Now,

13

when people emphasise a statement like that, bet your life that nine times out of ten it's a cover-up, and it was in his case. Huh, moderation! There had been fourteen of us: three were born dead, four died before they were twenty. That left seven: my three older brothers, two older sisters, me and then'—he gave a little toss to his head now as he said—'Gwendoline. Moderation in all things. If he had had his way there would have been twenty, but Mother potched him by dying. Oh, he gave her a great send-off and he himself gave the oration from the pulpit.'

'You didn't like your father?'

'No, I didn't like my father, Miss Barrington, and I make no bones about it. Yet'—he turned his head to the side and looked up at the racks of unevenly stacked books—'it's only at times when I unbury him, and it isn't when I've imbibed my refresher'— he held the cup up towards her—'no, it's generally following some event, and a while ago I had a last exchange with my arch-enemy Riley. Oh, you'll know about Riley, everybody does. I suppose it revealed more clearly to me life's incongruities. There's Riley, he's a bully of sorts and he's from a poor family. His father is incapacitated with a bad back, although his wife doesn't believe him; she says he's work-shy. There's another three besides him, all girls. Yet, as a boy I would have swapped places with him any day, work-shy dad an' all, because in our rambling domain up in the hills, under my father, we, in comparison, led a hell of a life. So much so that I wasn't the only one among us who thought those who had died young were the lucky ones, because we all knew about his secret tippling, and also that he followed, to the letter, be

14

fruitful and multiply and replenish the human race and subdue it, which he did by subduing my mother into a pregnancy each year. And subduing is the word . . . Oh, don't look like that, my dear. I'm terribly sorry, I'm boring you to death.'

'Oh no. No, please no, you're not boring me to death. It's very odd, it's very odd.' She now looked down into her almost empty glass and her voice was just a mutter as she said, 'As you feel about your father I . . . I do about my mother.'

'No! Really?'

'Yes, yes really. My sister and I were stifled by middle-class snobbery. But . . . but go on. Please, Mr Beardsley, go on.' Her head was bobbing now towards him and she was smiling. 'Tell me more about your family.'

'Oh, there's not much more to tell, except that we all got out as quickly as possible after Mother died. One brother went to Hong Kong. He's done pretty well for himself. Two in Australia have done even better. They have a ranch out there, breaking in horses. As for the girls . . . oh, you could say one married well and one didn't. One married into the upper class, the other married a man who wore a belt around his trousers.'

As he laughed she thought, There he goes again, but she didn't mind. No, she didn't mind in the least. She had never seen him in this light. He was different.

'But I'd like to bet Lucy is happier than May,' he was saying. 'He is a very good chap, is Robbie.' He pursed his lips before continuing, 'You know, you're having a very strange effect on me, Miss Barrington, because I can take four drinks and never feel warm. Now here I am talking to you

15

about my family. Now that is strange, because I never talk about it except to a member of it. And I was on the point of telling you about Gwendoline. Now, that is a strange story.'

'Why? What is the matter with her? Is she ill in some way?'

'No. Oh no; far from it.'

She was waiting for him to go on, but when he remained silent, she asked softly, 'Is she married?'

'Married? Oh no ... well now, I say no, in the official sense Gwendoline isn't married, but in another sense Gwendoline has been married many, many, many times. You look puzzled. Oh well, you would be; and you would like to ask what she does for a living, wouldn't you?'

'Huh!' she said; then in a laughing voice, 'Yes, please.'

And then he answered her, saying, 'Well, putting it plainly, she is on the streets.'

The silly smile left her face and her body stiffened slightly: he was saying that his sister was a prostitute, saying it openly like that.

'Now you're shocked.'

'Oh no; no I'm not shocked. Surprised, yes, but not shocked, no.'

'I'm glad. I'm glad that ...' His voice had a sober sound now and his face had a sober look and, turning slightly on the top of the stool, pushing aside some books he leant his elbow on the shelf and rested his head against his hand, then, as if to himself, said, 'Oh yes, she was a lovely girl was Gwendoline. Beautiful, beautiful inside and out, and she had an abundance of charm, her main desire in life being to give although not to just one ... well, one man, no. She must have known

16

from the beginning that it would be fatal to get married and that she didn't need to shop around . . . oh no; they came after her like bees to the hive. And, of course, that didn't please dear Papa. She was his last child and he wanted to possess her; and she knew this, so what did she do? As soon as she left school she left home. She had it all arranged and, being Gwendoline, she didn't leave alone; and when he heard with whom she had gone off and he threatened to ruin the man, what did she do? She came back home; and there we were, the four of us and old Eliza—she had been with the family from a girl—and there stood Gwendoline in the dining-room doorway. Eliza had just served dinner, and we just gaped. The lads were about to jump up when my father cried at them "Stay!" and for a moment we stayed and stared at the beautifully dressed creature as she said to us, "Hello there, troop!" Then turning to her father, she added, "If you dare to lift one finger against John or his business I will expose you from the pulpit of the church, that very pulpit from which you spout so much pomposity. And what'll I tell them when I stand up there? I'll tell them that I've gone on the streets or I shall be shortly, because I'll not be long with John. John isn't the first, by any means, Papa," she said. "Oh no; I've done it under your nose, because I'm made that way: I want to give, not get and grab and fill with fear, and live a false life, like you have. And I'll ask the congregation what they think their deacon got up to on his visits to York? It certainly wasn't to attend a quarterly solicitors' meeting. I'll ask them where the money came from to help Mary Addison's family to go to live in London. Well . . .

well, who knows? She may have taken up my profession or I've taken up hers, one or the other. Only you could tell, dear Papa."

'When he sprang to the fireplace and grabbed up the poker we were on him, the two lads and I, and Eliza had to get Gwendoline out. We often talk about that day, she and I.' He was nodding towards her, but she remained silent. She couldn't believe what she was hearing, and that it was Mr Beardsley who was telling it. It was as if he was dragging up some dark secret from the depths of him.

'Say something.'

'I . . . I don't know what to say.'

'Well, ask me why I'm spilling the beans at this time, because I'm not tight; it takes more than two large ports to push me over the border. I'm asking you because if I asked myself, "Why the devil am I talking to her like this?" I'd have to search for the answer bit by bit. I might tell myself, "Perhaps it's because she's a reticent person, and, as I am myself at the moment, rather lonely." Gwendoline would have made it clear in two shakes of a lamb's tail and in a few words. She wouldn't beat around the bush as I'm doing. She would be able to tell me the real reason I am opening up an old sore.'

She found herself draining her glass, and when she leant forward and placed it on the desk, he said, 'I'm not going to offer you any more. Two's enough for a starter on port, oh yes.'

She didn't come back at him and say, I wouldn't have accepted another. But what she did say was, 'Is your sister . . . I mean . . . is she still alive?'

'And kicking, and well-to-do. We see each other whenever we can, and always in the best hotels, let me tell you, or at her flat; but I prefer not to go

18

there because I don't want to be the one to recognise Lord So-and-So or Sir Somebody-else. Oh yes,'—he nodded—'you look surprised: there's nothing but the best for Gwendoline. They call them boyfriends or girlfriends today, but she'll put the real name to her end of the bargain: mistress; and mind you, she's forty-six. She was mistress to one particularly well-known man for ten years, and since he died three years ago I don't probe.'

They now sat looking at each other in silence, and he may have been surprised if he could have read her thoughts because she was asking herself if she herself had ever lived. And the answer was no; and yet once she had thought she was about to start living in a month's time. That was some years ago. How many? Eight, nine? Eight and a half. She was twenty-six then. They had been engaged for three years, and there was only a month to go before the wedding when he told her that he was uneasy inside about their future: he didn't know if he was ready to settle down. And oh no! What a suggestion to make: he wouldn't dream of asking her to live with him. What would their friends think, and his mother, not forgetting Father Ramshaw; and marriage, you know, in the Catholic Church, was not to be taken lightly. His mother hadn't recognised divorce and he shared her opinion.

She could visualise him standing before her, and asking herself why she had ever loved him. Yes, she knew his mother did not believe in divorce, which was why his poor father had to continue to give her a generous allowance and as a result to work all hours that God sent to keep his new family going. And she remembered asking herself why she hadn't

19

before seen him as an image of his mother. She had realised at times that he was pi about so many things, but she had overlooked this side of his character. No-one was perfect; and so, on looking back, his jilting of her hadn't been as painful as it might have been had she been passionately in love with him. So why was it that she had to act as she did and stupefy him into amazement by first slapping his face, both sides, then screaming at him as she hit him with a vase. After she had seen the blood pouring from his brow, her mind had gone into a state of confusion, and her father had held her in his arms and rocked her as if she were a child again, while her mother attended to her battered suitor. What had followed after, they said, had been a minor breakdown, followed by a number of temporary teaching jobs, until she had found a position in industry. But now here she was sitting in this cluttered room with this man, he who had altered out of all appearance from how she had seen him and viewed him over these past months.

He was holding her hand and saying, 'Are you all right? I'm an absolute fool. I've disturbed you by talking as I have. I don't know what came over me; I'm so sorry.'

'Please . . . please, don't say you're sorry. You've done something for me.'

'Yes?'

His face was close to hers now and she nodded, saying, 'Yes, you've opened up an old sore and scraped it clean . . . Good Lord! Now I'm using some of your metaphors,' and she smiled at him.

'Oh, my metaphors. They must bore people to death.'

'They've worked in my case.'

'I won't say I couldn't imagine you having an old sore, because I think that you have and if I, as you say, have scraped it clean, I'm more than pleased; and so I say our drinking has not been in vain.'

He pulled the steps closer towards her and seating himself again, he said, 'When are you off?'

'Tomorrow, sometime.'

'Same here.'

'Have . . . have you anything planned?'

'Not really, not booked. I usually travel, but this year I think I'll keep to southern Europe. I've only myself to please, so sometimes I walk and sometimes I indulge in a good hotel near a nice beach and swim and do a bit of boating and such.'

They were looking straight into each other's eyes now when he asked, 'Have you ever been in love?' and to this she answered, 'Yes, at least I thought I was for four years.'

'Were you married?'

'No, but I was about to be.'

'And you changed your mind?'

'No, he did.'

'The stupid bugger.'

It was she who first let out the peal of laughter; then, as if reluctantly, he joined her. She was wiping her eyes when he asked softly, 'How long ago was this?'

'Oh . . . seven, eight years ago. Something like that.'

'And you've kept it buried all this time?'

She looked thoughtful for a moment before she said, 'Yes, I suppose you could say that.'

'Well, I know how that feels; I did the same.'

Her mouth fell into a slight gape before she said,

21

'I can't imagine you brooding.'

'Well, no'—he smiled wryly now—'I didn't exactly brood, but I nearly went along the line for my reaction.'

'You mean, went to prison?'

'Exactly. We were married for four years. We were said to be young and foolish. But I've never really felt young in my life, nor foolish. I had the example of my parents not to follow, so I went the other way: I was too considerate, too kind, too trusting; and, you know, I was only three hours earlier than she expected when I returned home from London, and there they were. I'd gone upstairs quietly. I had a special present for her and I thought she'd be resting. She had been off-colour, rather fragile, couldn't be touched, waited on, and fussed about, yes, and she required a lot of sleep. But, to put it bluntly what they were doing at that moment needed a lot of energy.'

When her head went down he said, 'I'm sorry,' but she brought it up swiftly, saying, 'Don't be. Please don't be. Go on.'

'You know something? My heart actually stopped beating. Really stopped beating. I think if it had gone on for another few seconds like that I'd have had brain damage. Sure I would. Well, I must have had it for a time because what I did to that fellow and her was nobody's business. Yes, and her. By the way, he wasn't my best friend or anything, not even known to me in any way; I'd never seen him in my life before, but he turned out to be an old flame of hers, one of her first. Well, my last act towards them was to get them by the hair—there was nothing else to get hold of—and drag them down the stairs and throw them out of the house.'

'Oh, you didn't!' She was shaking her head.

'Oh, I did. I did. I tell you, my heart had stopped and it must have affected my brain for a time, but yes, I threw them both outside. Fortunately for them there was a bit of a garden with an iron railing at the end and it was nearly dusk, but it wasn't a warm day, and both Mrs Bradley on the one side and Mrs Newbank on the other apparently knew what had been going on under my nose: they had been behind the curtains and they got an eyeful and, being compassionate people, they covered them up and called for an ambulance.'

'An ambulance?'

'Yes, an ambulance. His jaw was broken, he had lost a number of teeth, and he was severely bruised about the body. I can't remember whether they were done by my feet or my hands. As for her, well, poor dear, she couldn't see out of her eyes for some days, and she had a broken wrist. Oh, it was a great sensation in the papers. It even made the nationals, third page, but it made them.'

'What was the end result? I mean about you almost going to jail.'

'Oh, the police were called, naturally, and I was charged with grievous bodily harm but given bail. Then the case was quashed. I think it was his people, his wife's people . . . oh yes, he turned out to be married with four children and the family were pretty well off, being in the grocery business, and evidently they didn't want any more scandal concerning their son; but later his wife divorced him.'

'Were you living here at the time?'

'Oh no, in York. I had come down from university when I was twenty-two and I married the following year, so when I was twenty-seven or so I was free again, by which time I had sold my house and my little bookshop.' He was nodding again. 'Yes, I had a bookshop that sold nothing but books, no newspapers, cigarettes, sweets or anything else, just books. There aren't many such left today, not the small ones in side streets anyway, except for those dealing in rare volumes or antique or technical and science books. So the following six months to a year I spent the time abroad walking and seeing the places I had read about. I came back here'—he now pointed his forefinger towards the floor—'as a master and that's almost twenty years ago.'

Her words were slow and soft as she said, 'You should have been headmaster, everyone seems to think that.'

'Yes, plus me. I seem to think that too. If the old boy himself had not died but retired, I would've been.'

'From what I understand you've helped a number of boys to get on.'

'The academically inclined would have got on themselves: it's quite easy to help the bright ones. It's those like Riley that are the difficult cases; but in the end they give you more satisfaction when they come out on top in one way or another; except, of course in the art of stealing cars.' As they smiled at each other he said, 'All this talk makes me feel old. Look at my hair: it's going white.'

'No, it isn't, it's just grizzled.'

'Well, at forty-eight one can expect to be a bit grizzled—you're trying to be nice to me.'

'Yes, you could say that.'

They were again laughing together and, bending

24

towards her, he said, 'You know what I'd like above anything at this moment?'

She shook her head.

'A cup of tea.'

'Really?' Her face was one bright smile. 'So would I.'

'Well, what are we sitting here for? We can either go along to the common room and make one—there's bound to be some milk left—or we can go out and have it like civilised beings in a café. What d'you say?'

'We wouldn't be able to talk in a café.'

'No, we wouldn't; so come on.'

When he caught her hand and pulled her up her whole body resisted for a moment, not because she didn't want to go with him, but because she wanted to laugh again . . .

They sat by an open window with a small table between them and sipped at their tea. She was looking down on to the playing fields in the silence that had fallen between them when he said, 'How long is it since we bumped into each other in the corridor when you were coming out of your room?'

She looked at her watch. 'About an hour, or just over.'

'It can't be.'

She looked at her watch again, saying, 'Yes, yes I would say it's exactly an hour.'

'Your watch says that, the time says that, but to you, how long is it since we bumped into each other?'

She gazed at him, her head slightly to the side; but when she didn't speak he said, 'Does it not seem an expanse that cannot be accounted for, because during the time you call an hour I have

25

talked to you as I've talked to nobody for years, and that's the honest truth. You're the only one in this town or anywhere else who knows what dear Gwendoline does for a living; you're the only one who knows I still hate my father—his death three years ago didn't lessen my hate; you're the only one in this school to whom I have shown the other side of Grizzly Beardsley, as is my nickname. And you know, you yourself have explained the facade that you have held up like a shield, the words large-printed for all to read: this far and no further; and I think I must be the only one who has got behind the shield. Am I right?'

It was a long moment of exchanged glances before she muttered, 'Yes, yes you are right.'

'Well then, how do you really measure the time you have called an hour and in which I have come to know you and you to know me and I've still not called you Louise and you have not called me Fred?' He leaned further towards where she was sitting with her forearms on the table, the cup and saucer between her hands, and said, 'D'you know something? We'll never be the same again, you and I, after this period of unaccountable time we've just passed through. Are you with me in this?'

She made a small motion with her head as she said softly, 'Yes, yes I am with you, Fred.'

He drew in a long slow breath, then pulled his chair closer to the table so that he could lay his hands on hers, and he said, 'I am going to ask you two questions. The second one will depend upon how you answer the first. This is quite simple: will your sister and family be very upset if you don't join them for the holidays?'

She stared back into his eyes as she wondered:

would they be very upset? Yes, in a way. Yes, they would be. But why? Because her presence in the house enabled them to socialise more, leaving her to keep an eye on the two younger children, nine- and ten-year-olds. She didn't mind them; it was fifteen-year-old Susan she couldn't stand. No matter how she tried she couldn't like her niece. She had never shown it, at least she hoped she hadn't. Her sister was having a hard time with her, and her familiar response to Susan was, 'Well, you may go if Aunt Louise will go with you.' But then, which fifteen year old wants to go to a dance or such with an aunt as old as her mother? And so she said to him, 'No, they just like me to look upon their house as home. They carry on the same as usual when I'm there and,' she added without any touch of bitterness, 'spare aunts are always pliable people, you know: they can be asked to do things that one wouldn't ask of one's friends.'

'Oh, Louise. Your insight is over-keen. I think you have now already answered the second question: "Will *you* miss going and joining them for the holidays?" '

When she did not answer straightaway he raised his eyebrows in enquiry, and then she said, 'Well, in my case it all depends if I have something better to put in its place, something to fill up the time.'

She watched him bite on his lip, and when he said, 'I'm about to suggest something that could help fill up the time; but even though I now know you better than anyone else does, and that I've had the urge to know you since I first saw you, the reason why wasn't understandable even to me at first. I hadn't dared put it into words to myself until I'd been through this time-lapse with you, for I

27

know that nothing so enormous could have happened to me in just one hour. No, the seed was set a long time ago . . . well, months ago, in January of this year, and it dropped, I may tell you, on very hard and stony ground. Prepared ground, ground to resist the blossoming of any emotion. Oh yes. All emotion had to be covered by Beardsley's long tirades on this or that subject and that he had not much use for women either inside or outside the school. He was always polite to them, charming in fact, at times, especially on parents' nights, but they had been warned off by his cutting tongue. They knew just how far they could go and would warn others, as they did you, didn't they, Louise?'

'Yes, yes they did, *Fred*.' She had stressed the Fred, and they both chuckled.

'But you asked yourself, didn't you, Louise, what they could see in that grizzled fellow? He must surely be in his forties, late forties, you would say.'

'No, I didn't. I never thought that. I thought late thirties.'

'You were indeed kind. But for the moment that is going to mean all or nothing. Well, perhaps not all or nothing, but whether or not we can enter that time-lapse again. It's just this. I'm going to get in my car tomorrow morning and drive down to Dover. I'm taking the car across on the ferry, and then driving down through France, all the while asking myself why I am alone; and so this time, I wonder if I could have a companion on that journey. It could be,' he held up his hand now, like a policeman stopping traffic, and placed it just above her shoulder as he went on, 'it could be utterly platonic or utterly not. It would be entirely up to you. And if you wanted it kept quiet, again it

28

would be entirely up to you. I could pick you up anywhere in the morning and we'd be away. Otherwise things would be as they were before: Beardsley would go off on his own and Miss Barrington would go to her sister in Rye.'

She pressed her back tight against the chair and stared at him. He was offering her his company for six weeks. They would stop at hotels and laze on beaches. They would visit places she had never even dreamed of and, as he said, it could be platonic or otherwise. *Platonic or otherwise.* She would have to say ... what would she have to say? She had never felt like this in her life before. She felt elated, different, so different, free. Perhaps that wasn't the right word because that feeling of rejection she had carried with her for years was now no more. Somebody wanted her. They weren't saying, 'I've had four years with you and I can't face a marriage to you.' And when you are presented to yourself in that way you become as nothing, your emotions freeze, thawing only in the deep darkness of the night when the desire for love becomes overpowering.

Platonic or otherwise.

Her voice was as soft as the look in her eyes as she replied, 'Why wait till morning? It'll be light until ten o'clock or so.'

She watched his head droop onto his chest for a moment, and she heard him mutter, 'Oh, Louise, my dear, dear Louise.' Then he startled her by grabbing her hand and pulling her to her feet and around the table and into his arms. But although he held her tightly he did not kiss her, and his voice was thick as he said, 'This is jumping the gun and going beyond platonic and you haven't made up

29

your mind yet.' His arms dropping from around her, he gripped her hand again and was about to begin running when he turned and saw the used teacup and glass on the window sill; then he said, 'Oh, to pot! I'll see Robson as I'm going out and explain.' Then as they hurried out of the room he added, 'But I'd better not explain too much, had I?'

'Where are we going?' she gasped.

'Back to my room to pick up the book that you came for, Miss Barrington, and the remainder of the port. It'll only take us five minutes.'

She didn't care if it took them five hours, she felt so alive. She was living, she was running. She was running hand in hand with Mr Fred Beardsley and they were going abroad and they'd be together for five to six weeks. She was young again and she was in love. Yes, she was in love. Oh yes, she was, and with such a man, and he was in love with her. Oh yes, he was very much in love with her; and it had all happened within an hour or so. She tried to tell herself it couldn't have, it couldn't have; but it had, it had . . . *It had*. As he said, what was time anyway?

*   *   *

'I tell you I saw him come dashing out of the common room; and he had Miss Barrington by the hand, and there they were running along the corridor and into his room. By the time I'd washed up the cups they'd left in the common room and come out, there they were, dashing out of the main door and running again towards the car-park, still hand in hand.'

Mrs Robson looked out of her kitchen window

30

and said, 'I've been standing here washing up me baking things and I saw his car going out, but I saw only him in it.'

'Well, you would from this point.'

'Sure you haven't been drinking?'

'Woman! I'm telling you.'

'Yes, yes I know what you're telling me. But him with his yelling and shouting and swearing and letting out with his hands here and there, it's a wonder he hasn't been brought up by some of the parents before now. And you say he was running with her, that stiff piece? They were saying just yesterday—I heard them when I was washing up their tea things—that she wouldn't last and they wouldn't be surprised if she doesn't give in her notice during the holidays. She doesn't mix. She's a bit snooty.'

'She's never been snooty to me. I've always found her very polite, and she comes nicely dressed, not like some of those floozies who, to my mind, shouldn't be teachers at all.'

'Look, sit down and get your tea.'

'You don't believe me?'

'Well, I can't, can I? If it had been him you saw then it couldn't have been her, and if it was her you saw then it couldn't have been him. Beardsley and Miss Barrington. Oh lad, have some sense.'

Joss Robson sat down at the table, but instead of taking up his knife and fork and attacking the ham and tongue salad, he just stared down at it. It was as she implied, fantastic: old Grizzly Beardsley and young Miss Barrington. But on the other hand he wasn't all that old, and she wasn't all that young. And he had seen them, hadn't he? Or had he?

The yell her husband let out made Mrs Robson

almost drop the two cups she was taking down from the delft-rack: 'Bugger me eyes to hell's flames, lass! I did see them.'

Quietly now she went to the table and pressed him down into his chair again, saying, 'If you say you did, then you did; I'm not disputing it. Now get your tea.'

She really would have to get him to the doctor's on Monday and get a tonic or something, his nerves were all a-jangle; and whose wouldn't be with those young hooligans. Devils, half of them were. He never used to be like this, all nerves and jumpy. And now he was seeing things. Oh yes, he was seeing things all right.

CHAPTER TWO

The man was dressed in a white duck suit and a pale-blue silk shirt and a grey silk tie. The woman at his side was wearing a soft mauve two-piece, over which was a light fawn, three-quarter-sleeved, ribbed silk coat. Like the man's, her head was uncovered, but whereas his hair was grey, hers was a shining auburn and lay in a roll along the nape of her neck. They were walking up a narrow tree-lined avenue that led to the Champs-Elysées.

He stopped her at a flower shop and pinned a small posy of violets to the lapel of her coat, only to jerk his head sideways when he heard his name being called loudly from across the road. They stood staring at the running figure coming towards them: in fact there were two figures but the second wasn't running. Turning to the woman, the man said, 'It's impossible. Not here. Not here. Riley? No! It's impossible.'

'Hello, Mr Beardsley. Eeh! I couldn't believe it, I couldn't. We followed you along from the end of the street on the other side, but I said to me Uncle Frank here, "It's Mr Beardsley. There's only one Mr Beardsley in this world," and me Uncle Frank said, "There's dozens of men with grey hair," but I said, "Not like his." Not like yours. And your size an' all, Mr Beardsley.'

They had moved a few steps away from the florist's shop, but stopped again as Riley exclaimed in a high voice, 'Why! it's you, Miss Barrington. Eeh, my! I didn't know you.' He turned a laughing glance on Mr Beardsley, then brought it back again to Louise before looking up at the tall thin man at his side and saying, 'Miss Barrington is a teacher at the school.'

'Pleased to meet you.' The tall thin man's hand came out, and Louise took it and shook it. While smiling widely, she replied, 'And I to meet you.'

'What on earth are you doing in Paris, Riley?' It was the schoolmaster speaking.

'Oh well, sir, it's a long story. I won a weekend here, but me ma wouldn't let me come on me own. Well, I wasn't going to be on me own: they were goin' to give me a guide, sort of, but it was me Uncle Frank or no-one. He's a good guy, me Uncle Frank.' When Riley's elbow caught his uncle in the ribs, the tall man said, 'Now watch it, laddie. Watch it!'

'Have you just come over here, miss, I mean for the weekend, like?'

Before she had time to answer Beardsley barked, 'No, she hasn't just come over here for the

33

weekend, like.'

'Your voice, Fred,' Louise interrupted him.

'Oh, well,' he said, nodding at her, but added, 'I'm dealing with Riley, Louise, Riley. You remember Riley.' Then turning to the tall man, he explained, 'He was the one person I hoped never to see again in my life.'

'As bad as that?'

'As bad as that. And there's one thing I must make clear to you'—he was now digging his finger at the boy—'her correct title is Mrs Beardsley, not Miss Barrington.'

Riley's mouth was wide open and he didn't utter a word for thirty seconds, then he said, 'No kiddin'?'

Mr Beardsley drew in a long breath, pulled his chin into his neck, then seemed to sigh as he said, 'No kiddin', Riley. No kiddin'.'

'Congratulations, Miss ... Mrs Beardsley.' Riley's hand was now shaking Louise's very vigorously; and then, turning to the man at his side, he said, 'What d'you think about that, Uncle, eh? What d'you think about that? Mr Beardsley's married. Eeh my! When was this, Mr Beardsley?'

Fred and Louise exchanged glances and it was Louise who answered, 'Five weeks today.'

Riley apparently couldn't believe it, because after a pause he added, 'That must be just after we broke up.'

'Yes, just after we broke up, Riley.'

'Was it done in St Bede's? Wish I'd been there.'

Fred now answered, 'No, Riley; it was not done in St Bede's, but in Bavaria, in a little chapel in the foothills of the Alps.'

It was evident that Riley was amazed by this
34

news and he looked from one to the other, showing it, before he said, 'Eeh! God, in Bavaria.'

Fred replied, 'No, God wasn't there, Riley, but there were quite a few villagers looking on.'

Riley's uncle laughed loudly and Riley, also laughing, said to him, 'That's Mr Beardsley, you know, the one I've told you about; he gets the better of you every time.' And he turned to Fred again, asking, 'How did you get there?' and Fred replied, 'We walked to Dover, swam the channel, then walked through northern France, Belgium and on through Germany and, finally, footsore, came to Bavaria.'

They were all laughing now, but at the same time Riley was thinking, and he responded in kind: 'Aye, you would be footsore, and have gone through some boots I'd say, but . . . but it would take some time, nevertheless, sir, wouldn't it? And you must have had it all planned and nobody knew anything about it. I mean nobody in the school.'

'No, we didn't have it all planned, Riley. It was on the spur of the moment on that memorable day I told you how I couldn't wait to see you again, wasn't it, dear?' Louise, nodding at Riley, said, 'Yes, Riley, it was done on the spur of the moment and I may as well tell you it was you who started it all off.'

'What! me, missis?'

'Yes, you, Riley.'

Now Fred turned and looked at her, saying, 'You've never mentioned that.'

'No, I haven't; but do you remember your conversation with this young man?'

'Oh aye, miss,' Riley butted in. 'I remember it all right. Me farewell set-off. It was a stinker.'

'Yes, in a way it was, Riley; but it showed me quite a different side of Grizzly Beardsley.'

Riley's laugh rang down the street and turned heads towards them, and then he spluttered into the laughing faces, 'Fancy you calling him that! But you mean to say it started from then?'

'Yes, Riley, it did; but I would like you to keep it to yourself as a secret link between the three of us, because I've got a feeling, you know, that we may be seeing more of each other in the future.'

'Oh, not if I know it.' Her husband was shaking his head vigorously and Riley said, 'He won't have much say in the matter will he, missis . . . ma'am? 'cause husbands never do, if my mam's anything to go by.'

'By the way, Riley, what competition did you win to bring you this far?'

'Actin', miss.'

'Acting?' Fred's voice covered hers, repeating the word, 'Acting?'

'Aye,' Riley said. 'You're the one, sir, that told me on our last day that I'd got something; I mean, being a comic, like. Well, there was a competition: it was running for three weeks in Fellburn at the theatre there and it was for talent up to seventeen. Coo! Lord; you've never seen anything like the queue. Me dad said I hadn't got a hope in hell but me Uncle Frank said, you go ahead and do your stuff naturally; pick on somebody; didn't you, Uncle?'

Uncle Frank nodded, saying, 'Aye, I said that. Be yourself, I said, but pick on somebody you know well and that you can imitate.'

'So that's what I did,' said Riley.

'And who did you pick on?'

36

'You, sir.'

There was an astonished silence for a moment; then, 'You what!' came out as a bellow, and again Mr Beardsley's wife had to intervene: 'Fred, you're in the street, people are stopping; they think we're fighting.'

'Well, that's what there's going to be in a minute, dear, I can tell you, if he's picked on me to make a fool of.'

'Oh, it wasn't like that, sir. Well, I mean, I just did you.'

Again there was silence; and now, trying to suppress her laughter, Louise said, 'How did you do him, Riley?'

'Eeh! Well'—Riley cast an apprehensive glance at his late opponent; then he gave a little laugh and said—'you see, miss, Mr Beardsley has different faces for the different things he says.'

At this Fred and Louise exchanged glances, he with his eyebrows raised, hers with her hand across her mouth. 'You see,' Riley continued, 'well, when he's listening to you and he doesn't like what you're saying, his eyes sort of narrow, go into slits like how a Chinaman looks; you know, and his long upper lip—you've got a long upper lip, you know, sir—' There was the sound of a deep intake of breath before Riley went on, 'Well, you pull it right down over your lower one like this'—he demonstrated—'and naturally your nose comes with it. It's as if you can't believe what you're hearing. You know, sir?' Louise could hold back her laughter no longer; it now rang down the street and caused passers-by to smile enquiringly. Fred did not smile, he just said grimly, 'Go on.'

'Well then.' Riley looked down at his feet for a

37

moment before he said, 'Your ears, sir. You know, when the lads mutter and they're not speaking, well, what you call plain English, you don't take any notice of them but you stick your finger in your ear and you shake it, and you keep on shaking it, and then you take your hand and you slap the side of your head like this. Then you say,' and now he went into a remarkable imitation of the master's voice as he said, ' "Dear! Dear! I can't hear a word, not one of us in this room can hear a word. Dear! Dear! What a pity. What a pity. And if that boy could only speak English, one day he might be able to earn a living." '

Louise had turned now and was leaning against her husband, and he had his head bowed and was trying vainly to cover up the fact that he was shaking all over, and Riley's Uncle Frank, too, was consumed with mirth.

'Well, how did they take *me*?'

'Oh sir, you brought the house down. And I was one of the ten they picked from the first lot; then one of the three picked from the ten.'

'All comedians?'

'Oh no. No, sir. I was the only one. I mean there had been dozens, oh dozens of funnies, so-called, as the man said, but ... well, they all did jokes as old as your granny, or ones that the real comedians had thrown out years ago, or they were just "I say, I say" ones. Those get up my nose. Well, one of the three was a singer and t'other one spouted Shakespeare. Mind, I didn't think I had a chance, because they were both good, the singer lad especially. He had a fine voice. I felt sure he would get it.'

'But he didn't make people laugh?'

38

'No, sir, no, he didn't make people laugh.'

'But when you imitated me, they did?'

Riley looked quickly from his uncle to Louise, saying, 'Well, he does pull faces, doesn't he, miss?'

'Well, truthfully, Riley, I haven't yet become acquainted with that side of him. You see, I haven't as yet upset him. Of course, I'll look out for them in the future. Are you set on going on the stage?'

'It seems to be all I'm able to do, miss. Well, sir there,'—he bounced his head towards Fred—'told me that's all I was good for; but it's funny that he should've said that 'cos it's the first job I've been offered.'

'You've been offered a job on the stage?'

'Oh no, no, sir. And anyway don't sound so surprised; I won the trip, didn't I? And what goes with it, and that's a job.'

'What sort of a job?'

Riley now squared his shoulders, and in a voice not unlike Fred's he said, 'Stage manager to The Little Palace Players.'

'You! Stage manager?'

'Well,' Riley, himself again, now said, 'assistant, anyway. It isn't all it sounds, sir, but they tell me it's a start. I didn't like the start when I first started it, if you get what I mean.'

'Making the tea, humping the scenery, sweeping up, and running errands, at everyone's beck and call.'

'You know all about it then, miss.'

'Well yes.' Louise now looked into Fred's enquiring gaze and nodded at him as she said, 'Amateur theatricals for some years. But even we had a stage manager and his assistant, and more often than not they themselves were inveigled into

39

doing a turn. Some of them were much better, I can tell you, than many members of the cast, and I'm sure it's going to be the case with you, Riley.' She was nodding approvingly at Riley now.

'Don't ... don't, my dear; that fellow's head's like a balloon that wants pricking, not blowing up.' Fred now looked towards Riley's uncle and asked quietly, 'Tell me truthfully what he's like on the stage.'

The uncle and nephew exchanged tight laughing smiles before the man said, 'He'll get there one day, I can tell you that. Of course, as I've told him, as you have many a time I hear, that's if he keeps on the straight and narrow and as you would say yourself, sir, it's no bad thing to have the power to make people laugh.'

Fred now looked at his watch and said, 'We're just off to have a meal. What are you two going to do?'

'Have a look round, before having a bite,' said Uncle Frank. He extended a hand towards Louise, adding, 'You know, missis, I didn't want to come on this trip, but it was forced on me. But I'm now glad it's happened, for it's meant meeting you and this good man here who I've heard so much about.'

After Fred had allowed his hand to be pumped with equal force there was an exchange of goodbyes; then he and Louise, smiling, turned away to continue their journey along the street, while Riley and his uncle went back across the road.

'I ... I feel awful leaving them on their own. They'll have a job finding some place to eat, except for the bars, and I don't think the uncle is a bar-type somehow; he doesn't seem that kind of a man.

40

Quite straight-laced really.'

'Oh, if he can't find his way about, Riley will.'

'Yes, and it might be the wrong way about.'

'Now, now, now! Look, why not ask them to come along with us.'

'You mean that?'

'Yes, yes, I do.'

'Huh!' Fred laughed gently. 'I was wishing the same thing but didn't want to put it to you, because you can't help liking him ... Riley, I mean. Something about the young devil.'

'Well, what are we waiting for?'

'Just use your usual voice now and bawl them back.'

But instead of calling, Fred put two fingers in his mouth and gave a shrill whistle.

As if he had been waiting for the signal, Riley swung round, answered with a wave; then he gripped his uncle's arm and ran him back across the road.

'Anything the matter?'

Fred looked at the uncle. 'No, nothing the matter, only we wondered if you would care to come along and have a bite with us?' he said.

There was a quick exchange of glances; then the uncle said, 'It's very good of you, sir, and missis, but look at us, we're very ordinarily dressed; I mean I'm in a suit but his nibs there, just a jumper.'

'But me jersey's plain; there's nothing written on it.' Riley was now thumbing his chest.

'No, but it isn't usual, going into a nice place looking like that.'

'You leave that to us; you'd be surprised how people dress in the best of restaurants here; and in the one where we're going I'm not unknown: I've

41

eaten here for at least one week in the year for a long time now. And, anyway, the proprietor has taken a fancy to my wife. We'll have the best seats in the house, I'm sure, and he'll advise us which show to go to where the language doesn't matter; the *Folies-Bergère*, I expect.'

'*Folies-Bergère?* Eeh, sir!'

'Never mind, eeh, sir! Anyway, you go on and walk ahead with my wife; I want to have a natter with your uncle.'

What happened next was to have a vital effect on Riley's life because Mr Beardsley's wife put her arm through Riley's. She actually linked with him and so astounded was he that, for a moment, he went out of step, but more importantly he could find nothing to say, because this lady was treating him as a man, not as the scallywag Riley. It was as if his life had suddenly changed and he had put on years. He could actually feel his future before him, and the prospect excited him: he knew for certain that he was going some place and, as his uncle said, on the straight and narrow. How narrow he was to live to find out.

PART ONE

CHAPTER ONE

The Little Palace Theatre was situated in a side street running off Fellburn market square. It had an inauspicious entrance, and if it hadn't been for its name depicted in eighteen-inch illuminated letters about halfway up the wall, it might have seemed that the two large green doors below the sign led into a warehouse.

The immediate entrance lobby was also inconspicuous, except for the ornamental arch leading into a surprisingly large and red-carpeted vestibule, with the booking office to the right, while on the left a flight of broad shallow stairs led up to the circle. Straight ahead were two ornamental doors which opened into the stalls.

That the interior remained almost as it was when first built more than seventy years before said much for the care of both the former owners and the present one, a Mr David Bernice. Besides being the owner, he acted as his own manager and director as had his predecessors. Such a situation was necessary if any profit was to be made: The Little Palace, like so many other struggling theatres, could hold an audience of no more than five hundred, crammed into its two boxes, the circle and the stalls. And this worked out only if such an owner put his heart and soul into all facets of the business.

David Bernice himself had never been a good actor, but he prided himself that he knew how to get the best out of whoever he had to deal with. He treated The Palace Players as part of his family, at

45

least for nine months in the year. They played everything from Ibsen to farce; not always brilliantly, very rarely brilliantly in fact, but always enjoyably for the audience; although now and again, as when Nonagon was at her best, a miracle occurred . . .

'The window was to the left of the desk. Now it's to the right.'

'Does it matter all that much, Vera?'

'Yes, Mr Bernice, it matters all that much. The light falls onto the desk in the wrong place. It's dim to begin with, coming from behind the window.'

Before he could make any further comment he was startled by Nyrene Forbes-Mason, that dear nonagon, that enigma of a woman, in a very sweet voice, so unlike her own, calling 'Yes, of course, Mr Bernice, it's bound to make a difference, for when it's on that side it won't show up her hair.'

There was a faint titter from the front row where members of the cast were sitting.

'I won't stand for it!'

'Vera! Vera, now, now!'

'Never mind now, now! It's getting too much. She's insulting . . . insulting. I'll leave. I tell you, I'll walk out.'

When there was no response to this David Bernice heaved another sigh, then shouted, 'Riley!'

Just as if he had been waiting for the prompt, Riley emerged from the wings and walked to the front of the stage. Gazing down at his boss he said, 'Yes, Mr Bernice?'

'Why did you alter that piece of scenery?'

'Well now, it's like this, sir. You see, I . . . er . . .' Riley looked towards the end of the row to the stage manager, and he waited for him to explain.

46

John Maybright moved to the front of the stage and, looking up at the leading lady, he said, 'I moved that, Vera, because where the window was it could hardly be seen by anybody in the audience, just those at the side; and what's more, the flaps looked dead. It's supposed to be an office wall, and so you'd expect to see a window in it. And what's more, Vera, you'd given orders over my head where the window should go, and I think in this business we all know our own jobs, and I know mine.'

'I won't! I just won't, I won't stand for this.'

At this the whole company witnessed a very strange scene taking place on the stage, a scene that had nothing to do with the play in hand, because Miss Nyrene Forbes-Mason, that lady who seemed to come alive only on the stage, whereas off it she was as icy as a refrigerator and shied from any friendly approach, was taking hold of the twenty-eight-year-old Miss Vera Fielding, who had been with the company for a mere nine months. She had come highly recommended, her latest play having run for six months in London. But here she was, being held gently by the tall imposing figure of Miss Mason who in a tone no-one had heard her use before, even on the stage, except when required of a character, was saying, 'Look, my dear, we're all on edge. I'm sorry that I allowed my grosser self to be bitchy. At your age, I would've had the same reaction to that window being moved. Now this is a good play, the best we've done for some weeks, so let's get on with it, eh? You'll hear no more quips from me, I can assure you.'

And taking her hands from the woman, she turned and looked down at Mr Bernice and said, 'Shall we proceed?'

'Yes, indeed, Miss Mason. Yes indeed.'

Riley, who during this time had been standing near the dead footlights, kept his eyes on the tall actress who now lifted her shoulders which made her back even straighter, and walked out through the far wings in readiness for her cue. As she did so he stepped back swiftly to his place beside Phillip Vernon, who was prompting for the leading man James Culbert, and there was a real quivering of excitement in him as he waited for Miss Mason's re-entry.

And there she was, sailing on to the stage, speaking over her shoulder in that haughty manner: 'I know my way, Johnson. I should do by this time.' It was a deep masculine voice. Dressed in an ordinary grey coat, her brown hair was piled on the back of her head in a large bun; but that wasn't what he saw: he was seeing her expensively dressed, and wearing a large hat, a feather curved on the brim. With the aid of a silver-mounted walking stick, she was limping; yet her body was still very straight. She stopped and looked at the young woman at the desk; then she moved a step nearer, turning her head one way and then the other as if viewing a statue. Then, in a deep, commanding and still haughty voice, she demanded, 'Who are you?'

The young woman behind the desk, rising slowly, said, 'I am Patricia Stace and I would like to ask the same question of you.'

'Oh, oh!'—the big head jerked backwards twice—'You would, would you? Well, I happen to be Lady Forester, known in this establishment, I understand, as Minnie. When did you begin here?'

'Two weeks ago.'

'Oh. Well, who are you? And why are you here, and in this room and at her ladyship's desk? Well, it used to be before she decided to . . . demise.'

'I happen to be Lord Fielding's cousin.'

'What! First I've heard of it.'

'Well, I suppose I should be more correct and say that my mother was Lord Fielding's cousin, I am his half-cousin.'

'Stop!' David Bernice interrupted. 'I would come round from the desk, Vera, when you say that, showing real indignation, then turn and look towards the door where James and Phillip are.'

And so it went on until David Bernice said, 'Fine. Fine. Let's have a break. We'll get going again at half-past one.'

There was now a general movement. Most of the cast, after they had donned their coats, scarves, or woollen hats, made for the pub at the far side of the square. There they would have the usual bar lunch and a drink.

Harry Morgan, the electrician and caretaker, lived on the premises. Being the caretaker, he occupied the three-roomed flat adjoining the theatre. His wife acted as dresser and seamstress. As for Mr Bernice, having lived in Fellburn for forty-eight years, he was well established in a house on the outskirts. This left only Miss Mason and Riley, and whatever Riley wanted to do in his dinner hour had to be done after he had seen to Miss Mason's needs.

This pattern had started about a year ago when the odd-job man Billy Carstairs had been taken ill. When he returned to duty Miss Mason had made it plain that she preferred Riley to go for her sandwiches.

49

As Riley had remarked to his mother, 'It was like being decorated by the Queen, because she's practically unapproachable once she comes off that stage. No chit-chat. She doesn't seem to talk with anybody except the boss; they seem to be old friends. She's been there twelve years, you know. All she eats is a tongue or a ham sandwich. I did suggest I should get her fish and chips, but she looked at me as if I'd come out with two four-letter words.'

Now, having tapped on the door of what was really the best dressing-room and been bidden to enter, it would have surprised most of the actors to witness the change in both the real leading lady of the company and that young whipper-snapper Riley. Nyrene was sitting, on what looked like a camp bed set against the far wall of the room and covered with a bright Indian rug. Riley greeted her with, 'Coo! You ought to put something on, it's cold in here. I bet he's turned the heating off again.'

'No, he hasn't; it's still on.' And her voice sounded so ordinary it was impossible to associate her with either the lady on stage or the one off it.

He now pulled up a chair and, turning it about, sat on it, his elbows resting on the back. Facing her, he said, 'It's enough to cut you in two outside. Now look; you want something warm in you. I'm sick of going for sandwiches. Now don't get your monkey up'—he wagged his finger at her—'when I mention pies and peas because that's what I'm going to have, and I can have them back here within a jiffy. You know Fuller's is just in the Town Hall Square? Come on, pies and peas, eh? I can understand you not wanting fish and chips, fish and chips are common, but pies and peas go back to Shakespeare. What about it, eh?'

'It's my birthday today, Riley.'

He hitched the chair slightly backwards from her, yet leant further over the back of it as he said, 'No! Your birthday, and nobody else knows?'

'You know, I was thinking just last night that you, Riley, know more about me than anyone else in this theatre; in fact anybody who has ever worked in this theatre, even our dear manager, producer, owner and benefactor.'

They looked at each other for a moment, Riley shaking his head, wanting to ask a question but not knowing just how far he should go; but she answered it for him: 'I am thirty-seven today, Riley.'

'Thirty-seven?' There was amazement in his voice, for he had thought she was well into her forties, but gallantly he said, 'I wouldn't have thought you were that.'

'Riley!' Her voice had a trace of the stage in it now. 'Don't spoil my picture of you. You thought I was much older, didn't you?'

'Aye . . . aye well, I did. But then I only see you on the stage and . . . well in here. I don't see you when you are your real self; and you must have a real self.'

Again there was silence between them before she said, 'I have no more real self than the one I show you, Riley. You should be honoured.'

'Oh, I am. I am, and I mean that. I told me mam, when you first spoke to me and asked me to go for your sandwiches, it was like getting an honour from the Queen.'

The laugh that greeted this was almost girlish.

51

'You didn't!'

'Aye, I did . . . I did, miss. And so . . . well, seein' it's your birthday, what about pie and peas, just for once?'

'All right, Riley, just for once and' her voice sinking now, she added, 'just for once I'd like to change my medicine today.'

'To what, miss?'

'I think I'll have a brandy.'

'All right, miss, a brandy. Sit there.'

As he rose from the chair she said, 'I've never asked you how you manage to get it each day without questions being asked; a young fellow like you'—she did not say boy but fellow like you— 'going in for miniatures.'

'Oh, don't worry about that, miss. There's two outdoor beer shops in the market, besides the Co-op, so I ring the changes.'

'You're very good to me, Riley,' she said, with a break in her voice that touched his own as he replied, 'Oh, miss, the boot's on the other foot; you've learned me a lot since I came here.'

'Taught you a lot, Riley, taught you.'

'Oh aye, taught me. I never seem to learn, do I?'

'Now, now, don't try to be modest; you've learned all right, every day, and it hasn't gone unnoticed by those that count. And I've got something to tell you, although you must assume you know nothing whatever about it. There's a part you may be offered in the near future, but it will be a difficult part. I know all about it, but I feel sure you can do it.'

'Me, miss! A real part? Not just actin' the goat, being the comic?'

'No, not just acting the goat and being a comic.

52

This is something ... well, it'll be very difficult. You'll have to learn about a new way of life, a dreadful life really. I can't go into it now; we mustn't go into it. I'll tell you later. But you know, Riley, I ... I ... I would do anything rather than spoil your chance in life, and you may have heard different stories about me. I am where I am today because I promised never to touch drink while on the premises, and I have broken that promise, and if I was found out I would have to go, and you too. I know there'll be no compromise, I've already been given too many chances, so after today, Riley, no more miniatures, and I won't need any more breath fresheners.'

'Ah, miss, miss ... I ... I can't see the harm in it.'

'No, neither can I if only one was able to stop when the mind says enough; but you know, in my case, I wouldn't listen to my mind and it was only because of Mr Bernice's compassionate heart that I was kept on.'

She now rose to her feet. There was no stateliness about her nor stiffness as she faced him and said, 'No, Riley, we won't make this the last time: if I'm going to stop it I'll do so from now. You go and get the pies and peas and I'll brew up a cup of tea.' She nodded towards the large square box standing on the table near the washbasin. 'Go on, bring them back hot. Then I'll tell you about the part, although it's got to be between just you and me for the time being. You understand?'

He stared at her without speaking; then he said softly, 'You're a great lady ... a great lady,' and, turning on a laugh, he shouted, 'Pies and peas, here I come!'

CHAPTER TWO

'Where are you off to the night?'

'I'm going across to see Mr Beardsley.'

'Now you don't want to make yourself a nuisance over there.'

'I don't make meself a nuisance, Mam.'

'How d'you know? They're too bloomin' polite to tell you.'

'What! Beardsley too polite to tell me when it's time to go?'

'Well, don't get too uppish; keep your place.'

'Oh God! Mam, I would have thought you'd have been pleased to hear I'm going to get a part in a play.'

'But you say you don't know what part it is yet.'

He turned away from her as he wound a scarf round his neck: he wouldn't dare tell her what part he had to play, she'd be up in arms. He didn't know himself if he could do it. But Mr Bernice seemed to think he could, and Miss Mason was positively sure, oh aye, she was, although he had pointed out to them both that he was perfectly at ease just doing his own kind of stuff such as taking the mickey out of this one or that. Why, he could imitate most of the voices of the cast, and their mannerisms an' all, but this other, drama, as they called it, oh my!

'They might be out,' said his mother hopefully.

'They won't be out, Mam, I've told you, they hardly ever go out, they don't like leaving the baby. You'd think it was the only one that's ever been born.' He turned and smiled at her now, then

54

added, 'But it's lovely to see them with it. Of course he had to call it Jason.'

'Why? What d'you mean?'

'Well, Jason was one of them gods, you know, that led this band of what they called heroes when they went after the Golden Fleece. They were called Jason and the Argonauts.'

Gods and Argos, whatever they were. Her lad was changing; not just since he had left school and had kept up a kind of friendship with Mr Beardsley, but more probably because of his mixing with that lot of actors and actresses. By the sound of things they were an odd lot of people.

She had only twice been to The Little Palace since he started there, and the second time nearly set her face on fire: the things they came out with. It might be what goes on today, but what goes on today she didn't hold with. Oh no, never would. She'd said as much to his dad, and when he had said, 'You want to wake up, woman!' she had let him have it. Wake up, indeed! That coming from him who would go sick with a bad back whenever a job tired him.

Looking at the small woman, Riley couldn't tell himself that he had ever loved her. She was a difficult woman for anyone even to like, bossy and hard, with a one-way view, and spiteful. And yet he had a feeling for her. At times he was sorry for her, especially when she had to go out to work because his father was at home suffering with his back. Even so, she wasn't the only woman round about who had to go out to work to keep things going.

Apart from all this he was wise to the woman in her. Not that he put it like that to himself; but he knew the real reason she went on about his going

55

so much to the Beardsleys' was that she was jealous of his liking for Mrs Beardsley—she thought her uppish. And then there was her definite jealousy of Miss Mason. He had happened to mention she was a lovely woman, one who would have done well in London if she hadn't once had a drink problem, when his mother had immediately come back at him with, 'How old is she?'

He recalled having to consider before saying, 'I think she's about forty or more, but it all depends upon what she's doing, because sometimes she doesn't look even thirty.' And then he had made the mistake of adding, 'She's a lovely woman,' which must have put his mother on her guard and had her galloping to the theatre to see what the woman really looked like.

Yet here he was expecting to play a part that would make her hair stand on end. Oh my, let him get out, he must have a talk with Mr Beardsley.

'Wrap up!'

'I'm wrapped up, Mam.'

When she pulled the scarf tighter around his neck he said, 'Hold on, Mam, leave me a hole where I can breathe.'

'Go on with you, and don't be late. I mean that, don't be late. Eleven, mind.'

'Oh, Mam!'

'Never mind, oh Mam. And don't play the big man with me: you haven't yet reached that stage.'

Outside, the cold air caught at his throat. Don't be late. Eleven o'clock! And then, you're not a man yet. In a couple of months' time he'd be eighteen; and if she only knew it, he'd been a man for a long time—his racing loins told him that.

Instead of taking the bus to the 'modern
56

residence' where his friends now lived he walked the distance, for he needed the twenty-five minutes it would take to think this matter out quietly. He couldn't see himself taking on such a part, he just couldn't; he wasn't made that way. Yet Mr Bernice and Miss Mason, particularly Miss Mason, were definite about his capabilities, and what was even more amazing was that the leading man James Culbert was agreeable.

He thought back to the scene in Mr Bernice's office that afternoon. There they were, four of them, each in his own way emphasising he could do it ... he was a mimic, wasn't he? Yes, he could mimic, but he had never acted, not really, he had only done one-liners announcing His Lordship, or some such. He had been tickled to death the first time he had done it and had had the urge to turn to the audience and say something funny. That likely would've brought the house down, and him with it for he would have been outside quicker than it had taken him to say his piece ...

He rang the bell, and when the door was opened the outsize figure of Mr Fred Beardsley greeted him with 'Sh! Come in,' then put out a long arm and practically lifted him over the threshold and into the hall as he said in a whisper, 'She's just got him off. That fella's getting too much of his own way ... no seven o'clock bed for him. Here, give me your coat. My, it feels almost stiff!'

'So would you be, sir, if you'd been out in that. It's gettin' worse. If only it would snow it would warm things up a bit.'

They were tiptoeing now across the quite large hall, and as they passed the stairs they both looked upwards to see Louise Beardsley now descending

57

and she, too, whispered her greeting: 'Hello there, Riley. You look frozen.'

'I am frozen, ma'am.'

It might have sounded strange to an outsider that this modern young fellow who had only recently left a school where the teachers were addressed by their Christian names should now call this one ma'am, and his one time antagonist sir. But, on the prompting of his Uncle Frank, after that evening in Paris, he had done so.

'Has he been playing up again?'

'Yes, he's been playing up again, Riley. You'd think he realised that I was out most of the day now I'm back at school.'

'Of course he knows you're out most of the day, woman. Even an idiot of a child would miss its mother; but that boy's no idiot. Oh no, he knows he's just got to yell and you jump. Well, it's time he learned different.'

'You're changing your tune, sir, aren't you?'

'What d'you mean?'

'Well, it isn't long since you were claiming that bairns know how many beans make five from the moment they draw their first breath and that they should be given freedom of expression. That was it, wasn't it, ma'am? Freedom of expression. He was always on about that, wasn't he?'

'Yes, Riley, always on about it, until he discovered that his wonderful son can't yet tell the time. It's since the clocks went back, you know, and it gets dark earlier, is his excuse for that.'

'Shut up, woman! And sit yourself down, because I'm going to, and if he yells he yells. Do you hear that, Mrs Beardsley? He'll yell until he's tired, and when he's tired he'll go to sleep.'

Louise Beardsley looked up at her husband, and behind the humour in her glance was a deep love that was very plain to Riley. He always liked to see her looking at her husband. It was a wonderful feeling to be with these two people. The atmosphere was so different from that at home, so different from that in the theatre; something beyond what was called love. But there was another matter he had to talk about.

'What's brought you out tonight? It's usually on a Friday we're honoured by a visit from you.'

'Fred! Shut up and get us a drink.'

Riley turned to the elegant woman sitting by his side on the couch, and he said quietly, 'I've come for some advice. I just don't know what to do.'

Fred Beardsley stopped pouring out the drinks and turned towards the young fellow. It was odd, but the boy seemed different tonight. In fact, he supposed he had been looking different for some time now, but he hadn't given it much thought. He didn't seem like an eighteen-year-old boy; sitting there, he looked like a young man in his twenties.

'You in trouble?' he asked.

'No, sir, I'm not in trouble, not the kind of trouble you mean, anyway. I did think about pinching a car; I passed a nice Jaguar on the road but I've lost the knack.'

'Oh, Riley!'

He turned to Louise, who was laughing at him as she said, 'You didn't really steal a car, did you?'

'Oh yes, ma'am, I did . . . I did all right. But I happened to meet up with a wall, and I just managed to get out before the thing blew up.'

'Really!'

'Oh, you know nothing about the past life of our

59

friend here.' Fred was handing his wife a glass of sherry, and another to Riley; then he sat down with his port and said, 'Well, out with it. What's your trouble?'

'It isn't trouble.'

'Well, if it isn't trouble why are you looking so glum?'

'Have you ever read a book called *The Golden Mind*?'

Husband and wife looked at each other and both repeated simultaneously, '*The Golden Mind?*' It was Louise who said, 'Yes. Yes, it was quite a sensation a few years ago. It became a stage play and ran in London for quite a while. It was written by an American. What about it?' But before Riley could reply, Fred said, 'Oh, don't tell me they're going to stage that.'

'Yes, and they're all for it.'

Riley watched his two friends exchange a long glance; then it was Louise who said quietly, 'And they want you to play the mentally retarded boy?'

'Yes, that's what they want me to do, ma'am, play the sixteen-year-old boy. I don't even like the sound of the words. There was a lad at the bottom of our road who was like that. I tried to avoid him, and he me.'

He looked at Fred. 'I'm the joker, you know, sir. You said yourself that I could make it with mimicking and comedy, and I know I can; I can make them laugh, but . . . but . . .'

'But what?'

Riley looked at Fred and said quietly, 'Miss Mason, you know Miss Mason?'

'Oh yes, I know Miss Mason very well and I value her opinion. What did she say?'

Riley concentrated his gaze on the carpet for a moment before he replied, 'She said it was harder to make people cry, and laugh as they were crying.'

There was silence in the room. The logs in the Adam-style open fireplace crackled. There was the sound of a car being started somewhere outside.

'You don't want to do it?'

'I . . . I couldn't do it, sir, could I? I mean *me*! I can play the fool. Well, you've got a lot of experience of that, haven't you, sir? And I'm out for laughs with my one-liners, and I've learned a lot from watching the others: when to pause, when to rattle on and when to finish and clear out; well, as you once told me, always denigrate meself and nobody else as I would get more laughs that way. And I do. I do. I've had them in stitches, the cast at break times, taking off one and the other; and so, imagine me playing something straight, so straight that I've got to act mentally retarded, and so straight that I've got to be sub-normal and act that way. They gave me the book; but I daren't take it home. I read a bit of it before I left. And boy, what that fella does!'

'Yes, what that fella does.' It was Louise nodding at him now. 'I've seen it twice. The actor who played the part was brilliant because he had to do so many things: he had to dance; he had to sing snatches of the songs that came into his head and spout the poetry that was passing through his tortured mind. He comes out of himself for a time and learns about love. Then when his parents bring him back home after so many years in care, the mother wanting him, the father aghast at the idea, there being an older brother and a younger sister to be considered, that is when the drama really begins. The brother reacts like the father, who can't stand him, and he teases him; but the girl has pity for him; in fact she loves him from the beginning.' She paused, then nodded towards her husband as she said, 'It's a very serious play for The Little Palace to take on, don't you think?'

'Well, they've staged Ibsen,' Fred said.

At this Riley put in, 'Yes, sir, they staged Ibsen but Mr Bernice did admit that Fellburn wasn't ready for it and that it was his mistake. Well, this sounds a much bigger mistake to me.'

'Oh, this is different altogether. This is a modern play, Riley, and the fact that they think you can do it means you must consider it an honour. They've recognised you've got something. God knows what it is,'—he now tossed his head from side to side—'I never found out.'

'Oh be quiet you.' Louise waved her hand impatiently at Fred. 'The scene with the brother and sister in bed is the real telling part. It is a matter of how it is played. When I saw it, it came across beautifully, or should I say, as pathetically beautiful?'

'Well, it didn't with me. Bugger me! It didn't with me; in fact, it had the hairs on my neck standing up.'

The room was now filled with laughter: Fred bowed his head over his knees, Louise lay her back against the couch and Riley, his hand covering his eyes, said, 'Well, I'm sorry, but that's put the tin hat on it; they're not getting me into that lark. Just imagine what me mam would say. Oh, lordy! Lordy! Turn her hair white.'

'It's all right, Riley. Really it comes to nothing. It's just how you look at it,' said Fred.

'It can be suggested as much as it likes. They're not getting me in a bed on a stage with anybody, let alone with a lass who is supposed to be me sister. Would you tell me what happens next?'

'Well, the parents find them there, and the father, thinking the worst, pulls his daughter from the bed and is shaking her like a rat when the boy tears himself from his mother's sheltering embrace and springs on his father. They both fall to the ground, with the boy on top of the man.' Louise paused, then she said, 'That was one of the most chilling moments in the play, for the boy, seeming to be possessed of great strength, lifts his dazed father by the shoulders and repeatedly bangs his head on the floor. I can still hear the audience gasp as they saw him stand up, the sweet smile returning to his face as his mind went back into itself, and he went into his dancing and singing routine; only to finish up sitting close to the floodlights and staring silently into the audience with a weird smile on his face. As I remember, it was some minutes before the curtain dropped, and there was a further period of silence before the audience applauded.'

And there was silence in the room now, until Riley burst out, 'Oh, ma'am! How would you expect me to go through all that, to create something like that? I could never do it. Never.'

'No, you couldn't.' Fred got to his feet now and refilled his glass at the side table before he added, 'Not with your attitude; at least, as it is now. But with coaching from your friend Miss Mason and plenty of rehearsal, you could do it. That's if you make your mind up and don't dither. You could either tell yourself outright you'll do it, or that you're not capable of tackling it; that it is too big

63

for you.'

Turning to Louise, Riley said, 'I don't know why I come and ask for his advice. Talk about being negative. If I wasn't negative when I arrived I'll certainly be so when I leave.' He shook his head slowly and, his voice dropping almost pathetically to that of a young lad, he said, 'But honestly, the very idea of acting that sort of part scares the pants off me.'

CHAPTER THREE

'That's it, don't blink; at least, not yet.' said Miss Mason. 'Keep the eyes half-closed; now gradually let them widen. That's it. Now the face should go into a smile. You may blink now; and keep your head going in that slight motion as if it were on a spring, jolting just gently. A bit backwards . . . a bit forwards, just a very slight bit . . . that's it now: think of a golliwog almost run down. Now you're looking out right over the audience. Keep your shoulders sloping and your arms slack. That's it; your whole body should be loose like that of a rag doll. That's better. You've been through it before, but don't forget you must continue to work on every part of it.

'Now back to the start: tap your forehead hard four times with your knuckles. That's it, that's it: and now blink hard, screw up your eyes, move your head a little as if you're trying to push something away, and then become still. Your expression changes to one of recognition and you look at your mother and you say, "Oh, Mama" . . .'

64

'I always feel daft when I—'

'Stop it, Riley! Stop it! No interruptions. You've recognised your mother; now you're looking at your father: the smile slowly fades; everything goes into reverse, and this is where your mother speaks and says, "Daddy's here." Your expression becomes blank, but your head nods as if in recognition. Then you hurry to the window and from there you turn your bright face to your mother and you say, "Birds, singing. Listen. Listen, Mama."

'She goes to the window and what the audience hears is a motor car, the sound of children playing or shouting, but you cock your ear to one side and say, "Beautiful. Beautiful, mind". Now start again.'

'Aw, miss! Miss, I know it. Yes, I know it. I should do.'

'You know it, Riley, but you're not living it. Oh, you know it word for word, but you're not living it. I tell you you must live every action in that part; especially your entry into that office where you see your mother and father who have just been told this small home is closed and that you cannot be sent to a smaller house with two or three others to be looked after by a house mother. And what the audience have to find out is if you are aware of the alternatives: you are either going home or being sent into an asylum. This has been made plain to your parents: your father's for the asylum, but your mother's for home. And now the continued discussion obviously puzzles you; but you do not seem unduly disturbed because you go into your dance, your ballet bit. By the way, I think you're excellent in that. How on earth do you manage to get on your toes so easily?'

'Oh, it's our dear Doris. She showed me how to

use my . . . flanges.'

'Oh yes, Doris would show you how to use your . . . flanges; you wouldn't mention toes to Doris, it would smell too much like athlete's foot.'

They laughed together now, and when Miss Mason said, 'Oh, let's have a cup of tea,' Riley went to the box on the side table and switched on the electric kettle; then he turned to her and said, 'We only have a fortnight; I'll never—'

'Shut up! Just shut up, will you? And don't ever say again "I'll never," or, "I can't" . . . you can! And you will! Anyway, as I said yesterday, just think I'm your mother, and I'll be on the stage with you most of the time; so what've you really to worry about?'

'Only dancing, singing, spouting rhymes, and being an idiot.'

When she began to laugh and her body to shake, he joined her. Then he said, 'You don't know how I feel.'

'Don't be silly, telling me I don't know how you feel. I feel like that every time I walk on from the wings.'

'No, you don't.'

They were looking intently at each other, and after a moment he said, 'You don't, do you?'

'I do every time; if you didn't feel like that you'd never get across to your audience. The greatest mistake in this business is to be sure of yourself. It has killed many an aspiring star. This play demands that you give it your body and mind. Forget about Peter Riley; you are a retarded boy, lovable, endearing, funny. And you know, a lot of the part *is* funny, and the comedian in you comes out at times, and is an asset.'

'Oh, I am Larry Meredith all the time; I am up

66

the lum half the time; and when I'm outside I want to hitch along the gutter, like kids do.'

'You're half him already, but only half; you won't be all of him until the first night on that stage when the light fades and you come on doing your dance. At first, not a sound; then you begin to sing; then quite suddenly the stage goes into total darkness.' She paused here and, as if to herself, she said, 'They've got to do it within thirty seconds; it won't work if it takes longer. Anyway,'—her voice rose— 'the following scene is going to be the really testing one for you. The high laughter has died away and as the lights get brighter the audience sees you sitting on the floor, your legs crossed, your hands lying limply on your knees. You are now a seven-year-old boy. Get down there!'

'Oh, miss.' Riley knelt on the floor; then tucked his feet beneath him.

'Now I'm walking up and down in front of you pleading with your father not to send you away, telling him that I can look after you. And he's telling me that you're growing and growing swiftly, et cetera, and that if you stay he goes; and then where will I be?' She paused and looked down at him. 'You must slowly turn your head to look at him as he yells at me, "He won't go to Golden's Private School for backward children, he'll go to the looney bin, where he should have been all this time. Just look at him now, and his antics: he's out of his mind." '

Now pointing down at Riley, she emphasised, 'The timing here must be right. As your father says mind, he taps his fingers four times on his brow, then adds, "It's Golden's or the asylum, take your choice." It is then that your hand moves slowly up and you tap on your brow, also four times, and you repeat, "Golden," then add, "mind." Then you smile and keep on tapping your brow while repeating, "Golden Mind" until he goes to pass you, when you grab at his trouser leg; and at this he shakes you off as if you were something repulsive. Then with the banging of the door you look up to me and you say, "Mind. Mind. Golden Mind," and again you tap your brow, and I take you in my arms and hug you.'

'I like you hugging me. But then, you're not yourself when you're on that stage. Eeh, my! I've never seen anybody cry to order like you do. They told me you could. They said that years ago you did a marvellous play where you went hysterical and cried, actually cried, and that it ran a fortnight.'

She gave a quick jerk to her head, saying, 'Never mind about me crying and bygone plays, it's you we've got to concentrate on now, and you mustn't take any notice of that lot down there telling you how wonderful you are and how you are fitting in to the character. I'm telling you you're not there yet, not by a half, and we'll not know for sure until the lights hit you on that first night. That'll be the telling point.'

'Ah, miss, have a heart, I don't want to feel really barmy, I want to live; I mean, live an ordinary life. And you know something? I'm petrified of feeling as you want me to for this play, I really am. It's too bloomin' deep for me altogether. It's not my style.'

'Shut up, will you?'

The words were said in a tone he hadn't heard her use before and caused the smile to slide from his face, and as he looked at her he thought, Why is she doing all this, so intent on getting me some

68

place away from here? Except for Mr David, I think I'm her only real friend, so why's she doing it? Oh, sometimes I wish I'd never come into this set-up. I do. I do. Oh, and when me mam sees this play . . . Damn, me mam! Oh my God! Fancy me saying that.

'What's the matter?'

'Nothing. Nothing, miss.'

'You thought of something then, didn't you? And it upset you.'

He gave a short laugh, then said, 'Aye, I did. I was thinking of what me mam would say about this play, and then I said, "Damn, me mam!" '

She laughed. 'That's healthy.'

'No, it isn't, Miss Mason, it isn't. I can bugger and blast about other people but not me mam. I tell you, this place is getting under my skin.'

'Good. Good. That's the best thing I've heard you say in days.'

His face straight now, Riley asked, 'But why do you have to keep going over these first scenes again and again? I know every action I've got to do, and I know every word you've got to say, but you keep repeating it, miss, day after day.'

'Well, in all the aspects of my particular madness there is method: and that is the word, method.'

'They go a lot by method up in the drama schools, don't they?'

'Yes. But my method means that if those first two scenes become engrained in you you're not likely to dry up later on, or if you do you'll be able to handle it, whereas, if you dry up at the start . . . well, I'll leave you to imagine the rest.'

'But I know every word I have to say.'

'Yes, you say and I say you know every word,

69

every action; but that's like having the paint without the canvas, and the canvas in this case is the feeling, the feeling that you are not just Riley doing a part, but that you're no longer Riley: you are a boy of sixteen who "goes back" to seven and you must bring that over in those first fifteen minutes. Anyway that kettle must be boiled dry now; make the tea. But candidly what I want is not tea but what a little miniature holds.'

'Shall I go and get you one, miss?'

'No, Riley. Thanks all the same. Let's keep it dry, at least until this play goes on . . . and comes off, long or short.'

CHAPTER FOUR

It was the last night of the play 'The Golden Mind'. It had run for four weeks, the longest run of a play at The Little Palace. The curtain came down at ten o'clock to a standing ovation which kept the cast on stage for the next twenty minutes before they all went down and mingled with the audience, and David Bernice had tears in his eyes as he kept repeating that his Little Palace had never known scenes like it.

The first week had brought rave notices in the local paper, which was unusual in itself. The second week had brought play-goers in from Newcastle, Sunderland, Gateshead and places round about. In the third week the fifty members of the Palace Club who, over the years, had worked so hard to keep the place going, willingly gave up their seats to queuers who had stood for hours. At the end of the

70

third week a scout came down from Manchester, and he saw the play on both the Friday night and the Saturday matinée, after which he had a long talk with Mr Bernice, followed by a surprising talk with Riley; surprising, at least, to Riley, for he was being offered a part in the pantomime at Christmas with the possibility of a part in a play that was to go on tour towards the end of February.

David Bernice's reaction was: 'Well, we'll wait and see. This has got to be talked over,' and this surprised Riley because Mr Bernice had said to him after the first week, 'Don't be surprised, lad, if you get offers to move.'

During the fourth week the scout returned accompanied by what Riley would call a gentleman: good manners, well-spoken and well-dressed. After seeing the play, he came to David Bernice's office and confirmed his agent's opinion that this boy had it in him to go places and that he would suit the character they were looking for in the new play. After further discussion Mr Bernice agreed that it was a great opportunity for the boy and assured Riley he would waive his year's contract. However, to the amazement of the four concerned, Riley did not jump at the offer but requested an hour or so to think it over.

During that hour or so he rushed over to Mr Beardsley, and after gabbling his news, he said, 'I would take it, but it's me mam. Look what she did when she came to the play. She's hardly spoken to me since.'

'What did she do?'

'Well, it was in the scene when I was lying on the bed. While Lily was leaning over me and stroking my hair, I heard a commotion down in the stalls

71

and I knew it was her; and there she was stalking out, and not quietly either; and when I got home there was a hell of a row.

' "You're not doing any more of that slush," she said. "They should be locked up for putting it on." And on and on she went. I pointed out to her it was the only scene of its kind in the play and that nothing happened anyway. She said that although it was all suggested, I might as well have been stripped naked. And then, me playing an imbecile and looking like one, and she said I'd never be the same again. And, you know, perhaps she's right there, for Larry, the young boy, has got under my skin.'

At this, Fred Beardsley had taken him by the shoulders and shaken him none too gently saying, 'Don't be a bloody fool! Your mother's a narrow-minded woman and she's fifty years behind the times, so get back there and say, "Thank you very much, sirs." And be grateful for it. And there's another you should be grateful to, all the way along the line, and that's Miss Mason. You could never have got through that show of emotion on your own, not without her coaching. I saw that from the start. She's an amazing actress, that woman. I don't know why she stays there, really. Now you've got to make a stand against your mother. She's not the kind of woman to let her only son get away from her apron strings, especially with your father as he is now. She sees you as the man in her life and she'll move hell and high water to keep you there. Where's the pantomime? Manchester?'

'Yes.'

'Well that's a good place to start. The next step could be London. Here you're acting to the same

72

audience week after week, but out there you'll be facing a different horde, and you'll find you'll have to respond to them in different ways. You'll gain more on that circuit than you would by going to drama school and you might just as well have gone there, because Louise—and it's strange, but you might have gone there—and I have had thoughts about putting that to you.'

Riley's reaction was to shake his head at the kindness of these two people.

So it was agreed that first he'd play in the pantomime for three weeks. Then go on tour.

It was late that night when he got home. Susie and Florrie were already in bed, but before his mother or father could say anything, sixteen-year-old Betty ran to him, crying, 'Have you seen the evening papers?'

'No, let me get in.'

'It says you're being offered a pantomime and a tour and you've accepted.'

Apprehensively he looked at his mother, then at his father, before he said, 'They couldn't have got it in tonight; I've only just agreed to do it.'

'Well, it says it was offered to you and only a fool wouldn't accept it and as me dad's just said, you're no fool. Oh, I *am* excited. D'you think I'll get on the stage if I—'

'Shut up and get yourself away to bed!'

'Oh, Mam.'

'Never mind, oh, Mam.'

'You know what, Mam? You're enough to make people run away.'

When her mother's hand came up her father cried, 'I wouldn't do that if I was you.'

Betty looked at Riley, and when he made a little

73

movement with his head, she turned and went swiftly from the room.

He now watched his mother go to the fireplace, take up the poker and vigorously stir the glowing coals, and his voice was quiet and even placating when he said, 'I was bound to make a move sometime, Mam.'

She was around in a flash, the poker still in her hand as she cried at him, 'Yes, maybe, but into something decent, not travelling the country with that dirty lot.'

'Which dirty lot?' His voice was as loud as hers now. 'I don't know them. They're a troupe of actors very like the ones I'm working with now, I would think. Which dirty lot are you talking about?'

'They're all a dirty lot, all of them.'

'Oh . . . h!' Riley's voice sank deep into his chest now as he said, 'You know, Mam, I was ignorant, oh yes I was, as ignorant as a pig when I was at school; but I've been educated since I was among that dirty lot, as you call them. Let me tell you they're a fine lot of people and I've learnt from them, and I'm glad I've met them and I'm going on meeting them. So I'm going on the road with them, whoever these others are, and I'm going into pantomime, and I hope I'll be able to make people laugh. And, Mam, I'm going to tell you something else, you've forgotten how to laugh, and because of it you've made everybody else miserable.'

The poker went limp in her hand; then she turned back to the fireplace and laid it down before turning to her husband and saying, 'You've been right all along, you know. You've told me that I had ruined him, that I looked upon him as the only one of any use in the family. Well, you've been right

74

because I never dreamed I would listen to my son telling me I made everybody miserable.'

Riley watched his parents glare at each other but whatever he expected his father to say it wasn't what came out of his mouth: 'Well, you're right on both counts: yes, I have said that you consider him the only one in the family, and he's just said you've made everybody miserable, because it's many a long year since I had a really civil word out of you. Oh, I've got me faults, I know, and if you've told me once it must have been a thousand times that I like work so much I make it me bedfellow, all because of me back. You shouldn't be surprised to hear that you've made people miserable. Oh yes, yes, your son's become a man long before you wanted him to be one. You've always wanted to keep him a naughty boy so you could see yourself as the caring, guiding mother, going to the school and siding with Beardsley for the beatings he gave him; not that he didn't deserve them, but it wasn't your place to go, it was mine; but I never got a chance. Oh no.'

When his mother turned to him Riley saw utter bewilderment in her face; but she turned quickly back to her husband and said, 'I can't believe this, not one but two of you. Perhaps you'd like to go along with him,' and she nodded towards Riley, and in reply his father said, 'I'd give me eyeballs for the chance. Me back would soon be better then, I can tell you.'

'God in heaven! It's a night of truth. Oh, it's a night of truth all right.' Mona Riley now turned from them both and walked slowly towards the far door; and there she stopped, holding the door handle for a moment as if she were about to say

75

something; but she changed her mind and left the room, without banging the door after her.

Riley looked at his father. He had never before seen him in this light; and his father had never before seen his son in this light; and he said to him, 'You're doing the right thing, lad. Get out while the going's good, because if you stay here for much longer you'll never get away. And I'm telling you, for women like your mother are the very devil, they're the bloody devil himself. Oh aye. Oh aye.'

For a time they stood staring at each other, until Mr Riley asked quietly, 'When are you off?'

At this moment Riley was so bemused that he couldn't think. This was his dad talking to him as if he was a human being, and for the first time in his life he was seeing his parent as a frustrated man. Frustrated by whom? His wife. The world had gone topsy-turvy ever since he took on this play.

Then they were both startled when the door was again thrust open, and there stood his mother. She did not enter the room but stood within the opening, and she screamed at him now: 'Go on your tours with that lot of harlots and play your filthy plays.'

Riley almost ran at her, but stopped within only an arm's length, and cried at her, 'It wasn't a filthy play, it was a magnificent drama, and everybody says so. It's only you that says it's filthy.'

'Not filthy, lying on a bed with your sister, and being about to . . . ?'

'About to do nothing. I was retarded, Mam. I was a child and incapable of doing what's in your mind, and she was comforting me in the only way she knew how. As it was in yours, so it was in the father's mind too.'

'My mind's clean, clean! D'you hear? And I've tried to keep yours the same way, even if I've used me hand to do it; but let me tell you this, half of those people you are joining are out of work for years at a time, so don't you think you'll come crawling back and find shelter here when you're doing what you call resting. You can find some harlot among them to give you another bed to lie on, because I won't have you back in this house: I've got three girls growing up and I don't want them contaminated.'

Again she swung about, and this time the door clashed behind her.

Again the father and son stood looking at each other, and when Riley said pityingly, 'Dad, what's come over her?' Alex replied, 'You, lad, you've come over her: she's lost you, you've beaten her, and she can't bear it. If she had played her cards right she could've always had you; but she doesn't see it that way; she's your mother, but she's a narrow-minded bitch of a woman. Always has been. Now my advice to you is go and get your few things together and go along to those friends of yours, because it'll be hell if you stay here for the next few days, or until you're due to go; and such are her wiles, she could change and be the sorrowing mother tomorrow, crying all over you; and the end of it would find you giving it up just to please her. Go on, get your things. She won't know what you're doing; and you'll find a taxi in the stand at Bing's Corner. There's always one there. And I know you'll find a room with Mr Beardsley, because he's a good fellow. I've always known that.'

'Oh, Dad.' It was almost a childish whimper. Here he was losing a mother and finding a father

77

after all these years. He couldn't believe it. He had the most odd feeling that he wanted to cry. Oh my God! No, he mustn't cry. That would be the finish of him.

He turned quickly from his father and went to his bedroom, a small room just off the passage. He had always slept downstairs, and the girls upstairs. Fifteen minutes later he came out carrying a suitcase and two plastic bags, together with an overcoat.

His father said in a practical way, 'Put the overcoat on and then you can put your mac on top of that. You needn't button it.'

Almost like a young boy now, he did as he was bidden; and when he saw his father take his own coat off the back of the door and pull his cap onto his head, he said, 'Oh no, Dad, it's bitter outside.'

'Well, I've been out when it's been bitter before, haven't I? Come on. Take the case; I'll take the bags. I'll see you off.'

His father opened the front door quietly, and when Riley was about to step out into the street he turned about and looked into the room again. He couldn't believe this. No, he couldn't believe this. It was as if he were still deranged or had become mental, because his mind was denying that his mother could have turned out to be the woman he had just witnessed, the woman who had just thrown him off as it were.

The door closed, his father said, 'It's no use looking back, lad; you're starting out in life and with the chance in a million, so make the best of it.'

They found a taxi, and as his father closed the door on him he said, 'Keep in touch, lad, will you? Let me know now and again how you are. If you give a message to Mr Beardsley I'll be sure to get it.'

He could only nod at his father. He looked different. It wasn't only the street lamp or the taxi lights that had softened his face, but there was something different about it. It held what he could almost call a loving look, and he didn't look so small and wizened.

As the taxi was about to move off he called to the driver, 'Oh wait a minute!' and jumping out onto the pavement, he put his hand in his pocket and drew out an envelope, saying, 'Give her half of that and get something for yourself. It was for me keep and more. I . . . I got a bonus.'

His father said nothing, not even thanks, but just held the envelope in his hand and watched his son jump back into the taxi. 'Keep half for yourself, I've got a bonus.'

Alex Riley gazed at the envelope: it meant such a lot, the lad had given him back some of his self-respect.

CHAPTER FIVE

They were all gathered for the last time. The audience had reluctantly dispersed and the whole company was engaged in erecting two long trestle tables in the hall, covering them with cloths and piling on them all manner of home-made pies and cakes, and even more evident was the number of bottles standing at the ends of the tables. Each member had brought a friend and a bottle or two. As well as the players and their friends, there were outsiders, including Fred and Louise and the newspaper editor, and the owner and barman from The Globe, who had served most of the cast with pub meals six days in the week. Altogether there were more than forty people ready to sit at the tables.

After Riley had told Fred what had transpired between his mother and father and himself, Fred expressed his amazement saying that he had always thought she was such a wise woman; Louise wasn't as surprised. Earlier, she too had wanted to meet the mother of this young fellow who was so full of character and impishness; but having then made her acquaintance she found that she was very disappointed in the woman. She understood, from the first, that Mrs Riley didn't mind her boy having men friends such as Fred, but she couldn't tolerate him showing any friendly affection for another woman. Both she and Fred, however, were pleased that Riley had found his father, albeit late, as the boy himself had said.

Fred had suggested that Riley ask his father to join them on this last night, but Alex Riley had refused, saying that it would hurt his mother still further.

A crowd now stood around the piano singing everything from 'The Blaydon Races' to 'Keep Your Feet Still Geordie Hinny', interspersed with 'The Old Bull and Bush', 'Won't You Come Home Bill Bailey', and choruses from every musical one or other raked up from the twenties and earlier.

And so the jollification went on until David Bernice called for the attention of the whole company and friends and, standing at the end of the long table, said, 'Fill your glasses, ladies and gentlemen; I want to make a toast.' This done, he went on, 'First, to a most remarkable play acted in a remarkable way by all concerned, here's to "The Golden Mind".'

All raised their glasses and called, 'To "The Golden Mind".'

'Now, ladies and gentlemen, I would like the glasses to be raised again to one particular person, someone who came here as a young lad with a dirty nose. I am speaking metaphorically, of course!' he said amid laughter. 'My companions know what I mean; he was raw, very raw. He was looking, I think, for a director's job, but the only position I could offer him at the time was that of assistant stage manager. Well, we know the importance of assistant stage managers, because where would we be without the tea? Where would we be without our sandwiches? Where would we be without the sweeping brush being used? Where would we be without a strong pair of muscles to help move giant flaps, or climb rickety ladders on to a more rickety platform six inches wide along which to walk to replace an electric bulb?' Now the whole company was laughing and Nyrene Mason, who was standing next to Riley, put an arm round his shoulders and hugged him to her; but he didn't look at her, his head was bent.

Then David Bernice, raising his glass, said, 'To Larry, the boy who lived in another world: a world of golden thoughts, of music and dance; and who was so brilliantly portrayed that his acting has attracted to this theatre people of this town and round about who had never been here before; and not only that, his acting has lifted him not just to the first rung of the ladder to success but more

81

likely to the third or fourth. We all know of the offers that have been made him and each one of us, and I know I am speaking for the entire cast when I repeat, *each one* of us is happy for him, because he has proved to be a favourite with us all, and to one more so than the rest, our dear Nyrene Mason. It was she, he would tell you himself, who trained him every step of the way: she has been his mentor. But first, to you, our dear Riley: here's to further success in everything you do.'

Riley couldn't raise his head. His throat was full, his head was buzzing, not only with all that had been said but with the three sherries and the port and lemon that he had so far imbibed. He couldn't speak. He had no words of his own, for he had been Larry for so long. Was it just four weeks? Four months? Four years? He pulled his arm away from Miss Mason's and pressed himself back from Fred and Louise who were also standing close by, and in the small space that he had made he suddenly went limp. Then his head moved in the same little noddings as it had done for almost two hours every night during the past month. His arms came up into the form of limp wings, and the expression on his face became soft and sad, and everyone in the room gazed at him with awe. It was one thing to see an actor on the stage, but here was this lad becoming an idiot before them; and then in a soft quiet voice Riley began to sing:

I'd like to crown Mummy
with flowers of May;
Daddy says I have a golden mind,
But he does not smile.
Sad . . .

Not kind. Not kind,
As the birds and the fireflies and the bees.
All the birds,
I have nests in my mind,
They spin golden thread
To fasten my golden mind.
God is kind.
And so big.

When he finished his hands fell to his sides, his head drooped and he stood thus for a moment amid the utter silence of the whole company; and then when they applauded vigorously he put up his hand and said, 'I did that by way of thanking all those who have helped me to be Larry during the past month. Whenever I came to that part I felt I *was* Larry and governed by a great God; and I owe this to my dear friend.' He now put a hand out and caught Nyrene's. 'Without her daily bullying for weeks on end before, I would never have got there. There *were* times when I hated her guts.' This caused general laughter and more applause; and then he ended by saying, 'Thank you all from the bottom of my heart. Wherever I land up I shall never forget The Little Palace or its owner.' And pointing towards David, he ended with deep sincerity, 'Thank you, sir.'

When the applause had subsided and drinks began to flow, Fred moved towards Riley again, and said, 'Look, laddie, you've been drinking and not eating. If you want to keep on your feet, get something into you.'

And so he ate, and he drank a little more, and he chatted, and he laughed, and those standing close by laughed with him.

When he found himself standing near David Bernice, that gentleman said to him: 'One thing I would ask of you, Riley: keep in touch with Nonagon; I know she has a deep affection for you.'

'Oh yes, sir, I will. I could never forget Miss Mason.'

Oh yes, he would always remember her, because without her he wouldn't be going on the road in a very short time, or into any panto, which was putting it plainly. She had trained him, and she had carried him through those first two terrifying nights. Yes, he would always remember her. He could never forget her.

'By the way, sir, why do you call her Nonagon? It's only you who calls her that. Is it a nickname?'

'Well, I'd have to explain what nonagon means. A nonagon is a figure of nine sides; in her case, it refers to one over the eight. After a great disappointment in her life she took to the bottle. I suppose you've heard various versions of the story. As you know only too well, you've helped keep her supplied. But we won't go into that, not tonight, except to say, I nicknamed her that when she first went over the top, and now it's a term of endearment. And I'll tell you something else: she had an offer about the same time as you did, although not in Manchester but much nearer London; and she turned it down.'

'Turned it down? Why?'

'Don't ask me why, because I can't give you a reason, I can only suggest that she doesn't want to leave me and this little place. As you know, actresses come and go while they're learning their business; and she knows her business, yet wants to stay. What is more she doesn't want to leave her

84

home, a nice little house that she inherited from her parents. It's more like a large cottage than a house, but it's a pretty place, especially during the summer. It has a pleasant garden at the back, and an attractive frontage, and it's in a very good part of the town. In this trade, if you want to earn a living you've got to be on the move; and many actresses would turn up their noses at the little I am able to offer her some weeks. Perhaps you didn't know, because your *huge* pay packet was stable, whereas hers fluctuates with the sale of tickets and it's very rare that we're in clover. This last month, as you know, has been an exception; and why, young man, I'm telling you all this is because this is your last night in The Little Palace and I've drunk more than usual. In fact, we've all drunk more than usual, and it's a good job it's Sunday tomorrow for we'll all have sore heads. Ah,'—he nodded now towards the middle of the hall—'they're on the move, they're beginning to leave. Come on and say your goodbyes.'

For the next half-hour Riley said his goodbyes: some were tearful; and he had never been hugged and kissed so much in his life before. Now, apart from the caretaker and his wife and Billy Carstairs and his wife who were already clearing up, there remained only David Bernice, Fred and Louise, and Nyrene and himself.

Fred and Louise were already dressed for departure when they took Riley aside: 'We think you should stay back and see her home,' said Fred, inclining his head slightly towards Nyrene who was sitting in one of the plush chairs alongside the vestibule wall; and without waiting for an answer, he added, 'I'll give you a key to let yourself in.' He

85

was already taking a key off a ring he had taken from his pocket. And as he handed it to Riley, Louise said, 'And don't come in singing.'

'As if I would, ma'am, as if I would,' said Riley. 'Well, what time is it now?'

'A quarter to one,' said Fred; 'and our baby-sitter will have rung her mother and father and they'll be on the doorstep waiting to tell us just what they think of us.'

They now said their goodbyes to Nyrene, while Riley went to the cloakroom.

When he returned to the hall Nyrene was on her feet and David Bernice was doing up the top button of her coat; then having pulled up its fur hood over her piled auburn hair, he bent and kissed her on each cheek, and said, 'Sleep all day tomorrow. D'you hear?'

Nyrene did not answer, but smiled a wide, rather silly smile at him; and when she swayed he beckoned Riley to take her arm, the while saying, 'There's a taxi waiting.'

'Where are your keys?' Riley asked at Nyrene's front door.

'Where . . . where do you think?' She laughingly replied as she handed him her handbag.

He had to fumble in it for some seconds before his fingers found the key ring. Then, when he tried one in the lock, she pulled it away from his hand, saying, 'Give it here, stupid!'

It was the first time he had been in her house, and his initial surprise was at the size of the hall and, also, of its contents. They were pieces similar to those in the Beardsleys' house.

He followed her stumbling walk towards a door to the left of them, his own step somewhat unsteady, too; and when the light in this room was switched on he was again surprised. A crystal chandelier lit up the room, causing his eyes to blink, and as he hesitated to gaze around, Nyrene pulled him towards a couch set at right angles to a fireplace in which was a large electric log fire.

'Switch it on!' she said, pointing to the fire. 'I'm . . . I'm fr . . . freezing.'

Within a few minutes the artificial logs were glowing and the fan was sending heat into the room. She was sitting at a corner of the couch when she said, 'A drink, eh? A drink?'

'Oh no! You've had more than your share; and so have I.'

'Coffee, man! Coffee!'

'Oh, coffee. That's different. Where?'

'Ah.' As she sighed and pulled herself towards the front of the couch, he rose quickly in order to help her up; and she led him out of the room, across the hall again and into the kitchen.

When the light came on here, he shook his head. This was an oldish house, but this was a very modern kitchen. A lovely kitchen.

She staggered to the far side of the room and pulled a percolater, already filled with coffee and water, towards her and switched it on; then, turning a laughing face towards him, she said, 'Four minutes dead flat. Cups!' She pointed to a glass cupboard, and when he opened the door and was about to take two cups from an array of china, she laughingly called to him, 'No! Not tea cups; two . . . two mugs, eh?'

He reached up and took down two mugs from another shelf; then stood by her as she put them on a tray, with a bowl of sugar.

Five minutes later they were back in the sitting-room drinking the steaming coffee.

She had half drained her mug when she said, 'Ah, that's better! That's better. Still leaves room for a proper drink.'

'Oh no, me lady! No more proper drinks tonight. I have spoken!'

They were lying back against the soft cushions of the couch, and she turned her face to him, saying, 'Riley,' and he answered, 'Yes, miss?'

'Don't call me miss any more.'

'Oh? What will I call you?' Nonagon immediately came to mind, only for him to dismiss it. Then she was stammering, 'My name is Nyre . . . ne! Why does everybody call you Riley, never your Christian name?'

'Don't ask me, Nyrene.' He was laughing. 'I think it was, well, Mr Beardsley. He always said Riley. And me dad calls me Riley. You know something? I've found a dad. Today, I found a dad. No, not today, but yesterday. We're in another day now. Look!' He pointed to an open pendulum clock on the mantelpiece. 'Half-past two.'

'You know, Riley, your mother is a stupid woman . . . narrow, stupid . . . woman.'

'No, I won't have her called stupid; narrow, yes. Oh, narrow, yes. You're right . . . narrow, yes.'

'My mother died when I was twenty. Did you know I was born in this house? Yes, I was born in this house, upstairs. But she died . . . she died when I was twenty. I was in London then . . . you know. Did you know that, Riley?' She pushed her face close to his. 'London. L-o-n-d-o-n, London. Three years in drama school, and I'd been in this play. Big success it was. I wasn't leading. No, no, no, not at

88

all, but I was noted by the press. Oh yes, yes, yes, I was. And then my mother died; and my father was helpless without her. You see, Riley, some couples care for each other and . . . well, when one dies the other dies while still livin' . . . living. "Don't forget to sound your gs, miss." That's what the teacher used to say to me.' Her voice trailed away. ' "Don't forget to sound your gs." Well,' and now as if talking to herself, she went on, 'I gave up London, came back home to see to him. I loved him. And there was The Little Palace, and there was Mr David Bernice, and he gave me a small part. Then he gave me a bigger part; and then, after the comings and goings of other leading ladies, I was leading lady at The Palace. And leading men came and went, until one came, and stayed. He was different.'

She stretched her legs out and thrust her arms above her head and yawned, and when she repeated, 'Different,' it was almost a yell.

'He wasn't a good actor, no; and I don't give myself any false claims, Riley, but I carried that man for eighteen months. He looked about thirty; yes, about thirty. Oh no, a bit more. Handsome, very handsome and couldn't forget it, but he was nearer forty. His trouble was that he played himself every time, played himself because he liked himself, and oh, grateful to me, yes, so he said.' She turned now to look at Riley and she asked him, 'Has anyone yet said to you, Riley, "I love you. I adore you. You are the most wonderful person in the world"?'

He was laughing now as he replied, 'Not yet. Not yet, miss . . . Nyrene.' He stressed her name.

'They will. Oh, they will. And you'll believe

them. Oh yes, they will.' She was shouting again. 'Oh yes, you will, 'cos I did. And you'll talk of marriage, you know; and you'll come into this house ... no, not you, he did. And he was pampered and looked after and worshipped. Yes, you silly bitch of a woman, because you weren't a girl, were you?'

She was sitting up now nodding her head as if to someone standing before her: 'No, you weren't a girl then, twenty-seven you were, twenty-seven. Then one morning you woke up.'

She turned again towards Riley who was still leaning back on the cushions but staring fixedly at her, and she wagged her finger at him as she said, 'A letter through the box there,' and she pointed towards the door. 'A letter to me thanking me for ... for our friendship. That's what he called it, friendship. Yes, that's what he called it. But where was he going? Australia? As far away as he could get ... Australia ... with a touring company, as you are. He said that by the time I received his letter he'd be on the boat. On the boat!' She almost spat out the last words.

'You see, it was the free week that we have now and again at The Palace, and he had pre ... presumably—I must make a better attempt at that—presumably? That's it, presumably been home to make arrangements for me to go and ... wait for it, Riley ... visit his people down in Cornwall.'

She allowed herself to slump back into the corner of the couch, and her voice was soft now as she said, and again as if to herself, 'Yes, she nearly went mad, and I did, Riley, I nearly went mad because no-one knows what I had done for that

90

man. I had carried him: he could never remember his lines. When I think of the hours I spent in this very room going over them and the times on that stage when he fluffed and I ad libbed to save his face. Countless . . . countless. It was only his face, his good-looking face, that kept him on the stage, that kept him in a job. And his voice. Oh yes, his voice. He practised it; he loved listening to it.' There was a bitterness in her tone now; but it fell away when she said, 'I could have forgiven him practically everything except for what that experience turned me into, a soak; and that's what I became, a soak. If David hadn't been the man he was and still is he would've sacked me; but no, he put up with me until it became unfair to the rest of the cast, when he sent me away for three months. Three long months.'

She paused; then with her eyes on Riley now, she said, 'I wasn't cured, but to a certain extent I had it under control; but then I found myself alone here, and you know, Riley, the quickest way to hell is to drink alone. Very soon there would be days when I found that I just couldn't get by without it. I'd go out to lunch and I'd have just one or two. But David could see where it was leading again, and so he put it to me that either I gave it up, at least when I was in the theatre, or I got out. He didn't put it as plainly as that, but I understood him; and so I used to have my sandwiches sent in. Then you came, Riley. You were a godsend in more ways than one; in a way, you saved my life. It wasn't only your getting the drops for me, it was also something about you. I don't know what. Oh yes, I do, I do. I do.' She pulled herself quickly up from the couch saying, 'Look, I think we'd better get to

91

bed . . . have a nightcap and get to bed.'

'You better get to bed, miss; you're the one who's going to bed.'

'But I must have my nightcap; I . . . I wouldn't sleep. Stay there,' and as he attempted to get up she pushed him back on the couch; then went from the room, her back straight as always, but her step decidedly wobbly; leaving him to gaze at the glowing logs, again feeling that he wanted to cry, only this time to cry for her and her wasted life, because if she were in her rightful place she would still be top of the bill in London or America. She was beautiful . . . and she had something to which he could not put a name. And just as she had carried that ungrateful swine, so she had carried many others since, most recently himself. Oh yes, without her he would never have been able to play that part and would never have had this new start in life. But everything had to be paid for, and in his case the payment had been his mother; the compensation of finding a father did not really level things up.

At the sight of her entering the room again carrying a tray, he jumped up and took it from her. On the tray were two bottles and two glasses, and as he went to take the tray from her, he said loudly, 'Now no! No more tonight. Have a heart.'

'I always have this nightcap. I've got this much in common with our dear Beardsley, we both know that the best pick-me-up, the best nightcap is port and brandy mixed. And it's also a remedy for the morning-after-the-night-before.'

'Not for me, thank you.'

'Well, if you won't, Riley, I can't; and I'll not be able to sleep. I know I've got a load on. Oh, yes I know. But I still won't be able to sleep.'

He watched her pour into each glass a measure of brandy, an equal measure of port, then swill the glasses round, and as she handed one to him she said, 'Go on, taste it. You've never tasted anything like it before, I bet.'

He tasted it, and she was right, he had never before tasted anything like it. He'd had a mixture of drinks tonight, oh yes, he had, but this was different.

They were now sitting on the couch together, grinning at each other as they sipped from their glasses; then presently she lay back and relaxed or seemed to relax. And after emptying his glass, Riley said, 'I'll have to be careful or I'll fall asleep here.'

She turned to him now, saying, 'You could sleep here. Nice bedroom upstairs, and warm. I always keep the heater on upstairs, so it's always lovely and warm. You could sleep here tonight.'

'Don't be silly; they'll be expecting me back.'

'What! Expecting you back?' She turned and pointed to the clock, 'Two o'clock in the morning! They'll be dead asleep. You'd have to wake them. But then, have you got a key?'

'Yes, I've got a key.'

'Well then, they'll understand.'

Yes, he supposed they would; but nevertheless he was going back. He must go back . . . he must. What was wrong with him?

She put her glass down on a side table and said, 'Turn off the fire and help me upstairs.'

He turned off the fire, and supporting her with one arm, he left the room with her.

They took the stairs walking abreast, and when

93

they reached the landing she pointed to a door and said, 'Bathroom,' and pushed him towards it while she went to a door opposite, saying, 'Wait for me. Wait for me, mind.'

He went into the bathroom. It too was modern. Everything looked so bright. Perhaps, he thought, it was because he had a load on. He had never felt like this before. It was a feeling as if nothing really mattered very much. He could have started to sing, that was the kind of feeling he had; but Fred had said, 'Don't sing when you're coming in.' Need he go back there? He washed his hands and sluiced his face, and while he stood drying himself on the towel before a long wall mirror he could hardly recognise himself. There was something different about him. He had changed. That was the drink. That's what drink did to you: it made you look older. He wasn't yet nineteen, but he certainly didn't look that young tonight. Good Lord, no! His nose almost touching the mirror, he stared hard at himself. He looked like a man. Well, hadn't he felt himself to be a man for a long time now? Not like this, though.

The click of a door being opened brought him from the mirror. He pushed his hands through his hair before returning to the landing; but he didn't shut the bathroom door behind him because he was brought to a standstill by the sight before him. There before him stood a woman. She looked like a girl, but she wasn't a girl, she was a woman. She was tall and slim. The thick hair was hanging down below her shoulders. She was wearing a nightdress, a flimsy thing, and over it a kind of coat that was equally flimsy. She turned from him now and walked towards another door, saying, 'Come and

94

look in here. This is the best spare bedroom.' She drew him into the room, saying, 'There you are. You have everything here. I keep it ready for when my cousin and her husband come down from Scotland. A nice couple. Don't see enough of them.'

She was standing directly in front of him now and he couldn't keep his eyes off her. She was no longer Miss Mason, she was not his mother on the stage, she was Nyrene, a young woman. She had told him she was thirty-seven, nearing thirty-eight. No, she must have made a mistake. She hardly looked to be thirty; she looked beautiful, really beautiful. She was beautiful as Miss Mason, but standing here now was a soft girl, no woman. But she was no girl, she was a woman, a wonderful woman. He closed his eyes tightly, then blinked; and at this she put her hand on his cheek and said, 'You're dropping with sleep.' Then her voice almost a groan, she muttered, 'Oh! Riley, Riley, I can't bear the thought of your leaving. One more day, Monday, and you're off on Tuesday and out of my life. I can't bear the thought of losing you.'

'Oh miss ... miss, Nyrene, don't cry. Oh my goodness! Don't cry.' She was in his arms now; her head was on his shoulder; her body was shaking and he was holding it. It was thin and warm, and he looked round for some place to sit. There was only the bed and the chair in front of the dressing table. He sat her on the side of the bed and began to fumble in his pocket for a handkerchief, and when he could not find one he began to wipe the tears away from her cheeks with his fingers, saying softly, 'Oh my dear, my dear, please don't worry; we'll keep in touch. I'll come back. Oh yes, I'll come back. I'll have to, because I don't . . .' He shook his head and she said, 'Don't . . . don't worry. I'm sorry, Riley. Oh, I'm sorry. But you've become so dear to me and . . . and . . .' Again she was in his arms, and now his mouth was on hers and they were swaying together . . .

Much later, he couldn't recall exactly when he removed his clothes or when they got into bed together. He only knew that he was holding her and that she was wonderful and that he loved her and was telling her so.

'No more than I love you,' she said. 'They'll all say it's wrong; they'll say it can't be, thirty-seven and eighteen! Seventeen years or whatever, the gap is great, but so is my love, Riley. I didn't mean to tell you. Never! Never! You were to treat me as a friend, a sister, or even a mother. I could be your mother, you know. It is dreadful to think of, but my love for you isn't dreadful.'

Just when had he begun to love her? He didn't know. He only knew that he was loving her now, that he was feeling like a man and if he lived to be a hundred he would never be more of a man than he was in these moments of loving her, and the moments went on and on.

And after he had loved her, and she had loved him, taking him into realms of passion that he had never even dreamed of during his adolescent yearnings.

Which one of them fell asleep first neither of them knew . . .

He came to himself slowly with a voice calling something quite ordinary. But he didn't feel ordinary. He felt different, wonderful . . . oh, wonderful! He stretched his body down the bed. It

96

was a long body, a man's body, and it was firm and still vibrant. He was recalling the feel of her, the smell of her. No smell of brandy or port or wine, but her body smell. Smell wasn't the right word, nor was scent or perfume, nor yet aroma. It was something intangible yet with a substance of its own; and he knew he must always smell it. Oh yes, he couldn't go away now. Never! Never! Mr Bernice would keep him on; he would be only too glad. After all, he hadn't yet signed anything with the others. That was to be done on Tuesday. No, he could never leave her now.

'Are you going to drink this cup of tea or are you going to sleep the clock round?'

He flung the bedclothes from his face and sat up, showing bare to the waist; then a wave of youthful shyness returned and he pulled the bedclothes back up about him as he looked at Nyrene.

She was handing him a cup of tea. She looked different. She was dressed, fully dressed, in a grey woollen dress with a soft-scarlet suede belt at her waist. It appeared to be a small waist. It *was* a small waist; he knew all about her waist. He continued to smile at her softly, until she said, 'Fred's been on the phone. I told him you were still asleep. He's going to call round for you about twelve.'

There was something strange about her voice. He said softly, 'Nyrene,' and to this she answered quickly, 'Look, you're spilling the tea. Drink it. Haven't you got a thick head? I thought I was the only one who never had a stinker the following morning; and yet I must have had an extra load on last night. What time did we get in?'

He pulled himself further up the bed, the clothes

97

with him and his eyes narrowed as he said, 'About ... about one, I think; I can't remember rightly. What time is it now?'

'Oh, about twenty minutes to eleven, I think.'

'*What!*'

'Well, you were carrying a load too, and you're not used to it, are you? So you needed to sleep it off. Anyway, go and have a bath; there's plenty of water. I haven't cooked a large breakfast; I didn't think you would need one this morning. Just some fruit and toast. Now drink your tea while it's hot.'

All of a sudden, the woman standing before him was not Nyrene but Miss Mason. What was the matter with him? Had he been dreaming? Was *this* a dream?

After the door had closed behind her he put the cup down on the bedside table, then stared towards the foot of the bed. He *hadn't* been dreaming, it *had* happened: she *had* stood there—he turned and pointed to the middle of the room—in that gauzy nightie and coat, and she had cried, and he had held her. He remembered it so clearly. He had been tight, yes; but he could remember that. But what he could remember even more clearly was ... He dropped his head onto his chest, and for some seconds there was quietness all around him. It was as if his mind had gone blank or had become a golden mind, as Larry's had. Oh my God! He was sitting up straight again. Had he taken on the mind of the boy and imagined it all so vividly? Because the woman who had just gone out of the room was not the one who had lain with him last night; that had been Nyrene, that beautiful, beautiful woman who had talked about her love and who had loved him. Oh yes, she had, and he her. Well, if thinking

98

like this was madness let him be mad.

His face was screwed up now trying to recall further events of the night; and he remembered that he had gone into Larry's soliloquy about the birds, a sad thing. If the drink could have done that, could it also have turned his mind and allowed him to act out what must have been a secret desire? Because he knew now that what he recalled, be it hallucination, dream, or imagination, spelt the same thing: he loved her, yes, yes, he loved her. He had loved her before he had taken her in his arms last night. He had known it then.

He threw back the bedclothes and stood up naked on the rug, and now he muttered to himself, 'I *wasn't* dreaming. I couldn't have been, but either she doesn't remember or she doesn't want to.' Oh but last night she had wanted to remember. He could hear her plainly now crying out her love for him, and how it had grown and that it didn't matter about the years between.

He dropped suddenly onto the edge of the bed. The years between. He wasn't yet nineteen, and there were nearly twenty years between them. How could they be in love? Yes, how could they be in love? She was nearly as old as his mother. His mother was only forty. It couldn't have happened. No, it couldn't have happened. Well, if it couldn't have happened it was the drink that had given him the experience and he should be grateful for it.

He pulled on his pants and gathered the rest of his clothes; then he crossed the landing and, as instructed, he took a bath. They had a bath at home, but it was a council-house bath, and a council-house bathroom, a room that was nothing like this. He hadn't imagined that she lived like

99

this. Altogether, it was a much better house, better furnished, better equipped than Fred's and Louise's new one, and in a way he could understand her not wanting to leave it; and this must have been her reason for not accepting the offer.

He was lying in the bubble-capped water of the bath when he suddenly sat up. No, it certainly wasn't hallucination; he could remember Mr Bernice talking to him, and then all the handshaking and even the feeling of loss he had had at parting from the cast; and he could remember the surprise he felt when he entered the hall of this house. But he didn't remember much that occurred after that until they were in the bedroom. He thought they had made coffee, and he could just remember coming upstairs. Oh yes, he remembered seeing her on the landing. And then she was sitting on the bed and he had his arms about her. It was neither a dream nor an hallucination. His hands splashed the water and the bubbles flew and he looked towards the door as if expecting his mother to come in and demand, 'What are you playing at, boy?' But he wasn't a boy, and he wasn't a lad, and the experience he had gone through during the night had taken him much further than ever he had imagined . . . by yes! He'd say it had. But there she was, denying everything by her very look, that coolness and the very stance of her. She was Miss Mason of the theatre, and her entire appearance had denied the whole experience he had gone through . . . she had taken him through.

He dried himself, then partly dressed, and, as of habit, washed out the bath and left the bathroom as he had found it. That was his mother's training. Oh, his mother! My God! If she were to get wind of this. But how could she? Unless he opened his mouth. If she had thought part of the play was dirty, what in heaven's name would she say about this, with a woman as old as herself?

Back in the bedroom, he finished dressing, and then, as he had done in the bathroom, he tidied everything. At his final effort, straightening the bed, he knew for certain that he had not imagined any of the incidents of last night.

In the kitchen, Nyrene turned from the toaster, smiling, and said, 'Did we have a brandy and port last night?'

He paused a moment as if thinking, then said, 'I can't remember.' If it was to be a game then he must play it her way; even if it wasn't a game, he still must play it her way.

'Well, we must have done because you don't seem to have a very thick head this morning.'

'What time did you get up?'

'Oh'—she turned and looked at the clock—'at about half-past eight; and when Fred phoned he said he had a thick head, as had Louise, and that when they got in the baby-sitter was sound asleep and that her people hadn't phoned to find out what was up. "So much for parental care," he said. And so, he'd had to take her home . . . One or two slices of toast?'

'Oh, I'll just have a cup of tea.'

'You'll not have just a cup of tea, you'll have something to eat with it. And first of all, get that grapefruit down you.'

He ate half of a fresh grapefruit, followed by a slice of toast. As he was drinking his second cup of

101

tea she sat down opposite him at the table, her elbows cupping her face as she looked at him and said, 'Oh, Riley, I am going to miss you.'

It was a comment that one friend would have said to another and if he wanted any proof that she recalled nothing that had happened earlier, this was it: 'Oh Riley, I'm going to miss you.' Just that. He could have been any one of the cast who was about to leave.

A deep hurt swelled inside him, gnawing its way up between his ribs, it gathered into a tight band just below his windpipe. So painful was it that he put his hand on the front of his shirt and rubbed it. She remarked on it, saying, 'What is it? You have a pain there?'

'Sort of. It's like indigestion. Too much drink. Does drink give you indigestion?'

'Oh, drink can give you all kinds of symptoms.'

Now her hand was across the table and holding his, and she was saying, in the voice that was not Miss Mason's, 'Will you miss me, Riley?'

He couldn't bear it. He gripped her hand with both of his so tightly that she winced, and he said, 'Oh my dear, I'm sorry, I'm sorry,' and he found his throat to be so dry he couldn't go on further; and when his head drooped, she said, 'Now, Riley, I know you feel indebted to me but there's no need. You have so much talent it was bound to come out sooner or later; you would have discovered it yourself without anyone's help.'

'You . . . you don't know how I feel. I—' He was shaking his head slowly from side to side now and his eyes were looking into hers when she replied, 'I do, Riley, I do. But you are so young. You know that? You are still so young.'

'I am not young.' His voice was deep as any man's now, and he went on, 'I have never felt young in the brain department; I just put it to the wrong use, as Mr Beardsley ... Fred has pointed out so often; and since I've been at the Palace I've felt I'm a man. And I know this much: only a man could have played the part in "The Golden Mind", and only a man could have followed where you led. I know I have a lot to learn, and I keep learning it; but I am learning it as a man, not as a boy or a callow youth.' He stood up now, because the pain had turned into anger, and he almost barked at her, 'I won't let anyone treat me as a boy or a youth in future. I'm telling you.' And with this, he stalked out of the kitchen, leaving her gazing towards the door, her clenched fists pressed tightly against her lips as she groaned inwardly: 'Oh my darling. My darling.'

Not until she heard his footsteps coming down the stairs did she enter the hall, to see him dressed for outdoors; and she hurried towards him, saying appealingly, 'Oh, Riley! Please don't go like this.'

'It's all right. It's all right. I'll look in before Tuesday. I'll walk round to Fred's now.'

She had him by the shoulders and was staring into his eyes, her voice held a soft, agonised appeal as she said, 'Please ... please! I beg of you, don't leave me like this. This is the last time I will have you. Just stay until Fred comes for you. Please! Do this for me. Let us sit down together quietly and talk. Please, Riley! Please.'

His whole body seemed to be bent in two. He allowed her to take off his coat and scarf; he threw his hat on to the chair; then together they made their way into the sitting-room.

The log fire was already lit. There was the couch they had sat on last night; and now they sat on it again, and she took his hand and pleaded, 'Leave me a memory to fall back on, please. Please, Riley!' She had his hand on her lap, and when he let out a long deep sigh she remained silent for almost a minute. Then she said, 'You must keep in touch. When you're on the road, as you will be, there won't be much time for writing. But wherever you are, just send me a card; then I'll know you haven't forgotten me.'

When she felt his whole body shudder and move as if away from her, she said, 'You won't have any idea of how long the tour will be or where you are going, but do let me know. You will, won't you?'

He slowly nodded his head just as a child might and, as she went on talking, he listened to her much as he might have done to his mother if she hadn't been such a narrow-minded woman; the man in him slipped away again and he was the boy he had denied, the boy whose one desire at this moment was to put his arms about this woman and to bury himself in her.

CHAPTER SIX

His first week in Manchester was spent in rehearsal for the pantomime. When it finished, three weeks later, rehearsals for the tour began and continued until the end of February. The rehearsal for the pantomime and the show itself he enjoyed to the full, which enabled him to stifle the pain of Nyrene, but the play itself he found less engrossing. He read it twice, and went over his part dozens of times. There was no Miss Mason to guide him this time. His part wasn't very large but it was important. For half of it he played a drunk; for the other half he was the youngest son of a notable family who was being kept at home to check his philandering. He was a cadger, and the fact that he needed money was the crux of the play. It dealt with family intrigue, divorce and a death to be investigated; it had some good fights, and one of the highlights was an Irish Ceilidh held, when the family were away, by the servants and himself as the youngest son. This was where he had to let himself go in song and dance.

He knew he was capable of playing all these parts, but there was one snag, which was why he had had to read the script over and over again. It was his voice and his northern accent. He did not speak as a Geordie might, but nevertheless he used the idiom, and the inflection at times was strong; and so for a full fortnight he had spent two hours a day with a voice trainer, and afterwards reading his parts in a highfallutin twang, as he put it. The only time he would be able to let himself go would be in the Ceilidh, when he would imitate the antics and twangs of the staff and the household. He had soon discovered the cast were very different from those at The Palace. There wasn't as yet that co-operation and warmth between them, although no doubt being on the road would bring that.

He had three days before setting out on the enterprise that would surely reveal to him what real touring was about, and he phoned Fred to ask if he could go through for a couple of nights, and Fred had bawled back, using no polite language, 'What are you talking about? You went off with the key of the door, didn't you?' . . .

Riley arrived at three o'clock in the afternoon during a heavy snowstorm. Because of the weather, the school had been closed so Fred was at home. He greeted Riley with open arms. As he helped him off with the heavy grey sheepskin-lined coat he said, 'My! My! Things are looking up already.'

'Second-hand. They know all the tricks in Manchester. Four pounds complete with lining.'

'Never!'

'Oh yes. Likely it was pinched; but what matter.'

'Hello, my dear.' Louise came from the sitting-room, her arms held out towards him, and after kissing her on both cheeks he said, 'French fashion: it's the in thing.'

'Go on with you. It's been the in thing in France since the first Napoleon was a lad.'

'What weather! It isn't snowing in Manchester or anywhere else.'

'Well, if it isn't, then the radio weather report is lying. But come on into the kitchen and have a cup of tea first. Are you hungry? I have a meat pudding on . . . a pot pie, as you call it.'

'Good. I love pot pies with plenty of gravy.'

'Sit yourself down.' Fred went to push him into a chair, but then stopped him from sitting by grabbing his shoulder and, holding him at arm's length and looking him up and down, he exclaimed, 'You wearing high heels or artificial soles?'

'Not when I left this morning, no.'

'Well, you seem to have put on inches since we last saw you.'

'It's my manly bearing, and haven't you noticed

my upper-clarss accent? I've had to learn how to . . . articulate correctly since I left you lot. I told the language lady that my awful way of speaking was due to my teacher; he was so broad.'

'How dare you! I have never spoken broad in my natural northern life.'

'Stop it, you two! Anyway, you stop it,' and Louise pushed at her husband, then turned back to Riley and said, 'Come on, give us your news.'

So he told them about the pantomime, the cast and the big names that appeared in it, then added, 'It strikes me as most odd, you know, that these top stars—after they've made it—want to play in pantomimes. They practically fight for the parts. Lord! If I was where some of them are they could keep their pantomimes.'

'Well, wait till that time and see how you feel then. Go on, what about this play. Do you think it's any good?'

'Oh yes, it's good; but it isn't "The Golden Mind". In a way, you know, I'm sorry I ever did that; I find myself now looking for faults and picking out niggly things in other people's work.'

'Well, that's all right, only keep it to yourself.'

All the time he had been talking he had been wanting to ask one question, and now he could resist no longer: 'How is Nyrene?' he asked, and his tone was even.

'Oh! Our Nyrene is in fine form, never better, but, mind, for a couple of days after you left we didn't know whether she had locked herself in or left the house. The Palace of course, as you know, was closed for a week, but she wasn't to be found. I had a suspicion then that she had gone on the bottle again, but later we found out we were

107

wrong.' He glanced at Louise now, and it was she who, nodding at Riley, said in an exaggerated whisper, 'She has a boyfriend. She told me yesterday. As you know, she has a married cousin in Scotland and although they come down at times, I've never met them, though Fred has.'

Fred nodded now, saying, 'Yes, and they're a nice couple, very nice. Well, apparently the boyfriend is a friend of theirs. He's a traveller in plastics. The two days I thought she was on the binge she must have spent with him. Aha! Aha!' and he nodded at Riley, a broad grin on his face; but then, the grin disappearing, he said quite seriously, 'I'm glad for her. She's been on her own all these years. I don't know how she's put up with it at times, because she's an attractive woman. Likely she's still harping after that rotter.'

He felt sick to the pit of his stomach. He was experiencing a feeling something similar to that he had had when he woke up that morning and found that she had changed from a wonderful loving woman back into Miss Mason.

During these past weeks he had tried in every way to get her out of his mind. The days had been bearable because there was so much to do, so much to think about, so much to learn, and with so many people milling around, but from the moment he dropped into bed in Mrs Wear's boarding house and longing for sleep the torment would begin again.

It had happened.

It couldn't have, judging by her expression as she stood there handing him a cup of tea.

But it had, it had.

Well, if it had, it had happened with a drunken

woman who had forgotten all about it, a thought which made him even more sick and brought the picture of her down to a level against which he would physically screw up his eyes; and now, here they were saying she had a boyfriend.

'What's the matter?' Fred was looking at him intently, and he answered, 'The matter? Nothing. Nothing.'

'You're shocked at the idea she should have a boyfriend.'

'Shocked!' The reply came out on a yell. 'These days? Where do you think I've been for the past weeks. Shocked, man? You know nothing about it.'

Louise put in quickly, 'What are the girls like in the cast?' To which he answered, 'Two of them are very pretty and fetching, another is old in the tooth behind her make-up, and one of them is married to the leading man.'

'Well, if there're two pretty ones still at large—'

'Oh, they're not at large, Fred—' He always had difficulty in calling this man by his Christian name, having been so used to Mr Beardsley or sir, but he went on, 'They've got sleeping partners in the cast. Perhaps I should be more modern and say boyfriends. But it's funny about lasses nowadays, they all veer towards much older men. Not understandable, is it?'

'Well, it isn't, looking at him,' Louise said, slapping her husband gently about the ears. 'But he's canny,' she said lovingly.

'I still maintain though, you must have been hard up at the time to take him.' She joined in his laughter when she said, 'I was; I was very hard up; but he was the best that was on offer, and so I jumped.'

When Louise's fingers went through Fred's hair he looked at Riley and said, 'A fella's got to wait until a certain age before he really becomes attractive and knows what it's all about.'

'Oh my. Oh my,' Riley sighed, and Louise came back with, 'Don't worry, Riley, the only thing they're sure about, men of this type'—she again patted her husband's head—'is that age gallops on them around now. Anyway, we're going to dinner at Nyrene's tonight to meet the gentleman in question, that is if he manages to get here from France in this dreadful weather. I'll phone Nyrene and tell her you're here. I'm sure she'd love to see you again.'

He rose from the table abruptly now, saying, 'I could do with a bath, Louise. Then I'll look in on the nipper. Is he up in the nursery?'

'Yes, but pay your visit first to the nursery. His lordship is at the painting stage, so look out for your suit. I would take off your jacket.'

Fred and Louise looked at each other and Fred said, 'Well, what do you think?' to which she answered, 'I don't know. I really don't know, except that he's changed.'

'I'll say he has. I could still see the lad in him when he left but it's there no more.'

'Do you think he's worrying about his mother and being here instead of at home and what she'll be thinking?'

'I wouldn't know, dear, I just wouldn't know; it could be, but I noticed a change in his expression when the boyfriend was mentioned.'

'Well, in a way I can understand his reaction because, you know, she's made a lot of him over these past two years. He might have been her son, although she's never acted like a mother towards him, more like a—' They looked at each other for the explanation, and when it wasn't forthcoming, Fred said, 'Yes, more like a what? She was his mother in the play all right, but off it, no. In spite of her drinking she never looked her age; and these last few days . . . well, I saw her twice last week and she was beaming.'

'Well, all I can say, dear,' said Louise on a laugh, 'is if this man can make her beam, long may he shine on her.'

'Oh, that's a stinker of a pun.'

'Yes, I know it is; but anyway, we'll see what he's like tonight and we'll take particular note of our friend's reaction'—she looked upwards—'that might give us a clue.'

'I hope it doesn't give you the clue that you've got in your mind.'

'Why not? Why not?'

'Don't be silly. The age difference between people of thirty and fifty doesn't matter so much, but he's nineteen, and Nyrene must be nearly forty, if she's a day.'

'Well he's an old nineteen. He was an old sixteen when I first met him. Stranger things have happened.'

'Well, all I can say at the moment,' said Fred, 'is that I hope such a strange thing hasn't happened to them.'

*   *   *

They were in the sitting-room. The artificial log fire was burning brightly. The chandelier wasn't lit, but the light from two gold-shaded standard lamps and six wall lights merged the colours of the carpet, the drapes, and the loose covers on the Chesterfield suite into a harmonious whole.

Louise and Fred were seated one at each end of the couch; Riley was sitting in an armchair at the other side of the fireplace.

The room looked different from how he remembered it. In fact, the whole house looked different. But at that time his main view had been through a white light of love, created by a wine haze.

The far door opened and he watched her enter the room, and coming in, pulling off a white apron to reveal the complete blue woollen dress. Again she was wearing the red suede belt at her waist. Her hair wasn't in its usual bun at the nape of her neck, but was loose and tied with a blue ribbon, making her look like a teenager from behind. However, from the front she certainly didn't have the appearance of a teenager; she looked a woman, a very, very beautiful woman. Her skin was clear, her eyes were bright. He hadn't before noticed that they were grey. Previously, he had thought they were green. But no, they were definitely grey. And her mouth was wide and laughing. Had that mouth ever kissed him, not only kissed his lips but kissed him all over? Oh, for God's sake, man!

'I don't think one can get any further down the culinary scale than to ask friends to dinner and offer them a meat pudding,' Nyrene was saying.

'Don't you believe it.' Fred nodded from his corner of the couch. 'If I'm to believe what I read the other day the self-appointed moguls are sick of chicken, game and turkey and are actually asking for steak and kidney pud . . . as grandma made it,'

112

he laughed. 'But it isn't everybody that can make a proper meat pudding. I love what I call the jelly part, where the steam has softened the crust.'

'Well, I'll give you a good helping of the jelly part, Fred. What part do you like, Riley?' She was standing by the side of his chair looking down at him.

'Oh.' He looked up at her without smiling as he said, 'Any part that fills me up.'

'Well, I can promise to fill you up, because I've made two man-sized ones.'

'Come and sit down, dear.' Louise patted the cushion to her side. 'You've been buzzing about like a bee. It isn't seven yet'—she pointed to the clock—'and you said he'd arrive about seven.'

'When did he say that?' Fred asked, and Nyrene answered, 'Yesterday morning.'

'Yesterday morning?' he repeated. 'Well, look what the weather's done since yesterday morning; it's gone barmy, and it will be a wonder if his plane will have been able to take off, let alone land on time.'

It was at this point that the bell rang. Nyrene had been about to sit down, but now she straightened up quickly and looked from one to the other in surprise, and then she muttered as she hurried to the door, 'He . . . he could have got in.'

Fred and Louise were facing directly towards the door but Riley was only half-turned towards it, and although he told himself not to do so he looked directly at her when she returned carrying an enormous bouquet of flowers.

'His flowers have come,' she said, 'even if he hasn't. I've only just got rid of the last lot.' There was a shy note in her voice now. 'Excuse me for a

113

minute; I'll go and put them in water until the morning.'

As she hurried out the three of them exchanged glances, but it was Fred who remarked, 'Thoughtful bloke. Talks big at least with flowers,' and turning to Louise, he added, 'It used to be a single red rose in my time.'

'But that was many, many years ago, dear.'

'Watch it woman! Watch it!'

Riley watched them chipping each other, their love-making hardly disguised.

At half-past seven Nyrene, glancing at the clock, said, 'I'll give him another quarter of an hour. If he's not here by then we'll eat, because the puddings will be getting soggy.'

The next fifteen minutes was taken up mostly with question and answer between Fred and Riley, Fred being the questioner, and just as Nyrene rose from the couch saying, 'Well, that's that! We're not waiting any longer; he can have it warmed up, or sandwiches or something. Come on,' the phone rang. It was as if she hadn't heard it for she made no response. It was Louise who said, 'That's the phone, Nyrene.'

'The phone? Yes, of course. What's the matter with me?'

She ran down the room and into the hall, and the three of them stood listening to her saying, 'Hello, dear,' followed by a silence during which they all concentrated their gaze towards the open door into the hall. Then Nyrene's voice came again: 'Oh, I am so sorry, dear. Still it can't be helped. Until tomorrow then; that's if possible. Yes dear . . . Oh, yes indeed, dear. Indeed . . . Oh, please don't worry . . . don't attempt tomorrow if the roads are bad. I understand. Of course, I do . . . Oh, what is a meat pudding! Yes, my dear. Yes, all right. Good-night. Good-night.'

She came back into the room unsmiling and saying flatly, 'He's stuck in Manchester. He's just got down. They've been going round and round for ages. They were an hour late leaving. I'm sorry.'

'What's to be sorry about? There'll be other times. What's worrying me at the moment is that pudding getting soggier and soggier.'

'Oh, you!' Louise pushed Fred and he fell back on to the couch and sat for a moment looking up at them and saying, 'And only one port. That's all I've had, one measly glass of port.'

'Oh, get up! And come on with you. You're like that man in the films who used to turn into the Incredible Hulk.'

'Well, I like that!' Fred pulled himself up from the couch and nodded towards Riley, asking, 'Do you remember him?'

'Oh yes, yes. And his eyes went funny just as he was about to change personalities. Yours go a bit odd at times you know.' And on this light note they made their way, laughing, to the dining-room.

There were no starters; they went straight into the meat pudding, together with sprouts, glazed carrots and mashed potatoes, and the quality of this course received its due appreciation.

But the sweet was more elaborate: jellied fruits in a ring of puff pastry and topped with fresh cream and spikes of angelica. This, too, received its share of appreciation; and when Fred said, 'All I can say, Nyrene, is that you'll make a good wife for some man one of these days,' Nyrene answered in the same vein, except even more lightly, 'Well, I hope so.' What could be said to be a tactless remark was passed over, yet all the while Fred was cursing himself for his stupidity and Riley was thinking, She wants to be married; you can see it in her face. She's glowing. Yes, that's the word, glowing . . .

It was ten o'clock when they left. Fred kicked a path through the snow on the pavement to the car door. The night was bright and clear. There was a stillness everywhere, and when Fred shouted to Louise as he walked back to meet her on the garden path, 'Come on then,' his voice rang down the street like that of a night watchman.

Riley was left standing in the doorway gazing at Nyrene. Her face, which up till now had appeared so bright, had taken on an almost sad look, and when she put out a hand and cupped his cheek he wanted to grab it and pull her towards him, only for him then to ask himself what she was playing at. Her bloke hadn't turned up and she was disappointed, but she had played the hostess all night, hadn't she? But now . . .

'Oh, Riley! Riley! It's been lovely seeing you. Don't forget me, will you? Don't forget me. And don't think badly of me, please.'

He was about to say, 'Think badly of you, why?' when Fred's voice boomed out again, 'Come on with you! Let her get in out of the cold. She'll freeze.'

She was pushing him gently now on the chest, but his eyes remained tight on her silhouette until he felt his arm gripped none too gently by Fred who was saying, 'What's up with you? Louise is freezing. Come on, man! Come on!'

Sitting in the back of the car, he looked out of the window. She was still standing there . . . 'Don't

116

forget me,' she had said. 'Don't think badly of me.' That look on her face. It was so different, at least from what it had been all evening whenever she had looked at him. But, until that moment, she hadn't looked him straight in the eyes.

'Don't forget me.' Why did she say that? Why did she have to say that when she was full up with this other bloke? Foreign calls, flowers, and skipping around all evening like a teenager. But the woman he had loved hadn't been a teenager, she had been a woman, and at one time in their love-making she had looked at him with that same expression that she had had on her face just a few minutes ago.

Shut up! Drop it! You'll drive yourself barmy, man. All right, all right. Perhaps you weren't dreaming. Perhaps it did happen. Well if it did happen, as you've admitted before, it was with a drunken woman who has forgotten every blasted minute of it.

Or had she?

Dry up! For God's sake.

CHAPTER SEVEN

Spotting Nyrene walking along the pavement, Louise pulled the car into the kerb and, lowering the window, she called, 'Where're you off to at this time in the day?'

'Oh, hello, Louise.' Nyrene bent down to the face that was upturned to hers and, smiling, she said, 'I've cut the rehearsal; I was feeling a bit

117

groggy.'

'And meaning to walk home?'

'No, madam, I wasn't, I was making for the taxi-rank at the end there.'

'Well, get in, and I'll charge you only half-price.'

'Thank you very much, ma'am. Will you come in and have a cup of tea?'

'Yes, and I'll be glad of one; I've been shopping. That young fellow of ours outgrows his pants, his sleeping bag, the lot, every week it seems.'

'Well, Fred calls him his bouncing boy, and that's what he is.'

'There's a pair of them.'

Five minutes later they were sitting in Nyrene's kitchen, and Louise said, 'I'll see to the tea. Sit down; you look green. Have you eaten something bad?'

'Could be; I'm eating too much altogether these days.'

'Well, perhaps you are.' Louise looked at Nyrene intently for a moment, then said, 'I thought you were putting on a bit of weight. I said so to Fred but he said, not you; you've been like a rake for years.'

There was no response from Nyrene for a moment until, her head slightly drooped and her gaze directed towards the table, she said, 'Well, pregnant women are known to put it on, aren't they?'

The cup and saucer jangled in Louise's hand, and she said, 'What did you say?'

'You heard what I said, dear: pregnant women—'

'You're pregnant, Nyrene?' The question was soft and awe-filled.

And Nyrene answered it in the same vein, her

voice scarcely above a whisper, saying, 'Yes, Louise, I am pregnant.'

'Well, well!' It was as if Louise was just emerging out of a doze or a dream: her eyes blinked, she moistened her lips, then said, 'How far are you gone?'

'Oh.' It seemed that Nyrene had to consider; then she said, 'Oh, just over two months.'

'Well, well! Two months.'

'Yes, Louise, two months; and don't try to reckon up. I know I went up to Scotland for a weekend at the time Charles was there.'

'You call him Charles? That's the first time you've mentioned his name.'

'Well, that *is* his name; and I've been up to Scotland since.'

'Does he know?'

'No, not yet.'

'Will he be pleased?'

'Of that, my dear, I'm not certain. It's slightly worrying.'

'Oh, Nyrene.'

'Don't say, oh, Nyrene, in that tone, Louise, because that part doesn't matter.'

'What d'you mean? You don't mind if he cares or not?'

'Oh yes, I do; but it's not all that important. What is important is—' she paused and a smile came over her pale face as she said, 'having a baby, the wonder of having a baby, something of your own, something belonging to you, something to cherish. You know what? It doesn't matter to me what I have, boy or girl, twins or whatever, it will be a baby, something of my own.'

'Oh my dear.' Tears were in Louise's eyes, then

119

onto her cheeks as she rushed around the table to put her arms about Nyrene. And when Nyrene got to her feet, they held each other tightly, and Louise, the tears flowing now, said, 'I know what you mean. Oh, I know what you mean. After I was dumped: and you know all about me being dumped, don't you? I am sure his lordship has told you. Anyway I went a bit berserk; I had to go away for a time, you know. And it was strange, but that too was the thought in my mind during my bad periods: I'll never have a child. I'll never have a child. It would repeat itself, and when Jason first came and I knew that he was there inside me'—she now patted her stomach—'it was as if . . . well, God himself had visited me.'

'Yes, that's what it's like, Louise, you've said it, just as if God himself had entered into you. Well, I can tell you it's the most beautiful thing that has ever happened to me in my life, ever, ever, and if he wants it, it'll be marvellous, but if he doesn't want it, well . . . it'll still be mine.'

'Oh, my dear. My dear.' Again they were enfolded; and now Nyrene's face was wet. Then when Nyrene said, 'The best way to express happiness is to cry,' they both laughed; and she added, 'An old actor said that to me once because, you see, I rarely cry off the stage although I can cry to order on it. In fact, it was due to being able to cry at will on the stage that I once got an offer to go to London.'

'And you turned it down. Oh, I know all about it. I wonder what Fred will say.'

'I think he'll be pleased for me.'

'Oh, he'll be pleased for you, all right. Oh yes. He's very, very fond of you, you know. I told him once that if he'd had any sense he would have cocked his cap at you years ago.'

'You didn't!'

'Oh yes, I did. I love him to distraction but he can be a very irritating man, can our Mr Beardsley, when he gets a bee in his bonnet. And then it turns out to be the whole hive, not just a single bee. Oh, let's have another cup, eh?'

Later, at the front door, Louise turned suddenly to Nyrene and said, 'But what about The Palace and Mr David?'

'I've told him.'

'You have?'

'Yes.'

'How did he take it?'

'He was pleased for me and said I could take as long off as I needed, that there'd always be a hole in The Palace for me to crawl into. He's a good man, is David. Always has been; at least he's been good to me.'

'I wonder what Riley will say. I had a card from him this morning.'

There was a pause before Nyrene said, 'Yes, so did I, from Eastbourne. They've done Wimbledon, Bournemouth and Worthing. I don't know exactly where they're bound for next.'

'Oh, I think it's Reading, then Oxford, Birmingham, Coventry and so on. Fred's got it all written down. He's very, very fond of Riley, you know, Nyrene, and he's got it into that big head of his that it was he who started him on his career.'

'Well, I'm sure he did. Has Fred had a letter from him recently?'

'Yes, about a fortnight ago.'

'Oh. Did he say when he's likely to be here

121

again?'

'Perhaps towards the end of next month, or the beginning of May, when they end up in Newcastle after doing Sunderland. I think, too, they're booked up for Scotland, and perhaps Ireland, too. It isn't a controversial play, so it might take on there. And do you know something, Nyrene? His father comes round every now and again to see if there's a letter for him, and there usually is; and I'm sure there's something in it by way of paper money. But I don't think he comes just for that, he seems genuinely concerned for him. Fred asked him once about his wife, had she softened towards Riley? But his father said, not a bit; hardened if anything. And apparently their daughter Betty is bearing the brunt of it. If Riley had gone on drugs or got a girl or two into trouble, well, you could understand it, but as young fellas go today he's kept as clean as a whistle, to voice my husband's much used phrase. Hasn't he written to you, I mean anything besides the cards?'

Nyrene gave a small laugh as she said, 'No, just the cards, and always with the same message: he hopes I am well. Although sometimes there's a little change when he says he used to look forward to weekends, but that now Sunday means scene shifting, followed by a train journey to some other oasis in the desert. The one I received this morning said he was going to write a book on seaside landladies, particularly theatrical ones.'

Louise laughed as she said, 'On Fred's this morning he wrote, "Why didn't you educate me, Beardsley, when you had the chance, instead of thrusting me out in the cruel wide world, where people talk proper?" He's still the natural

122

comedian. Well, I must be off, and I'm dying to pass your news on to him.' But Nyrene thrust her hand quickly out and grabbed Louise's as she said, 'Oh no! Don't, please. Don't tell him; I'd rather you didn't.'

'Fred? Not tell Fred?'

'Oh yes, yes, Fred; I thought you meant Riley.'

'Oh no, no, I'll leave that to you, dear.'

Nyrene nodded. 'Yes, leave it to me.'

After the door had closed on Louise, Nyrene stood with her back to it and drew in a long shuddering breath before putting her hands on her stomach as she repeated, 'Leave it to me.'

CHAPTER EIGHT

At about four o'clock in the afternoon on a day in the middle of May, Riley rang her doorbell. He expected her to be at home about this time. The air around him was heavy with the smell of May as it drifted from the large hawthorn tree in the next garden, its branches obligingly stretched over the dividing fence.

When there was no immediate reply he again put his finger on the bell, but this time, before his hand had dropped away there she stood, this strange woman. She had evidently just pulled an apron from her waist: she was dressed in a shapeless blue cotton dress; she had no stockings on and her toes showed through openwork sandals. Her mouth was agape as she whispered his name: 'Riley.'

He did not say, Hello, Nyrene or Aren't you

123

going to ask me in? He just remained still and looking at her. The last time he had seen her she had been as thin as a rake; now her face was showing plumpness. She was big all over.

His eyes came to rest on a stomach that seemed to be gently forcing her dress out of shape, and the sight of it caused him to say, but to himself, 'No. No.' Then, 'Good God, no!' And again, 'No. No.' It was as if there was a shout coming out of the top of his head crying, 'Good God, not that! And at her age!' Well, what age was she now? Thirty-eight come thirty-nine? They had bairns at forty-five today, and after. But . . . but her.

'Aren't you coming in?'

'Oh yes, yes.' He turned and looked at the May branch, then remarked, 'Nice smell that, May.'

She nodded. 'It is a beautiful smell. No-one has yet been able to reproduce it. When did you get in?'

'Oh, about an hour ago. There was no-one in'—he jerked his head to the side as if indicating the Beardsleys—'except the cleaning woman, to whom I had to prove my identity.'

It was strange. He was speaking differently: 'to whom I had to prove,' he had said, not who I had to prove my identity to, but, 'to whom I had to prove'. He looked different: so much older. Oh yes, so much older. And he looked so smart. He was handsome . . . a young man.

'The house looks the same.' He was walking into the sitting-room now. 'This hasn't altered, but'—he stopped abruptly and turned to face her—'you have, haven't you?'

'Yes, yes, Riley I have. A blind man could tell I have. Are you shocked?'

'I don't know. To tell you the truth I don't know how I'm feeling. I can't imagine you with a—' He couldn't say kid, he couldn't say child, he couldn't say bairn, he had to force himself to say, 'baby.'

'I couldn't at first either, but . . . but I can now.'

'You want it then?'

'Want it? Oh, Riley, yes, yes I want it. As I've never wanted anything in my life before, I want this baby.'

There was that sick feeling in him again. He had a desire to yell at her, Why? Why? Why? But need he ask why? That damned nightmare was still with him. At this moment he would like to take her by the shoulders and say, Tell me, don't you remember? Please tell me that you remember something of that night, just something, and he would go on to say, because that night has bloody well altered my life. I should be enjoying myself as only a male my age knows how, but what do I do, turn me nose up. There's a girl in the troupe just breaking her neck to jump into bed with me. But she now thinks I'm a poof, in fact she's nearly said as much. And married women; well, those with boyfriends, you'd think they'd be satisfied with one, but no. And I can't let myself go. D'you hear that? I can't let myself go. All because of that bloody nightmare. Or was it a nightmare? You're the only one that knows. Instead, he found himself asking a question, 'Does he want it?'

She turned her head away from him, saying, 'Not really.'

'What?'

'I'm still within an arm's length of you, Riley, so don't shout. Lots of men don't want to be saddled with children, but he's willing that I should have it;

125

he didn't want me to have it taken away. In any case, I wouldn't have, never! Never! Anyway, would you like a cup of tea?'

There was a long pause before he said, 'Yes, yes I'd like a cup of tea.'

'Then why are we standing in the sitting-room? Come on into the kitchen. And don't look so amazed, Riley; these things happen. Have you learnt nothing from your stage experience?'

'No, not a damn thing that'll do me any good.'

'Well,'—she laughed now as they crossed the hall towards the kitchen—'it doesn't show: you look very much the prosperous actor. David tells me there was quite a good report from Manchester about the way you're shaping up.'

'Oh really? Well, all I can say is you hear things that I don't; and whatever it is, I hope the rest of the cast don't hear of it, because they're very touchy as regards their positions, and if that northeast youngster is sucking up, well he'd better look out.'

'Are they like that?'

'Well, perhaps I'm exaggerating a bit, but the prestige battle of the stage shouldn't have to be explained to you. Now should it? You've had some.'

'Well, from what I've been given to understand you're not the lead, you're not even the stand-in.'

'No, but the black sheep of the family in this play is an important spoke in its intricate wheel. That's what I was told by my Manchester boss and that I've got to put my all into it, just as I did into Larry; and that's what I do.'

'Ah well, that explains it . . . your all. Anyway, do you like touring?'

126

'To that I could answer yes and no. I like it when I see a new audience and a full house, but I don't like it finishing on a Saturday night and then having to travel on a Sunday so as to get down to it again early on Monday morning. And what I also don't take to is changing digs. Although I must say some have been good; but others . . . oh, far from it. You see, if you can't get into some place that is used to dealing with the roadsters and instead you go into an ordinary boarding house and they learn that you're from the stage, well, you must be making a mint, and so they charge accordingly.'

They were sitting opposite each other at the table now, with a cup of tea in front of them, and all he could do was stare at her. There was so much he wanted to say to her, so many questions he wanted to put to her. One of them was, when was the child due? He worked towards it by saying, 'How long are you going to go on working?'

'Oh, I'm only,'—she paused—'about four and a half months gone; I think I can go on for at least another two months. During the next two plays I'm twice a grandmother and once a pregnant . . . lady. That'll fit in nicely. I'll leave after that, I think.'

'Why aren't you getting married?'

'Because I don't want to.'

'Well, the child'll be illegitimate.'

'Yes, it'll be illegitimate, like thousands of others; but that doesn't create a scandal these days.'

'No, but the kid—whether male or female—will know it hasn't a legal father, and no matter how you polish it up, it and thousands of others will feel they've missed out . . . illegitimate . . . bastards.'

They seemed to rise to their feet simultaneously

and whatever he was going to say by way of apology was cut off by her voice, which seemed to be coming through her clenched teeth as she said, 'Riley, I have put up with a lot from you, but not any more. Do you hear? Not any more, because whatever my child turns out to be—' and now her voice rose to a shout, 'it's got nothing to do with you! Understand that? Nothing at all to do with you. Now will you please go!'

His whole body was shivering. It was as if she had struck him; yet he was crying out inside, I'm sorry. Oh, I'm sorry. I never meant to say that. Never, never!

But when he did speak his voice was a croak, 'Nyrene, believe me, please! Please believe me, I had no intention. I don't know what made me.' He bowed his head and closed his eyes, but there was no soft or pardoning ring in her tone as she replied, 'It was in your mind or you wouldn't have said it. Now go. Please go. And I don't want to see you again.'

His head jerked upwards and he said, 'Don't say that. Whatever I've done, however I've hurt you, please, please don't say that. You see, I—' He paused, turned from the table, pushing the chair back so violently that it toppled over. After he had straightened it, he gripped its back and bent over it and almost whimpered, 'Don't say you don't want to see me again, please, please, Nyrene, because I must see you. Somehow I must see you.'

She let out a long drawn breath that touched on a cry and her voice was low now as she said, 'Just leave me for now then, please.'

'I've got three days. May I come back?'

'I don't know. I'll . . . I'll be working.'

'Oh, Nyrene!' As he now went round the table towards her she backed away from him, saying, 'Don't, Riley. Don't touch me, please, not at this moment. I'm sorry, but I must ask you to go; I just want to be left alone.'

He stood looking helplessly at her before turning and walking slowly from the kitchen and out of the house.

*　　　*　　　*

'You said what?'

'I didn't mean it.'

'You must have meant it, you bloody fool! It's been in your mind.'

'How could it be in my mind? I didn't know she was pregnant until I saw her about fifteen minutes or so ago. No, it wasn't in my mind.'

'Well, all I can say is you'll have a job to convince her that it wasn't. In any case, as with thousands of others today, she's as well as married to him. She was up in Scotland again last week-end. Oh, Riley, you shouldn't have said that.'

He turned to her, crying, 'I know that, Louise. I know that; but after all, it's really a fact, isn't it? Those born out of wedlock are still illegitimate, new birth certificate or not, and the other name for them is bastards. For our next tour, the manager is considering a controversial script, which brings in illegitimacy. The cast in general isn't for it; too tricky. When I come to think of it, likely that was in my mind when I brought the word out. Anyway,' he looked from one to the other, demanding now, 'why can't he marry her? Is he already married?'

'No, I understand he isn't married.'

129

Riley looked at Fred and said, 'Have you met him?'

'No, I haven't met him.'

'Have you?' He had turned back to Louise, and she answered, 'I haven't met him but I've spoken to him on the phone.'

'What's his name?'

'Charles Kingston.'

'Is he a Scot?'

'Yes, at least he sounded like a Scot during the short time I was talking to him. I picked up the phone when Nyrene was upstairs. He said "Nyrene?" He sounded puzzled; and I told him, no, I was her friend Louise. And I asked if I was talking to Charles; and he laughed and said, "Yes, definitely." It was then she took the phone from me, and they laughed, I think about him recognising that I wasn't her. Anyway, let it drop for the moment; the dinner's waiting to be eaten and Mrs Roberts is waiting to get washed up and away. So, come on with you.'

Towards the end of the meal Fred, looking across the table at Riley, said, 'How did you find your father?'

'Find him? What d'you mean?'

'Haven't you been to the hospital?'

'I don't know what you're talking about. Is he in hospital? I didn't know. When was this?'

'All right, all right; go on, finish your pudding.'

'No. No, I don't know what you're talking about, Fred. What has happened to put him into hospital?'

'Well, I understand it's his back; and he certainly hasn't been kidding all these years from what he told me. I think they froze him, and it wasn't very

130

pleasant; and they did something to his spine or the back regions. He wasn't himself very clear about it. He was out for three weeks and in dreadful pain, so they took him in again and operated on him. That was about a week ago. You haven't looked in at home at all then?'

'No. No, I haven't. I didn't want to be shown the door again, and I was going to get word to me dad where to meet me.'

'Why hasn't somebody written to you?'

'Well, what would be the use? Now I ask you. Moving every week, there's no fixed address.'

'Well, you could've told them as you told us, to send a letter to Manchester, to be forwarded on to wherever you were.'

Riley looked down and said, 'Dad's no letter-writer.'

'Well, you've got a sister.'

'Yes. Yes, Betty would've done it; but I never thought. What time is it?' He glanced at his wristwatch.

'It's too late now; visiting hours are from seven to eight-thirty. You wouldn't make it, but you've got tomorrow. You tell me you're not linking up with the troupe until Sunday, in Leeds, isn't it?'

'Yes, yes, in Leeds.' He nodded absentmindedly now; then looking at Louise, he said, 'It's something, isn't it, when you're afraid to go home and face your own mother? Cowardly.'

'No, I wouldn't say that.' Fred was nodding at him. 'I'm thinking of some of the mothers I've come across. Given the choice, I'd take the front of an army patrol in a wood any dark night.'

As they moved from the dining-room into the hall Fred put his arm around Riley's shoulders as he said, 'It isn't your day, laddie, is it? And it's no good saying to you as everybody else does, not to worry, it'll all pass. Passing takes time and it's the hell of the moment that matters.'

'Now if you're going to start quoting and preaching, Mr Beardsley, forget it, and go back and bring the drinks tray into the sitting room. And you, Riley, do something for me, will you, dear?'

'Anything in the world, Louise, anything.' He smiled at her.

'Go to the kitchen and have a word with Mrs Roberts will you? Because you're a local hero to her. You're an actor and you've been in the papers. Have you got a pen on you?'

'Yes, yes, I've got a pen on me.'

'Well, sign something for her, a paper napkin . . . anything. Now go on. It isn't the first time you've had to do this, I bet, is it?'

He looked at her for a moment, then said, 'You know, Louise, most women are mad. They are, they're mad and they should be locked up.'

'I agree with you, Riley, I do indeed; and I wouldn't mind being put away as long as I had a man with me. And by the way, when you have seen Mrs Roberts, will you, please, go upstairs and say hello to my son. He'll still be awake and waiting for you. It's a wonder he hasn't yelled out before now.'

'Go on!' He pushed her gently; then made his way to the kitchen.

When Fred entered the sitting-room with the tray Louise said to him, 'I'd pour him a stiff one, dear, because he is very, very low. Nyrene must have been in a tear if she told him to get out. Dear, dear, dear! There's something there that troubles me.'

132

'What d'you mean, something there? Where?'

'In that set-up.'

'Which set-up are you talking about now?'

'I mean between Nyrene and him.' She jerked her head back towards the door.

He now placed a hand on her shoulder and very quietly he said, 'You're not the only one, Mrs Beardsley, who thinks along those lines; and we must talk about it, and soon. Myself, I keep putting two and two together, and I daren't believe what the four makes ... or the five with this Charles man.'

*   *   *

He stood by the door of the ward. It was small, with three beds only along each side. The patients on the left each had a visitor; the three on the right were without visitors, and of these the man in the middle bed was leaning over and talking to the patient lying prostrate on his left, and they were both laughing. The third man was also lying flat with his face turned towards the window through which he could see the top branches of a tree waving about.

When Riley stood at the foot of the bed the head turned towards him and he saw his father's face light up as he exclaimed, 'Peter!' It was a strange sound somehow to hear his Christian name being used; he rarely heard it. Even when he went to Manchester he was introduced to the company as 'Peter Riley, generally known as Riley.'

'Hello, Dad. How are you?'

'Fine, lad, fine. Sit down. Sit down. My! You've grown so tall, I hardly recognise you.'

133

Riley pulled a chair nearer the bed and gazed at the face on the low pillow. It looked different, a little thinner but brighter.

'When did you get in?'

'Yesterday, but I didn't know you were here.'

They were looking at each other, both smiling; then Riley asked softly, 'When did all this happen?'

'Oh, the hospital business started just shortly after you left, lad; but when it first started really I can't remember. I seem never to have been without a backache; but you know, Peter,'—his head moved on the pillow—'nobody would believe other than I was swinging the lead. I suppose they would've gone on believing it if it hadn't been for that little woman doctor. My, my!' He started to chuckle now. 'The one that dished out me pain killers every week was away. This one was a new hand. There are five of them, you know, in the practice. Anyway, the first time I saw her she said, "Strip off and get on the couch." Just like that; that's what she said'—he was nodding his head now—' "Strip off and get on the couch." And I did just that, and she started to feel all over me back. Then she got me to walk up and down the room starkers. I felt like a ninny. Then she said, "You'll go for an X-ray tomorrow." As quick as that. You've normally got to wait weeks … months. Well, they had me X-rayed and three days later there I was in here, lying on me belly with me back being frozen, or something. Oh, I can tell you it wasn't pleasant, lad; but I didn't mind, 'cos something was being done. And oh,'—his voice now dropped and there was a sort of sadness in it when he said—'I've never known such kindness, such attention. They're all marvellous. They are, lad, they're all marvellous.

134

Anyway, that didn't seem to work. The pain was . . . well a bit much, so back they had me three weeks ago, and there was a lot of examining done. Then ten days ago I was in theatre. What exactly was done I can't tell you, but I do know that, since, I haven't felt better in me life. But I've got to do what they tell me, and that is to lie still here. They got me out yesterday and standing up. It was weird being on my feet again. Talk about you growing, I felt I'd grown; and you know something, Peter?'

When he didn't go on, Riley said, 'No, Dad; tell me.' He had never heard this man talk so much.

And Alex Riley went on, 'The outside world has changed towards me an' all. Everybody seems different. Your mam, you know, she wouldn't believe but that I was swinging the lead all those years. There were days when I could hardly crawl out of bed, lad; but it was put down to laziness, that I was born lazy. Well, I was born something all right'—he nodded—'apparently me spine's been out of shape since I was a bairn. It's been nipping nerves here. And, also, I've got arthritis. But in a way I feel it's the best thing that's happened to me. I mean it being proved that I am misshapen there.'

As Riley looked at his father he saw him down the years being belittled, being held up as a no good, work-shy individual.

He put out a hand and gripped the thin one that seemed to be waiting for it, and his father's eyes were bright with moisture as he said, 'And there's Betty. She's a good lass, is Betty, and full of spunk. She'll stand up and say what she thinks; your mam will never be able to browbeat her. One night she brought out the cards you had sent her from different places through Mr Beardsley, and she showed them to the bairns.'

'I bet that created havoc.'

'Not until the bairns were upstairs in bed; but then she collared Betty and told her if she did that again she'd be out of the door.'

When his father began to laugh, Riley said, 'Well, what happened?'

'Justice, lad. Betty never said a word, but she went upstairs and packed a bag and came down with her hat and coat on, and she said, "I'll go now, Mam; it'll save a lot of time." Just like that, "I'll go now, Mam; it'll save a lot of time." '

They were laughing together when a nurse came and placed a large vase of flowers on the table, and Alex Riley, looking up at her, said, 'My flowers? Who sent those?' The nurse nodded towards Riley, saying, 'I understand he's your son, isn't he? Well, he was too shy to bring them in and he pushed them at me, saying, "Those are for Mr Riley." '

Riley who was now standing by the bed, his face tinged with pink, said, 'It was Mrs Beardsley's suggestion: she said men in hospital never seem to have flowers sent to them.'

'She was right. She was right.' The nurse was nodding at him now. Then looking him straight in the face, she said, 'You're the actor, aren't you?'

'I'm on the stage, I don't know about acting,' he answered her, laughingly.

'Well, it didn't say that in the papers. I know it's some time ago now, but you were splashed all over them. I saw you in that play. Your last one here, wasn't it?' And she nodded, waiting for him to say something, but he could only smile at her. And so, looking at the man in the bed, she said, 'I thought it was amazing, I did. It must be the most difficult

136

thing in the world to act like someone barmy, when you're not like that naturally, I mean.'

Riley could contain his laughter no longer, and the nurse laughed with him; and then she said, 'Who do you take after? Where do you get it from?' and Riley looking at his father, said, 'Him likely. He's as daft as a brush.'

The nurse let out a loud giggle and placed a hand over her mouth before, bending over the bed, she patted Alex's cheek while looking at Riley and saying, 'He's a canny lad, and the best patient we've got.'

'Go on with you.'

Standing aside, Riley saw his father's beaming face, his hand flapping towards the nurse. He had never seen this man so happy: his mental picture of him back down the years was of a miserable little fella. And yet he could recall walking with this man across the fells. It would be on a Sunday, and there would always be a surprise from his dad's pocket, a bar of chocolate, a Mars bar, or some humbugs, always something. But the walks had stopped when, at eleven, he had moved to the comprehensive. 'You married?' the nurse interrupted those recollections.

'Me married? No, no.'

'Oh, then there's still hope, I'm only thirty-eight. Well, you'd have to know the truth sooner or later, forty-three; but off duty and with a bit of war paint on I'm a teenager. Eeh!' The laughter suddenly went from her face and she turned quickly to the bed and said, 'Is there anything you require, Mr Riley?' and her voice dropping several tones, she added, 'The Sister's just come on duty. Here we go!'

137

As she passed Riley her expression was still blank, but she winked at him.

Seated by the bed again, Riley said to his father, 'She's a card.'

'Aye, lad, she is a card, and a good 'un. She's lovely. As to age, she's forty-four, and she's been married and widowed and has brought up three bairns. We have a crack now and again. She was on nights the last time I was in, and when the going was rough she would sit by me and wipe my face with a flannel. You know something, Peter? For the first time in me life I was able to talk to a woman, I mean really talk about life and things. And you know, I'm only a year older than her, forty-five. And she's made me think along the lines that there's more fish in the sea than there's ever been caught; and it's funny too, how a lot of women take to small men. You know, you get tired of being nagged and looked down on. For years now I've been made to feel useless.' His hand came out again and gripped Riley's. 'Will you be able to come in the morrer?'

'Oh yes, yes, I'm not going back till Sunday.'

Some time later, when he was about to leave, Riley said, 'Is there anything I can bring you, Dad? Mr Beardsley said you're not allowed to smoke in here.'

'No, that's right. But it's funny, I've gone off them since the op, and I'm going to keep it up; but I'll tell you what I like, lad, those chocolate walnut whirls, you know?'

'Oh yes, I know, Dad. All right, you shall have a box tomorrow. Now is there anything else?'

'No, no, nothing else, lad; only let me say this, I'm very proud of you and I'm glad we can talk, you

138

and me. You know what I mean? And I want to thank you for those bits of paper you put in your letters; they're a godsend.'

'That's all right, Dad.' And Riley bent over his father and they gripped hands again.

He was smiling as he walked through the hospital gates.

* * *

It had just turned seven o'clock. He had had the questionable pleasure of bathing Jason and, as Louise remarked, it was also questionable who was the wetter after the routine.

He had the further pleasure of reading a bedtime story to the young man, and being continually interrupted with the question why: Why was Jack the giant killer so big and Tom Thumb so small?

'Because they were different stories.'

'Why?'

Some time later, in the sitting-room, he looked at Fred unsmilingly and said, 'No-one would need to ask who that fella,'—jerking his head upwards— 'takes after. He never stops talking.'

As Fred was about to answer this in his usual pithy way the phone rang and he stuck a finger in Riley's chest, saying, 'I'll answer that statement at some length when I come back.' And Louise smiling, said, 'I've told him, Riley, that a blind identification panel could prove the relationship.'

They both turned and looked towards the door as Fred came hurrying back into the room, saying, 'That was Nyrene's cousin Ivy, Mrs Wakefield. She's been trying to get Nyrene since late on this afternoon. It appears that Charles is rather ill, very ill by the sound of it, after a heart attack.'

'Where could she be?' Louise looked from one to the other. 'I know she's not working this week, but to be out all day.'

'If she *is* out. Perhaps she's stuck in there not answering the phone.'

'Why would she do that?'

'Don't be silly, woman! After what happened yesterday between this one'—he jerked his head towards Riley—'and her, she's likely still feeling sore.'

'Don't you be silly, too. And she's not a silly girl, either. She was likely mad at the time, but she's got over that; we all have to get over such things, Mr Beardsley.'

'Oh dear, dear.' He shook his head. 'Anyway what should we do?'

'I'll go along and see if she's really in.'

'You?'

'Yes, me!' Riley's voice came out almost on a shout. 'And if she's in I'll apologise in the only way I know how.'

'If she knows what's happened she won't have time to listen to you. Anyway, I'll go along with you,' Fred said.

'Well, that's sensible.' Fred turned towards his wife, a half-smile on his face, as he said, 'And I'll deal with you when I come back.'

Riley noted that the path was now strewn with May blossom for there had been a strong wind in the night, and the scent of the May was almost overpowering as he watched Fred ring the bell. It was the smell he would never forget, the smell of May; it would always be associated with a pregnant woman.

After his third ringing of the bell, Fred turned to Riley, saying, 'We'd better go round the back way and look through the windows. The curtains are drawn there.' He pointed to the side.

They had just reached the gate when a taxi drew up to the kerb, and to their amazement out stepped Nyrene, carrying two mauve-coloured bags with the name of the shop printed in deep black letters across them. They watched her put the bags on the pavement, pay the taxi-driver, bid him good night, then turn towards them. Taking them both in her glance, she said, 'Is this in the form of an honour or a deputation?'

'We've been worried. No-one could get in touch with you. A phone message came through from your cousin.'

He was taking the bags from her as she said, 'What about? What about? Charles?'

'Yes. That's what she said, Charles. Come on, get in the house first.' He pressed her through the gate, and when they were all in the hall she turned to him and asked sharply, 'What did she say about him?'

'He's not very well. He's had a heart attack. I . . . I think she wants you to go there straightaway.'

'Oh my. When did this happen?'

'I . . . I'm not sure. Some time today, it seems. She's been trying to get you since late on this afternoon.'

Nyrene put her hand to her head and bit on her lip. Again she looked from one to the other, then as if to herself she said, 'Oh dear, dear.' Then turning from them and running towards the stairs, she was about to mount them when she stopped

141

and, looking back to Fred, she said, 'There's a train goes to Aberdeen somewhere around nine, I think. Could you ring the station and find out, Fred, please? I'll just pack a few things.'

'Well, don't rush yourself. If it doesn't go till nine there's plenty of time. Now don't rush.'

Nyrene paid little heed to these words and ran up the stairs as if she were carrying no weight other than that of her own body.

'Ask her if she would like a cup of tea made.'

'What?'

Riley poked his head close to Fred's, and repeated, 'Ask her if she would like a cup of tea made. She'd take it from you better than from me.'

Fred pushed Riley in the chest; then going to the bottom of the stairs, he shouted, 'Nyrene! can you hear me? Would you like a cup of tea?'

After a moment her voice answered him, saying, 'Yes. Yes, please, Fred. I could do with one.'

On hearing this, Riley went into the kitchen and set about making a pot of tea, and it was ready on the table when Nyrene entered the room wearing a different coat and shoes. Fred greeted her with, 'There's an Inter-City to Aberdeen at eight forty-five. That gives you nearly an hour, and it's only a ten-minute drive to the station, so sit down and have this drink. Do you want anything to eat?'

'No. No, I just had a meal in town.' And she smiled wearily as she added, 'It's harder work shopping than acting; I'll be glad of the train journey.'

'Have you very far to go after you reach Aberdeen?'

'About eight miles, on the way to Banchory. I can get a taxi.'

'Has he had a heart attack before?'

She was sipping her tea and she didn't answer for a moment; but then she said, 'Well, not that I know of.'

'Did you know he was in Scotland?'

She paused again before saying, 'Oh yes, yes, I knew he was there. Oh.' She suddenly rose from the table, a hand patting her chin now as she said, 'I'd better phone David . . . what time is it?' She glanced at her watch. 'Oh, he'll be in the midst of it.'

'I can slip round and tell him,' said Fred.

'Would you, Fred?'

'Yes, of course.'

'Thank you. Would you tell him I'll phone from there tomorrow? Say I don't know how long I may have to stay.'

'Are you on next week?'

This question came from Fred and she said, 'Yes, but in a very small part. They'll be able to fit someone into that. The week following will be more difficult because I'm playing myself, a pregnant woman.'

Riley turned away towards the stove to refill the teapot, asking himself why his stomach should react as if from a blow every time he heard her refer to her condition. He listened to her now exclaiming, 'Oh, I'll have to inform the police. I always do when I'm away for any short time. They ask you to, you know.'

'Sit yourself down again and leave that to me, I'll do it now,' said Fred.

Riley did not turn round from the stove until he knew Fred had left the room, then he went swiftly to the table and, looking across at her where she

143

was sitting with one hand supporting her face, her elbow on the table, he said hurriedly, 'I . . . I've got to bring it up, Nyrene. I'm sorry, deeply, deeply sorry I upset you. It's the last thing in the world I would want to do. You know that. Forgive me, please. I'll not know any peace until you say you've forgotten it.'

Her hand came down from her face and she held it out towards him, and as he gripped it tightly she said, 'Don't worry, we all say things we shouldn't; we all get mad about nothing at all. I'm sorry too, and I've forgotten it.'

'Oh! Nyrene. Nyrene.'

'Now, now. Remember our parts,'—she smiled widely at him—'the budding actor and his mentor.'

He shook his head violently as if dismissing such a description of their association; then quietly, he asked, 'May I write to you?'

'Yes, if you wish. But . . . well you know the circumstances.'

'Yes, I'm aware of the circumstances,' he said, 'very much so.'

When Fred's voice saying, 'Thank you. Thank you,' came to him he quickly let go of her hand.

Fred was laughing when he came back into the kitchen, saying, 'Give them their due, they're always polite on the phone, so why can't they be like that when they stop you for speeding or for parking on a yellow line?'

Nyrene looked up at him. 'Of course you would answer them gently, wouldn't you, Fred?' she said.

'Now, now, Nyrene, I've got one at home like that. Have a heart. Anyway, the time's getting on. Are you all locked up, I mean all the doors, windows?'

144

'Yes, and I always close the curtains.'

'Well, I don't know whether that's a good thing.'

The train was in the station and time was taken up walking through the carriages trying to find Nyrene a comfortable seat near a window. This done, there was still time for small talk; but they were all relieved when the whistle blew. As the train moved, Riley left Fred and walked alongside the window, and Fred's eyebrows lifted when he saw Riley's hand reach up to the window as if he were touching her.

Slowly Riley walked back towards Fred, and when they met no words were exchanged, but their glances were held for some time.

*   *   *

Later that night, in the bedroom, Fred continued his questioning of Riley's behaviour: 'Why,' he again put to Louise, 'should Riley walk alongside the train and act as he did?' He was no longer a lad. He'd always said he never had been; but now it was as though he were a fully-fledged man, not some callow youth who had a pash on his teacher or some older woman.

'That's the point, isn't it?' he almost demanded as he addressed Louise.

She was sitting up in bed, a book open on her knees, looking at him standing in his pyjama trousers.

When he kicked off his slippers he did not immediately get into bed, but sat on the edge and leaned forward, dropping his hands between his knees and, more to himself than to her, he said, 'Every movement, every look was the act of a lover.

145

And she was aware of this, I knew she was. And the way she said to him "Goodbye, Riley," just before the train left, something in her voice seemed to suggest a deeper relationship. But she's having a child by this other fellow. And that's another thing, none of us have clapped eyes on him. We don't even know if he exists.'

'Don't be silly, dear; I've told you he exists all right, I've spoken to him.'

'Oh aye.' He turned towards her; then sighing deeply, he climbed into bed, and when he pushed himself close to her she put an arm around his shoulders and said, 'What could there be between them, dear? She must be nearly twenty years older.'

'I'm years older than you.'

'We've been through this before, haven't we? It's different with a man.'

Again he sighed deeply before saying, 'I wish I could get to the bottom of it; I hate mysteries and there's a mystery there all right, something funny, something fishy. I can smell it.'

'Darling, even the *word* fish has the power to make me retch. You know it has.'

'Oh, I'm sorry, love. I'm sorry.' He pulled her into his arms, saying, 'I must be up the pole. Why do I worry about anything or anybody except you because there's only you and the child in my life, nobody else, nobody else.'

As he snuggled up beside her, she thought whimsically: Just you, and the child, and all the children at school, and of course Riley. And so concerned was he that everything should go right for Riley that he was puzzled about the association; and she was too. Oh yes. In a way, she was more puzzled than he was because she had her own ideas

146

of what was between Nyrene and Riley, ideas which her mind kept refuting. Anyway, it would all work out, she thought; just as her own life had done.

*　　　*　　　*

It was a quarter to four on the Sunday when the phone rang. It was Ivy's husband Ken. He said he was distressed to tell them that they had lost Charles. That's how he put it, they had lost Charles. He had died at ten o'clock that morning. Nyrene had sat up with him all night and was with him when he passed away. He said they had been so very fond of each other, and what was more Charles had been his wife's and his best friend for many years. He said that Nyrene had fallen into an exhausted sleep and they didn't want to wake her, but she had indicated that they would like to know what was happening. She herself would likely phone them tomorrow, but she would be staying for the funeral.

Then he said something that to them was quite natural: apparently, Charles's last regret was that he wouldn't see the baby. But he had ended in a rather puzzling way, adding that anyway she would never need to work again. He had always said that the house was hers and all that was his was hers too, seeing that he had never been married.

Fred had tried to relate the conversation to Louise and Riley as he had heard it.

They had all remained silent until Louise said, 'I . . . I think she must have known him for a long time and they had only recently got together again.'

'Did she ever say how old he was?'

Louis looked at Fred and shook her head. 'No,

147

not really,' she said, 'but I seemed to get the impression that he was quite a bit older than her, fiftyish perhaps, and I also got the impression that she had known him for a long time; that he was a family friend; but I had assumed he had been married and had lost his wife, and that's why they had come . . . well, together.'

Riley had made no response and Fred said, 'Well, Riley, what's your opinion? What do you think?'

Were Riley to tell them what his thoughts really were at this moment, they would be shocked, because he would have said, I'm glad the fella's dead. And what's more, he didn't feel bad thinking this way. What he did was to lower his head and mutter, 'I don't know what to think,' and only just stopped himself from adding, She's going to have a child but she's free again.

He turned from them and walked to the fireplace and looked down on the artificial log fire.

Fred said, 'Your train goes around six, you said, didn't you?'

He turned and said, 'Yes, five past.'

'Then we'd better have a bite now.'

'Oh, look I had a huge lunch; I couldn't eat anything now, I can assure you.'

'You're not going to get very much, so don't worry.' And Louise bounced her head towards him. 'You'll have a cup of tea and a bun.'

'Suits me, madam. Suits me.' And when Riley smiled at her, she tossed her head and flounced round like a young girl in a huff, saying, 'I'm tired of slaving after unappreciative males.'

'Unappreciative males indeed!' Fred went into one of his huffing and puffing acts, which didn't

148

deceive Riley at all for he knew quite well they would have liked to face him with the question, What is going on between you two? and he wondered how they would react were he to say, I am under the impression and have been for months that I slept with a woman and made passionate love to her and she to me for hours on end, and when I woke up to a glorious day it was to find only that her mind was blank about the whole occasion: she had been drunk during it all; or, at least, she had made out she was. What would they think of that? One thing he was sure of: they wouldn't believe him about the glorious love-making, for what could he know about such things? In their eyes he felt he was still a lad. They would put it down to his fantasies. Yet what about her fantasies? for at about the same time she must have been with him ... that Charles fellow who had just died, he would have been, too.

He wouldn't let Fred drive him to the station, his excuse being he wanted to break the journey and have a few minutes with his father before leaving. He had seen him earlier in the day, and although it wouldn't be visiting time the nurses, he was sure, would be lenient with him; being an actor, he'd found, carried prestige.

He had thought that, once clear of the house and of his two dear friends, he could sort out his thinking and compose the letter he intended to write to Nyrene. Not of condolence, no; he wasn't going to be a hypocrite.

But the matter came up again in the hospital. He had said to his father, 'I have only five minutes, I have to dash for the train; but I just wanted to leave that with you,' and pushed an envelope into

149

his father's hand, adding, 'Keep it for yourself, d'you hear?' to which his father replied, 'Thanks, lad. Thanks, I'll do that,' but had then added, 'I get very little for meself but abuse. Your mother was in this afternoon—she's been different since I came in here—and there she was going off the deep end again. She was saying that that actress friend of yours, Miss Mason, is it? Well, she'd heard that she's pregnant. And I had to shut her up, 'cos she thinks you stay there, you see, and not with Mr Beardsley. But is she pregnant?'

'Yes, Dad, she's pregnant.'

'Is she going to be married?'

'I think she was, but he died this morning.'

'Oh my!' his father jerked in the bed and bit on his lip.

Riley said, 'Be careful, man. Be careful.'

'Well, it's what you said, how you said it, just like that: "he died this morning." Poor lass. Poor lass. Anyway, she's got good friends; and you're one of them.'

'Aye, Dad, I'm one of them.'

They smiled at each other; then Riley said, 'I must be off. Now take care of yourself. I've left an address in that letter. It's a Manchester address, and Betty can write to me there if you need me.'

His father said nothing, but just pulled one lip over the other, and nodded and lifted a hand in farewell . . .

Is she going to be married? No, he died this morning. Is she going to be married? No, he died this morning. The wheels of the train took up the beat in his head and the words became almost a song.

He'd have to pull himself together. What

difference did it make now that she was free? She had been free on that Sunday morning before Christmas when she became Miss Mason again and handed him a cup of tea.

He wished he was back at The Palace; he hated these journeys.

He hated the jumping from one town to another.

He hated the set of different faces glaring up at him night after night.

He hated what went on among the other couples and in which he could share were he not such a damn fool.

He took a deep breath, opened his eyes and stared out of the window into the flashing blackness rushing to nowhere; and that's where he was rushing, to nowhere.

When there came over him a longing to be back at school and to hear Beardsley's voice bawling at him, he said to himself, 'Come on! Come on! Snap out of it. Whatever you want or whatever happens you've got to finish this tour.'

It was almost as if Beardsley was going for him again, so he closed his eyes and pretended to sleep, as the other three passengers were doing.

CHAPTER NINE

Towards the end of the first week in September Riley saw Nyrene again; but there were no words to express his feelings at the first sight of her on this day. His mind put it crudely: she was like a woman standing behind her stomach, for it looked enormous. He had heard the expression carrying it high, regarding pregnant women. Well, Miss Mason was certainly carrying her child high at this moment.

He saw that she was surprised to see him and not over-pleased, for she stood stock-still looking at him as she said, 'You're back then.'

He made himself smile, saying, 'I think so.'

'Oh! come in.' She made an impatient movement with her head, then walked before him, leaving him to close the door. He followed her into the sitting-room where he could see she had evidently been lying on the couch, for a rug lay crumpled on the floor. Looking at it he said, 'Oh, I'm sorry if I've disturbed you. Were you resting?'

'I always seem to be resting these days, Riley. Sit yourself down. I'll come to in a minute; I was dozing.'

He drew a chair up to the couch but not too close to it, and as he watched her reach out and pull the cover over her feet he saw that her legs were so swollen as to be almost unrecognisable. Then, his eyes seeming to skip the mound of her stomach, he looked at her face. It, too, was swollen and looked so white and strained that it forced him to ask, 'How much longer have you got?'

'Four weeks.' She sounded hesitant. 'Perhaps five.' He watched her close her eyes.

Five more weeks with that mound; she would surely burst.

He asked, 'Do you see the doctor often, or go to the clinic?'

Again there was a pause before she answered: 'No, I don't go to the clinic; but yes, I see the doctor often. He's very good. He looks like his name, Fox; he's got side whiskers and a beard.' She

152

opened her eyes and he saw there was a smile in them now as she said, 'He's very like Fred: proverbs, platitudes, and poetry all mixed up to hide a very sensitive and thoughtful nature. Have you just come from there?'

'Yes. I've been back since the end of last week; you see, we finished in Sunderland on Saturday.'

'Oh, the run's ended?' She sounded interested and pulled herself slightly further up on to the head of the couch.

'Yes, before it starts again. But that certainly won't be for a few weeks, I should think. There's a lot of kerfuffle going on in Manchester because there's not enough bookings in Scotland; but there are a few in Ireland, and still a number in this country that we could use, but it's how to fit them in. You know the kind of thing: one wants it this week, another wants it the same week, and a third says if they can't have it that week they're not having it at all. Still, it doesn't really matter, for I don't know if I'll be carrying on with them.'

'No? Why not?' She had hitched her body slightly round towards him.

'Well, I've had an offer, or I should say a promise of an offer, a big hint of a part, opening in December. I'd have to go up to London at the end of next week for an audition, like the rest of them, but the hint was that I stood a good chance. Yet I don't know, because if nothing comes of it and I haven't signed up for the tour then, like two thirds of the profession, I'll be taking a nice rest. Anyway I've got to work it out.'

'Yes,' she nodded, 'it's your own decision.'

She lay looking at him, and he returned her gaze for some time before he said quietly, 'You got my letters?'

'Yes, Riley, I got your letters.'

'But you never answered one of them.'

She hitched herself onto her back again, gave a deep sigh and said, 'No, I didn't answer because . . . well, I didn't seem to have anything to say. It had all been said.'

There was another silence before Riley said, 'I understand from Fred that he's left the child well provided for.'

Her head jerked towards him, and she said, 'Yes, I suppose you could say that, but it was me he left well provided for. I understand that that was always his intention long before the child came upon the scene.'

'You had known him for some time then?'

She nodded her head now, saying, 'Oh yes, you could say that I'd known him for some time.'

He looked about him now. The room was tidy and as bright as he remembered it, and as he couldn't see her doing it he asked the obvious question: 'Have you got a woman coming in to see to things?'

'Yes, she's a Mrs Mary Atkins, very good, motherly. Spoils me, she's out shopping now.'

'Which hospital are you going into?'

'I'm not going into any hospital, I'm having it here.'

'Is that wise nowadays?'

'Wise? I don't know what you mean; but where did women usually have babies but in their own home; and they had them with them from when they were born, not whisked away and put behind a glass case. Where did your mother have all of you?'

'As far as I can gather she had them in a hospital,

The General.'

'Well, everybody to their fancy. How is she these days?'

'I don't know, I never see her.'

'You must be a big disappointment to her; yet from what I understand, you've become a source of light to your father.'

'You're right about what you understand, but I wouldn't have phrased it that way, a source of light.'

'Fred says he's a different man nowadays.'

'Yes, I think he is too, but that's with the operations: he's now free from pain, at least for most of the time.'

Hearing someone crossing the hall, he turned towards the door, and when the woman entered the room she looked from him to Nyrene saying, 'I've just got back. Oh, you've got a visitor.' Then coming closer to Riley, she exclaimed, 'Why! it's Mr Riley the actor. Oh, I'm pleased to meet you.' Her hand went out and he took it, and he said, 'And you, too, Mrs Atkins.'

'Oh, you know me name?' And saying this, she turned and looked at Nyrene. 'You look as if you could do with a cup of tea,' she said. 'How are you feeling?'

'Fine. Fine.'

'No, you're not; don't tell lies.' Mrs Atkins turned again to Riley, saying now, 'She's always fibbing. She must feel like nothing on earth, you'd think she was carrying two-ton Tessie.' She turned away laughing. 'You could do with a cup of tea an' all, I suppose,' she said to Riley.

'Yes, Mrs Atkins, I could do with a cup of tea too. Thank you.'

155

After the door had closed on Mrs Atkins, Nyrene sighed and said, 'Who could be sad, lonely or unhappy with a Mrs Atkins about? She's a marvel. She can do everything except stop talking.' She smiled now, adding, 'I feel very fortunate in having her. She's a widow with no family, so I think she's adopted me just for something to do.'

He sat looking at her now in complete silence, his hands grasped tightly around his crossed knee to prevent his arms, in spite of that lump, going out and around her; and then putting his lips on hers, and not only on her lips. He wanted to kiss the weariness from her face, the sweat that was now appearing on her brow. It was this last which caused him to say, 'What is it? Are you all right?'

She did not answer, but laid the fingers of one hand tightly across her mouth as if to prevent herself from speaking or, he realised, crying out.

'You've got a pain?'

He was on his feet looking down on her, and she looked up into his eyes and muttered, 'Call Mrs Atkins, please.'

He did not move from her as he muttered now, 'I don't think it's Mrs Atkins you want, it's the doctor.'

'Get Mrs Atkins.'

He actually ran out of the room, across the hall and into the kitchen: 'Mrs Atkins!'

The urgency in his voice turned her from the sink and she said, 'Aye? Aye, what is it?'

'She needs you! I think she's got a pain.'

'Pain. Well, I'm not surprised.' She pulled a towel from the brass rail above the fireplace, quickly dried her hands and arms, then hurried out, and he after her.

156

Yet when she reached the couch her voice sounded quite ordinary: 'Now what're you up to, ma'am, eh? What're you up to this time?'

'Help me upstairs, Mary.'

Mrs Atkins went swiftly to the end of the couch and helped to lift the swollen legs; then turning to Riley, she said, 'Get to the other side of her, lad, will you?'

Nyrene made no objection when his arm went around her, and it was on him she leant heavily as they made their way out of the room and across the hall.

It was he alone who guided her up the stairs because they weren't broad enough to take the three of them, and so on the landing Mrs Atkins darted before them to the bedroom to pull the clothes down and push up the pillows.

He had got her to the bed and was helping her down, when what happened next he was to remember always as the beginning of a new life, his new life, for she gave a gasp and a groan and, bending sideways, she leant tightly against him, her fingers digging into his.

Mrs Atkins was on the other side of him now and she said hastily, 'Ring for Dr Fox, you'll find his number in the book; and for her friend Mrs Beardsley; and Nurse Boston, although you'll likely not find her in this morning, as she gives time to the open clinic. Still, get the doctor and her friend.'

Nyrene was sitting on the edge of the bed now and she looked up at Riley and between gasps she said, 'I'm . . . I'm sorry.'

'Don't be silly, woman.'

Then she murmured, 'Ring the doctor first; he'll just be finishing morning surgery at about . . . this

157

time.'

With one last look at her he now hurried out of the room, and he had no need to look in the small telephone book lying on the side table to find out the doctor's number, or that of the nurse, or that of Mrs Louise Beardsley; they were on a notepad written in large letters.

Yes, the doctor was in; he had just finished surgery. A minute later he heard a man's voice saying, 'Yes? What is it?'

'It's Miss Mason; she's having severe pains.'

'Oh, all right, I'll be there in a few minutes. Have you got her to bed?'

'Yes.'

'Who's with her? Is the nurse with her?'

'No; only Mrs Atkins.'

'Well, phone the nurse right away.' The phone went dead and he stood looking at it for a moment before replacing the receiver and then dialling the nurse's number.

No; she wasn't in. She wouldn't be in till half-past twelve or thereabouts; and so he left a message that she should come at once to Miss Mason's house.

When lastly he phoned Louise and explained the situation, she said, 'She can't be; she's not due till the middle of next month.'

At this he put in, 'She's enormous; I can't see her lasting out until then. It's impossible. I know very little about it but ... anyway, will you come over?'

'I'm on my way, Riley.' Louise's voice was sharp, and when the phone banged down he stood for a moment, his head hanging. Everybody was so abrupt, as if they didn't believe him. It was like a morning at a bad rehearsal, everybody on edge. God above! You could say that again, for here he was in the midst of the last place he'd wished to be, near her when her child was about to be born. He would go when the doctor came.

He was standing as though in a daze when Mrs Atkins came skipping down the stairs like a young girl and cried, 'Did you get through to them all?'

'Yes, but the nurse isn't in.'

'I knew she wouldn't be, but as long as the doctor's coming and her friend. Look, come and make yourself useful, because it strikes me that this is the day, and the hour practically. The middle of next month, she had said. Nonsense! I've said that all along: nonsense. Look there'll be tea to be made and such like; the doctor likes coffee. Anyway she'll drink between spasms, so make a pot of tea. The things are on there.' She pointed to a side table. 'The trays are underneath. I'll leave you to find them.'

She was practically running out of the kitchen again when she stopped and turned and, a broad smile on her face, she said, 'Funny, isn't it, how things turn out? Its father's dead; I mean the bairn's, and when it comes, you'll be in the house. It's always nice to have a man in the house when a bairn's born. Makes things right somehow.' And with a bounce of her head towards him she was gone, leaving him clutching the end of the table well aware that he was no longer the actor whom she had treated with deference. To her now he was just a young fellow who happened to be in the house at an opportune time.

He thought back to Larry and 'The Golden Mind' and at this moment he wished he could slip away into him and forget everything that was happening in this so-called normal life.

*   *   *

It was late in the afternoon. The doctor had come and gone but was now back again. The nurse had been in attendance since one o'clock. Mrs Atkins had been in attendance all the time, as had Louise, and he himself was still here.

How long had he been here? He had made his call at eleven o'clock, which meant he had been in the house for five hours, although it seemed more like five days, five years. He had never been out of it, yet each time he had heard her groan or cry out he had wanted to make for the front door. Seeing his white face, Louise had smiled at him as she said, 'It's natural. I screamed the place down. Fred couldn't stand it; he went for a walk.'

When he had said, 'I would like to go for a walk, Louise,' she put a hand onto his head and looked into his face as she said, 'No, you wouldn't, not really. Somehow it was meant that you should be here.'

'No, no!' He was strong in protest. 'It was never meant that I should be here and her like that.'

'Well, you have it your way and I'll have it mine; and another tray of tea is called for. Better go to the shops before they are closed.'

'Do . . . do you think there's any chance she'll die?'

'Oh! Riley, don't be ridiculous, be your age, and that in your own mind is about thirty. Die? Of course not!'

'But she can't keep going on like that much

longer, can she?'

'Yes she can, and she will. It could go on till midnight or till tomorrow morning.'

'Well, I couldn't stand that. I really couldn't stand that.'

'Oh, poor fellow. Poor fellow.' She was now laughing at him.

'Don't laugh about this, Louise. I can't tell you how I'm feeling. And another thing: she isn't the first pregnant woman I've seen. I have sisters, you know, and although I wasn't there when they were born I saw my mother just before the ambulance came. She was in a bit of a state, but nothing like Nyrene has been.'

'How d'you know? Apparently your sisters were all born in hospital, and so you can't know exactly what state your mother was in then. She might even have had a Caesarean or forceps ... Oh my goodness!' She pushed him into a seat now, saying, 'Oh, I am sorry. I am sorry, Riley. Look! Sit quiet; I'll get you something.'

More than ever she was realising what had prompted them not to tell Nyrene he was back, and also to dissuade him from visiting her, their excuse being that in her advanced condition she did not welcome any visitors. And he had given them no indication that he was going to visit her today.

Within minutes she came back holding a wine glass and said to him, 'Drink that. Go on, drink it up.'

He gulped at the brandy, then drained his glass; and after a moment, his head drooping, he said, 'Good God! I was for passing out.'

'Well, you wouldn't have been the first, nor the last.'

161

As she finished speaking the door was thrust open and the doctor stood there, saying, 'I'll have to be gone for an hour or so, but I'll be back. In any case, she's got a good way to go yet.'

Louise walked towards him now, saying, 'She should've gone to hospital, shouldn't she?'

'Yes, of course, she should've gone to hospital! But like most women she thinks she knows best.'

They were walking into the hall now when she said, 'But is there really any danger, Doctor, it being so premature?'

There was a long pause before the answer came, and Riley heard it, for the doctor was now on his feet moving towards the door. 'All I can say to you, Mrs Beardsley, is, premature my foot!' Then he was gone, and the door banged behind him before Louise turned and saw Riley standing at the kitchen door. 'What did he mean, "premature my foot"?' Riley said.

She blinked, wetted her lips, then said, 'I don't know. And I want a cup of tea for her,' and she pushed past him to go into the kitchen, leaving him standing and looking towards the stairs.

Premature my foot.

*　　　*　　　*

At a quarter past twelve he was standing on the landing with Fred when he heard the first cry of the child. They looked towards the bedroom door behind which varying sounds could be heard. Fred was smiling when he turned to Riley, but Riley wasn't smiling, and there was no way in which he could describe his feelings at this moment; they were such a mixture. He only knew that he was

162

relieved she had got rid of . . . it, and would now be herself again. So he imagined.

'I wonder what it is.'

He glanced towards Fred, saying, 'What?'

'I said, I wonder what it is; she's got the nursery'—he nodded towards the far door—'ready for either blue or pink.'

With the sound of Mrs Atkins's high laugh the bedroom door opened and out she came holding something in her arms and looking towards him and saying, 'Oh well, here it is! Did you ever see the like of it? Look at the size of him!' And she suddenly pulled the blanket from the child, and they both looked down on to the firm compact body of a baby boy.

'And look at his hair! We'll have to send for the barber tomorrow. Did you ever see the like! By! he's a lovely bundle.' She switched the blanket this way and that and the baby was covered up. Then she was looking at Riley, saying, 'Like to hold him? You're likely used to holding bairns, having all those sisters below you.'

He didn't remember holding his arms out, he was sure he hadn't, but he had to put them out to stop the child from falling; and there he was looking down into a round, crinkled face.

'Well, don't stand there gaping at him, bring him along. He's got to have a bath; then he'll be ready for a feed if I know anything.'

In the nursery, after handing the child back to Mrs Atkins his arms felt very odd, tired as if he'd been carrying something heavy. Yet it hadn't been an unpleasant feeling.

They stood watching Mrs Atkins sponging the child, and when she said, 'Well, instead of you two standing gaping there, the doctor and the nurse will want some kind of refreshment, and I don't think it'll be just coffee or tea because they're both worn out. She had us all worn out, herself into the bargain. I think she'll sleep for twenty-four hours.'

When Fred moved towards the door he looked back to where Riley was still standing near the high table; then he shook his head. During the past weeks he had become tired of putting two and two together, and then discarding the answer. A while ago he'd had a few words with Louise, and she had repeated the doctor's statement, 'premature my foot!'

'Well it all adds up now,' Fred said, and she had answered, 'Yes, I'm afraid so. But what's going to be the outcome? And where does Charles come in?'

'And there *was* a Charles, wasn't there?'

'Oh yes, yes, no doubt about it, I spoke to him, I've already told you, and he sounded a very nice fellow.'

'And he died.'

'Oh yes, he died.'

'I give up.'

*   *   *

Riley did not see Nyrene until the next day when she was sitting up in bed with the child by her side, and the first impression he had of her was that she looked radiant. He had never seen her look so happy; and she greeted him as she hadn't done for a long time.

'Hello, Riley!' she said. 'Well, it's all over bar the shouting, and we've had plenty of that. He's got

164

lungs on him like a coal hawker. Isn't he lovely?' She pulled the clothes back from the baby; then picking him up, she said, 'Hold him.'

The last thing he wanted to do was to hold the child again, for he still hadn't been able to analyse his feelings he'd had the first occasion. He was thinking it was partly resentment against her, because she was no longer alone and in need of him, or of anyone else apparently. All he wanted to do now was to take her hand, touch her face and tell her that she looked beautiful.

Nyrene lay back on her pillows and looked at the tall young fellow holding the child, and when she said softly, 'You must be his godfather, Riley,' he almost answered her flippantly, I'm not supposed to be old enough to be a father never mind a godfather, but then, he supposed, godfathers came at all ages.

'How are you feeling?'

'Wonderful.'

'You look it too.'

Her reply, which was actually a question, had no coyness in it: 'You think so?' she asked simply.

'Oh yes. Yes, taken years off you.' He was smiling at her now. 'At least nine months.'

Her expression changed, as did her voice as she said, 'It was early, premature, almost five weeks or more.'

Five weeks or more. He was shutting down on a question in his mind, a ridiculous, stupid question, one that came to him whenever he experienced that particular dream; maybe not so often now, but nevertheless still there.

Riley was still holding the baby, and when he made a whingeing sound he moved his arms up and

165

down, as he had seen his father do with one or other of his sisters; then he handed him back to her, and she was placing him by her side when he said, 'It's a pity his father'll never see him.'

She turned her unsmiling face quickly towards him as she said, 'Yes, it is, a great pity; but there, these things happen, and I have him.' She turned her head away again and, looking down at the child, her fingers moved through the tuft of hair.

Presently she said, 'You go for your audition next week then?'

'Yes, but as I'll likely be one of a hundred and one the result will be, "We'll ring you. Don't ring us." '

'But from what you said I thought that it was almost sure.'

He smiled at her now as he said, 'Well, you above all people should know what in the theatre "almost sure" means: nothing is sure until you've signed on the dotted line—not even then. But we'll see. It doesn't matter, anyway, if I'm not there; I'll be on the road again. That's still open.'

'You sound as if you're in two minds about the whole thing.'

'I am. I am. Yet if I gave it up what else is there for me? I've got to eat. More's the pity.'

'What else could you do? What else are you fit for now?'

He looked at her. She was Miss Mason again, as when she wasn't in a good mood, and he answered with equal stiffness, saying, 'Well, I could do like many another does, become a waiter, get on the buses, go on the dole, probably go in for adult education. Oh there's lots of openings.'

'Oh, Riley!' She was still Miss Mason. 'I could

166

slap you when you talk like that. You're made for the stage, and you know it, and that'll be your life, so get it into that stubborn head of yours and don't let me down. I spent more than two years on you altogether, drumming that into you.'

He felt his jaw stiffening and he wanted to reply in her tone: Yes, you drummed it into me, but as a cover-up for your miniatures. But she was still ill, and there was the child, and anyway, he could never have said that to her. So what he did say was, 'What are you going to call him?'

'Charles.'

'Why Charles?'

'Because it was his father's name, Charles Geoffrey Kingston.'

They were looking at each other in silence when the door opened and Mrs Atkins said, 'You've got visitors, Miss Mason, all the way from Scotland: Mr and Mrs Wakefield, and Mr Beardsley is with them.'

'O . . . oh no! No!'

'What is it?' He was bending over her. Her face had gone pale and she was nipping on her bottom lip, and when he said, 'The Wakefields? Mrs Wakefield is your cousin, isn't she?' she nodded, saying, 'Yes, yes, she's my cousin. Yes.'

'And you don't want to see her?'

'Oh yes, of course I do, but . . . oh but, do something for me, Riley, will you?'

'Anything. Anything, my dear.' His voice was soft.

'Go downstairs, and take Fred home straightaway. But before you go, send them up. Do that, will you, take him with you straightaway?'

'Of course. Of course.' He was puzzled, and he

167

showed it by shaking his head; but he repeated, 'Yes. Yes, I'll do that. I'll see you in the morning then?'

'Yes, Riley. I'll see you tomorrow.'

In the sitting-room he said to the elderly couple, 'Good evening. I'm Peter Riley.'

'Oh, how d'you do?' The man was nodding at him. 'We've heard a lot about you, Mr Riley.'

Before more could be said, Riley looked at Fred, saying, 'Could I have a word with you?' Then he asked Louise: 'Would you please see Nyrene's friends upstairs?' and to them he said, 'She's waiting for you anxiously.'

'Well, what word do you want with me?'

'Nothing really. The only thing I can say to you is, she obviously wants both of us out of the way for some reason or other, so she asked me to go home with you now.'

'Haven't you any idea?'

'No, I haven't, but I'm puzzled.'

'Well, where ignorance is bliss it's a folly to be wise, and we'll leave it there, Mr Riley, for the moment. And without being pushed I'm going home, and I suppose you must come with me.'

'I have no other choice, have I?'

'Oh yes, you have, mister. You have a number: our being sent home is a poor substitute.'

'Oh, don't get on the Mr Beardsley tack, please, Fred. I'm all worked up inside. Why the hell I should be, I don't know.'

At this Fred laughed, put his arm around Riley's shoulder and led him to the door.

CHAPTER TEN

Riley had just returned from London and the audition and, because of the result, he knew exactly what he was going to do once he reached the Beardsleys' house, where for some days, the atmosphere had been strained, and strained was putting it mildly. Even Fred hadn't been able to maintain his forced jollity.

Then there was Nyrene. Her happiness with the child seemed to be overshadowed by ... was it anxiety? Well, it was worry of some kind.

Before he had left for London, two days before, she had said to him, 'Oh, I do hope you get it. And if you're offered it, let nothing stop you from accepting it, even if they want you to go to Brazil or Hong Kong,' and to that he had replied, 'As far away as possible, you mean?'

And her answer had come softly, saying, 'Oh, Riley, don't twist things.'

Well, his mind was made up; he knew what he was going to do.

He entered the house by the kitchen door and the greeting Mrs Roberts gave him was genuine: 'Nice to see you're back, Mr Riley. What was London like?'

'Bedlam. A thousand times worse than Newcastle.'

'Oh well, that's saying something. You're just in time for a cup of tea; Mr Beardsley's just got in.'

As he left the kitchen and entered the hall he saw Louise coming down the stairs, and she exclaimed, 'Oh! You got back then?' Then at the

169

foot of the stairs she called out, 'Fred! Our lodger has returned.'

Riley said nothing, but forced himself to smile: the jollity was beginning again.

'Hello, Riley! Well, you've got back then.'

Riley stared at this big, outsize man and, reverting to a boyish voice, he said, 'You know, Mr Beardsley, that's the most silly thing that could be said to anybody ... so you've got back then. Who do you think, Mr Beardsley, is standing in front of you?'

Fred's hand came out none too gently and pushed him roughly forward, saying, 'Smart alec! And you're not yet too big, you know, to have my hand across your ear,' to which, and in his natural voice, Riley answered, 'And you're not big enough, Mr Beardsley, to do it.'

They looked at each other, then laughed.

Rather anxiously, Louise put in quickly, 'I'll bring some tea in.'

Seated in their usual places, Fred looked at Riley and said quietly, 'You've made up your mind about something, haven't you?'

'How did you guess? But you're right: yes, I have.'

'Well, it might surprise you, laddie, so have we. It's been very testy for a while, hasn't it?'

For the moment Riley was stumped with the plainness of this statement; then he said, 'Oh, you've noticed then.'

'We'll keep facetiousness out of it for the next half-hour, Riley.'

There was something about the tone of his friend's voice and the look on his face that caused Riley to withhold any comment he might have made; but as Louise entered the room with the tray he got up quickly and took it from her and placed it on the side table, and as she poured out the tea she chattered about the doings of Jason at nursery school that morning.

Fred put his cup and saucer none too gently down on a side table and, addressing Riley, said, 'Well, come on, how did it go?'

'I didn't get it.'

The husband and wife exchanged a quick glance, and then Fred said, 'Why? I thought it was to be handed to you on a plate.'

Riley gave a small laugh as he said, 'You can never trust the waiters in this profession. Anyway, again I got down to the last three, and the best of us got it. He was older than either of us and he had a presence gained from quite a lot of experience, I should imagine. The other fellow was about my age, just on twenty.'

'Well, you're not just on twenty.'

'I'm not all that far off; but what does that matter?'

'Well, as I see it, it must have done in this case; likely they thought you were too young.'

'They didn't think I was too young. Apparently they knew nothing about me.'

'What about the man, Mr ... what was his name? Who told you to go up there?'

'He was one of four and he was a voice in the wilderness. I knew this from the moment I got inside the theatre. He was going on my appearance in "The Golden Mind", and that's all he knew about me. It wasn't enough against what the others had done, well, what the man who got it had accomplished. Anyway, I've made up my mind, I'm

171

going to take the tour offer; I don't like resting.'

Again Fred and Louise exchanged a glance, and when she nodded at her husband, he said, 'Well, we've made up our minds too; at least you've made up our minds for us. We've got something to say to you, Riley, and it all depended upon the result of your London trip: if you had been given the part we would've let it go at that, because, once in London, that would've been a stepping stone to bigger things. We both felt this, and that being so we weren't going to enlighten you with anything that might have impeded your career. And we were not the only ones who thought along these lines, oh no. I'm going to ask you a question.'

As he said this, Louise got to her feet, almost gabbling now, 'I . . . I'll get some more hot water.'

Fred looked at her for a moment and smiled, then said, 'All right, dear. If you wish to save him embarrassment, then go and get some hot water.'

'Oh, Fred!'

As she went quickly from the room Riley asked tersely, 'What is this? From what embarrassment could you save me?'

'I'm going to ask you a question. You remember in part the Christmas party and your farewell do last year?'

Riley made no answer, but he felt his whole body stiffening, and when Fred said, 'You were tight, and she was tight. I know that much, so I'm going to put the rest to you plainly without any frills: did you sleep together?'

Riley's body was stiff; he felt he was red from the roots of his hair to the soles of his feet. Fred had said they were both tight, then asked if they slept together. It sounded crude, even nasty.

172

'I'm asking you a question and you're bound to know: did you sleep with her?'

Riley was on his feet now and although he wanted to yell his answer, Yes, I slept with her; and I can't forget I slept with her, but she forgot it, he said nothing.

'Sit down. Sit down, man. I've got my answer. And look, believe this, I'm not blaming you or her, no; neither is Louise; but as for Nyrene, all she is worried about is that you should be free to continue your career without feeling responsible for anything. You're so young compared—'

'I am not so young, Fred, compared with her. I've told you before and you've said it yourself, I've never felt young. And what d'you mean, she wants me not to have the responsibility for what?'

'Sit down. Sit down, will you?'

He sat down, and they looked at each other in complete silence while the word responsibility ran through Riley's mind. Responsibility for what? Couldn't be. But yet it was. He had hoped and hoped; but then there was this Charles. Yes, there was still this Charles, and now he said, 'What responsibility should I have?'

'Well, if you refuse to reckon, I can't reckon for you. You know when you were together, and you know when the child was born.'

Riley again made to rise but Fred waved him down with a sharp motion of his hand.

'But it was premature.'

'Premature be damned!'

'What . . . but what are you saying? What about this Charles, her boyfriend? Don't tell me he was imaginary, because Louise said she spoke to him.'

'No, no, he wasn't imaginary, Riley; he was
173

Charles all right, full name Charles Kingston; and she loved him very dearly, because he happened to be her godfather.'

'What?' The word was small, soft, but penetrating.

'Yes,'—Fred nodded his head slowly—'her godfather. Her father and Charles Kingston had been in the war together, were great friends. He remained a bachelor all his life, and he was ... well, very comfortably off, with a nice house on the outskirts of Peterculter, near Aberdeen. This, I understand, had been the family residence, but he was the only one left. Nyrene's cousin Ivy and her husband Ken were also close friends of his; they were his nearest neighbours, I understand. These were the two, you know, from whom you tried to guide me the other night on instructions from Nyrene; but she had forgotten about Louise, and Louise later got the whole story over coffee. Not that they thought they had any story to tell, for they had nothing to hide, not like our dear Nyrene. And so Louise found out that Nyrene had spent every holiday possible with her godfather, and that after her parents died she became closer still to him and she spent every weekend possible up there with him, even ... when she was on the bottle. In fact, it was he who helped her to recuperate after she was thrown over by the handsome slob. You used to wonder, didn't you, where she got to at the weekends? We did, too, at least we understood she went up there to stay with her cousin. Anyway, our dear Nyrene not only has her own house but she now owns a much better one, in Scotland, as I understand it from the photographs; and she has enough money to keep her in considerable comfort

174

for the rest of her life, even if she never wants to put a foot on the boards again. And he didn't forget her cousin either, which they considered very kind of him.'

'How old was he?' His voice sounded dull.

'Eighty, I think, one or two; not quite sure, but eightyish.'

'Eighty!'

'Yes, eighty. But that's beside the point now. The question is, what are you going to do about it? From our side, I can say we are in her confidence, but on the promise that we didn't tell you anything. Things were to remain the same. However, right from the beginning both of us knew it was a false promise, because we felt you were entitled to the truth, but this would depend on the path your career would take. By the way, do you now feel anything for the child?'

'No, it's been a bombshell. The only person I think about is her. She has burnt me up all along. And during these past few months it's been hell. People talk about being burnt out by their feelings, their emotions, well, I know what it's like, and believe me'—now he moved his head back and forth slowly before adding—'it's no boyish attachment. I've known her since I was sixteen, and from the beginning, right from the beginning when she was a star up on that stage and I, like all assistant stage managers, was only a dogsbody, a glorified tea-boy. And something else I've realised lately.' He paused here and looked down at his hands before saying, 'I had never experienced the falling-in-love stage; I was never excited or stirred by the girls I knew. My role in life seemed always to act the clown or play the big fella, be centre stage,

175

as you well know'—he was nodding at Fred now—'but what I have felt for her from the beginning, and what has grown seemingly daily, I feel will be with me till . . . well, I sound like my dad now or my mam, to the end of me days. But that's how it is. I feel I could swear on it.'

Fred now lay back in his chair and sighed as he said, 'I wouldn't, Riley, I wouldn't swear on it; but your emotions are high where she is concerned, and I can understand that. She's a very attractive woman and doesn't look her age. However, I'm not going to say I'm warning you, but the years play havoc with emotions, they change them in spite of all the good intentions. Well, if they don't exactly change, they cool down, turn into something else: fondness, friendship, kindness, compassion, a mixture, which in the end, and I'm speaking from age now, is much more satisfying than the burning up elements. But then, who am I to be talking like this? You've got to live your life before you come to that, and she'll help you to meet it, that's if she takes you on.'

'What d'you mean, takes me on?'

'Oh, you'll have to convince her of a number of things: first, that you not only love her but that you want the child, because, let me tell you, that child at the present moment is number one in her life, probably because it's partly you, but perhaps more so because it's something she never thought to have. Would you hope to marry her?'

'Yes, of course, of course. What else? What are we talking about?'

Riley's voice had risen, as Fred's did when he replied, 'I know what we're talking about, laddie, I know what we're talking about, and I'm going to tell you, if you do marry her you'll have to receive some flak, and not only from that little spitfire of a mother of yours but from the local public at large. This is a small town. You don't live in it but you are known because of your acting. One has no private life when you take to the boards. Everything you do comes out illuminated in print.' And with a forefinger he started to write imaginary words in the air: 'The young man who played the imbecile boy so successfully in "The Golden Mind" at The Little Palace Theatre and who is not yet *twenty*'— there was great stress put on the word—'is to marry Miss Nyrene Mason who is now forty years old—'

'She's not forty.'

The imaginary finger still went on writing: 'He denies she is forty, so let that pass. However, Miss Mason has been one of the stars at The Little Palace for fifteen years, and has recently given birth to a son.'

Riley was again on his feet, but Fred, his hand dropping on to the arm of the chair, lay back again, saying, 'And that's being kind to you, laddie. It just wants your mother to come round intending to knock blazes out of this old woman who is corrupting her son, and there you have it. Now Nyrene is aware of all this, much more so than I am, and that's what you've got to get over.'

'With your help?' There was bitterness in Riley's tone, and Fred answered evenly, 'Yes, with my help. In talking to you, as I have during the last ten minutes, I have acted as your best friend; and you'll never have a better, let me tell you.'

On the opening of the door, Riley swung round and faced Louise. There was no hot water jug in her hand and she went straight to him, her arms outstretched, and hugged him to her, and felt his whole body crumbling and he muttered, 'Oh, Louise. Louise. What am I to do?'

She took her arms from around him, put her hands on his face, then she kissed him, saying, 'Now come and sit down here between us and we'll think something out, because although I know he'll already have thrown the whole barrelful at you, he's done it for your own good.' Then she pushed him down onto the couch as she added, 'She's not the only one who loves you, so just remember that. And you also, Mr Beardsley, don't forget it was only because of Riley that I took *you* on.'

'Shut up, woman, before I skelp you where it hurts most!' And Fred pulled her gently down between them; then in a more serious voice, he addressed Riley again: 'Listen to me for a moment. Put yourself in Nyrene's place. You are over there in the house, you've got the child, you're in love with a fellow half your age. As you see it, he's got his life before him but you love him too dearly to check it in any way; but if, for instance, he were to come to you and tell you that he didn't care a damn about age and let the future take care of itself, what would you do?'

Unhesitating, Louise turned from him and looking at Riley she said, 'I'd fall on his neck.'

'Oh, Louise. Louise.' Riley was holding her hands, and his head was bowed as he muttered, 'You really think she would?'

'Why not put it to the test, and without any more hesitation? Go on; get on your pins. Then come back here and tell me straight you're going to take your things. And you could say, "Do you mind, Louise?" Go on!' And as she went to push him up, he turned to her and took her into his arms; but looking over her shoulder at his benefactor, as he had always been, first as Mr Beardsley and now as Fred, he said, 'May I?'

'Go ahead. Go ahead. Who am I to stop you?'

At this Riley leaned forward and kissed Louise on the lips; then he swung himself up and hurried from the room.

'What are you crying for?' Fred pulled Louise tightly to him, adding, 'I knew there was a gentleman in Riley somewhere, and that last act proved it. Another of his breed would have kissed you, and that would have been that, but not our Peter Riley.'

*　　　*　　　*

Mrs Atkins greeted him as Mrs Roberts had done, 'So you've got back, then?' and, not waiting for any answer whatsoever, she went on, 'The miss is upstairs. By! His Lordship's been at it today, divils fer garters he's made. I told her not to worry, it's wind, and not to pick him up every minute, either. Oh, he's all right if you walk the floor with him. I bet you could do with a cup of tea.'

'No thanks, Mrs Atkins; I've just had one at Mr Beardsley's,' and quickly he ran up the stairs.

At the nursery door, he hesitated before gently pushing it open, only to find Nyrene wasn't there, and he paused before walking slowly to the cot to look down on what he was sure was his son.

A suffocating tightness gripped his throat, causing him to open his mouth wide and to gasp at the air; and not until the tears welled from his eyes could he close his mouth again and grope in his

179

pocket for a handkerchief.

This was his son ... his. He had created this baby, this child, this was his son. The enormity of it overwhelmed him: this child had been conceived in a rare passion of first love, even through drink-bemused senses. Yet, the drink hadn't obliterated the essence of what had taken place; nor had there been a day since when he hadn't thought about it. He should have known. He should have guessed. Did it matter now? Did it matter?

There was a sharp intake of breath behind him, and there she stood in the doorway looking at him. She did not move towards him, but he did to her. It was at a run and on tiptoe, and, grabbing her hand, he pulled her into the corridor and along to her bedroom.

Inside, he stood with his back to the door, and held her close.

She had not uttered a word, not even when he had said, 'He's mine, isn't he? I should've known from the start. Oh, Nyrene, Nyrene.' He was kissing her as he had done that first night and never since.

When at last she pressed herself from him she gasped, 'They promised.'

'Yes, I know they did; and if I'd got the part in London they would've kept their promise.'

'You ... you didn't get it? I thought it was sure.'

'Well now, darling,' he now pressed her face tightly between his hands and placed his mouth on hers again before he said, 'You above all people should know there's nothing sure in this business unless you're coming out of the wings to say your first line.'

'Oh, my dear. My dear Riley.'

180

'I am not just your dear Riley, from now on I am your dearest Riley.'

'All right. All right, you're my dearest Riley. Yes, you are. Oh yes, you are. But now look, nothing has really changed. We must be sensible about this. There's the public to think of.'

'Damn the public!' His voice expressed the look on his face. 'And I mean that: damn the public! Oh yes, I know what they'll say: "Him not twenty and she near forty," I've just had it rubbed into me, back there.' He jerked his head. 'But you're not near forty; you don't look thirty and I certainly don't look nineteen-kicking-twenty. Beardsley didn't even give me that; he stuck to the nineteen; but I've never been nineteen, I've never been eighteen, nor seventeen, nor sixteen. I felt like a man before I left school and my dear master's questionable protection. If anybody made me into a man through my mind it was Fred himself; so let's wipe age out of it.'

'We might, dear, we might,'—her voice was sober now—'but David won't. Nor will The Little Palace Theatre, nor will the people of Fellburn. And there is your family.'

'Damn, my family! Anyway, what family have I? I have no home there.'

'You may not, but from what I understand, your mother will have a lot to say.'

'She can say what she likes. Dad will be for us, as will Betty, and that's all I care about.'

'We must talk, dear, we really must, there's so much at stake.'

'Who for?'

'You, of course. Oh, it's all right, it's all right saying you'll love me till the day you die. In ten years' time you won't be thirty and I'll be fifty. Let's face it.'

'And of course, in between that, you've forgotten to mention the seven year itch, haven't you?'

She laughed outright now.

'There's only one more thing I want to ask you, Nyrene, and just give me a straight answer. Do you love me, I mean really love me?'

'Oh, Riley! Oh, my dearest, dearest, Riley! If I live to be fifty'—she gave a smile now—'I'll never be able to tell you just how much. But wait, wait,'—he had been about to kiss her again—'listen to me. No matter what my feelings are for you, there is always the age gap, and we've got to live in the world, and the world is a cruel place. One can say "I don't give a damn!" but one does. Not that I would really give a damn for being blamed for baby-snatching—and, mind, that'll be the saying—but the fact that you have a career before you and that I am a hindrance and will continue to be so as the years go on. And I couldn't bear that.'

'Sit down here.' He pulled her onto the side of the bed. 'Now listen to me. I want to marry you. Not only that, I am going to marry you, and you are going to marry me; either sooner or later you'll marry me. Now, until you do I am your lodger, because I'm bringing myself lock, stock and barrel into this house tomorrow. Fred and Louise want it that way too, they want rid of me. Seriously though, they want, above all, our happiness, and I can't be happy without you, my dear, and you can't be happy without me. I know that. You're a very good actress and you've fooled me some of the time, but you'll never fool me again. I can see you standing with that cup of tea by my bedside on that morning

182

when I woke feeling glorious and there you were, turned back into Miss Mason, so much so that I had to believe you. Oh, I was an idiot. Now there it is. I have it all set out in my mind. I shall finish the tour, and this'll give David time to get used to the idea of Mr and Mrs Riley being on the stage together once again.'

'Oh no! No, my dear. Oh no, my dear! Never! I couldn't bear that, not here.'

'Well, that's the only way I can see us being together all the time, and that's the only way I want to live, being together all the time. And, also, I want to get to know my son. Oh yes.'

'I must tell you something.' Nyrene took hold of his hand now and pressed it to her breast. 'There is nothing more that I would wish for than to act on the stage again with you, but since Charles died, I've already given up the idea of the stage. Oh, dear Charles!' She smiled now. 'You would have liked Charles. As you know so much, by now you'll know who he was. Well, you'll also know, I am sure, that he left me pretty well off, with a very nice house near Aberdeen. It's a charming place; just a short run. Fred and Louise don't know yet that I have already put up this house for sale and that I'm going to live up there.'

'Wonderful! Wonderful! I don't mind being a kept man.'

She shook him now as she said, 'To me it's like a script to a new life, but would you mind living there?'

'From what you've said, it sounds marvellous to me, simply marvellous. And there're bound to be theatres in Aberdeen ... but I thought you loved this house so much.'

183

'I do; but then I know Charles's house too. I spent half my childhood at The Little Grange. It's a lovely place, and not all that far from the actual Highlands.'

'But what would you do with yourself while I was working?'

'Oh my dear, the things I could do with myself happily. First of all, keep the home as beautiful as Charles always kept it; or at least as Old Sally Nolan kept it for him for years before she died. Then I'd have the joy of bringing up my,'—she inclined her head towards him—'our son; and lastly, the garden will require a lot of attention. It's a very large—well, there are five acres of land around the house. Two have been cultivated into a garden; the rest is made up of a little woodland and meadows, looked after by one Hamish. Charles used to ride a lot in his younger days, and so there is stabling for a horse, and the meadowland for grazing. Can't you see our life there?'

'It sounds too good to be true. Oh, much too good, dear.'

'It can be, for, apart from Ivy and Ken and the other three houses within a mile or so of us, we'll be on our own and accepted by those whom we choose as friends.'

'But listen, Peter—I'm not going to keep calling you Riley—listen. There would be one provision I would have to make, and that is, on no account must you give up your career. I know it'll take you away from me at times, but I'll be there waiting. And in between times, on your own, and really on your own: no Fred and Louise, no Dave, none of the company. And remember that everyone of it is of your own kind, someone with whom you can talk shop. What about life then?'

She looked hard at him now, no softness in her face as she said, 'You're thinking of my weakness, aren't you? Well, let me tell you: from the day I knew I was carrying the child I swore I would hurt it in no way: I've never smoked, so that was no obstacle; but I have been a drinker and, I admit it, more than was good for me, and what damage I have done to my body that has got through to the child is out of my hands now. I promised that I would only be able to live with myself if I could give it up entirely, and this I have achieved so far. I didn't even join Louise and Fred in drinking a toast to the new addition, and I look at it this way: if I could keep dry for that length of time during which I often felt so lonely and wretched, not to speak of feeling ill, then I cannot see myself succumbing to it with all the happiness in store for me even if you should have to go away.' She went to him and, bending down, put her arms around his shoulders and, looking into his face, she went on, 'I'll hear your voice on the phone every night, I'll have your letter in the morning. Oh yes,'—she was nodding at him, smiling now—'I demand that I have a letter every morning. You see your career is set and so is mine. It only remains for us to leave here and start life in The Little Grange.'

'After we are married.'

'Yes, after we are married.'

His arms went around her waist and he laid his head against her breast and murmured, 'I can't believe it. Not really, I can't.'

*   *   *

185

The following day Fred dropped Riley off at the house together with his luggage.

He was greeted by Mrs Atkins with, 'Come for your holidays, Mr Riley?' and he answered, 'Just that, Mrs A., just that,' and he dropped his cases in the hall.

When he returned to the pavement to take up the rest of his luggage, he looked at the man who was sitting grinning at him and said, 'Thanks, Fred, I'll be along tomorrow,' and Fred, looking past him, called to Nyrene, saying, 'Hello! I'm running a taxi business now, madam. Any time you need a car I'm at your service, any time.'

'Thank you, Mr Beardsley, I've got your number.'

And at this Fred laughed, then called back to her, 'If that school bell should ring before I get there, I'll lose me job this time. See you later, Nyrene.'

'Yes, Fred, see you later.'

The car moved off and she was about to close the door when she stopped and said, 'That man across the road, Peter; that's your father, isn't it?'

Riley had gone back to the doorway, and he exclaimed, 'Good Lord, yes! It is me dad. Hang on a minute, I must go and have a word with him.'

But she brought him to a stop by gripping his arm and saying, 'Why don't you bring him in?'

They exchanged a deep look, and he said, 'Thanks, dear. Thanks, I will.'

He walked across the road and approached his father, saying, 'Hello, Dad! What are you doing up this end? Anything wrong?'

'No, no, lad, nothing. I was just coming back from the hospital and I took this street and

186

there ... well, I saw you.' And he laughed before he added, 'And seeing that I know you, I couldn't help but stop, could I?'

'Come on over.'

'Eeh, no! No, lad, no. You're ... you're gonna stay there?'

'Well, that was my luggage going in; Mr Beardsley's throwing me out.'

'I could never believe that.'

'Come on. Don't stand there. Come on.'

'No, lad. What I don't know I can't talk about.'

'You can say what you like, Dad; and you'll have a lot to say after you've been in. Come on.' Riley took his father's arm and drew him across the road and into the hall, where Nyrene was holding out her hand to him and saying, 'Hello, Mr Riley! I'm so pleased to meet you,' and she indicated the sitting-room door, saying, 'Come along.'

Meanwhile, Riley, throwing off his overcoat, turned to Mrs Atkins, saying, 'Now you leave those alone; I'll take them up in a minute.'

'Yes, I know you will. I wasn't going to touch them.'

'Don't tell lies, woman.' Then he stopped and said quietly to her, 'That's my father.'

'I'm not deaf.' And she smiled warmly at him, then said, 'What's it to be, tea or coffee?'

'Oh, a cup of tea, I think.' And when Riley entered the sitting-room Nyrene was saying, 'Do take off your coat, Mr Riley; you'll feel the benefit of it when you go out. I know we're only in October but it's surprising how cold it's been all day.'

Riley looked at his father. He had never before seen him in an overcoat, not as far as he could remember. He must have got it from Oxfam, which meant he had gone there himself. His mother had been a customer of Oxfam for years, but she had never, to his knowledge, brought anything back for his father. There seemed something different about him. His hair had been cut shorter; his face was clean-shaven; he looked, as they say, 'well set up'. He hadn't ever been the kind of man who could ever look smart, yet here was a different man altogether from the one he was used to. His appearance seemed to match the character that had come out in the hospital.

'Would you like a cup of tea?'

'I've just told Mrs Atkins, dear.'

Alex Riley looked from one to the other. He was bewildered by what he was thinking. She was a lovely woman, all right, but she was in her thirties, around thirty-five he would say, and Peter wasn't twenty yet. Oh, he'd heard of these things happening, but not with such a big difference in age. Yet there was a change in his lad since he had last seen him. He was a man already. Perhaps it was his height; he was nearly six feet. He thought it was odd that here he was, five-feet four and a half at his best, with a son like this and one who evidently could pass in the best of company. And it seemed no time at all since he was a young scallywag and always in trouble. Look at that car business. Well, since he had won that competition and had been championed by Mr and Mrs Beardsley there had certainly been a change in him. Look at him now in this lovely room acting as if he had been used to it all his life, and it looked as if he was going to be used to it, for some time ahead, anyway. By gum! When he took everything into consideration he was lucky, he was, with a woman like that. She was lovely, lovely. Yet there had been rumours that when she was an actress she'd had a drink problem. But people would say anything. People were wicked, especially women. Oh, didn't he have experience of that. Wait till she heard of this! Oh my! He hoped he wouldn't be around at the time, better still that they wouldn't be around.

'Dad, would you like to come upstairs a minute?'

'What? Upstairs, up here you mean?'

Riley was laughing, and so was Nyrene, and it was she who said, 'He wants to show you something, Mr Riley. He's a show-off, and who should know this better than you.'

As the older man rose to his feet she said to Peter, 'Don't stay too long; Mrs Atkins will be in with the tea in a moment.'

When they were on the landing Mr Riley stopped and looked about him and said, 'It's a lovely house this, isn't it?'

'Yes, Dad, it's a lovely house, but we're leaving it.'

Alex Riley noticed the we, but all he said was, 'Aye? Where for? I mean, where are you going to?'

'Scotland. Nyrene has a nice house there too.'

Here was his lad saying he was going to Scotland with this woman who had another house there, Nyrene he called her.

'It's a lovely name, Nyrene,' he said.

They were in the nursery now and standing each side of the cot, and the child was awake and was gurgling so much that the saliva was running out of his mouth.

As Riley wiped the baby's mouth with a soft tissue he said quietly and seemingly to no-one in particular, 'He's mine.'

Alex Riley looked down at the baby, then up at his son, and he said, 'What's that you said, lad?'

'I said, Dad, this child is mine.'

'Dear God! You mean that?'

'Yes. Yes, I mean that.'

'Eeh, lad! How did it come ... ?' Alex Riley closed his eyes in embarrassment for he had been about to ask how had it come about, and Riley answered gently, saying, 'In the usual way, Dad. And we love each other; we always have. From the first moment I saw her, I think. I know there's a big difference in age, but she's not old in herself and she doesn't look her age, not by half. I don't look mine either; no-one would take me for only nineteen come twenty.' He laughed out loud now. 'If Beardsley was here he would stress the nineteen and cut out the come twenty. My dear friend deals with stark facts, but I'll soon be twenty and feel thirty, if a day.'

Alex Riley was staring down at the child and muttering, 'I can't believe it. This makes me a granda.' His head came up and his eyes were bright and moist, and he said, 'That's something, isn't it? Eeh my! That's something. Oh, lad,'—his hand went out across the crib—'I'm gonna say this: I've not said it much before but of late I've thought it a lot, I'm proud of you.'

Then his whole expression changing, he said, 'But dear God, lad, dear God! What's gonna happen when she knows?'

He had no need to explain the 'she', and to this Riley answered, 'It's got nothing to do with her. She can do what she likes or say what she likes.'

'That's it, lad, but what she says and where she'll say it are what will matter. She'll come round here storming the place. You know she's got no sense of decency, not where you're concerned anyway. I could go to hell's flames and it wouldn't matter, but you ... oh, you were going to be her bright boy. Well, you've turned out to be a very bright boy but not hers, not under her thumb. She could see you staying at home for years, and I could see her putting her foot down on one lass after another. No-one would suit her. Some mothers are like that. There's more divorces caused through mother-in-laws than enough. It's got nothing to do with class, 'cos the middle class have the same kind of trouble; but they react to it in a different way from what the likes of your mother will do. Oh aye. She loves to hear her own voice bawling in the street. She's done it to me more than once, until I've become dumb and let her have her own way because I couldn't stand the disgrace of being shown up again outside. Many a time she's gone and hung the washing out and yelled my defects and my laziness so that all the backyards on both sides could hear her. Anyway, I'm ... I'm glad for you, lad, delighted; and I know somebody else who'll be an' all, that's Betty. She missed you when you left, you know, 'cos she and you are very much alike, and she has a hell of a time with her mother. You're not there to go at, but Betty is, as a kind of whipping block.'

As they were about to leave the cot the older man bent over and touched the little fist and, laughing down on the wide-eyed child, he said, 'I'm your granda. What d'you think of that eh? Oh, not much. Not much.'

'Come on with you!' Riley tugged his father towards the door, but on the landing Alex Riley drew him to a stop and, looking him straight in the face, he said, 'I'm thinkin' of leaving your mam.'

'You're what, Dad?'

'Well, you heard; and do you blame me?'

'Oh no, no, I don't; but how has this come about? I mean, where would you go? What would you do?'

'Oh, just as you've settled your life, I could settle mine the morrer; I've got a . . . a woman.'

His dad had a woman! Well, well! The things that were happening.

'She's a widow with three daughters, but they're all well set up: two are married and one's away at college. Oh yes,'—his head was wagging now—'she's no common piece. You remember the nurse that was nice to you in the hospital when you came to visit me, when she joked with you?'

'Oh yes, yes, Dad, I do. And that's her?'

'Yes, yes, that's her, lad. She's three inches taller than me, and what she sees in me God alone knows, but she seems to see something, so much so that she put it to me. I couldn't believe it myself. Me thoughts were goin' that way, but they would've just stayed that way, they would've had no outlet. But there she was telling me I was worth something. She's got a nice house and a good job, and she's state registered, well, I mean she's a fully qualified nurse.'

'Has Mam an inkling of this?'

'No, not an inkling, lad, although she's wonderin' why I've tidied meself up of late. When she used to come to the hospital to see me and I was pretty bad, I thought things might have changed; but no, that was just a phase: she had to show people that she was a very thoughtful wife. Once I was home

192

again, it was my old chores being left for me, the hooverin', the washing up, the lot. Yet I was the one who never worked. She went out in the morning, did her job, and that was that; the rest of the day was hers, except for the actual dishing out of the dinner I had prepared. Oh no, I never worked; I never did anything. That was her cry. And everybody believed her, except perhaps one or two of the close neighbours who have always been decent to me.'

'Well, Dad, no matter what way your life goes, it'll be up to you from now on, but you'll both always be welcome wherever I am. And Betty too. You tell her that.'

'I will, lad. I will.'

And then the most strange thing happened. His father suddenly put his arms about him and hugged him, and as Riley returned the embrace he thought the world, as it was at present, was a wonderful place.

*　　　*　　　*

Since his operation, he had forced himself into the habit of keeping his back straight when he walked, and today it was straighter than ever and his walk was sprightly, almost a march, in fact. He had just come from Peter's, as he now thought of the house, and they were to be married tomorrow. They wished him to be at the Registry Office, together with their friends Mr and Mrs Beardsley. It had been kept very quiet, the only other person in the know being Mrs Atkins, and she was well acquainted with everything. She was to go with them for a month, to see if she would like the life in

193

Scotland. She had no ties and only a small flat, and they'd told her they would like her to stay with them permanently.

It seemed that everything was happening at once, for he had made his mind up about his own future life. Being only forty-five, yet knowing he looked fifty, he still considered he had a number of years ahead of him in which to live a peaceful and happy life. He felt that was assured with Maggie. Everything was arranged. He would see Peter married; then he would tell Mona that he was going. He felt no compunction in leaving his other two children, Betty could look after herself. They were all in their teens now, anyway, and the attitude of the two younger ones towards him was a pattern of their mother's. She would certainly bring up the matter of their keep. Well ... well, according to her, it had been a long time since he had subscribed to their upkeep. All he had brought into the house for years was his sick pay, and she could claim that he wouldn't miss it, because he had never had it; she had seen to that.

There was a feeling of elation about him, of having just come alive, yet, as he pushed open the back-garden gate and heard her voice coming from the kitchen, his heart sank. She must be at Betty; it was her half-day from the hairdressers.

As he opened the kitchen door they both turned and looked at him. Betty's face showed white and she seemed to be on the point of crying, but his wife's face was scarlet, and he noted immediately that she was preparing to go out: not only was her hat and coat lying across the head of the couch, but she had a comb in her hand, and the combing back of her black wiry hair always preceded the putting

194

on of her hat. He had always felt she was the only woman in Fellburn who still wore a hat, even when she went out shopping. As she once had said to him, she considered it a sign of respectability, only drabs wore headscarves. He had reminded her on that occasion that she was on sticky ground there: what about the Queen?

The tone of her greeting was as usual: 'Where've you been all morning?'

'Out.'

'Don't come that with me. Well, while you've been out, have you heard the latest news about your son?'

He had also noted of late that it was his son, not hers. 'This one here's let it drop that he's no longer with the Beardsleys, so where d'you think he is?'

'You tell me.'

'Yes, I'll tell you: he's lodging with that actress trollop who's just had the bairn, a bastard one at that.'

'Shut your mouth, woman!' And at this her mouth actually sprang agape, for she did not recognise either the voice or the man, for he advanced towards her, not stepping away as he usually did, but coming straight at her; and what he did next amazed her further because he thrust his finger none too gently into her brassiere-tight breast, saying, 'Don't you use that word about the child, or anybody else's for that matter!'

Recovering somewhat, she now slapped viciously at his wrist as she said, 'I'll use what language I like. I'm talking about your son.'

'Oh yes, *my* son. He's ceased to be *yours*, has he? Then if he has just become *my* son, why don't you let me deal with him? What business is it of yours what he does?'

'It's my business when he shows us up before the whole town, going to live with that—!'

'I'm warning you.'

'You're what?' Her head came forward, and when, without moving, he repeated, 'I'm warning you: quieten your dirty tongue or else you might be sorry for it,' it was evident that his wife was now really amazed, because she turned to Betty, who also looked amazed, albeit gleefully, for she was actually smiling, until her mother bawled at her, 'Get that grin off your face else I'll wipe it off for you!'

'Oh no, you won't, Mam. Oh no, you won't. Not again you won't. You want to listen to me dad a bit and you'll learn something more.'

'What's this?' She looked from one to the other. 'Hand-in-glove with him, are you? Well, you might be, but that makes no difference to what I think and what I feel. A bit of a lad like that in the clutches of—' She stopped and drew in a long breath, and at this he said, 'That's it, think on it before you spit it out; and it'll be well for you if you do that in the future an' all.'

'I don't know what you think's come over you but I'm goin' to tell you this: you're not goin' to shut my mouth up where he's concerned, and her an' all. Oh no, you're not. He's still a bit of a lad.'

'He's nearly twenty.'

'He's still a lad, and he's given us a bad name.'

He laughed now. 'Given us a bad name? If anybody's given us a bad name ... well, I mean in the vicinity of this house, it's you, missis. To the rest of the town, well ... what are you? You're a charwoman for Mrs Charlton, but round about

196

here they have a number of names for you. Did you know that?'

'Well they might have a number of names for me, but I've got a number of names for them, and there's truth in mine because most of those who are for you are a common, drunken, swearing . . . and, yes, a whoring lot.'

'Yes, yes, perhaps you're right, but they're doing one thing that you've never done, they're living. They're enjoying some part of their lives, and it wouldn't matter so much about you not enjoying yours but you've stopped a number of other people from enjoying theirs, and I'm thinking right back to your own mum and dad. I've realised for some time now they were glad to get rid of you even when you stooped, as you thought, so low to take me on. What a pity you didn't catch the verger from St Bride's. You ran hard enough after him. But he was wise.' When her eyes darted from side to side he knew she was looking for something to lay her hands on. Her teeth were clenched, her eyes were blazing, and when she muttered, 'You'll pay for this!' he came back at her with, 'Yes, I might, but not through you, not through you ever again, my dear wife.'

Once more he watched her looking towards Betty as if her daughter might be able to explain what had come over this man, this mouse-like, docile, gutless individual, as she thought of him; and then he began to tell her.

He started by saying, 'I was going to leave this news until the day after tomorrow because tomorrow's a very special day. My son . . . Do you hear what I'm saying? My son is to be married tomorrow and I'm attending the ceremony. Then,

197

the following day, I was going to tell you something else, and this is what I'm going to say to you now. I'm going to leave you. You see, I've got a woman. I'll try later on for a divorce, but until that comes about we're going to live together, and in this town, on the outskirts, but definitely in Fellburn.'

He watched her jaw drop while her cheeks seemed to move upwards and she half-closed her eyes. Then her face straightening out and she said, 'Oh, come off it! Don't you think you can frighten me with that: you with a woman! Then the stars fell down.'

'No, they haven't fallen down, have they, Betty?' He turned to his daughter and she, looking at her mother, said, 'Yes, he has a woman, Mam.'

He watched her now lean her back against the sink, as if for support and to give her time to digest what he was saying, actually saying, that this little squirt was going to walk out on her and he had a woman. That was the difference that had come about him of late, the difference she had been forced to notice. He had taken a new interest in himself and how he looked, and she had thought it was because he had been in the hospital and that they had made a fuss of him, because his back really was in a bad way. But it was a woman. Who? But what did it matter? Whoever it was, it was a woman, and he was going to leave her just like that, her still with two to bring up, which is what she flung at him next: 'You can't walk out on me; you wouldn't dare with two to bring up.'

'The two still to be brought up, as you put it, are in their teens now; and I have never brought them up in any way, you've seen to that. In any case, you can't get blood out of a stone, you'll get my sick pay and that's all there is to it. But I can tell you you'll have to fight for that, because I've got to live wherever I go, and the authorities are well aware of it. Anyway, you've still got child benefit, you've still got your job, and you're not above claiming any other thing you can get out of the government. Oh, you'll manage all right. And I'm going to tell you another thing: you keep on leading Betty here'—he jerked his head to the side—'a hell of a life, as you've been doing lately, and I'll take her along with me; and she'll come because she's met the woman and they like each other.'

He watched her now turn her glaring eyes on her daughter and mutter, 'God in heaven! I cannot believe this is happening. I just cannot. I don't deserve this.' There was an actual break in her voice; but he came back at her harshly now, almost yelling, 'Yes, you do! You've been let off lightly, because all our married life you've done nothing but bawl and browbeat me from the time you tipped me out of bed and I lay on the floor all day and couldn't straighten out, and I would've been there all night if it hadn't been for me brother coming in and was told I had been lazing it upstairs all day, and he found me and got the doctor. But still you wouldn't believe it, oh no; not even when I went before a medical board, and then your slogan became, "You can work if you want to. Other men have to." Anyway, I'm going to talk no more, for all I have to say has been said.'

There was silence in the kitchen for a moment before, gathering her forces together, she pulled herself up straight and, glaring at him, she said, 'You mightn't talk any more but I haven't started yet, because I'm going along there and what I'm going to say to those two is just the beginning until I come back to you.'

Grabbing up her hat from the couch, she thrust it on her head without going to the glass at the side of the sink, as she usually did, then pushing her arms into her coat, she stood buttoning it as she continued to glare at him. But when she made for the door, he was there before her with his back pressed against it, one arm stretched across it.

'Before I let you go down there and break them up with your dirty tongue and dirty mind I'll go out in the street with you here this minute, and I'll raise hell, and I'll hit you. For the first time in my life I'll hit you; and I realise now it's something I've left too late. And so get back in the kitchen there and take off your badge of office.' He made as if to pull the hat from her head, but she caught him a sharp blow across the wrist, and this brought him upright and from the door. She did not attempt to open it, but backed away from him.

In the kitchen again, she faced him, crying, 'You can stop me now but there'll be other times that'll be open to me.'

As he glared back at her he knew this to be true. Once she got him out of the way he could see her dashing down there, banging on the door, confronting and covering that lovely woman with abuse, and the abuse she would use was bound to take the shine off the brightest love, for if the difference in age between Nyrene and her young husband-to-be wasn't troubling her much now it certainly would after Mona had opened her mouth. He knew that one said to oneself, 'Oh let people think what they like,' but it's when they voiced what they were thinking that the knife was thrust in.

He had never realised, not until these last few weeks, how much he loved his son, his only son, for up till now she had driven a wedge between them. She had done that since she had first noticed they were growing close, taking walks or going to the football match together, and what would happen now that she couldn't have him tied to her apron strings, he wouldn't dare to think, except that she would destroy him in the only way she knew. He knew that his son had found something that was rare. When he was a very young lad he himself had dreamt of such a love but this had soon been knocked out of him, for he was to learn they were but fancies of the night; real life had no place for such feelings. Yet here was his son aglow with them. It shone out of his face. He had always been a good-looking lad, but now there was something more in his countenance, something which radiated from him especially when he was with her or holding the child. He mustn't lose this feeling, he mustn't, and nothing must happen to mar it. The years might take their own toll, but that was in their hands. He . . . he'd have to bargain with her. Aye, that was it, he'd bargain with her. He turned from her now and, going to a chair, he sat down and said, 'I'll bargain with you.'

'You'll what?'

'You heard what I said. Sit down a minute.'

'I'm not sitting down and I'm not bargaining with you.'

'Well, have it your own way. If you go along there, I walk out; you hold your hand and let things ride and—' He looked towards Betty who was staring wide-eyed at him, then as if half-ashamed of what he was about to say, he muttered, 'I'll stay on with you; and that should save your face, because you'd be unable to stand the racket of your neighbours knowing that your despised husband had left you for another woman. In this quarter, there's still a code that you are expected to live up to. You must stick it out together, endure the hell and all else. Anyway there it is: I'll stay if you'll leave him alone, so what about it?'

He watched the muscles of her face twitch. She was moving one lip over the other; then her mouth opened and closed before she turned away from him and went towards the window, where the net curtains across the bottom half shut out the view of the street, and she stood staring at them, as if she could see through them down into the future. She knew that all he had said was true, and she was already feeling the scorn of her neighbours. She knew exactly what the verdict would be: she deserved all she was getting and more; he should've walked out years ago. No, she would be unable to bear that.

Turning from the window, she looked at him still sitting by the table; and being who she was, she had to remain herself, even in defeat, for she cried at him, 'Don't think you've got me where you want me in this, not by a long chalk. There'll be other times,' but she did not say, I agree with your proposal, or put it in her own words; her answer was to pull off her hat and coat, then march to the door and into the passage, and they heard her feet almost pounding the stairs.

Immediately the door banged overhead, Betty, reaching across the table, gripped her father's arm, saying, 'Oh, Dad! what are you going to do now? Maggie expects you.'

'I know that, lass, but she'll have to understand, and you understand, don't you? I couldn't let your mother go round there. It would break them up, even after they're married. But, don't worry—' he now stood up and in a whisper, he said, 'They're leaving on Friday for Scotland. They've sold the house to the daughter of the people next door and Nyrene's given me lots of things.'

'You know, Dad, I can't help feeling sorry for Mam.' She jerked up her head and added, 'She's miserable. To the very core of her she's miserable.'

'You're telling me, lass. She's been miserable all her life.'

'Oh, I know, Dad. I know. But what'll happen when she knows about the bairn?'

'God knows. Oh, God knows, dear! I'll keep that for later, I mean when they're well away and she won't know where they've gone, because you don't know, do you? I'm the only one, and Mr and Mrs Beardsley.'

'You'll still see Maggie, won't you, Dad?'

'Oh yes, of course. Of course. Nothing'll be changed in that way. And she'll understand, I know she will. She'll know it's only a matter of time.'

Betty straightened up now, and there was a smile on her face as she said, 'I don't feel old enough to be an aunt; but that's what I am, aren't I?'

Alex Riley now got to his feet, saying, 'Aye, lass, you're an aunt. And I'm a granda; and it's a lovely feeling to be a granda.'

CHAPTER ELEVEN

A pile of luggage had been put in the guard's van. Mrs Atkins, carrying the baby, had taken her reserved seat in the first-class compartment and she was now looking down at Peter and Nyrene on the platform talking to Mr and Mrs Beardsley and Mr Riley.

'I'm going to miss you both,' Alex Riley was saying to Nyrene, 'and the bairn. Oh aye, I'm goin' to miss him; I feel I've known him for years.' He gave an embarrassed laugh here, and Louise put in, 'And you won't be the only one, Mr Riley. We'll all miss him.' It was noticeable that Fred said nothing.

'You all know well enough you may come and see us as often as you like.' Nyrene looked fondly from one to the other.

With the sound of banging doors came the shaking of hands and kissing between the women. Riley suddenly grabbed at his father's hands but seemed unable to speak. It was his father who was the more composed: 'It's all right, son,' he said, 'everything's goin' to be all right. Don't worry about this end; just look after her.' And he nodded as he smiled at Nyrene, then added, 'Just give me a thought now and again, because I'll be thinkin' of you.' He now pressed Riley towards Fred.

Fred had remained strangely silent all through the parting. Even now he did not break it. Instead, he thrust out his arms and hugged Riley to him for a moment, then pointed to the porter now standing at the open carriage door.

Riley had been about to say something, but

turned hastily away and jumped into the carriage.

The door banged, and shortly afterwards the train began to move. His eyes following it, Fred had the feeling it was carrying away a son; or, at least, a friend he could never replace . . .

Twenty-five minutes later, Alex Riley entered his house to see Betty there, in a state of agitation. It was unusual for her to come home during her lunch hour.

'What is it, lass? What is it?'

In answer to his question she asked, 'Have they got away? I mean the train, are they on the train?'

'Aye, lass, they're well on their way now.'

She let out a long-drawn breath. 'She's gone over there to the house.'

'What's made her do that?'

'She met Mrs Naylor on the road. You know, she cleans at the theatre; and she congratulated Mam on being a grandmother.'

'Oh my God!'

'I'd popped home because I couldn't help but feel sorry for her. But there she was, like a mad woman, ready for going out. She was calling our Peter all the filthy names she could lay her tongue to. I've never heard such language. She said he must have been only eighteen when he went with that drunken old hag, and she said you weren't goin' to shut her mouth, no matter what you threatened. And that's the last I saw of her; out she went. Dad, she seems insane.'

'No, she's not insane, lass, she's mad but she knows what she's doing. You can put people away when they're insane mad, but when they're just mad with possessiveness and jealousy, envy, the lot, as she is, they can appear normal for most of the

205

time. She knows what she's doing all right. But don't look so worried, lass. I've told you, if things get unbearable for you here you've just got to leave, because this will have cleared me of the bargain. I had said if she didn't go round there I would stay. Well, she's done it.'

And with this he went from her and hurried up the stairs.

It was almost one o'clock when Mona Riley stormed back into the house. There was no other way to describe her entry, and when she saw her husband standing with his coat on and a case and a canvas holdall by his side, she said nothing. It was he who spoke, saying, 'Well, the bargain was that if you didn't go round there I stayed. Now you've been round there, so I'm going.'

Still she said nothing, and her silence was more menacing than any words she might have used. Then, seeming to spring to the Welsh dresser, she grabbed up the glass rolling pin that Peter had won at a fair when he was a lad of fourteen. When she half-turned from the dresser and her hand swung up he knew what she intended, but he wasn't quick enough to avoid her aim, and when the rolling pin grazed his brow it felt as if a hammer had hit him. He staggered back, and it was only the armchair that stopped him from falling. When he felt the warm trickle of blood through his fingers he thought he was about to be sick. Her screaming voice seemed to be coming from a distance; then, the mist clearing from his eyes, he saw Betty holding her mother back against the dresser and she was yelling to him, 'Get out, Dad! Get out!'

Slowly, as if he were walking in a dream, he grabbed the two bags and ran out the back way into

206

the garden shed. There he dabbed the blood from his face with a handkerchief, before leaving the house that had been a virtual prison for so many years.

Betty looked at her mother sitting at the table. She had taken off her hat and coat, and the coat lay crumpled upon a nearby chair. Her head was drooped between her resting forearms and clenched hands. She had been like this for some minutes; nor did she move when Betty said, 'I'll make you a cup of tea, Mam.'

Betty made the cup of tea and brought it to the table, and she looked down somewhat apprehensively on the still figure, for her mother hadn't moved an inch.

'Have this cup of tea, Mam.'

When her mother slowly raised her head and turned and looked at her, for a moment Betty felt pity overflowing and she had the desire to go and put her arms about her and assure her it would be all right. But she knew that nothing could or would ever come right for her; and the desire was swept swiftly away as her mother began to speak. Her words coming from deep within her, she said, 'I'm goin' to live. I'm goin' to live a long, long time, and I'll get my own back on him. You see if I don't. I hate to think I gave him birth. He's filthy! Like her. Eighteen years old and goin' with that drunken slut and givin' her a bairn. God! I'll see my day with him. As for the other one just gone, his turn will come. And there'll come a time when I'll dance on their graves. By God I will. I'll swear on it.'

Oh dear Lord! Betty's hand was tight across her mouth now and she turned swiftly away and went back into the scullery. She had never before felt afraid of her mother, but she did now. She had said she would dance on their graves, and she meant it, meant every word she said. Well, there was one thing sure, she herself couldn't stand this life. As soon as possible she would get out. Oh yes, she would get out, she'd go and join her dad.

PART TWO

CHAPTER ONE

She stood inside the gate. It was all of four-and-a-half feet high, but she hadn't leaned on it, although she had been standing there for more than an hour. Her body was still erect and tense, her gaze directed over the bucolic scene ahead, nevertheless her troubled mind was taking her back down the years. Years filled with mental torment, hate and tragedy, but all the time supported by a devastating love. Love, love that had always held pain through fear of losing it but had finally become a torment.

Nyrene Riley was now a woman nearing fifty who looked her age, and she was well aware of it. Yet on the day of their arrival here, when Peter and she had stood at this very spot and gazed over this same scene towards the river, she had imagined she was a young girl again, a feeling which had persisted for weeks, months, yes even for the first three years. There had been a feeling of youth and gaiety within her.

When Peter had been forced to leave her for his tours she had filled her days with looking after her beloved child, helped by Mrs Atkins and supported by their unique gardener-cum-handyman, Hamish McIntyre, who came from Peterculter, just a short distance away towards Banchory.

With Ivy and Ken she would take a weekly trip into Aberdeen or Banchory to do the shopping. Aberdeen in particular was full of interest, and now and again they would go to a play. Then there were evenings when Claire and Mick Brown, near neighbours of Ivy's, would pop in, as would an

211

amusing middle-aged bachelor, Angus Clarke.

Perhaps it was after the child's third birthday that the change began, although it did not affect their love.

At that time she wasn't taking into account the years to come; and now her tortured body and mind were taking her back down them.

CHAPTER TWO

She had met him at Peterculter station and managed to restrain herself from running to him when she saw him jumping down from the carriage. But he ran towards her, only to pass her, shouting, 'I've got a box in the guard's van.'

A minute later, standing by his tightly packed holdall, his usual travelling case and a wooden box, she said, 'What on earth's all this?'

'Mind your own business, woman. Here, let me hold you.'

'No, no! Look, there's the lady from the—'

'Damn the lady from the—!'

He kissed her, then said, 'Do you think you can lug my holdall?'

When she picked it up, she said, 'Just what have you in it, bricks?'

He did not answer, but, picking up the suitcase, he pointed to the wooden box, saying, 'I'll get someone to come and fetch this. Is the car in the yard?'

'Yes, of course.'

Ten minutes later they were on the main road when he gave a great sigh, leant his head back, thrust his feet out as far as they would go and exclaimed in a high falsetto voice, 'Ain't life wonderful!' She burst out laughing, then said, 'What's happened to make it so wonderful?'

'Don't be stupid, woman,'—he had assumed the voice of Fred Beardsley now—'I'm home, aren't I? And you're but inches from me. What more explanation do you want?'

'Oh, Peter!'

Her tone brought him upright and, leaning towards her, he kissed her neck, creating danger for an on-coming car. 'Don't be . . . don't be a fool! See what happened? I bet that fellow's cursing me.'

'He wouldn't dare.' He lay back again and looked out of the window as he now said quietly, 'I love this countryside. And to think I can wallow in it for the next, oh ten weeks, more if I want to.'

'Really?'

The car swerved again.

'Yes, Mrs Riley, really.'

'What about the pantomime?'

'I turned it down.'

'You didn't! You love pantomime.'

'Yes, I know, but if I'd taken it I wouldn't have seen much of a woman that I've been after for some time.'

'Oh! Peter . . . Peter don't,' and when he went to move towards her again, she said, 'No, don't move! I'm going to put on speed and get home. No more antics, or we'll end up in the ditch.'

As they turned off the main road on to a root-lined narrow way, bordered by woodland, he sat up straight, misquoting, ' "And does the house now stand above the field above the Dee, and will we have tea at three?" '

After they had passed a copse of Scotch firs bordering the path to the left, to the right was a high green hedge that was checked abruptly by a huge wooden-framed gateway leading to a drive on to which Nyrene now slowly turned the car, saying on a laugh, 'Poor Rupert Brooke. He didn't deserve that.'

The drive was broad but short, only about a hundred feet long before it opened into a large paved square, bordered on one side by the end of the house. Opposite, a row of outbuildings containing three stables, a tack room, and a wood store, and at the far side was what looked like a large barn, running from the end of the outbuildings to where it was cut off from the house by an archway leading into a kitchen garden beyond.

The stone and partly timbered building was now used as a garage, and as the car approached it there emerged from the wide open doors a tall thin man wearing a red woolly hat that hosted a big pompom on its crown. The skin of his long face was not unlike a paler shade of the hat for it was what could be termed ruddy.

Almost before the car had come to a stop he pulled open the door and, looking at Peter, he said, 'Well, ye've made it again I see.'

'Yes, Mac, I've made it again, and not before time.'

'No, as you say not afore time. Four weeks is long enough to be gone.'

Riley, now standing in the yard, stretched his arms whilst saying, 'Oh, this air, this air! Everything all right, Mac?'

'Now, Mr Riley, sir, would ye be expecting it to

214

be different? Your good woman is fine, there she is fine as ever; your linty is as spring-heeled as ever; he's along with his Aunt Ivy at this minute; and as for Mrs Tommy Atkins ... well, would ye expect her to change?'

As Riley lifted a case from the car boot he laughed as he said, 'She'll give you "Mrs Tommy Atkins" one of these days when she hears you.'

'But then, she does na' hear me. She is Mrs Atkins to me in public as I am Mr McIntyre to her in the same, but as ye already ken, weel I said it afore, she's the most fear-filled creature that I would expect to find in a long day's walk through the gullies.'

'Well, who's to blame for that?' put in Nyrene, with a laugh. 'You will tell your tales of goblins and woodfolk; it's a wonder that Charles, too, isn't scared to death by them, the stories you keep telling him.'

'Now there's a funny thing—' But as Mac went to pick up the wooden box from the boot, the weight of it diverted his thinking and he said, 'My! My! There's some scrap iron ye've got in here by the weight of it. Where do ye want it put?'

'In the corner of the barn; and don't let the linty near it, it's a real model train with all the accessories for his Christmas stocking.'

'My! My! 'Tis good, that is. That'll delight him.' Mac lifted the box and took it into the barn.

After he had returned, he said to Riley, who had already lifted the cases from the boot, 'Give them to me here,' and then returning to his earlier conversation, he said to Nyrene, 'As I was about to ask ye, have ye ever seen the linty go pale with me stories? Dances around me, he does, as if he had joined the woodfolk hissel. By the way, I've just come out,'—he bobbed his head towards the house—'I've made up the fire. It's flaming nicely now. That woman! She'd let it go out in front of her. But she had the good sense to leave the coffee table all set quite near it. It looked comfortable. Yes, it looked comfortable.'

Both Nyrene and Riley laughed as they watched him carrying the cases towards the kitchen, then, their arms about each other, they walked round the side of the house and approached the main door.

As he always did, Riley stood back from the door and gazed up at the façade of the outsize cottage that had thrilled him the first time he had seen it. Constructed of stone, topped by timber, it had hand-chiselled beams of oak linking with each other up to the eaves, which overshadowed the deep set windows.

The roof had a distinction of its own, being covered with huge stone tiles with the ridge leading to two ornamental chimneys, one at each end of the long house.

They were crossing the threshold when he pulled her to him and said, 'You know something? I think I love this house better than I do you.'

'Yes, I know you do, that's why you married me.'

When she was pulled against him she gasped, and when his lips pressed hard on hers she returned his kiss for a moment; then pushing him away, she said, 'Let's get in.'

She ran from him, down the long room and through a door and into the kitchen, leaving him standing and pulling off his scarf and overcoat. As had been his experience in the yard, it was as if all this were new to him.

The room—it was more than a hall, for it was furnished as a sitting-room and dining-room—was all of fifty feet long and twenty-five feet wide and, together with the adjoining kitchen which at one time had also served as the byres, was vaulted. The great beams supporting the roof were held in place by equally impressive timbers. To his left a shallow flight of oak stairs led to a narrow gallery from which led a number of doors. The stairway was supported by four oak posts, allowing usable open space.

He walked slowly across the room towards the wood fire blazing in the low basket set on a stone hearth, and bordered by two large iron dogs, against which were stacked a number of equally large fire-irons, a poker, a toasting fork, and a pair of tongs used for arranging the hot logs. The inglenooks beside each iron dog were too near the fire for comfort.

The stone mantelpiece held only one pair of brass candlesticks, between which was set an array of pewter mugs. On the stone wall, at each side of the fireplace, a large painting was hanging; one depicting eventide with a beautiful peasant girl standing, a sheaf of corn across her arm; the other a painting of richer hue depicting a French lady at court, bare-bosomed and bedecked with lace so real one could imagine it could be picked up from the canvas. The authenticity of its being a Boucher had been debated. Were it so, it would nowadays be worth a fortune.

The whole room was stone paved, glimpsed only in small areas, for three large and brilliantly hued Chinese washed carpets covered most of the room. In front of the fireplace was a long white rug, and beyond it was a deep-seated couch, with matching armchairs at each side. Various pieces of antique furniture were scattered about the room.

The suite was upholstered in a soft shade of blue velvet which matched the curtains at the two long windows each side of the front door. There was a third window at the very far end of the room towards which he was now looking, for set in front of it was the long trestle dining table with its high, hide-backed chairs.

There were no pictures on the walls at this end, the light from the window reflecting from the highly polished furniture giving enough variation of tone.

Riley's face had taken on a serious expression as he continued to stare down the room. When he had first come into this house, he could remember standing as he was now, amazed by the uniqueness and beauty of it. The room looked exactly the same, nothing had changed, and he recalled his thought: God, I'm lucky. The words had been said almost in the form of a prayer, and his mind still voiced them. He had her, that wonderful wonderful woman, and she had this house. He had this house now, too, and he was Mr Riley, Mr Riley, sir. It was Hamish McIntyre who had first addressed him like that and without blinking an eyelid at his youthful appearance. He liked Hamish, he was a good man. He had a deep sense of humour and he would give the impression that he cared for neither God nor man, yet Sunday found him at his church or, as he said, the kirk. And if the travelling parson happened to be preaching on a particular Sunday and came out with jokes, surprising for a parson, Hamish would seek him out in order to relate them to him. There would be nothing nasty nor even risqué in these jokes, but as he was wont to say, few women understood what made a man laugh.

Yes, he liked Hamish, and he loved this house, and he adored her. The more he saw of her the more fiercely did his love grow; but such love had a hungry side. He missed her so much when he was on tour. Time and again he would feel like giving up the whole business, dashing home to her and saying, 'I'm going to go local, at least team up with an Edinburgh company, so I can get home at least for one day a week,' only, when this feeling was at its height, to tell himself to stop acting like some youth who had just fallen in love. He had a wife and child to support. Oh yes, she had plenty of money of her own, but he wouldn't touch a penny of that. Oh no! That was the only thing that they had disagreed on, the use of money, her money. She could buy what she liked with it, but he would provide for their living. She had once come back at him and reminded him there were such things as resting periods that hit the best of actors, and he had said he was well aware of that and would take odd jobs at such times.

Taking this stand had mentally helped to pile the years on him. He could consider himself a man now. But hadn't he always felt a man?

'What's the matter, dear?'

He turned and blinked and said, 'The matter? Nothing. What could be the matter? I'm home . . . I'm home . . . I'm home.' Again he was holding her; but now she pressed back gently within his arms, saying, 'You look worried.'

'Worried? What have I got to be worried about?'

He now let go of her, turned and dropped on to

219

the couch, then pulled her onto his knee, saying, 'Nyrene ... Nyrene. What am I going to do about you?'

'The same as you always do about me, give me my own way: lie to me from the minute you come into this house until it's time to go.'

He stared at her for a moment, then put out a hand and softly stroked her cheek, saying, 'I adore you and I need you. Oh, how I need you! I need you so much at times that I wish, sincerely wish I'd never clapped eyes on you. I do ... I do. At one time I used to despise all those yarpers on the television and the radio always on about love. I used to switch them off in disgust; yet here I am so soaked up with it that at times it becomes unbearable. I look at the girls in the cast. They don't walk properly, they don't hold themselves right, they don't talk right. They've got no idea that you can put more into a pause than you can into a sentence, they're gauche.'

There was no smile on her face now as she said, 'They're only gauche, dear, because they're young, and I only walk straight, talk correctly and know my pauses because I'm a middle-aged woman.'

He laughed now as he kissed her, then said, 'Well, how would this middle-aged woman like to come up to bed right now, this very minute? I must find out if she's started to spread yet.'

'Certainly not! I want a cup of tea and they'll be in at any moment, and I shouldn't wonder but Ken will bring them. Let me go.'

Frustration. Frustration. As he let her go he nodded up to her, saying, 'I'll have a headache tonight.'

'Do, Mr Riley. Oh, do have a headache. That'll

suit me fine.'

In the kitchen Nyrene put the kettle on the Aga plate, then put the tea in the pot and stood waiting. It would take only a minute for it to boil. It was now three o'clock. It would be another five hours before they could go upstairs, at least to bed, and she didn't know how her body could wait that long. He had said he adored her. What name could be put to the feeling she had for him? Consumed would be a better word. His absences were a torture to her, and she could give him no hint of her pain because although she might want him with her, she knew that acting was his life and that he'd be lost without it. She had imagined her feelings would ease over the years, fall into a pattern, perhaps even become motherly; but no, if anything they had become fiercer, stronger; and she now found herself constantly asking what would happen if anyone were to come between them, and it could happen. Those gauche girls he talked about were all attractive. If they had nothing else they had youth, and that could pay off any day against age.

Then again, what if he were killed in a train crash or a motor crash or whilst crossing a road. Well, she could suffer that. Yes she could suffer that, but not another woman. She hoped it would happen like that, rather than he would live to see her as she really was, for then he would turn kind, no longer loving. Oh, what was the matter with her? Here he was, and she was going to have him for weeks; and she must tell him what Fred had said was happening to The Little Palace. Now there was a solution, that is, if it ever got off the drawing board. Oh yes, that could be the solution. Don't be silly! What did it matter? She was brought from her dismal thinking by the sound of a commotion in the yard. Presently the door was flung open and there bounced into the room a small, startlingly fair and beautiful-looking boy and now he almost overbalanced Nyrene as he flung himself against her, crying, 'Mama! Mama! Bruce came. Bruce.'

'Careful. Careful. Bruce came?' Nyrene was looking at Mrs Atkins who was divesting herself of her coat and balaclava hat, and that lady said, 'Mr Wakefield will come traipsing across for him tomorrow,' only for her voice to be cut off by Hamish McIntyre saying, 'Nonsense, woman! That dog knows the road better than his master any day in the week. He'll be snuffling at the door come dawn. Mr Wakefield just likes an excuse to visit.' Then after a pause, he went on, 'I'll be away, ma'am. I'll be away. No need to wish ye a good night; ye've got your man back, and the linty there. By, he'd tire a troop of horses, he would that! Good-night to ye. Good-night.'

Nyrene was smiling and her voice was soft as she said, 'Good-night, Mac.' And whatever else she might have said by way of thanks for his escorting the little troop home, her son's voice cut her off now, crying, 'The morrow, Mr Mac, the morrow, high . . . high jink.'

'Aye. Aye, me linty, it'll be high jinks tomorrow. But keep it to yersel, laddie. Keep it to yersel.'

When the door closed on the Scot, Nyrene, who was now sitting on the couch with the child on her knee, took his face in her hands and whispered 'What is this, high jinks tomorrow? What are you two up to?'

As the child gurgled with laughter, Mrs Atkins put in, 'That man, ma'am, he gets up my nose. We could find our own way, but there he was standing at the beginning of the wood for all the world, I tell you, looking like the stag at bay. You know, there was a picture in me grandma's house and it showed you a great elk standing on top of a hill surveying the world, and there he was: give him a pair of horns, ma'am, and a couple more legs and you've got a stag all right, a rutting one at that, eh! The things you hear about that man.'

Nyrene was shaking gently inside. 'What's the latest this time?'

'Oh, he's chased a widow from Peterculter or somewhere near, got her run off her feet.'

'Oh, Mrs A., it must be all talk; what time has Mac for chasing anybody? He's here nearly every hour of the day, except Sundays. Then he's been known to look in on that precious day too. It's all talk.'

'Never smoke without fire, ma'am. Anyway, where's Mr Peter?'

'I'm here,' a voice said from along the far end of the room, 'but nobody takes any notice of me. Not when the love affairs of the great Scot are being discussed.'

The child, springing from Nyrene's knee, raced up the room and with a leap landed in Riley's arms, causing him to fall back against the stanchion of the stairs and to cry out, 'Hold on, there! Hold on, you wild horse!'

'Daddy-man.'

The child was holding Riley's nose now and repeating, 'Oh, Daddy-man, home.'

'Yes, your daddy-man is home.'

The word man tacked on to Daddy had come about by the fact that the child, who had seen Riley

223

only at intervals during his first and second year had addressed him each time as man, and it had taken both Riley and Nyrene some time and a lot of repetition before he was made to understand that the man was his daddy. However, it had seemed that, although he accepted this fact, his parent's name couldn't be complete for him unless he added the man. The man. At first he had said the words separately, 'Daddy man', but as time went on they were merged and now the Daddy was more than taken up with man, and as Hamish had been heard to say, the title wasn't far removed from that English idiot's little diddy-men, the only difference being that the i in diddy was replaced by the a in Daddy.

Riley was now being pulled back down the room by his son, his progress punctuated by small leaps.

At the end of the room, the boy let go of his father's hand and ran to Mrs Atkins and tugged at her skirt, crying, 'Peeano!'

'He wants to play the piano,' Mrs Atkins said.

'He wants to play the piano?' said Riley. 'But we haven't got a piano.'

'No, but his Uncle Ken has and he showed him how to play "Oh, can you wash your father's shirt?" with two fingers. And he loved it. We couldn't get him away from it.'

'What?' both Peter and Nyrene were laughing now.

'Well, it's a piece, you know, that you play with two fingers. And it goes:

"Oh, can you wash your father's shirt?
 Oh, can you wash it clean-oh?
 Oh, can you wash your father's shirt

224

And hang it on the line-oh?" '

His face alight with merriment the child sang the end line again: 'And hang it on the line-oh.'

Of a sudden, the child began to race around the couch and in and out of the chairs, jumping and leaping as he went, until Riley, grabbing him, said, 'Now, now! No more. You know what Mummy says: walk in, jump out. Inside the house you walk, outside the house you jump. Come on, say that: walk in, jump out.'

The child said nothing. He was standing looking up into Riley's face, his arms now extended towards his father's shoulders, and his voice became strangely quiet with a pleading note in it as he said, 'Daddy-man.'

Riley quickly picked him up, and hurried back to the couch and placed him in his mother's arms. The child's laughing expression had changed into one that could be called sad, yet the strange thing about him was that his whole body seemed to be at rest. It wasn't limp; one could say it had gone quiet. It was a state Riley found disturbing, although Nyrene was more used to it. The doctor had been unable to tell them what really was wrong with the child, except to say it was a kind of relaxation following the exhaustion brought on by extreme activity.

Looking down at Nyrene, Riley asked quietly, 'How many of late?'

'None since you were here last.'

'Really! Then you think it's the sight of me?'

'Don't be silly. The previous month he had four, one as I told you lasting for hours. That's when I called the doctor again.' She tapped her son's cheek, saying, 'Come on, darling. D'you think you can walk up to bed? You're a big fellow now, you know.'

'Mummy.' The voice sounded clear, and when it added, 'I'm tired,' the words had lost all childish lilt.

There was another strange thing about these turns that puzzled them. While in them he would speak without hesitation. Generally these periods were short, lasting perhaps an hour or two, but occasionally one would last a day.

During the longer periods it was noticed that he always wanted to hold on to a hand. Mostly it would be Nyrene's, sometimes Mrs Atkins's, who often objected to Hamish McIntyre taking charge of the boy on such an occasion, for, she said, it did the child no good to listen to his jabbering on about the best places for fishing in the river and how young deer were bred. What disturbed her most was his description of the woodfolk and their antics; made her hair stand on end, he did with that talk. However, her mistress was all for McIntyre, and so it was no use talking.

'I'll carry him up.' Riley took the child from Nyrene's arms, and she followed them up the stairs.

After the child was undressed and tucked up in bed Riley sat by his side, the small hand within his, and quietly, he said, 'Would you like me to tell you a story?'

The reply was equally quiet but definite. 'No, Daddy-man, no.'

Riley looked down into the eyes staring up into his. They were full of something he could not define, in fact he could not put a name to the expression on the face. It wasn't angelic, no. The cheeks were rounded and of a pale cream colour, and in contrast, the mouth was a soft rose, like two petals dampened with dew, slightly open and showing the gleam of small teeth.

If Riley had been nonplussed and made somewhat sad by this curt reply from his son, the feeling was swept away when the child said, 'Daddy-man?'

'Yes? Yes, dear? Yes?'

'Don't go away.'

He was looking down into the child's eyes and what he saw in them now was a deep appeal. His child had said 'Daddy, don't go away,' not as a child might, but in a tone that an adult would have used.

He swallowed deeply, then said, 'I'm not going away for a long time now, weeks and weeks, and we'll have some fun. And I'll tell you what.' He bent closer down to the face now and, his voice a whisper, he said, 'We'll get a piano and you'll learn to play all by yourself "Oh, can you wash your father's shirt?" Eh?'

There was no answering smile on the child's face, in fact his whole expression had changed again, and Riley, drawing himself slowly upright, knew that the boy had gone into one of his silences.

A few minutes later, Nyrene came into the room with a bedside tray all daintily set and holding a boiled egg in a china-cock egg cup and a plate of narrow strips of thin bread and butter. After placing it on a bedside table she came and stood by Riley's side, and he, without looking up at her, said softly, 'He won't have that now; he's gone into a sleep.' Yet when he went to draw his hand gently from the child's, the boy moved uneasily for a moment before once again settling down. His eyes

227

were closed, his breathing was even, his whole body was relaxed, and he had the appearance of a child in a deep sleep. They looked upon it thus the while realising it was not a natural sleep.

The door opened again and Mrs Atkins came and stood by them, saying, 'Go on down, the pair of you. Your tea's all ready. I'll stay with him. I've done your eggs. They'll last you over till dinner time. He looks as if he's in a fast one this time; and I'm not a bit surprised, for he's worn himself out racing around since we left the house this morning.'

Fifteen minutes later they had finished their tea and were sitting side by side on the couch. Riley being unusually quiet, Nyrene took his hand and, bringing it up to her chest, she held it tightly, saying, 'Don't worry about him; I'm used to this. He's perfectly all right. As Mrs A. says, he wears himself out. The energy he expends when outside and in the wood and running around would tire a man in no time.' Then sighing deeply, she added, 'But having said all that, I think we should take him to a specialist. What do you say?'

Riley stared at her for a moment before replying, 'Yes, dear. I'm with you there.'

'Shall we leave it till after the holidays? I doubt we would get an early appointment now.'

After a moment's thought, Riley agreed. 'Yes, dear. Yes,' the while he was thinking, In her own heart she's really not for it, but did not add, she's afraid of the verdict, as he knew he was too.

There was silence between them for a moment. Then Nyrene, leaning back, said, 'I must tell you all the news. First, The Little Palace is coming down.'

'Coming down? Demolished, you mean?'

'Yes. The whole street's to come down. There

was talk about it years ago. They want to widen the market. Apparently, though, there is a good side to it. Did you ever hear of a family called Pickman-Blyth?'

'Oh yes. Yes, they had that enormous house at the top of Brampton Hill; in fact, it was said that they owned all Brampton Hill at one time, and half the town.'

'Well, did you know that there was just a Miss Pickman-Blyth left and she is a friend of David's?'

'Mr Bernice? David Bernice?'

'Yes, Mr Bernice. David Bernice and she are friends; old friends, I understand. It seems they have joined forces. It's in the papers, and Louise is sending one on. As far as I can gather, the old Town Hall was for sale and David was for buying it, but in she steps and puts in a bid for the whole place, which was mainly offices. Well you know, the old Town Hall hadn't been used for years. It was boarded up soon after I first arrived at The Little Palace, and the offices adjoining were used by squatters for a time. They were the old rates office and such like. Well apparently, Louise said, David couldn't stand up against her buying the block, but he must've put it to her about the Town Hall itself. I don't know the ins and outs of it, but they've gone into a sort of partnership: she's interested in the arts, and he's going to turn the Town Hall into a theatre which will be marvellous, you know, because it had the most beautiful ceiling and a gallery, if I remember rightly, but the offices will be turned into a restaurant, and the end of the block into flats, two sections of four. Louise said it had passed through preliminary planning stages, with certain details to be finalised. But just think of The

Little Palace coming back to life, Cinderella turning into a princess. David must be excited.'

'My, my! I can't believe it.' Riley shook his head, then said, 'I hope they still call it The Little Palace.'

'Well, again from what I remember, it could be two and a half times the size of The Palace, and just think of the gallery. My, my!'

She pulled herself from the back of the couch as she said, excitedly, 'It would be worth your going back there for a time, wouldn't it?'

When he said nothing, she turned to him and said, 'Oh, I know you couldn't.'

'I could. I could if I hadn't a mother. Anyway, to get a thing like that off the ground'll take years.'

'They hope to have it all ready and running in two and a half years at the most.'

He too pulled himself forward on the couch now, saying, 'Well a lot can happen in two and a half years. Me mam might have pegged out by that time.'

'Oh, don't say that. Don't say that, Peter. It isn't like you.'

'Well, I mightn't have said it a year ago, but she's at her old games again and leading Dad a hell of a life, and sending that woman filthy notes. A lighted paraffin rag was pushed through the letter box one night.'

'Never!'

'Oh yes. But they couldn't pin anything on her; there's already a pretty rough crowd of lads round there who would get the blame for it. But then, as Betty said, those lads have got nothing against Maggie or Dad. Anyway, they had to call the fire brigade, the house was full of smoke. Betty's having a time of it, too. Mam started to turn up at the

230

hairdresser's around six o'clock to try to stop her meeting up with Harry Wilton, who's sweet on her. One night she actually went for him loud-mouthed, but he gave her as much as she sent. He told her he was getting a flat and was taking Betty with him. Apparently, that night Betty stayed at Dad's, and in the morning he went and saw Mam and warned her that if she laid hands on Betty again, as she had been doing, he would go to the police. And what was more, he had put in for a divorce. Following this, she went to Harrogate to her brother Frank's place. You know, he's been on that new estate only six months and apparently he wasn't very pleased to see her. She kept emphasising that he was all she had and that she wanted him to come and talk to Betty. He told Dad he had sent her away with a flea in her ear. Dad says he's well out of it, and so, you can't see me going back there, dear, can you? Anyway you wouldn't want to leave here would you?'

'No, I'd never want to leave here for good; but at times Peter, it becomes very lonely. Every day is like a year when you're away and I long for something to take up my time. Oh, I know there's the child and my new interest in the garden through the perpetual coaching of our dear Mac. And there's Mrs Atkins. But they don't fill my life,'—she turned to him now—'not even the child. Peter, there are times when I long for a glimpse of you, to hear your voice.'

She was buried in his arms now and he was kissing her passionately. Then holding her at arm's length, he said, 'It's the same with me, darling, exactly the same with me. When women come slavering round me, I want to push them on their

231

backs.'

Her eyes widened now as she said, 'They come slavering round you? Young or old?'

'Oh, you know what it is: some of the old ones are worse than the young 'uns. Then there are those crazy youngsters who wait for you coming out at night. Really! Was I ever young?'

'It's a long time since I was young, dear, but not so long ago since *you* were young.'

'Shut up! I have never been young, as I've told you. You know'—he now stroked her hair back from her forehead as he said—'you're the most wonderful teacher this business has ever had. Just look at me. What was I before you took me into the world of "The Golden Mind" and showed me how to act, not just be a funny man. I had come to think that was my forte; all I was good for. It still remains with me, you know, the feeling of that play. You did a Mrs Frankenstein on me, oh yes, you did. But now, look at you: your talents are being wasted. Only the other day I was thinking about that barn outside there, how wasted it is, and what would we do with it in the future. And you know what I think now—well, it's just since we've been talking—that barn could fill your days, for you could start a drama school.'

'Don't be silly. For one thing, just look how far we are from the town. And what is more, you have to have training.'

'You have training, you were at drama school in London.'

'I have no certificates or—'

'Damn, certificates! What need have you for certificates? All right, engage someone with a certificate and you take charge. It's an idea, and it's a good idea, and it would ease my mind if I knew you were doing something like that, something in your own line because you're wasted, you know. Oh yes, you are. Don't shake your head like that, you are wasted. Grant Forbes is putting us through our paces for a new play, and I often look down on him and think, You don't know the first thing about it, and I'm big-headed enough to feel, having come up under you, I could take his place and do it on my head.'

'Yes, of course you could dear.' Laughing, she now ran her fingers through his hair, saying, 'And your head gets bigger every time I see it.'

As he went to pull her into his arms again, she said, 'No. No. I'm going to slip up and see how he is. In the meantime, go into the kitchen and brew a fresh cup of tea. I won't be a minute.'

As she opened the nursery door, Mrs Atkins held up a finger to her, and when she tiptoed up to the small bed and looked down on her son she saw that he was in a natural sleep. She whispered, 'You can leave him now, Mrs A. Come along, he'll be all right.'

They did not speak again until they were on the landing, when Mrs Atkins said, 'It's just lack of energy, ma'am. You should've seen him over there. I wonder he hasn't had a turn sooner. That big hulk of a man eggs him on in all ways. I didn't tell you before, but he had the child up a tree and sitting on a branch, and they were swinging their legs and could have fallen backwards. I yelled up at him and told him so, and you know what he said, ma'am? He said that if they were to fall he would see that they fell on something softer than me. Oh, that man gets up my nose!' Then as she preceded

233

Nyrene down the stairs, she said, 'And another thing, ma'am, at times you'd think he owned this place, you would indeed. He pointed out to me that I was damn lucky to have that lovely flat above the stables, and I pointed out to him that it was me that had made it into a lovely flat, made those three dirty old rooms into a lovely flat, and he came back saying, well, they were wasted on me, there should be grooms up there and horses in the stables, as there once was. Oh, ma'am, if I ever disliked a man in this world it's that one.'

Nyrene, trying to hide her smile, said, 'I don't believe you, Mrs A. Underneath all this you're fond of him. Look what you did for him last year when he had that cold: wouldn't hear of him going home to his bare shack, as you called it, without a good meal in his stomach and a nice little parcel of goodies in case he should be unable to come back the next day.'

'I would do that for a sick dog, ma'am.'

'Go on with you; you can't hoodwink me.' Nyrene pushed the older woman by the shoulders towards the kitchen door before going to Riley where he was now lying on the couch with his eyes closed, and, sitting down beside him, she said, 'You're not asleep?'

'No.'

'You didn't make the tea, then?'

'No. She's on about Mac again?'

'Yes, she's on about him again. She fancies him, you know.'

'Oh, I wouldn't go as far as to say that.'

'I'd go farther. I'd say he fancies her too.'

'What! Mac fancies her? Never!'

'Oh, yes he does.'

234

'Madam, you know nothing about human nature.'

'No, of course not, sir; I haven't been around like you.'

He still had his eyes closed when he said, 'What's this titbit you've got to tell me about Louise and Fred?'

'Oh that. It's more than a titbit. You know I wrote and told you that Louise asked if she could come for a day and stay overnight with the boy, and I said I'd be glad to see them both. Fred was going on one of his trips to London again; they're usually short from the Friday night till the Saturday, but from this one he wouldn't be back until the Sunday. He goes to see this sister of his, Gwendoline. Apart from him she's the only one still here of a large family, for the rest are scattered all over the world. And he happens to be very fond of her. Even so I was surprised to know that Louise has never clapped eyes on her. I said of course I'd be delighted, so she came with Jason. He's not as lively as our spring-heeled Jack. Anyway, it was a very interesting short weekend and I learned some very odd things, all about the wonderful Gwendoline. Louise said she first heard about her the day you were leaving school. Fred had gone for you, and she and Fred had got together and started talking. He spilled a lot of family beans he must have been nursing for years. It seems the only member of the family he liked was Gwendoline. Well it should happen . . . are you listening?'

'My eyes are open. I am looking at you, dear, and I am listening.'

'Well, dearest Gwendoline started life as a prostitute, high-class one, of course.'

235

'What?'

'I said, Fred's dearest Gwendoline started life as a prostitute.'

'You're kidding!'

'I am not kidding, sir, and you haven't heard anything yet.' And Nyrene proceeded to give him a detailed description of what Louise had told her about the dining-room scene with Gwendoline and her hypocrite of a father, after which she went to London, becoming the mistress not only of one but of a succession of very wealthy men, very important men. The last, and with whom she lived for some years as his wife, died and left her a splendid house and a small fortune. But then she went on to say, 'What Gwendoline didn't tell her dear brother during one of his many many visits to her was that she has a daughter, who is now twenty years old. At present, she is living with her in London and she wanted Fred to meet her. She said to me then that she had never seen Fred so shaken or so piqued, he had thought he knew everything about his dear Gwendoline, he had been her confidant and friend during all her escapades. The father of this child was an American business man living in Paris with his French wife: their liaison in London was short, but the result of it was a child. And the remarkable thing is, on hearing of it, he decided to adopt the child. His wife, who was childless, was in agreement: being a French woman she accepted her husband's peccadillo. Over the years Gwendoline was even allowed to go and see her daughter and to spend some time with her. And now this young miss is on the loose. Her father died a few years ago, and then last year the adoptive mother, too, died, and Gwendoline felt that although her daughter was no longer a child she still needed a home of sorts and a guiding hand. And from what Louise says of Fred's impression of her, she'll certainly need that. Anyway, they seem to be getting on like a house on fire.'

'Good Lord!' said Riley. 'It sounds fantastic. Fred would be taken aback. But how did he find the young *mademoiselle*?'

'Oh that was another thing. Louise said he found great difficulty in describing her; in fact, it would seem he had never met anyone like her. Beauty alone couldn't describe her; she seemed to possess some extraordinary attraction . . . all legs, loins and licence was how he put it.'

'What?' Riley was laughing now. 'All legs, loins and . . . ?'

'Yes, licence: legs, loins and licence. What he inferred by the last I don't know. Neither did Louise. It appears, though, that when she suggested it might mean she would follow her mother's trade, oh dear! Mr Fred got into a paddy and apparently there were words.'

'Good gracious! I couldn't imagine Fred ever saying a rough word to Louise.'

'Nor can I, but then we haven't met Gwendoline or her offspring. Anyway, Fred was informed of his niece's education, three years in a French convent followed by a year in Switzerland at a finishing school, and now she is finished. Well, has been for the past year or more and is tossing up whether to marry a count, whose title is foreign, and assets invisible, or an industrial tycoon. By what I gathered from Louise's tone on the phone the other night she's not looking forward to their visit.

They're coming to stay for two nights early in the New Year. They then go off to spend the winter in Austria. It appears that they both ski well.'

'Poor Fred, all this must have come as a kind of shock.'

'I don't know so much about poor Fred, dear, I'd say poor Louise, because I think over the years she's got a little tired of hearing about dear Gwendoline. She hated the times Fred went up to London to visit her, and although he occasionally asked her to go along with him, she had always refused, feeling that he must have blown up this sister into a romantic being out of all recognition and she did not want to come face to face with her. Still, she'll be seeing them both soon, and I'll be waiting by the phone from then on to hear what impression she gets of the legs, loins and licence piece.' Nyrene slanted her gaze towards Peter saying, 'I wonder why he tacked the word licence on to her?'

'Likely no reason, only the slight alliteration with legs and loins. You know him and his quotations and such. He can hardly finish a sentence without a quote from someone or other. Anyway, darling, enough of big Fred, sweet Louise, darling Gwendoline and her leggy daughter. What about bed? Come here.'

'I won't come any nearer to you.' Nyrene was now edging firmly away from him. 'Mrs A. has a meal prepared outside. You're going up to have a bath; then we're going to act like civilised people. After Mrs A. has done her chores and has departed to her homestead across the yard, then, Mr Riley, we may sojourn.'

'Oh, come on, girl, have a heart. Come on.' He

had edged closer towards her and was holding her tightly now. 'Just ten minutes, come on. I'm aching for you, woman.'

She looked into his handsome face, and saw that he belonged to her, and that he was wanting her as she at this minute was wanting him; she told herself to stop acting the young teasing wife and remember what Mac had quoted yesterday, apropos of nothing that had been said in the conversation:

'Hold tight the Spring,
Clutch its birth before Summer dies
And Autumn weeps
And Winter withers age.'

CHAPTER THREE

Christmas was a gay and jolly affair. It really began the day before Christmas Eve when Riley and Mac and the child brought in armfuls of holly and set up the tree in a tub at the foot of the stairs; followed by the tacking of balloons to the beams, hanging strips of coloured lights between them and, finally, covering the lower part of the windows with 'A Merry Christmas' in cotton wool snow.

Nyrene told Charles that Christmas Eve was a secret day because his father and Mr Mac were in the barn and he must keep away, as they were making a place for Father Christmas's sleigh and reindeer. He would be stopping to drop off presents and to have a glass of hot punch to set him on his way again.

As Mrs Atkins listened to this story being repeated and expanded and altered she remarked to Nyrene, 'You're getting as bad as the monarch of the glen, ma'am.'

When later it began to snow, it formed a frame to the picture of their Christmas.

*   *   *

It goes without saying that Riley and Hamish McIntyre and the child spent most of the morning of Christmas Day in the barn. The child's amazement and delight at first seeing the trundling engine pulling a train behind it had been something to witness. Several times he cried his delight and hugged his father. Then when Nyrene and Mrs Atkins entered the barn he screamed his delight at them; and they almost returned it because it was the first time they had seen the train set working.

It was some time later when Mac handed his own Christmas box to the boy who, after tearing open the wrappings, lifted the jangling item from the cardboard box and looked up, first at Mac, then at the others and exclaimed quietly, 'What . . . 'tis?'

At this there was laughter; but then Mac, taking up the strings attached to what looked like oddments of wood, pulled it upwards to disclose a beautifully painted and dressed miniature replica of a Scottish soldier. The shoes and tartan socks were painted, as was the red and gold tunic, but the kilt was made of a bright tartan, and the Glengarry cap sported a big red pompom. Then stooping down to the box again, Mac picked up another set of strings and behold, there appeared at the end of them a dog wearing a plaid coat, and as Mac

240

danced it and the soldier towards Charles, the child cried, 'Bruce! Bruce!'

'They are beautiful.' This came from Nyrene, and she added softly, 'Did you make them, Mac?'

'Aye, mistress. This clever fellow by the name of Hamish McIntyre can do anything he sets his hand to,' casting, at the end of this self-explanatory praise, a shy glance towards Mrs Atkins, and she, although she was smiling, shook her head.

'Can you work them, Mac?'

'Well, Mr Riley sir, I can in a way, I can in a way, but it's better to be leaning on something like this.' He now stood on a box and putting his arms over a low beam he caused the soldier to dance and the dog to follow him, to the delight of them all.

'Let me! Let me, Mr Mac! Let me!'

'Yes, of course. Come, laddie, they're yours. But I must tell you that you must name them before you use them. The soldier is Mr Jock and the dog is Mr Jig. Now, who are they?'

The child looked up into the long red face and his own was alight as he said, 'J-J-Jock and Jig.'

'Mr Jock and Mr Jig.'

'Mr Jock and Mr Jig.'

At this clear pronunciation Riley and Nyrene exchanged an appreciative glance; then they watched the big Scot manoeuvring the child's hands to make the soldier and the dog dance on the box at their feet . . .

All together it was a delightful day, made more so, they all agreed, by Mrs Atkins's dinner. This lady was in high fettle, having received a beautiful full-length lamb's wool lined coat from Nyrene and knee-length boots from Riley, together with gloves and a tam-o-shanter from the child. But what did

241

the Scot give her? A jumper and she couldn't believe it, nor could Nyrene, when he told her he had knitted it himself, for it was made of fine wool and the pattern was in a number of shades. When, later, Nyrene, exclaiming in wonder, said, 'That man can do everything,' for once Mrs Atkins did not contradict her, but she did say, as if to herself, ' 'Tis a wonder he's not spending the day with his friends; he's always nattering about this one and that one,' and to this, Nyrene, looking straight at her, said, 'Perhaps he thinks his best friends are here.'

The tart retort to this was, 'Of course he would, 'cos you and the master are too soft with him. He thinks he runs the place, not counting the boy.'

These latter words made Nyrene realise that she didn't know at times what she would do without the big rough Scot's attention and care for the boy, for deep within her, she acknowledged the child's never-ceasing activity wore her out at times.

*　　　*　　　*

After dinner, which they ate in the evening and at which they had all sat down together, they were entertained by Mac and the puppets, and, too, by Riley, who got them all singing; he then caused further laughter when he went into the part he had been playing during the past six months on tour, performing a dance whilst in a half-inebriated state. But by midnight the house was quiet.

Mac was up in the hayloft, surrounded by bales of straw, which he said he found much warmer than his cottage bed. He had slept here before when the sudden heavy falls caused drifts and prevented him from returning to his home.

Nyrene and Riley had loved and loved again, and now he was saying softly, 'You know, I think this is the happiest Christmas I have spent in my life. Last Christmas you had the flu, and the Christmas before I was held up in Ireland. Remember, the boat wouldn't sail because of the storm?'

Did she remember? Whenever they were parted, always she would go through a particular agony. There could be a girl holding him, one of the cast. He was so young, so attractive. This is what frightened her, his attractiveness. He had something else besides his good looks, a particular attraction which, she knew, did not affect only herself.

She was aware that their love was unusual: generally, within a year or two, the fires of first love would lessen into glowing embers before smouldering into grey warmth, but their love had remained at its height, and at times she became afraid, knowing it was too good to last.

But now, life was wonderful, except ... except for the child. The love she held for her child was a thing apart, but it was coated with a worry deep within her. What her concern was based on she couldn't say: she only recognised that he seemed to be different from all other children of his age. He played differently, he talked differently. Oh yes, he talked differently, incoherently at times, yet in his quiet periods his diction was so lucid, it was as if he had suddenly aged. She must talk it over with Peter; in fact, more than talk it over, she must come into the open about her real fears on the matter. But she must go about it gently.

'What're you thinking about?' Riley said, interrupting her thoughts.

'You,' she lied glibly, 'and that I've got you for nearly another four weeks.'

After his lips had gently traced her face, he muttered, 'This road business is no good for either of us, you know, dear. I keep telling myself I must get fixed up somewhere permanently; and yet I feel I should consider myself damn lucky I've got a job at all. There they are, out of RADA and begging for small parts. I am lucky you know.' And now, leaning over her, he held her face and said, 'Here I am: first, I have you. Yes ... yes, that's the main thing, I have you. Then the boy; then this lovely house to come back to, and a job waiting for me. And that is the point: a job waiting for me. That is brought home to me strongly every place we stop. Always a queue forms outside hoping we need extras. We have to advertise before we reach the next town for two men and a girl for walk-on parts, which results in a queue, and I often think, there but for the grace of God, Fred Beardsley, and you, go I ... But wouldn't it be marvellous if David should get that Town Hall going ... There I go again. What am I talking about? I always forget my mother.'

Yes, yes, his mother; that vicious, dreadful woman.

'Darling,' Nyrene's voice was soft, 'We've been through all this. Let's get to sleep. There's another day tomorrow ... and tomorrow is today, and I love you.'

*   *   *

244

Christmas had been a most happy time all round, and it led to the excitement of New Year's Eve and its attendant jollification.

The child was asleep upstairs, but Nyrene and Mrs Atkins were busy loading the long table with all kinds of eatables from veal pies to mince pies, and Riley was busy trotting backwards and forwards bringing bottles of beer and the hard stuff from the small cellar, entry to which was through a hatch outside the kitchen door. When at last he was finished, he almost jumped into the kitchen exclaiming loudly, 'Whew, it's going to rain icicles!' Then he shouted up the room, 'Nyrene! Look, will that be enough?'

When she came hurrying towards him, he said, 'A dozen and a half beers, four whiskys, one rum, one gin, and two brandies.'

'I should hope so; if they get through that lot we'll have to put them up for the night. There can't be much left down there.'

'Just a few.'

'How many do you think Ken'll bring with him?'

'Oh, you never know with Ken. Of course there'll be Ivy, Claire and Mike Brown, and definitely Angus, Angus Clark, and he'll likely have one of his women tagging on to him. Then there are the Fitzsimmons'. Well, how many are they?'

'Well, that's eight, and the Lord only knows who they'll collect on the way. I wonder who Mac is first footing tonight?'

When Mrs Atkins's voice from the far end of the table muttering derisively, 'One or more of his lady friends, I shouldn't be surprised,' both Riley and Nyrene exchanged a laughing glance and pulled a face at each other, and now Riley said, 'Oh, I shouldn't think so, Mrs A. He seemed to have a bit of a cold on him this morning, and it's more likely he's keeping company with one of his old cronies from The Stag.'

'Yes, you've said it, one of his old cronies, Mr Peter. Yes, just as you say. But you can be thankful that your whisky will be able to live a little longer,' and she flounced down the room.

Riley whispered, 'I think someone should tip that fellow the wink,' and Nyrene whispered back, 'Well, don't let it be you; things will work out in the end. Mind your own business, Mr Riley; Mac wouldn't thank you for any help in that quarter, I'm telling you . . .'

It was just on five minutes to twelve when Nyrene pulled the lambswool collar tightly around Riley's neck, but when she went to draw down the woollen flaps over his ears, he said, 'Don't cover up my lugs, woman, I won't be able to hear.'

'You'll not have any lugs left if you go out there bare-faced, Mr Peter.'

'Oh, that won't make any difference,' put in Nyrene quickly, 'he's always been bare-faced . . . Somebody's outside. There's somebody coming along the front.'

They became quiet, listening, and when the footsteps stopped outside the door they waited a moment for the knock. It didn't come, but a voice said, 'I ken ye'll be standin' there, Mr Riley, sir, all ready to come out.'

They exchanged quick glances and there was a muttered, 'Who would believe it?' from Mrs Atkins, and when the voice said again, 'Ye can come out and join me, but I ken if such was ye did, and your good lady was going to have a bairn 'twould sure be twins.'

Nyrene closed her eyes and covered her mouth with her hand, while Riley bit tightly on his lip before calling, and in a good imitation of Mac's voice, 'Well, man, I'm not after wanting twins, so I'll bide awhile and let you freeze a bit longer.'

'Shush, now! Here it comes, the New Year. The New Year.'

At this distance from the towns there was no ringing of church bells or of tooting hooters, other than that from the television set behind them, and they weren't laughing, not even smiling. It could be said there was a sad and enquiring expression in their mingled glances; that is until the hammering came on the door and Riley, quickly pulling it open, let in the tall, rimed figure of Hamish McIntyre, and he, holding up a piece of coal in one hand and a bottle of whisky in the other as if in blessing, said, 'Let there be nowt but peace and happiness in this house in the coming year.' And there followed the exchange of greetings: 'Happy New Year. A Happy New Year.' And Riley took Nyrene into his arms and kissed her hard; then held her for a moment away from him and looked deeply into her eyes; and she returned the look, before he swung round to Mrs Atkins and, putting his arms around her ample body, he kissed her, which brought a giggling laugh from her: 'Oh, Mr Peter! Mr Peter. A Happy New Year. A Happy New Year.' Then she turned to the big ruddy Scot, and when he said, 'I'll take no such liberties with ye, ma'am; for they wouldn't be to your liking; but I'll take your hand and I'll implant my lips on it in wishing ye all ye wish yourself,' and at this he grabbed her hand and carried out his intention.

'You big drunken dopey!'

Mrs A.'s words could hardly be heard for Nyrene's and Riley's laughter; and Mac, wagging his finger at her, retorted, 'Careful, now! Careful, woman! I am far from being in me cups as yet. Another two hours and who knows, the hospitality being lavish I could claim then to be what you English diddies call slightly intoxicated, but as for now, I could stand on one leg and gesticulate while reciting my dear Robbie's rhymes and not totter an inch.'

Mrs Atkins's derision and the ensuing laughter set the pattern for the next hour; and this was enlivened by Hamish taking a flute from the inside of his greatcoat which was now hanging on the back of the kitchen door and, even to the amazement of Mrs Atkins, playing it expertly.

'I didn't know you were a musician,' said Riley, to which Hamish answered, 'Ye don't know the half of me, nor of this.' He tapped the flute. 'Bridie here cost me seven days in jail, all because I tried to measure a polis's gullet with her. She didn't get very far, and she couldn't speak up for herself, so they gave me seven days in which to learn her. And she paid for her keep because she kept the lads happy.' He now turned swiftly towards Mrs Atkins and added, 'I'm a bad wee Scot,' and she answered as quickly, 'You're a big-headed thick galoot, if I know anything.'

It was just on one o'clock when the company arrived. There were ten of them altogether, and Ken explained the reason why Angus was carrying a fiddle case was because they knew there was no piano in the house, and they would need something to jig to; you couldn't rely on the silly television.

Nyrene was to remember this night as the jolliest she'd ever had for, to the tune of the fiddle and the flute, they danced reels and jigs: the Gay Gordons, Spanish Tangos, and even a Knees-Up Mother Brown, until four o'clock, by which time most of them were sprawled either on the couch or on chairs or lying full length on the rug. But, led by Hamish, they were still singing chorus after chorus. That man seemed to know every chorus that had ever been written.

After downing mugs of black coffee, unlaced now, the company left at five, in single file, hand on shoulder, endeavouring by song to break the glass in ten green bottles.

When eventually their voices faded away and the door was closed, Riley leant his back against it and shuddered with the cold. Mrs Atkins, whose eyes were unnaturally bright, pointed to where Hamish was sprawled in a big chair to the side of the fire, his voice fading on the line 'When one green bottle should accidentally fall'. His head momentarily drooped to the side and Mrs Atkins said again, 'Well! What about him?'

'Leave him where he is,' said Nyrene. 'We'll put the guard round the fire; he'll be all right. And you'—she now pushed Mrs Atkins down the room—'get yourself well wrapped up and over the road, and don't think about food till dinner time tonight.'

'I'll see ye across.'

The voice came from deep in the chair, and at this Mrs Atkins said, 'I have no need to be seen across, I can still walk straight,' only for Riley to put in, 'Stay where you are, Mac, I'll see to her! Now look! Go on!' He pushed the man back into the chair. 'Stay where you are and do as you're told for once: get yourself to sleep. We'll be upstairs in a minute.'

Ten minutes later they were upstairs and in bed, and as Riley held Nyrene in his arms he said, 'I am sorry, Mrs Riley, but I've got a headache.'

'I'm so glad, Mr Riley,' she replied, 'because I've got two and a bit.'

'A Happy New Year, my love.'

'A Happy New Year, dearest.'

'It's been a wonderful night, hasn't it?'

'Wonderful. Wonderful. Life is wonderful, everything is wonderful.'

CHAPTER FOUR

It took the rest of New Year's day to get over the early morning's jollifications. Little was eaten and less drunk. There had been various phone calls; a long one from Fred and Louise, others from their early-morning guests, all with thick heads.

They had agreed on an early night. The child was asleep. Mrs Atkins had just bidden them good night and gone across to her rooms. Hamish had made a short visit during the day, long enough to leave a good stack of wood outside the kitchen door, and to take the youngster for a scamper through the grounds; more than ever today his energy had worn them out indoors. It would appear that the rule 'run outside and walk inside' had gone by the board, excused by Riley saying it was holiday time.

He was on the point of walking to the front door

to drop the old-fashioned bar into the slats when the phone rang. He picked it up and a little impatiently said, 'Yes? This is . . . Peter.'

'This is Betty here.'

'Betty? Oh! Hello, Betty. A Happy New Year to you. How's everything?'

'Peter, I'm ringing to tell you that Dad's very ill.'

'What?'

'I said, Dad's very ill. He was taken into hospital first thing this morning and he's going to be operated upon tomorrow.'

'Dad? What's the matter with him?'

'It's cancer of the bowel.'

'Good God! How long has he known about this?'

'Oh, I think for some time; but he wouldn't have anything done; he said it was just cramp and one thing and another. Here's Nurse.'

It was odd, but no-one spoke of Alex Riley's girlfriend or common-law wife, however you looked at it, in any other way than as Nurse, and Riley said immediately, 'Hello, Nurse. This is awful. How bad is he really?'

'I would say pretty bad, Peter; but they won't know until they get inside, not really. He's had these pains for ages; but you know what he's like, he's stubborn and he doesn't like hospitals or doctors. Last night, when I came in off duty, I found him writhing on the floor in pain. He insisted it was just cramp. Anyway, I got the doctor first thing this morning and within an hour he was in hospital, and after an examination they said he's for the theatre tomorrow morning. Peter, there's something I'd like to ask you, put to you. He's never said openly he would like to see you but he keeps talking about you and . . . Oh, I think it would make a great difference when he came round if you could be there, if only for a short time.'

'Yes. Yes, Nurse. I'll get away first thing in the morning. I don't know as yet how the trains are, it being holiday time, but once I get to Edinburgh I'll be able to get one straight through, I know.'

'Thank you, Peter. You can stay here as long as you like; there's plenty of room.'

'Thanks. Thanks, Nurse. I'll see you some time tomorrow.'

'I'll put Betty on again.'

Betty's voice sounded tearful as she said, 'I feel awful about him. He never seemed to have a chance. He could be so happy with Nurse 'cos she's a lovely woman and she cares for him, but Mam keeps sending her filthy letters. You remember how she once tried to set the place on fire?'

'Oh, yes.'

'Dad wouldn't let me tell you details about the letters, but they've become so offensive, Nurse has put them in the hands of a solicitor.'

'Good gracious! I can't believe it.'

'Oh, you'd believe it all right if you saw her, Peter. And since I've left home she sends the girls round here, supposedly to see their father. Susie's all right, she's no tale-bearer, but Florrie is, so we give her plenty to carry back. Susie's dying to come and live here, but I think Mam would kill her if she even mentioned it. It would be the last straw. I'm going to be married, Peter, to Harry on me twenty-first birthday, but we daren't let her know because God only knows what she would do. We've got a flat, but she practically parades there at night-time to see if I'm staying with him. I'll be glad to see you, Peter, and have a talk.'

'Me too, Betty, me too. I didn't know all this was going on, and I'm so sorry.'

'How much more holiday have you got?'

'Oh, another three weeks before I'm due for the road again.'

'How is Nyrene?'

'She's marvellous. Marvellous.'

'Will she be coming with you?'

'I'll have to see: there's the boy, you know, and he's a bit of a handful. He's never still, and he likes plenty of space. Anyway, we'll see. In any case I'll be there tomorrow, dear. Good-night.'

'Good-night, Peter. And thank you. Oh,' she said, 'just a minute. I'll be going in first thing in the morning and I'll tell Dad; it will make all the difference before he goes down to the theatre.'

'Do that, dear. Do that. Good-night.'

'Good-night, Peter.'

He turned to Nyrene where she was standing at the foot of the stairs, and she said simply, 'Your Dad?'

'Yes. He's due for an operation tomorrow, cancer of the bowel.'

'Oh, my goodness! Oh, I'm sorry.'

'And by the sound of it, my mother is playing hell with the lot of them, sending filthy notes to Nurse now.'

'Never!'

'Well, that's what Betty's just said.'

He went towards her and put his arm around her shoulders and said, 'It was too good to last, three weeks at home, but I'll have to go.'

'Of course. Of course, dear.'

'Will you come with me?'

253

She paused for a moment. 'I'd love to. Yes I'd love to, if you think we could leave the linty for a few days.'

'I don't see why not: there's Mac and Mrs Atkins, and there's Ivy and Ken; he'd be well looked after. Come on! Let's go to bed; we'll work out the timetables in the morning.'

How often had she thought about dashing away to some far-off place to be with him on a Saturday night and for a few hours on a Sunday. But it was always the child who had stopped her. But this time, she felt it imperative she go with him dismissing from her mind the times she had left the child for a day to go with Ivy and Ken into Aberdeen for a day's shopping, only, on her return, to hear that the child had gone into one of his silences and to be greeted by him with: 'Not leave me, Mummy. Not leave me.'

She always had to reassure him she would never leave him, that she was just going shopping. He could be away from her all day in the woods with Mac or go down to Ivy's with Mrs Atkins and not show any such agitation, for he knew she would be in the house awaiting his return. But this time was different. She had longed for these weeks when Peter would be here at home; not so that he took the pressure of the child from her, but that they would be together. She knew that if she didn't make a stand—against what?—she wouldn't give voice to the thought in her mind—she would be tied for ever. And so, this time she must go with him. She needed him so much, not only his passionate loving but his daytime presence, too; the sight of him, the sound of his voice. She loved to watch him walking or running; his body was so lithe, indicative of vitality and youth. Oh yes, youth, that frightening thing, youth; he was growing better-looking every year and he was speaking differently too. He had a naturally deep voice, and she no longer had laughingly to pull him up about errors of pronunciation. She had never corrected him openly, but when he mispronounced anything she would tactfully bring it into the conversation a little later on; and he was clever enough to pick it up. There had been his habit of saying ad-vertise-ment instead of advert-isement; he would pronounce the w in wholly; and not forgetting fil-um. He was on twenty-three now, but he looked older. Oh, if only he were thirty, or more. Here she was, close on forty-two and the middle years were thickening her body, no matter what she tried to do about it. She ate very little, she drank less, she kept very busy, but apparently to little effect. At one time her breasts had been like shells, now they were full to the hand, but not drooping yet. That was to come.

'You're sure you won't mind coming?'

'Oh, darling, don't be silly. You want me to go with you, don't you?'

'Oh, you know I do.' She was in his arms now. 'To think of Fellburn for the next three or four days and on my own. Oh, I want to see Dad. Yes, I want to see Dad. I've become very fond of him, but all the time I'll be petrified in case I run into Mam.'

'Well, my dear, if she gets up to any abusive ways towards us, there's only one thing to do, and that's to go to the police. By the sound of it she wants the fear of God or somebody put into her.'

'I can hardly believe she tried to set fire to Nurse's house.'

255

'But she did.'

His thoughts moving along another channel, he said, 'I'll have to get in touch with Mac first thing: he never gets here before eight. He'll have to sleep in the loft while Mrs A. sleeps upstairs with the child. Now don't look so worried; it'll be all right. He's got to be left some time.'

'I'm not worried, darling. I'm not worried.'

'Then your face is lying.'

Neither of them suggested to the other that they should take the child with them, nor did they question themselves as to why.

*　　　*　　　*

It was almost four years since they had last been in Fellburn and immediately they were both made aware of its drabness. Perhaps it was the slush-covered streets and the close proximity of the buildings; even the hospital on the outskirts seemed to have shrunken in size; or perhaps it was just the striking comparison with the place they had recently left, because, from the air to the tongue of the people, all was different.

It was late in the afternoon when Riley saw his father; and then for such a short time. The small shrunken figure was unrecognisable.

Back in the waiting-room, he took Nyrene's arm and led her out of the hospital.

'Did you find out what they had done?' she asked.

'I don't really know; I didn't get much out of the nurse. She said I should come and see the doctor in the morning, but that he was quite comfortable.' He sighed, then said, 'You know the routine; if the patient is not dead he is quite comfortable. What he's going to feel like when he wakes up, God alone knows.'

Endeavouring now to sound reassuring, he said, 'Let's get back to the house and have a word or two with Nurse. Then we'll slip along and see Fred and Louise.'

As they neared the house Nyrene said, 'Hasn't Betty grown? She's quite a young woman now. She's very like you in lots of ways.'

He made no reply: he wasn't thinking of Betty, but was, in fact, wondering how he'd stuck this town for so long. Perhaps when the sun came out and the streets were dry he would see it differently.

Back at the house, Nurse, Mrs Maggie Fawcett, reassured Riley about the state of his father: 'Oh they all look like that, Peter,' she said. 'He'll be different altogether tomorrow when you see him, and things aren't as bad as they might have been. They've performed a colostomy, which should help. Your father's a good man, Peter, a kind good man. He's had a rotten life and he's still having it with that woman. I don't know what'll happen when she knows you're in town. We'd better keep on our guard, all of us. I'm telling you, I don't think she's right in the head. Anyway, the meal's already, and afterwards you can have the house to yourselves. I'm going back to the hospital tonight. I . . . I want to be there when he comes round fully. Oh, he'll be glad to see you, tomorrow; I know he will.'

After they'd had their meal and unpacked their bags in the bedroom, which was exceptionally bright and cosy, they told her that they would be going round to see their friends, Mr and Mrs Beardsley, and at this she said, 'Well, your time's your own. I'll give you a key and you can let yourselves in and out when you like. Betty won't be back till half-past six; it's late night at the shop tonight.'

*　　　*　　　*

When Fred opened his door to them he let out an exclamation, not as a blasphemy but as a statement of surprise. 'God Almighty!' he said, then added, 'Where've you two sprung from?'

'Where do you think?'

'Louise! Louise!'

When Louise appeared at the top of the steps using the same words, 'Where've you sprung from?' Riley said, 'Well, let's get in and we'll tell you.'

After embracing Nyrene, Louise helped her off with her coat and said, 'You look marvellously tanned. Where've you been?'

'It's the wind up in the wilds.'

'Well, it's doing you good. Come in. Come in. Oh, I am glad to see you both.'

Louise now pushed Riley sidewards, adding, 'As Mrs Roberts says, there are some people who are like one's own soul, and that's you two at this moment. What's brought you here?'

'Dad's very ill,' Riley said, and Louise's manner changed immediately: 'Oh Lor! Oh, I'm sorry. Really bad?'

'Yes, by the sound of it: cancer of the bowel.'

'Good lord!' Fred said. 'He doesn't want anything more than that. Has he been ill for long?'

'I suppose he has, but I didn't hear of it until yesterday, last night, in fact: and I hadn't time to phone you.'

'Have you had anything to eat?'

'Oh, yes. We've had a good meal at Nurse's.'

'What about a drink then?'

Fred looked from Nyrene to Riley, who said, 'It would go down very nicely, thanks.'

'The usual?'

'The usual.'

Louise now dropped on the couch beside Nyrene and caught hold of her hand, saying, 'Oh, you don't know how glad I am to see you! You're like a breath of fresh air,' and she glanced towards Fred who was looking at her warningly now. 'I'm not sorry: I'm going to say it because you know yourself you're longing for tomorrow when they'll be gone.' Then addressing Nyrene again, she said, 'We have company, you know. Gwendoline,'—she paused—'and her delightful daughter, Yvette.'

'Oh yes?' Riley said, turning to Fred, and adding, 'Sounds interesting.'

'You've said it,' said Fred. His head was bobbing. 'Interesting is the word. Amazing is another, not to mention fantastic. And one must ask why? Why the devil are such people put into the world to create havoc in males from budding youths to old men with damp underwear.'

'Oh, Fred!' Louise's voice was a reprimand. 'You get more coarse every day.'

'Well, I'm honest enough to put it into words. All you do is smile and play the hostess and say, "Oh yes, dear. You must call in any time you're this way." Hypocrite.'

'You're talking about your niece?' said Riley.

'Of course I'm talking about my niece. Who else? I wouldn't have believed it. I can believe everything her mother did, and tolerate it, but this

259

one's been brought up in a convent and a finishing school and the rest. If Gwendoline had told me she had put her in a brothel when she was seven, I could probably have understood it.'

'Be quiet! You never know, they might come in at any minute.'

'What odds! Gwendoline knows what I think. I've told her already what she should've done with that one when she was a young girl. She should have skelped her from the bare backside up to her lugs.'

To this, Riley didn't say, She sounds interesting; he never joked about other women in front of Nyrene.

When there was the sound of a door opening and then voices were heard, Fred said, 'Speak of the devil. Gird your loins, lad.'

At this Riley laughed outright; then he turned to Nyrene and shook his head.

The sitting-room door opened and there entered a very tall woman. She could have been in her middle forties, or even in her fifties, Riley thought. All he could take in at first was that she was very tall, dignified, and beautifully dressed. And from where he was now standing, he saw she had an unwrinkled skin and was auburn-haired. And then came the voice, high, clear and bell-like, exclaiming, 'Oh, I'm so sorry, we're intruding.'

'Don't be silly! Gwendoline, get yourself in. You've heard about Riley and Nyrene; well, here they are. Peter Riley, my sister Gwendoline. Nyrene, his wife, Gwendoline.'

As Nyrene was shaking the woman's hand they looked deeply into each other's eyes, and in the depth of Gwendoline's Nyrene saw herself as she

260

might be in a few years' time: likely not as beautiful but of an age that could not be hidden by cosmetics because age, she had found, was expressed by the eyes.

'Tra-la-la! Tra-la-la! The plane leaves at nine in the morning from Newcastle.'

No-one spoke; they had all turned to look at the figure entering the room. She too had stopped. What age was she? Sixteen? Seventeen? No, she was twenty or more. And there were those long legs that Fred had talked about. He had said legs, loins, and licence; it was all there. The legs were beautifully shaped. Clothes were being worn down to the calf this season but her dress, of a light soft woollen material, was inches above the knee and clung to her upper body like a skin. Her breasts were small although full and pointed, and the nipples were almost visible through the thin wool. But at this moment his eyes, as were Nyrene's, were fastened on her face, which was long and thin and peach-tinted, and the features were such that you had to take them individually: the finely marked eyebrows etching the oval eye sockets. The eyes were dark, their colour unfathomable. The nose was straight, and the mouth below was over-full and wide. The lips were slightly apart now, showing a gleam of teeth.

'Company! Oh, how lovely!' There was just the slightest note of a foreign accent to the words and the voice was unusually deep. 'And me, such a mess! Look at my hair.' She ran her fingers from her shoulders up through the pale gold strands, exclaiming, 'I must go and change.'

'Don't be so silly, girl! These are our friends.'

'Oh yes. Oh yes.' Her whole manner changed: it

261

was as if the young woman, the sophisticated being, had slid back into a seventeen-year-old, for she practically skipped up the room now, saying, 'I'm sorry. How do you do?' She held a hand out, first to Nyrene who, when she took it, felt a strange shudder pass through her, causing her almost to tug her hand away.

When the hand was held out towards Riley, he shook it, but said nothing, even in reply to the girl's, 'How d'you do?'

Just as everybody else, on meeting this girl, was affected by her, Nyrene felt that Peter, too, was being bowled over. But what could you expect? She had never seen anyone quite like her. And that voice and that manner, that air. As Fred had so crudely suggested, she would affect even the senile. Yet what it was about her she couldn't put a finger on. It was the total combination of her presence.

Riley's thoughts were running along similar lines. Good God! he thought. It's a good job she won't be around here for long.

'You're the actor?'

'Yes. Yes, I'm the actor, so called.'

'How exciting! I met Maurice Ducan in London last year. Do you know him?'

'No, but I've heard of him.'

'He wanted me for one of his plays, but there was a "bastard" of a woman there who said I had too much of what it takes, so I didn't get the part. What do you think of that?'

'Yvette! Behave yourself. Sit down.'

'Mama, I usually behave myself. It all depends upon the company I'm in. This young man'—she turned and looked at Riley, then glanced back towards her mother, saying—'he's an actor. They all talk like that, don't they?'

'No.'

'No?' She was slightly taken aback, as the tone of her voice implied, and when he went on, 'You've a wrong conception of actors, I would say; at least of how they talk in public. They might use slang, but they don't come out with "bastards" unless they're provoked. I'm speaking from my own experience, of course, with our company.'

'Oh. Oh.' She smiled slowly at him now as she said, 'You sound funny, you know, different from how you look, because you're so young. All right, Mama, all right: I'll sit down and I'll behave myself. What shall we talk about? This fascinating town?' She now threw herself into an armchair.

'What'll you have to drink?' Fred was standing near her now, his face straight.

'Cognac. You should know by now, Uncle; there's nothing to match cognac.'

Riley looked at her, then he sat by Nyrene on the couch; and after Yvette had taken a sip from her glass, she said 'I understand you live in a sweet place in the wilds of Scotland and that you have a small son and a Scottish servant. Interesting, I should think, with a name like Hamish. What else could one expect but something unusual: Hamish McClusky.'

'His name is McIntyre'—there was a cool ring to Nyrene's voice now—'and he's an ordinary kindly Scotsman. There are many such like him there.'

'Oh. Oh, I'm sorry. Are you of the clan?'

'No, I am not of the clan, I am English. What are you?'

The question seemed to startle them all, not least the one to whom it was addressed; and her

263

whole attitude now changed as, sitting up straight in the chair, she looked at her mother and said, 'That was straight from the elbow, wasn't it, Mama? What am I? I am your daughter and you hail from Northumberland. Now my father, my real father'—she was nodding her head now—'was, I understand, an American. But then he was of mixed blood! part Irish, but the other half, we have never got to the bottom of, have we, Mama? Whether it is Maltese or Malaysian; something that begins with an M. Now my adoptive mother is a French lady, or was. I miss her. Yes, I do,'—the voice had changed again—'I miss her very much. She was an enlightened and charming woman. Yes, I do, I miss her very much.' She turned her head to the side now and for a moment appeared a different person altogether; but then, looking at them once more, she finished, 'But the truth of it is, I don't think my mother knows exactly what I am; she only knows what she herself is or was. Isn't that right, Mama?'

'Yvette, you become more impossible every day. Now whatever we are, we are here, and among friends, my brother, sister-in-law, and his friends. Now can I ask you to behave like a normal person for one evening?'

'You always want the impossible, Mama. By the way, where is Jason?'

'Yvette, please!' Gwendoline's voice was stern now, and the girl turned on her mother and said, 'Oh, be quiet, Mama! We're not children, we're adults. I am an adult and I wish to be treated as such; in fact, I would like to say that I am more worldly-wise and worldly-conscious than any one of you in this room, and I hate to be treated as if I

264

were a numskull; and I would repeat that this young man to me doesn't appear, by his looks, his voice, or by his manner to be a comedian, not in the manner of those I have heard on the television, the radio, yes and on your London stages for the past eighteen months. Remember, Mama, I've been at large for eighteen months.'

She stood up now. Her face had again changed and, her laughter ringing out, she said, 'It's odd . . . it's odd, I've never been in a family, and yet this appears like a family and that we're having a family row because Mama's ménage'—she jerked her head back to Gwendoline—'is anything but homely, whereas here we are five people daring to express our opinions and be contradicted. Definitely, it is what I imagine as home life. I was eight when my dear French Mama put me into the convent. Ten years later I was taken out and thrown into the maelstrom of a so-called finishing school. You know, no brothel,' she glanced towards her mother before she repeated, 'no brothel could have educated me more in a way of life than the dormitory of that finishing school where we were never allowed to see a pair of trousers, although what we didn't know about men wasn't worth learning.'

'I'll go now,' she said, 'and hold a reasonable conversation with Jason, which will give you time to discuss me.'

Every muscle in her sylph-like body seemed to ripple as she walked away down the room, leaving behind her an embarrassed silence, until Gwendoline sighed, which in itself spoke of weariness, then said to Fred, 'I'm sorry, Fred, I should never have brought her. But I must say she's

265

not always as fractious as she appears now. She's very bored; we'll be better when we get to Austria. She has many friends there and the skiing always does her good.'

'Then all I can say, Gwendoline, is that I hope her friends keep her there, because she's an impossible young snipe.'

'That, I suppose, is my fault.'

'No, it isn't. Some lasses would give their ears to have a convent education, followed by a year in Paris and all the things that she's been given. What's she going to do with her life? Does she know?'

'Marry, I hope. There are two or three possibilities in the offing. One is very charming, very entertaining, very everything other than responsible, and has no money. The other is a middle-aged businessman who can give her most of the things she thinks she's entitled to, and that can be put down to my fault, and perhaps to her French adoptive-mother's because every holiday she would take her away to a different country. I think she's toured half the world by now. You know'— Gwendoline now turned to Riley and Nyrene, who had been looking at her intently whilst she was speaking, and said—'this is not a case of the sins of the fathers being passed on, but the sins of the mother: knowing that I didn't want a child, why did I have her? And when I had her, why did I let her go to her father? At the time I thought it was a marvellous idea, a way out for me, and besides, she was brought up knowing my relationship to her. She accepted me in a funny kind of way, funny to me that is, because she still saw my friend's wife as her mother.'

Gwendoline, too, now rose and, inclining her head, first to Nyrene then to Riley in farewell, she turned and followed her daughter from the room.

Nyrene had noticed the term 'my friend's wife'. How many friends' wives had that woman distressed in her time? she wondered, because they must have known of her, and looking at her now it wasn't hard to see from where her daughter sprang. She had her looks, and she certainly had a sexual drive oozing out of every pore. She now thanked God she had come with Peter this time, because that girl could eat a man alive. And yet, would her Peter have allowed himself to be eaten? Not as he was now, no; but who could tell what he might do in the years ahead? That girl could hold her youth everlasting, while she herself developed into . . .

Oh, for the Lord's sake, stop it! There's plenty of time to meet that. 'What did you say, dear?' Riley asked.

'Nothing. But I was thinking it's about time we got back to Nurse's house; Betty should be in by now and she'll be alone.'

'Yes. Yes.'

'Oh! Nyrene, and you, Peter, you haven't been here five minutes. We haven't had a talk, not our kind of talk.' Louise had emphasised the last words; then looking at her husband, she said, 'I can tell you now, I'm just living for tomorrow morning and that plane going at nine.'

'Well, I can tell you too, madam, that I'm of the same mind.'

'Don't worry, Louise,' Riley said, 'we'll pop in tomorrow. The air will be clearer and the atmosphere not so electric, and we can talk about the big fellow's half-term'—he jerked his head back

267

towards Fred—'and see if you would like to pop through and stay with Nyrene for a time. Charles would love being with Jason again. They had the time of their lives before.'

'How is Charles?' Louise asked, and Nyrene said, 'Oh, as live a linty as ever; in fact, more so; he never stops. I've got him a little tamed inside the house; outside he's unstoppable. Anyway, we're going to see a doctor; that is a specialist about him. He's using up too much energy all the time.'

'Is it still causing the faints?'

'Yes, sometimes,' Nyrene said. 'It's sheer exhaustion of energy; but it's the source of the problem we must sort out.'

At the front door Fred said to Riley, 'You can now understand what I meant on the phone the other night, can't you?'

'Yes. Yes, Fred, exactly. Only thing is, you should have added "man-eater".'

'Yes, you're right. It's a good job this town doesn't attract her and we won't be troubled with her much, if at all, but we mustn't be deceived, and I've said this to Louise and to Gwendoline, she's not just the precocious little piece she makes out to be; there's a strong will buried there, and all I can say is, God help any man she gets her claws into. Look, Riley, let me run you back.'

'No, Fred. Thanks. We want to walk; we've got a lot to think about.'

'You're right. You're right.'

'Good-night, Louise.'

'Good-night, Peter.'

'Good-night, my dear.' Louise now kissed Nyrene, and she, her voice soft, said, 'I don't envy you in any way, Louise, at this moment.'

They laughed together; then more good-nights were exchanged.

They were some way from the house when Riley broke the silence saying, 'Well, what did you think of that?'

'The question is, dear, what did *you* think of it? You're a man.'

'Well, if you want the truth, I think she's beautiful, she's magnetic, she's everything they write about, but she's a spoilt brat and she wants pulling down to earth; and I just hope she comes across some fellow that'll keep her in her place or beat it out of her if he can't. I really do, for she'd likely drive a fellow crazy. Even her dear mama's far from happy. You can see that.' He paused a moment. 'I wonder what Fred thinks about his dear sister now? She doesn't look anything like a whore, does she?'

'What do you think a whore looks like?'

'Oh I imagine someone rather gaudily dressed, common, loud. She's none of those things; in fact she's got a ladylike air about her.'

'Well, that's likely rubbed off from the gentlemen she's been associated with over the years because from what Louise tells me she's gone through a number. Anyway, I don't think we will see much of either of them. As for Fellburn, she has already washed her hands of it, and it should be thankful for that.'

When they reached the house, Betty greeted them warmly; yet Riley noticed that she seemed agitated, and he said 'Have you heard anything further from the hospital?'

'No. No, we really won't know anything about how Dad is until tomorrow.'

In the sitting-room, Riley said, 'Are you expecting Harry round tonight?'

'No, he's on night-shift and he'll just be getting up now; he didn't go to bed till about one. He's been very good, you know, since Dad took ill, with so much toing-and-froing. And there's been Mam to contend with. You know, Peter, I think they should put her away. The things she does, and they can't be pinned on her. She's so sly, and she's clever. I'm worried at this moment, and I think I'd better tell you why. She knows you're here, of course. She sent her snooper round, and Florrie's just like her. But what's worse, not only does she know you're here, but she now knows where you live. We've so far managed to keep it secret. Anyway, Sue was waiting for me coming out of work. She'd just had a do with dear Florrie and she'd left her mark on her face. It should happen that the schools had been having discos once a month and Florrie must have plied Mam with all her wiles to get her to let her go. But no. Well, you know what Mam would think about a disco. And Sue said, with being off work early, naturally she went straight home, and there was dear Florrie titivating herself up in the bedroom. At first she wouldn't say why she was wearing her good frock and piling on make-up. Anyway, when Florrie had her coat on, then got into her wellies and wrapped up her shoes, Sue said she got suspicious and wouldn't let her out; she wanted to know how she had earned leave to go to the disco. But she could get nothing out of her, so Sue said she herself had nowhere to go, so she would stay with her until Mam came in, and that could be seven or eight o'clock. Well, it was then that Florrie started to cry, and to cut a long story short, it would appear that the day Dad collapsed she was at the house and, of course, Nurse had to go with him in the ambulance, and she had to ask Florrie to lock up for her and to leave the key at Mrs Green's at the end of the row. But before she locked up, Florrie must have gone into the bedroom and found a letter from you. All she could remember of it was that the house was called The Little Grange or something like that, but then she couldn't get her tongue round Peterculter. Anyway she got enough of the address to be able to tell Mam, and Mam must have put some value on that information to let her go to the disco. So you see, Peter, either of you could start getting those letters and things could happen which, as I have said, you'd be unable to pin on her.'

'Oh, wouldn't I! Don't you worry, Betty, if anything happens at our end both a solicitor and the police will be informed. I wouldn't hesitate for a moment. And you've been to our place, haven't you? It's very difficult to find. And really, I can't see her going all that way. It's a long journey, however you take it. But, nevertheless, thanks for putting us on our guard; you can't be too careful where Mam's concerned.'

Betty, relaxing against the back of the chair, said to Nyrene, 'You know, I get frightened at times because I think she's capable of doing any bad thing, wicked thing that comes into her head. I mean, she could've burnt the house down that night she put the lighted paper through the letter box. It was terrible.'

Nyrene nodded, saying, 'It must have been, my dear; and I think you have good need to be frightened of her, and careful, because she's eaten up with bitterness and jealousy. I know that Peter was the beginning.' As she caught his hand and held it, he said, 'Oh no, I wasn't! Dad was the beginning. I can see now that he must have gone through hell for years, for she never spoke to him without denigrating him. There are times at night when I start thinking back into the past and I can hear her voice going on incessantly in the room above my head. The dull murmur of it used to drive me almost mad. What it did to him, I daren't think. It's really a wonder that he hasn't tried to do her in. Many a man in his place would have, because she constantly put him to scorn.' He turned his head away and looked towards the fire, adding, 'A man can stand most things but not to be belittled, as he was.'

*   *   *

The following morning as he stood by his father's bedside and looked down at the waxen face topped by the high brow, receding hairline and the tufts of grey hair sticking out from above each ear, he was overwhelmed again by the sadness that had pervaded his thoughts last night as he had gazed into the fire when, for a time, he had seemed to become inbued with the feelings his father had endured throughout his married life. Now here they were again and swelling his throat.

He watched the pale lids lift, then his father's body made an effort to rise onto the pillows, before flopping gently back again. The effort checked his speech for a moment, but his left hand came up and across his body, and when Peter caught it and

272

held it tightly, he too could say nothing.

Presently, his father said, 'Hello, lad. I ... I didn't expect to see you.'

'Well,' Peter answered in what he hoped was a jovial tone, 'I can say the same to you. What d'you think you've been up to, scaring the wits out of folk?'

'Oh, lad. Lad.' The head moved slowly on the pillow; then in a low voice, Alex said, 'I understand it's not so bad as they thought it was going to be, and I thank God for that. Did they tell you about it?'

'Yes. Yes.' Peter nodded his reply, then said, 'And they've also given me a time limit; ten minutes at the most. It isn't visiting hours, you know, but this afternoon Nyrene'll come with me. She would like to see you.'

Alex looked at his son for a long moment before he asked softly, 'Things still going well with you?'

'Never better, Dad, never better.'

'You're lucky having her, you know.'

'Yes, yes, I know that, Dad. I'm very lucky. I'm very lucky in all ways. And look, when you're able to get on your feet you're coming to us for convalescence. Likely I won't be there, but Nyrene has it all arranged.'

'I'd like that. Aye, I'd like that, and to see the youngster again. How is he?'

'Oh, as lively as a cricket; or, rather, ten crickets; the difficulty is in keeping him down.'

'Oh, lad, don't say that, and excuse me for saying it to you; never try to keep anybody down. You know what I mean?'

There was a long pause before Peter said, 'Yes ... yes, Dad, I know what you mean. Now

273

look, here's the nurse coming straight for me, I'll go now, but I'll be back later. Rest, all you need now is rest.' Again they held hands.

The thin fingers clung to his for some seconds before letting go, and when Riley found himself in the corridor, and Nyrene waiting for him there, he did not speak in answer to her look but bit tightly down on his lower lip.

They were out in the slush-covered street before Nyrene asked, 'Did you have a talk with the Sister?' and he answered huskily, 'Yes, and thankfully it seems to be not as bad as feared. The colostomy could be reversed in a couple of years' time if the disease is kept in check. I told him he must come to you for convalescence and that you had it all arranged, even knowing that as things are it will be a long time before he can travel.'

'Well, you know, dear, I could take him at any time, I could look after him.'

'Yes, you could, dear. I know that.'

After walking on in silence for some way, Riley suddenly said, 'You know, Nyrene, at this moment I cannot fathom my true feelings for him. The only thing I'm sure of is that I hate my mother, because I can look back and see that, in a way, she deprived me of a father.'

Nyrene tugged his arm tighter against her side; then on a much lighter note she exclaimed, 'It's about time you had a new coat, this one's wearing thin.'

'Never! This one'll last me a lifetime and a half! When it gets threadbare there's always the lining. And anyway, what do you expect for four pounds?'

They both laughed gently together now; then when he felt her shiver he said, 'Are you cold?'

'I'm not very warm. What about a coffee? Let's go to Prims.'

Prims was a very smart restaurant known as the meeting place of the upper-class residents of the town; and so, naturally, the players at The Little Palace had found it much too expensive for their pockets, and it was laughingly said it was too starchy for those wearing tights.

As Riley pushed open one side of the double-glass door to allow Nyrene to enter, the other half was pulled open to allow a gentleman and his companion to leave. At the midway point both doors were held stationary and David Bernice's voice mingled with Riley's surprised exclamation of 'Just look who you run into on a wet day!'

The four of them were back inside now, and David Bernice introduced them to his companion, saying, 'Isn't it odd, Constance, that I should be talking about them only this morning, this very morning, even within this last hour, and here they are, Mr and Mrs Riley, the best players in their own way that ever put foot on the stage. And this is Miss Constance Pickman-Blyth.' David turned to the well-dressed, middle-aged woman at his side and said, 'Could you manage another coffee?'

'Of course. Of course. What else? You don't expect us to stand here chatting, do you? And don't worry, I'll pay for it.' She turned a mischievous glance on Nyrene and Peter and in a hushed whisper exclaimed, 'He's very mean.'

As they walked into the restaurant David exclaimed something unintelligible and the small lady, between Nyrene and Peter, said, 'He's a very careful man, as you likely know, and he can't stand being teased,' which caused them both to smile and

275

exchange a glance which said they were of a similar mind.

This seemed to set the tone of the conversation around the coffee table, together with enquiries from David about Riley's work. 'Now that you've learnt all that Mr Riley is going to do in his foreseeable future,' Constance Pickman-Blyth said to David, 'what about telling him of our plans? Or have you forgotten?'

'Oh, Connie! Of course I haven't forgotten. I was coming to that, working round to it.' He now grinned at Riley as he said, 'Perhaps you've heard that Miss Pickman-Blyth here'—he inclined deferentially towards his companion—'has bought the old Town Hall block, the Town Hall included.'

'No!' Both Nyrene and Peter expressed their feigned surprise.

'Yes. Yes, the lot. Well it's been in the papers. Anyway, I forgot to ask you, what's brought you to this end? Something wrong at home?'

'My father's ill in hospital.'

'Oh, I'm sorry. I'm sorry to hear that.'

'But go on, tell us more about the new enterprise.'

'Well, that's the word for it, enterprise.' He now smiled warmly at the woman sitting to his side.

'Yes, very fitting, I would say.'

'Well, it's like this—' David started again. 'We're going to reconstruct the whole area. I've had my eye on the old Town Hall for some time, but really it was out of my reach.' He glanced at his companion. 'It was a kind of dream. Anyway, I happened to be looking around it again when who should I bump into but another prospector,' again his head was turned towards his companion, 'and

Miss Pickman-Blyth here told me she was in two minds about buying the whole block, for her main interest was in turning the end offices into flats, shops, and a restaurant, but she didn't know quite what to do with the main hall itself. Did you?'

'No, but you weren't long in telling me.' She was smiling at him. 'The rest is a long story, but the main thing is we did a deal. He wanted a theatre, I wanted some nice flats put up in that part of the town, and a good restaurant. Anyway, I have always been interested in the theatre. The last time I was in The Little Palace you were there, playing in "The Golden Mind". I saw it twice. The first time I knew I had missed something. Oh yes, I felt tearful, but I laughed more at your antics. The second time I didn't laugh at all because I recognised the man inside the maimed brain of the child, and how you brought it over was simply wonderful. You have a talent, young man, which, as with health, all the money in the world cannot buy.'

The jovial atmosphere had changed completely, and Riley could not find words to give an immediate response. It was a few seconds before he said, 'Thank you, Miss Constance, you recognised what few in the audience did, that I tried to express the adult man probing through the skin of the disordered brain of the boy. But I could never have played that part had it not been for my wife, who coached, bullied and coerced me for weeks on end.' He turned a loving glance on Nyrene; then impulsively took her hand.

Now speaking directly to Nyrene, Miss Pickman-Blyth said, 'Yes, yes, I understand what you did for him. David has talked a lot about it since. And you know what I was saying only ... well not fifteen minutes before we met this morning? I was saying to my friend here,'—her hand went out now in a flippant gesture—'well, I was saying that wouldn't it be wonderful if you could get that young man back and also his wife! I really did say that, didn't I, David?'

'Yes, yes, you did, my dear.' David Bernice was nodding from the one to the other now. 'So, as there's nothing like striking while the iron's hot, I'm going to say, why not? But first, we were on our way round there, so how about coming with us, eh?'

It was noticeable that Riley immediately fell in with the suggestion with a nod of his head, but that there was no such acceptance from Nyrene.

CHAPTER FIVE

They were home again. There was the fire blazing; there was the tea table set to the side of the couch; there was Mrs A. and Hamish McIntyre; and there was the child.

Nyrene had not had time to take off her coat before the boy had thrown himself on her, crying and gesticulating wildly, the while talking incoherently and being watched by a tearful Mrs Atkins and a grim, smiling Hamish, who remarked 'Well, that's one good thing: he's come alive.'

'What is it, darling? What is it? Mummy's back and here's Daddy.'

Although Riley tried to take the thin arms away from Nyrene's hips, the boy still clung to her, crying, coherently now, 'Don't . . . don't, Mama . . .

don't leave. Don't . . . Mama. Don't . . . don't.'

'No, I'm not going to leave you any more. No, darling, no.'

'Don't . . . don't leave Charles, Mama.'

'Now, now! Stop it, Charles. Stop it, this minute!' Nyrene pressed the boy away from her, and held him by the shoulder and looked into the round almost angelic face of her son. It was bone dry: there was no sign of tears, yet there was agony in his eyes. And now when the child turned to his father, saying softly, 'Daddy . . . Daddy,' not 'Daddy-man,' Riley dropped on to his hunkers and took the boy in his arms and said, 'Yes, Daddy's here.'

'Mama . . . Mama not go?'

'No, darling, no, Mama won't go away again.'

The boy now put his arms around his father's neck and as Riley looked over the child's shoulder towards Nyrene, the look they exchanged had a new pain in it. They both knew they were troubled, very troubled about their child.

During all this Mrs Atkins and Hamish had stood silently, and it wasn't until Hamish gave an audible sniff and turned hastily towards the kitchen door that Riley gently unloosened the arms from around his neck. Then pressing the child towards Nyrene again, he followed Hamish to the kitchen and was greeted with, 'I'm always glad to see you, Mr Riley, sir, but never more so than on this day. It's me that's telling ye that that child can't live without the one or the other of ye.'

Riley had to force himself to say, 'Well, what d'you mean by that, Mac?'

'Well, to tell ye the truth I find it difficult to explain the feeling that's been in this house since ye both left; Mrs A. herself will tell ye, and such is the feeling that neither of us have said a wrong word to each other. Now that in itself will tell ye something. Very worried, she's been. Yes indeed, she's been very worried. So much so that if ye hadn't been coming back today she was for phoning ye to let ye know how things were.'

'Well, how were things, Mac? Hasn't he been playing or—?'

'Playing? No, no, Mr Riley, sir. Playing? I think I've seen him run twice since you left the place. Walk yes, quite sedately—more like an old un he'd walk by my side—but then 'tis no weather for walking. And when it came to running, he wasn't for it. No. When ye think how he usually gallops like any horse and jumps like any kangaroo, it's got to be noticeable, but there he was as sedate as an old un. But that wasn't the worst. That was outside. Inside he went into his quiet periods more and more. Well, you know them, but somehow again these were different, for he talked in spasms, I would say, and his words and meaning were distinct. It isn't no business of mine, Mr Riley, sir, and yet I contradict it, for I love the wee laddie, always have done. Where I come in his affections doesn't matter. The only thing I'm sure of is that I don't make up for either of ye, and neither does Mrs A. So again I say, although I know I might be speaking out of turn for ye've seen the doctor, but to my mind Old Johnson is the best friend the undertaker's got around here.' He now waved his hand, saying, 'Oh I know what ye and the mistress herself think of him. Perhaps I'm prejudiced; in fact, I know I am. The further away ye can keep from their kin the better. This is no time to tell ye something funny about the said man. Ye've heard me talk about Rubie Smythe the butcher, not Smith . . . ye know, but SMYTHE. Oh yes, he's very particular about the E. Anyway his wife got him to Dr Johnson because she was worried about the state of his health and everybody from here to Edinburgh knows it's drink that's wrong with the state of *his* health. All except her, and when, in all good faith she was asked what the doctor's findings were, she said it was something serious, something that the doctor wouldn't like to put a name to, but there was one thing sure he had said: her husband would never get out of this life alive with it. And she was as serious-minded as a monk at his beads. Well, the village has never had such a laugh for many a day. Rubie, ye ken, was a butcher for years until he retired, and the oddest one ever made because he used to apologise to each animal before striking the final blow. Mannie Pratt would have the bar in stitches doing an imitation of him. Mannie used to be his assistant, ye ken.'

He now joined in Peter's quiet laughter. Then becoming serious once more, he said, 'Ye could ask for a second opinion, couldn't ye, 'cos Johnson's opinion is that the boy'll grow out of it. His philosophy is, let children run themselves wild because they're not children very long. That's what he says, isn't it?'

Riley, also serious now, nodded to him, saying, 'Yes, yes, it is, Mac, and I know you're right; but one has to be prodded into facing up to these things. In any case, I must tell you we've already discussed it, and I'm making an appointment for a second opinion.'

Hamish, his voice changing entirely now, said

brightly, 'Perhaps he only wants a few special pills now and then to quieten him down; and if he didn't gallop so much outside he wouldn't need so much rest inside. At least, that's how I see it; but I'm a simple man, ye ken.'

At this Riley gave a hoot and, smiling broadly, he said, 'Yes, yes, I know, Mac, you're a very simple man. I guessed that the first time we met, a very simple man,' and on this he thrust out his fist towards Mac's shoulder; then turned and went back into the sitting-room.

'This tea will be dead cold; come and sit down.'

'Give me here the teapot!'

After Mrs Atkins had hurried from the room, Nyrene said on a laugh, 'Give me here the teapot! Give me here the teapot! She's becoming as bad, or as good, whichever way you look at it, as Mac. What have you been talking about?'

'Oh,' said Riley lightly, 'lots of things.'

He was again seated on the couch and had put his hand out towards his son who, at the moment, seemed oblivious of everything but the job of separating the piece of almond paste from the icing that topped the slice of Christmas cake on his plate. He wasn't fond of icing, but was very fond of almond paste, and he did not turn his head as Riley said to him in a raised tone, 'I'm thinking about tomorrow. I'm wondering if we should mend that sleigh or just build a snowman. What d'you think?'

Riley turned and looked at Nyrene; then they both looked at their son. He had put the last piece of almond paste in his mouth and was chewing it slowly as he returned their gaze, but he did not speak or refer to the arrangements being prepared for him on the morrow. His expression would not

282

have been unfitting in a much older person who was willing to go along with what had been said, not for his own sake but for theirs, which he seemed to emphasise when he turned back to the business of eating his cake.

CHAPTER SIX

It was the day before Peter was due to leave for the road again. They were in Aberdeen and he and Nyrene were sitting in the comfortable reception room of Mr Kramer, the children's specialist who had been highly recommended by Dr Johnson.

Mr Kramer was as tall as Hamish McIntyre but much broader, an outsize specimen of a man; but when he spoke his voice was a contradiction to his build, for he had what could be described as a small voice. In a sing-song way he said, 'You're quite a big fellow for your age. How old did you say you are?' The big face was beaming down into the child's and Charles was smiling back into it and there was a mischievous look in his eye as he answered the tall man, saying, 'They t-tell me, sir, I am four years old.'

There was a quick glance between Mr Kramer and the parents sitting at the far side of the desk; then the face returned and beamed again down on Charles and the soft voice said, 'They told you that? Well, I would've thought you were much older. When is your birthday?'

The child's glance wavered for a moment: it was as if he were thinking; then he said, 'Last year, before Christmas.'

'Fair enough. Fair enough.' The big man now moved uneasily in his chair as he said, 'I'm getting to be a very old man and stooping doesn't agree with me. Now would you object if I lifted you onto the end of my desk here so we could be face to face?'

He hadn't intended to wait for an answer, but when it came saying, 'No. No,' the big man was slightly nonplussed and inclined to smile, and he said, 'Good enough.' Then putting out his hands he lifted the boy up onto the end of the desk; and once there, Charles turned and looked at his parents sitting rather straight-faced on the other side and he smiled at them. It was a reassuring smile, and when his mother smiled back at him he said, 'Mr Mac would have laughed.'

The seemingly strange response brought a questioning look from Mr Kramer, followed by the quiet enquiry, 'Who is Mr Mac?'

It was Riley who answered, saying, 'He's our friend. He looks after the house and garden and helps my wife with anything she wants doing. He's very fond of Charles and Charles of him.' He paused here and smiled slightly before he added, 'They play a lot together.'

'Oh. Oh, I see.' Now the big face was close to Charles's and saying, 'Is this Mr Mac the one who jumps and gallops as quickly as you do?'

Charles's smile was broad now as he replied, 'Yes. Yes, sir. But . . . but he cannot jump very far.'

Charles now brought his arms above his head and they went into a flopping, waving motion, and his heels began to kick the back of the desk as he now said, 'We fly . . . or'—his head bobbing now—'we try to fly.'

Mr Kramer was now holding Charles's hands steady and bringing them down in front of the boy, saying 'Well, it isn't everyone that can fly. It's very difficult to do. Even the birds have a hard time of it, and you and Mr . . . Mac get very tired, do you?'

There was no immediate response; it was as if the child were thinking; then with his head to the side he said, 'Not really tired, I just want to—' When he stopped they all waited with him; then it was Mr Kramer who spoke more softly still, saying, 'What happens when you are tired? Do you just want to go to sleep?'

The answer came quite quickly and abruptly, 'No! Not to sleep, just to—' Again it was as if the child were thinking, then Mr Kramer, his voice rising, exclaimed, 'We'll forget about flying for the moment, but if you do ever manage to fly, you come straight to me and show me how to do it. Is that a promise?'

The twinkle was back in Charles's eye as he turned his head, and there was that old knowing look on his face as he gazed at his parents, and the answer he gave was a bright high laugh.

Mr Kramer now rang a bell, and when a door opened and a nurse entered he said, 'This is Master Charles, Nurse, and he would love to see all your toys, your blocks and things, in your room. Would you like to go with Nurse?'

The last words were addressed to the boy; and his face, now losing its bright appeal, took on a wary look. And now his gaze was directed towards his mother; but it was Riley who said, 'It's just next door or so, quite near. There are some lovely games. Nurse will show you.'

'You come, Daddy-man?'

'No, darling, you go with Nurse.' It was Nyrene speaking now, and the child, swiftly getting on to his knees on the desk, looked at his mother and said, 'No, Mama. Not just me go.'

Riley and Nyrene looked at each other in slight apprehension, before Riley addressed Mr Kramer: 'All right if I go with him, sir?'

'Perfectly. Perfectly, yes. I'm sure you'd love to play with the blocks too; and while you're away Mrs Riley and I'll sit here nattering. What about it, Mrs Riley?'

'Yes, that would be very nice, Mr Kramer, very nice.'

The nurse now led them out of the room and just a few steps along a corridor to another room where there were numerous small tables on which were coloured blocks and shapes of all sizes.

Meanwhile, back in the reception room, Nyrene was gazing at Mr Kramer and he was saying, 'Well, you can get one fear out of your mind, Mrs Riley, and it's the fear of all mothers I know in this situation: the boy is not mentally handicapped.'

The oh, thank God! wasn't voiced, but Nyrene said, 'But there is something not quite right?'

Mr Kramer leant back in his chair and put his fingertips together before he said, 'I mightn't be able to pinpoint it for some time; all I can say at the moment is, the child is intelligent and he has a thinking mind. Oh yes, definitely a thinking mind, but it is more active than his years warrant.'

'Yes. Yes, we have thought that many a time, especially when he's in his quiet periods.'

'Describe them again to me.'

This Nyrene did, and when she had finished he said, 'There have been no fits, nothing

286

spectacular?'

'No, nothing apart from extreme exertion beforehand.'

'What I think Nurse might confirm is that he is dyslexic.'

Nyrene was nodding quickly now, saying, 'Yes, yes I've thought of that too; we've both thought of that. But that isn't so bad is it? Well, I mean, there are actors and actresses and notable people who are dyslexic.'

'Oh yes, yes, definitely, you're right. And what's more, much can be done now to assist the child to cope with this. It's not a disease, it's an impediment. Now what I think we've got to go into and find out more about is this tiredness, or sleeping while still awake; and you feel it isn't only caused by extra exertion, but occurs when he is left alone; that is without one or other of you to hand. You say your helpers don't seem to fill the gap your absence leaves?'

'Yes. Yes. He loves them both; but recently when I had to accompany my husband back to his home, they had a most distressing time with him for three or four days. It was then he spent most of the time in what we call his quiet periods.'

'Well, I think this will have to be dealt with separately. But now let us go and see what progress has been made next door.'

Mr Kramer stood up, and she also, but she did not immediately move. Looking straight at him she said, 'Would the so-called quiet periods suggest he might have a rare mental condition?' and he, returning her gaze, said, 'Well now, Mrs Riley, I cannot answer that as yet. I shall have to see him here periodically for both physical and mental examinations; and the physical side has still to be gone into. But, don't worry. As I see him now there's no reason to suggest that he will not grow into a normal little boy.'

*   *   *

When, the following day, Nyrene reported to Dr Johnson the result of their meeting with Mr Kramer, it appeared he already knew something of it, for he surprised her straightaway by saying, 'Well now, he thinks there's no autism. I'd have thought there might have been; but there, you live and learn. And he knows what he's talking about, does Mr Kramer. As for dyslexia, that's nothing to worry about, not today.'

The previous night, as they lay in each other's arms and talked, she had asked Riley, 'If David acquired the Town Hall would you come back?'

'Like a shot, darling, quicker than a shot, oh yes. I've been thinking about it quite a lot during the past days. We could rent one of those flats they are proposing to build. Why shouldn't we?'

There had been a pause before she said, 'I couldn't come with you darling, could I?'

'Oh?' he questioned. There was another pause before he said, 'But he could be a lot better by then. I have faith in that man.'

'Yes, you're right. But until then, you could be home every weekend; and by that time I should have my,' she stressed the word, '*my* drama school running.' And she had laughed.

'Yes.' He had risen on his elbows and looked down into her face haloed by the pink shade of the bedside lamp and said, 'Now be serious about this, dear. You have marvellous scope here: the barn could make a wonderful setting and, as Mac said yesterday, there are two stables next door which could be turned into dressing-rooms with a shower. He seemed very keen on it so long as he's then able to extend the vegetable garden. Him and his vegetables! He'll have this turned into a market garden, you see, before he's finished.'

'Well, it wouldn't be a bad thing, there's all that land lying fallow.'

'Look, darling, if you get that school going you'll have more than enough on your hands. It's a marvellous idea. And if I could be settled again at The New Palace, well what more could we want?'

Her voice came low and thick, 'Only never to be parted at all, darling, because I ache for you every moment you are away.'

'Well, my love, how do you think I feel? There are times when I want to say, "To hell! I've had enough of this," and just walk out; and every time I look at another woman I'm comparing her with you, especially on the stage. You may not know it, Mrs Riley, but I've been accused of not showing enough affection in the love scenes.'

'I'm so glad to hear that, Mr Riley, because I . . . well I dread the day when you might look at another woman and there'll be no comparison.'

'Never! Never!' They were lying close now and he was making her breathless in his hold as he repeated, 'Never! Listen, woman: that will never happen to me. There's nothing or no-one can come between us. I know that right in the heart of me, nothing and no-one. Now get that into your silly head.'

She had said nothing to this, but she had loved

him and they slept, and the next day came.

CHAPTER SEVEN

After a week at the Sunderland Empire, Riley spent four happy days at home; but now here he was in York and it was Wednesday afternoon and the matinée had just finished. For the time being he had the dressing-room to himself, and he took from his coat pocket Nyrene's last letter. It was mostly about the child and the wonderful news that he had accomplished an A and a G all by himself. But the end of the letter, as always, was to the effect that she wouldn't be alive until she saw him again and she had never longed for another year to pass as she had the coming one when he would be installed back in Fellburn.

Riley noticed that, when referring to his return to Fellburn and the new theatre, Nyrene never mentioned his mother, but in his own mind she was ever-present as a threat. He was folding up the letter when the door was thrust open and a young actress named Evelyn Dowell, who was something of a comedienne, approached him on exaggerated tiptoe, saying in a hushed whisper, 'There's a man-trap downstairs wanting to see you, a vixen-wolf if ever I saw one. My, good job she's not in this lot, for our leading lady wouldn't stop at skull and hair!'

Thrusting his hand out towards her, Riley waved her away on a laugh, saying, 'I've heard you before, Evelyn, and I remember Coventry and the two antiquarians you saddled me with.'

290

'Oh! They were two old dears and good fun, but this one ... well! But this one, I'm serious. She's waiting. She gave a sort of French name, and when I tried to put her off she said to tell you that she was a Mr Beardsley's or Birdsley's niece.'

He was on his feet now, staring at the young girl, and what he said was, 'Oh Lord, not her!'

'Yes. Yes, her.' The young actress made a face at him now. 'So you know her? My! You are lucky; and to still be alive.'

'Go on with you!' He grabbed at his coat and pulled it on, ran his hand over the top of his hair, then quite inanely said, 'What does she want?'

'Well, if you were asking me that objectively, I would say you at the moment; but, at a push, any respectable-looking male within arm's length of her. So, laddie, watch your step.'

Again he flapped his hand towards her.

She was standing at the end of the middle aisle looking towards the stage on which men were busily moving pieces of scenery about, and he greeted her heartily with the cliché, 'Well, well! What's brought you to this neck of the woods, may I ask?'

'Oh. Hello.' She turned to him, her face bright, saying, 'I can put it briefly: a broken-down car, a placard advertising the matinée, and a ticket to allow me to sit through your play. But mind, I had to pay the full amount because I couldn't get in for half-price, not being an old-age pensioner.'

He laughed. 'That's a pity,' he said.

'May I sit down here?' She pointed to the end seat, and he said, 'I don't see why not, at least for the next few minutes anyway, for presently we are having a meeting before this evening's performance.'

'Oh, a meeting,' she said, indicating by a movement of her hand that she didn't believe a word he had said.

He, too, sat down, saying, 'What happened to the car?'

'Oh, it stopped talking to me when I was just outside the town, so I stopped at a garage and they said, "Apart from everything else, you need a new exhaust, miss". Well, I told them it wasn't long since it had had a new exhaust. I also said that if they could find anything else that I didn't know about, would they please see to it?' Then moving into a very good imitation of a mechanic, she said, '"Take a couple of hours, miss." And what I said to him was, fair enough; two to three hours, no more.' Her voice now resuming its natural tone, she said, 'They're daylight robbers, these garage owners; at least, when they think they're dealing with a numskull . . . I learnt that word from Uncle.'

Riley laughed now, then said, 'I understood that about this time you were away on a world tour with, was it the count, or a wealthy business man?'

'Oh.' She tossed her head now, saying, 'Oh the businessman thought better of it, or of me, and the count went on his way weeping; that was after he discovered I hadn't a private fortune. But . . . well, I've been in the market again. His name, by the way, is Percy.'

Again he was laughing at her, for her face was puckered up into what looked like a mischievous schoolgirl's as she went on, 'Shortly my dear mother is once more about to hear the death knell of her aspirations. That's why I'm on my way north, to break the news to her.'

He was gurgling in his throat as he said, 'What has Percy done to deserve the chuck?'

'Oh it isn't Percy, it's his people. Have you ever been to Surrey?'

'Yes, yes, I like Surrey.'

'Do you like the people? Well, perhaps you have never met Percy's family. He is in the ministry, you know; no, not the religious one. He has three unmarried sisters and three married brothers, and with his mother, of course, that's seven women altogether, and they were all there to view me. Poor Percy. I told him I had nothing against him; but to cope with seven females! They all live in the same area, and Percy was expected to join them, with me, of course!'

'D'you know something?' He was laughing outright now. 'I really feel sorry for that Surrey family.'

'Yes, I suppose you would; as will Uncle . . . yes, Uncle, and Mama. But it's their fault, they are pushing too hard.' Her voice now took on a quite different tone as she added, 'I'm quite an embarrassment to them, and they want me tied to someone who'll take on the responsibility of me. And you know, Pe-ter,'—she split his name and gave a little laugh as she reverted to her jocular manner—'I am not a bit like they imagine, not at all. I would like to live comfortably and to travel a bit, but I'm not after tiaras, diamonds or pearls. Anyway,'—her well-shaped mouth pursed itself before she said—'you know what I'd like to do? I'd like to visit them again in Surrey and to tell them quite seriously about my mother's history. Of course, that would be after grace had been said.'

As her laughter rang out through the empty

theatre the men on the stage stopped what they were doing and turned to look over the footlights towards her; and they all smiled at her and she smiled back at them, and as she did so Riley studied her. She wasn't a bit like that infuriating French piece they had met in Fred's house, and he could sympathise with her about Fred and her mother pushing too hard to get her off their hands. But then, who wouldn't in their place? She possessed something. Whether it was good or bad, she gave off something, and he could imagine men being stunned by it.

She turned to him now, saying, 'Did you know that my mother is aiming to set up house in Northumberland?'

'No. No, I didn't.'

'Oh yes, of all things, she is considering buying ... the old homestead.' She delivered the last in an American accent. 'It's been empty for two years and needs a lot of attention. Although Uncle Fred seems to favour the move, I am sure dear Louise is dead against it. And if I were in her place I would too, because, you know, Mother has always looked upon Uncle as her very special possession. I also understand from the grapevine that within a year or so you may be back there working at The Palace.'

'Yes,'—he nodded at her—'so I understand too. And I'm looking forward to it, because I'll be nearer home. I miss my home, especially, of course, my wife and my child.'

She was staring at him fixedly; then, her voice low, she said, 'She's a very lucky woman.'

'No, the luck is on the other foot, I'm a very lucky man.'

294

'Well it all depends how one looks at it, doesn't it? As for me, the way things are going, I see my time being taken up with evading marriage—although I don't mind suitors.' She laughed here, then added, 'In between them I'll take rests up at Mother's. That being the case, in the future we may meet more often.'

The sudden crashing to the stage of a piece of scenery prevented his making any remark at all to her last statement, and this was further aided by the appearance of Evelyn from the wings calling loudly, 'Meeting's in a few minutes.' And she looked down at the two figures sitting in the front row of the stalls and said, quietly, 'The meeting, Peter, is about to begin.'

He had to swallow twice before he could reply, 'Thanks, Evelyn. I'm coming.'

They were both on their feet now and Yvette was smiling at him, saying, 'And I didn't believe you about the meeting. I'm sorry. Anyway, it's been nice chatting to you.'

He was gallant enough to say, 'It's been nice listening. Goodbye.'

'Goodbye.'

Quickly he looked towards the stage, saying, 'I'll get someone to see you out.'

'No need. No need; I saw myself in and I can go out the same way. Goodbye, Peter.'

A few minutes later he was back in the dressing-room and Evelyn was saying, 'Didn't I do well? And didn't the fellows do their stuff?'

'Oh yes, you all did very well. But here I am stuck now and can't go out in case I bump into her. She's waiting for her car to be mended at some garage, but which garage? And I'm dying for a cup of tea.'

'Well, that's easily rectified, sir. I'll bring in a tray and buns and the leading man and the dogsbody will have a tête-à-tête in here. What about it?'

He laughed outright as he said, 'As you say, dogsbody, get going.'

With the dressing-room to himself again, he looked at his reflection in the mirror and said 'Lordy! What if Nyrene gets to hear of this visit? But if I don't tell her, that imp of Satan likely will.'

Yes. Yes that's what he would do, he would tell her, and make fun of it.

But he also decided to phone Fred ... Fred listened to his comical description of her visit; and then he said, in no light tone, 'Be wary, laddie. I'm telling you, the nicer and the more girlish she appears, the more sinister is her intent. She never does anything without a purpose. She's dangerous. And don't forget that in your case you will always have Nyrene's situation to contend with.'

'What do you mean exactly ... Nyrene's situation?'

'Don't be so bloody thick!' Fred replied tartly. 'Nearly twenty years is the situation.'

Riley could say nothing to this, and Fred went on, 'I suppose Yvette told you about her mother taking the old house? Well, I never thought I would say this, but in a way I'm glad, because Gwendoline needs more support now than ever she did, especially with that one around her neck.'

Riley was tempted to retort, 'What about Louise's situation? She'll have two to contend with.' But he let it pass, ending the conversation by asking how The New Palace was progressing, to which Fred replied enthusiastically. 'Like a house on fire,' he said. 'They're working from both ends. They've got four flats up already, and they're building the restaurant now. And they say another six months should see the theatre open. How about that? You must take that into your reckoning when you're signing up again. How much longer has this one to run?'

Riley answered, 'Well, they've extended it. We have three more towns to do before we go into Wales, then Scotland. Probably another four months. Yes, I think I must contact David again soon, and who knows, come spring, I'll be back there once more.'

*   *   *

Nyrene finished reading the letter. She folded it up and was about to return it to its envelope; instead, she opened it again and, her eyes scanning down the page of closely written words, stopped at the sentence which said, 'There she was, standing in the empty aisle looking a bit like a schoolgirl who had come to ask for an autograph. And, you know, that's all she still is in her mind, a silly schoolgirl. Straightaway, I told her I was surprised to see her and that I could give her only a few minutes as I was due to go into a meeting. She didn't believe me, but after Evelyn had convincingly done the meeting trick, she apologised for having thought I was lying. Anyway she was off to jilt another fellow; his name is Percy. She was very funny about him, but cruel at the same time. She's a symptom of the age.

'Now, my love, just think: this time next year I should be established on the home front and we

297

shall never again really need to be separated for longer than a week.'

The letter ended with, 'I can't just write I love you, darling, because my feelings for you extend beyond that. I could use "adore" and I do adore you, and always shall,' and on a more jocular note he finished off, 'And all this from a fellow named, Riley.'

Was she afraid?

Yes, she was afraid. Where he was concerned, she was afraid of all youth, but youth like that girl possessed was something apart, for it was a dangerous youth. She was clever, wily, and would be ruthless. Her car broken down! Why was she in York anyway? Had she been coming from London straight to Fellburn she could have stayed on the main road all the way.

Later, Nyrene was to look back to her reading of Peter's letter as the beginning of the dark cloud that came to overshadow her life and the house.

CHAPTER EIGHT

'Mummy! Mummy!' Nyrene rose and went into the hall, to see her son almost leaping down the stairs while holding a square of cardboard above his head. 'Look! Look, what I've done . . . dog.'

Nyrene looked at the large letters scrawled in red crayon in the middle of the board and she said, 'You've done that today?'

She now lifted her gaze to where Miss White was standing above the boy, her hand on his shoulder, and that lady said, 'Yes, and all by himself.'

298

'Dog. Dog, Mummy.'

Again Nyrene lifted an enquiring glance to the petite middle-aged woman who nodded, saying, 'On Monday we are going to find a name for him.'

The boy now turned and looked up at his teacher, and there was a tender expression on his face as he said, 'Yes, next week his name.'

Opening her palm, Miss White said, 'Tell your mummy what that is.'

The boy looked at the coin; then, his face bright, he said, 'Ten.'

'Ten what?' The teacher and pupil stared at each other; then the child went to turn quickly from her, his arms flailing, and she caught him gently by the shoulders and said, 'Look, Mummy's waiting. Tell her that is a ten . . . what?'

The mischievous look coming into his eyes now, he said distinctly, 'Penny. Penny.'

'No, not penny. What did we say up in the nursery five times? Didn't we five times say *pence*?'

And at this the boy yelled, 'Pence! Ten pence!'

'There you are.' Miss White nodded at Nyrene who was really surprised. 'Well!' she said. 'We're getting on like a house on fire.'

'Mr Mac, Mummy. Show Mr Mac?'

'Yes, go on, darling, show Mr Mac and Mrs Atkins, but Mrs Atkins first, as she's in the kitchen.'

The two women stood watching him run down the room, leaping and waving his arms.

Over the past month they had come to know and like each other. When Nyrene now said quietly, 'Did he count to ten?' Miss White replied, 'Oh yes. Numbers don't seem to bother him. What a pity he cannot attend a class with other children. They seem to pick up things that much quicker then. But

299

that's impossible, simply because of his high spirits. Then, as the specialist had implied, if they are forcibly subdued he could revert to longer sleep patterns.'

Miss White had always called his quiet periods reverting to sleep, even though when experiencing them, the child would continue to talk.

Nyrene asked her, 'Would you know if there are many others like him who don't take to games?'

'Oh yes, and many, even in their teens and highly intelligent, never take to games. Anyway, keep reading the story to him over the weekend and I'll test him again on Monday to see if he has remembered any part of it. But don't worry; he's doing splendidly and he's so bright. I have to laugh at some of the things he comes out with, they're so wise sounding, as you might hear from an elderly person.' She turned now to look fully at Nyrene as she said, 'He's unique, in his way, you know, and needs to be cherished.'

The sound of the car horn told them Hamish was at the door; and when, a few minutes later, as Miss White was about to leave, that lady turned to her and said, 'Don't worry; he'll be a comfort to you as long as the gods allow him to live.'

To say that Nyrene was shaken by this form of farewell was putting it mildly. After the car had drawn away, she went back in the house, and as she dropped down on to the couch Mrs A. came from the kitchen, saying, 'Oh, he's in his element, that one, when he can drive the little teacher to the station: he gets spruced up as if he was going to drive the Lord Mayor's carriage.'

'He's always like that, Mrs A., when he gets a chance to drive the car.'

'What is it, ma'am? You not feeling well?'

'I . . . I could do with a cup of tea.'

'Yes, in a jiffy. In a jiffy.'

What did Miss White mean 'as long as the gods allow him to live' and why had she brought it up again about him not being able to attend school in the ordinary way? They had talked this out from the first meeting, and the obstacles that prevented it, one of which had been herself. For Miss White, the main one was that the child seemed incapable of sitting still except when he was having one of his 'turns'. Earlier in the year, the final report from Mr Kramer, following on from a number of visits, had been somewhat enigmatic. It would appear that such behaviour as Charles's was probably due to a slight disorder of the brain. There had been no suggestion that it would worsen, but there was a possibility that during his teenage years there would be some alleviation.

Why could she not rid herself of the phrase 'slight disorder of the brain'? The very thought of it had made her feel sick at times.

*   *   *

The following morning, when the phone rang, she heard a voice say, 'Is that you, Mrs Riley? This is Dr Johnson.' She answered, 'Yes, Dr Johnson?' He went on, 'I've some bad news for you. It's come as a shock to me, yet I was in a way prepared for it. Our dear Miss White is no longer with us.'

For a moment Nyrene thought he meant she had returned to that college, the one she often talked about and where she trained. Then, her mind jumping to the real meaning of 'no longer with us',

301

she cried, 'No! No! You can't mean that she's . . . we only saw her yesterday afternoon; she was perfectly all right.'

'Yes, Mrs Riley, she appeared to be perfectly all right, as she did to everybody except to me and her brother, with whom she lived. She's had serious heart trouble for years and was well aware that her end could come without any warning. She must have had a very definite premonition that her end was imminent for during our meetings last week I recall being puzzled at one or two of the things she said. I put it down to that odd strangeness I espied in her from time to time. Are you there?'

With tears in her voice now, Nyrene said, 'Oh yes, yes, Doctor. I . . . I was very fond of her. We became friends; and she loved the boy.'

'Yes, she was indeed very interested in the boy; more so in his sleeping periods than his gallivanting antics. Oh yes, yes, she had her own ideas about your son. One thing she did say about him: he is highly intelligent and it is a sin that his intelligence is being thwarted.'

Nyrene made no comment to this. Miss White had never discussed the boy's quiet periods with her; well, she hadn't gone into them deeply.

The doctor was now saying, 'It's a great pity for all children so placed; she was a wonderful teacher. I know now that she hadn't been feeling too good, and I think she must have timed her exit. It took place in her sleep, and so I don't suppose she would have been aware of it.'

'When is she to be buried?'

'Tuesday or Wednesday, I'm not sure, but I'll get in touch before then.'

'Thank you, Doctor.'

'Oh, there was one thing she did say to me that stands out. She remarked that you could just as easily take over the child's teaching.'

'She said that?'

'Yes. Yes, she did, now that I recall. Anyway, I'll pop in early next week, unless I am needed before, of course, and then we can talk further on the subject. Goodbye, Mrs Riley.'

'Goodbye, Doctor.'

She put down the receiver, but her hand remained on it. She couldn't believe it. She turned her head slightly and looked up the room. The phone table was to the right of the door and placed under a high window. She could see herself saying goodbye to Miss White, then watching Hamish helping the small figure into the car. She remembered she had closed the door and moved to the window here at her side, which would give her a longer view of the receding vehicle. Then she sat on the couch and Mrs A. brought her a cup of tea. Was that only yesterday? And now that little woman was dead. And what had been her last words in this room? 'He is unique,' she had said, followed by that strange goodbye outside. For a moment she thought, They were both of the same mind, he and she; but now she was gone.

She went into the kitchen and stood by the table, her hands supporting herself against its edge and, looking to where Mrs Atkins was arranging some cooking utensils on the far end of it, she said in a low and hesitant voice, 'Miss White is dead; she died in her sleep.'

Some seconds elapsed before Mrs Atkins, who was staring at her, said, 'What?'

'Dr Johnson has just been on the phone.'

'Dear God! You never know the minute, do you? But there she was yesterday as bright as a button.'

'Apparently not; she's had heart trouble for a long time.'

'Oh dear me!' Mrs Atkins now turned away and, thrusting out her hand, she gripped the brass rod that ran above the fireplace and muttered, 'And . . . and I was never over civil to her, all because that one out there made such a fuss about her. I'm daft. That's what I am, daft.'

'No, you're not.' Nyrene was standing beside her now, her arm around her shoulder, and she said again, 'You're not daft; and he was just polite to her, that's all. You see she was a teacher and the Scots lay a great deal on education, and to them teachers are always people of importance, no matter what stage they're at, from primary to professor. Do you know where he is?'

Mrs Atkins now took up the corner of her apron and dabbed her eyes before turning to Nyrene and answering, 'I saw him going into the barn not a minute ago, with the child.'

As Nyrene now made for the door, Mrs Atkins said to her, 'Would you let me tell him? It'll ease the guilty feeling I had if I did.'

'Yes, yes, of course, my dear. Go on.'

The interior of the barn could no longer claim the name. The rough floor was now boarded and there was a low raised platform at the far end. Moreover, the stone walls had been roughly panelled to five feet up. Against one wall there were a number of folding chairs, and at the end of it there stood a small piano at which the child was now fingering out the tune of the first two lines of 'Bobby Shaftoe':

Bobby Shaftoe went to sea,
Silver buckles on his knee . . .

Following this the tune went somewhat astray in aiming to pick up:

When he comes back he'll marry me.
Hooray! for Bobby Shaftoe.

The boy did not turn from the piano except to glance towards Mrs Atkins as she entered the door, but continued with his erratic fingering.

Seeing he was deeply engaged, she did not give him his mother's order to return to the house.

Hamish McIntyre was looking keenly into the face of the woman standing in front of him and she was saying, 'I'm . . . I'm sorry about the news I have to tell you, but the mistress—' This was followed by some swallowing before she could go on, saying, 'The mistress has just heard over the phone that Miss White died in the night.'

'Miss White died?' Hamish said in a low voice, at the same time turning to look towards the piano. The child had stopped playing but his fingers were still on the keys, and Mrs A. said, 'He'll have to be told in some way; how I don't know. But I want to say this to you: I'm sorry, Mr McIntyre, if I was ever curt to her, I didn't mean to be.'

'I know ye didna, woman. I know ye didna.' Hamish said. 'But Miss White dead; I can't take that in. Yet, honestly, I'm not all that surprised.' Both were startled when the boy appeared as if he had sprung there, to the side of them. He was saying in an agitated tone, 'Teacher has gone?

Where she gone?'

'Oh dear Lord!' Mrs Atkins turned away, and Hamish said quickly, ' 'Tis all right. 'Tis all right. Leave him to me; we'll work this thing out. Come, laddie! Let's go for a wee walk and have a natter, eh?'

'A natter? Yes.' The boy nodded to him, then held out his hand and, like that, they went from the barn, leaving Mrs Atkins standing, one hand gripping the other forearm and her teeth dragging on her lower lip . . .

She was upstairs doing the bathroom when she heard Hamish McIntyre's voice saying to the mistress. 'A wee bit tired, he is, ma'am. We've been for a dander, but he's disinclined to hop, skip and jump this morning. To tell ye the truth, I am feeling a bit that way meself.'

On hearing these words Mrs Atkins gave an impatient toss to her head, then came out of the bathroom to see Nyrene leading the boy slowly towards the nursery, and she said, 'Should I stay with him, ma'am?'

'No, thanks, Mrs A. I'll see to him for the present: we're going to hear a story.' She inclined her head towards her son as she said, 'It's all about a poor tiger that has toothache, and the only time he gets any ease is when he goes to sleep.'

Taking up the inference, Mrs Atkins said, 'Oh, I like that one.'

At this statement Charles glanced at her and although he smiled his look could have said, Now, don't be silly.

The child's expression often bothered Mrs Atkins, and now she went downstairs and into the kitchen, there to prepare Hamish McIntyre's morning cocoa and buttered scone.

When, on the stroke of eleven, she did not hear the expected commotion outside the back door or the warning cough that told her both the interest and the irritant in her life was about to appear, she sat down at the table and sipped at her own mug. But after a further five minutes, she rose to her feet and, putting his mug of cocoa and the plate holding the scone on a tray, she went out to the barn.

The barn door opened noiselessly and she had taken two steps inside when she came to a halt, for there, at the far end, near the low stage, sat Mr Hamish McIntyre. He had one foot on the stage and his elbow was on his knee and his hand was holding his head. She was surprised that he did not move as she walked up the room towards him, but she was still more surprised, in fact startled, when as she tapped him on the shoulder he brought his foot so swiftly from the platform that his body fell forwards towards it, and, twisting around, he said harshly, 'Woman! Why didn't you speak?'

'I . . . I didn't think there was any need to, you would've heard me come in.'

As he straightened up he turned away from her and groped in his deep pocket for a handkerchief, then he blew hard on his nose.

When, turning towards her, he saw that she had placed the tray on the edge of the platform, he said, 'Oh, thank ye. I was just about to come over.'

She was staring at him. She couldn't believe her eyes. This big, burly, rough-spoken Scot, this annoying, pig-headed Scot had been crying. She couldn't believe it. But then he must have thought quite a lot about her to make him cry.

Her voice was very soft as she said, 'I'm sorry

you're troubled. I can't get over her going either.'

'Oh, woman! Woman.' But the words were spoken softly, and his voice remained soft as, looking down on her now, he said, 'Ye've got the wrong end of the stick. It's a habit with ye, ye know, to get the wrong end of the stick. I gave vent to my feelings just then, but not over Miss White as ye surmised: it was the child and his questioning and me trying to explain her going when he says to me, "What is dying, Mr Mac?" ' He shook his head slowly now; then he added, 'I ask ye, what answer do ye give to a wee lad who asks that? Then I thought I was a very clever fellow when, seeing a dying flower, its head hanging, I pointed to it, telling him, "It is when you become very tired like that flower." And the child looked at me, but didn't say a word until we had gone some distance, and then he said, "It sort of goes away?"

' "Yes. Yes, that's it laddie, it sort of goes away," I said. And then what d'ye think he came out with? He said, "I go away like the flower and teacher, don't I? But I come back. But one day I won't, after I have written my name and address, and I know everybody is happy." And straightaway he said, "I am tired, Mr Mac. Will ye carry me?" I'm telling ye, Mrs A., I don't know how I got that boy into the house, and then any moment I could have broken down in front of the mistress. I've always known that the child was fey ... oh, from when he went into his first quiet periods, because then he reminded me of a tale me grannie used to tell about a child such as he. He was the son of the laird, and as a young girl me grannie worked at the house. She said the child could prophesy things. I thought it all a tale until the first time I saw the linty here go into one of his quiet periods. Then there was Miss White. She was of the same ken, and I'll tell ye something that neither ye nor the mistress knows. I've heard them talking together, when they weren't talking like child and teacher. Twice I've heard them at it. It was in the orchard one day. They weren't aware that I was so near. She quoted some poetry. I had no idea of what it was 'cos I get no further than my Robbie, but I knew it was poetry and I knew that he capped the last two lines of it, and then they laughed together.'

He now reached out and took up the mug of cocoa which he almost drained at one go, then, wiping the back of his mouth on his hand he looked down at her and said, 'There's more things in heaven and earth than this world dreams of, is the saying, and there was never such a true one.' But now he put his hands out quickly and caught her arm, saying, 'Sit yersel down; don't look so scared like. Every now and again these things happen.'

When she sat on the edge of the platform he sat beside her, then lifted her hand from her lap and looked at it, the while stroking each of her plump fingers as he said softly, ''Tis about time we ceased our fooling and bickering and come into the open, don't ye think now? Because I've had kindly thoughts towards ye for a long time and although I do a lot of talking with me mouth, me head and me heart is lonely at times. I am fifty-eight years old. I have a cottage of my own and a pension, that's if ye wanted to go there. But if your thoughts were kindly towards me, we could continue on here and keep me cottage in what you call ... abeyance or some such ... anyway on the side, in case we should ever need it. What I'm asking of ye now is, would ye consider taking me on?

'It might seem to ye an odd time to put it after what I've just told ye about the boy, but that child is going to leave a big hole in my heart and life when he does go. It may be in weeks, months, or years. And it'll be the same with ye, I know, because ye've brought him up. I'm not thinking only of a lonely future, but also of a lonely now. Oh,' he paused and stared at her for a moment before he said, 'I can see by your face that ye need time to get used to the idea, so I'll leave ye now.'

'Stay where you are.' Her voice was breaking, her lids were blinking, her lips were moving one over the other, and the answer she gave him was, 'You know what you are, Hamish McIntyre? You're nothing but a great big blind idiot.'

After a moment of staring at her, his smile broadened, his arms came out and around her shoulders, and as he bent down to her he said, 'I am that. I am that.'

*   *   *

Nyrene was in bed, almost asleep, when the phone rang.

It was Peter, and his voice brought her upright. 'I've slipped out. You can't phone here in the day because everybody's got their ears cocked. How are you, darling? Did you get my letter?'

'Yes, yes, dear, I got your letter. But before we talk about it I must tell you something. It's been a very odd day here. Two surprising things have happened. The second not so, but the first very surprising: Miss White died last night.'

'Never! Miss White? She looked so sprightly.'

'Yes, I know, dear, but apparently she had heart trouble, and what is more she seemed to know when she was going. We'll discuss that part some time later. But the other thing is, wait for it, there's an engagement in the house.'

'Engagement?'

'Yes. Mac and Mrs A. are going to be married.'

'Well, I'll be jiggered! Who came to the point first?'

'I don't know, but they came to me like two teenagers who had misbehaved themselves. They're so happy. They've got their life ahead all arranged. As far as I can gather they mean to spend it mostly here, above the stables. They've got the alterations all in mind. We're going in tomorrow to buy a ring. Oh yes! They insisted that I and the linty accompany them. I phoned Ivy and Ken, and they phoned the others, and you can imagine what's going to happen: there'll be a ceilidh like never before.'

'Yes, I bet there will be. I'm so glad for them. Yet how strange it should happen on the day Miss White dies.'

'Yes, I thought so too; and more so after Mac said that it was Miss White who had paved the way for them through Charles. I couldn't ask him what he meant by that at that particular moment because Mrs A. was then telling me they would never leave us. He's going to rent out his little but an' ben. He looked so happy.'

Riley did not remark further on this, but said, 'What did you think about that cheeky piece coming to the theatre?'

She paused before she answered him, saying, 'Oh, I think she's keeping to pattern.'

'What d'you mean, dear?'

'Just that; she's the kind of person who will pop up into people's lives. Some places where she's wanted, and some where she isn't.' Then she added, 'I did get a laugh, though, about the meeting. That's come in handy a number of times over the years, hasn't it?'

'Darling.'

'Yes?'

'I miss you. I'm hungry for you.'

'And I for you, dearest.'

And so it went on until he ran out of change, which necessitated a quick exchange of, 'Good-night, darling,' . . . 'Good-night, my love.'

When she lay back on her pillow she felt wide awake, and she repeated to herself, 'Good-night, my love.' Love, love, love, that's what it was all about. Whether or not you were conceived by it, there was always that word love; and after all, what was it made up of? Pain, fear, anxiety, longing, jealousy all threaded together by flashes of ecstasy; and they were just flashes, because the essence of this word was so ephemeral there was no holding it. But obliterating all the other elements of it was the simple necessity of need. This word came under the heading of happiness. But surely you could have happiness without love. The nearness of the other's body brought comfort without the urge to possess it . . .

What was she talking about? What was she thinking? Here she was nearing forty-four and desire was in her and more aflame now than it had been five years ago.

Of a sudden she had a longing to be free of it, because then there would be no more wondering

312

whom he was holding in his arms on the stage that night, or whom he was kissing. Oh, the audience liked that, especially at the end of the play. They paid to see emotion, particularly in the raw, and if not in the raw you were expected to touch their hearts in some way sentimentally . . .

What was the matter with her? Why was she going on like this? She had him; he was hers. There would never be another in his life. He had said so a thousand times, and he meant it. Oh yes he meant it. He must mean it: in six years' time she would be nearing fifty and he'd be thirty!

Go to sleep, woman! Go to sleep.

CHAPTER NINE

They returned from Aberdeen at about four o'clock in the afternoon after what Hamish pronounced to have been a most joyous day. They were all singing as he swung the car into the by-road. Nyrene was sitting in the front passenger seat and Mrs A. was in the back holding on to the bouncing boy who was kneeling up on the seat against the window. In different keys they were singing 'Ten green bottles'. They had reached six when Charles's voice checked them, saying, 'Look! There's a lady. A lady in the wood, Mummy.'

He leant forward towards the window and waved his hand now, but by the time both Mrs A. and Nyrene had turned to look the car was well along the rutted road, and Mrs A. said, 'Likely someone's been to the house, ma'am; come in person to see about this drama business: how to become an actress in three easy lessons. That'll be the idea of some of them, you know, ma'am.'

'No doubt. No doubt.' Nyrene was laughing now. 'Film star in six months or money back.'

Nyrene said 'Don't drive in, Hamish, just leave the car outside the back gates because I want to slip over to Ivy's and I don't feel like walking.'

So it was because of this that Hamish stopped the car outside the back gates and almost before any of them had alighted the boy had jumped out and was dancing about, and now as he ran back towards the wood he cried, 'Meet the lady, Mummy.'

Nyrene stood watching him running down the rough road, leaping over exposed roots as he came to them, and she shook her head as she smiled. He'd had a lovely day. He was so happy, and he had behaved most admirably in the town, no running or jumping or leaping about then; and now, in his usual way, he was running to greet a visitor. It was a charming habit he had developed over the last year. The front doorbell just had to ring and he would rush to open it, then hold out his hand to whomsoever was on the step, saying, 'Hello. Mummy is in.' It was always just as well she was behind him because every now and then it would be a road hawker or a salesman of one sort or another; but whoever it was the child's action always brought a pleasant talking point, even if she refused to buy anything. So on this occasion Nyrene thought nothing of his galloping away to greet the visitor whom she herself hadn't seen, nor apparently had Mrs A.

Mrs A. was now leaving the boot from which Hamish had piled several parcels in her arms, and

314

on a light note she cried, 'Tea up, ma'am, in five minutes.'

'That'll be welcome,' Nyrene called back.

In the meantime the child had almost reached the end of the by-road, and when he saw the lady to whom he had waved, he shouted, 'Hello! Hello!' and at this she turned and looked at him.

As he stood before her he smiled. She wasn't very tall. He could see her face plainly and she wasn't smiling as he said now, 'Mummy's home,' and when he put out his hand to take hold of hers he received the first real shock of his young life, for the hand came fully across his face in a resounding slap knocking him flying onto his back where for a moment he lay stunned.

Charles's head was reeling; his cheek was stinging; there was a buzzing in his ear; but through tear-filled eyes he looked up into the distorted face of the visitor and let forth a loud cry: 'Nasty! Nasty woman! I'll tell Mr Mac.' And he shouted at the top of his voice, 'Mr Mac! Mr Mac!' He turned on his knees and stumbled up and as he went to turn towards home he saw Hamish running towards him, and he pointed backwards crying, 'The lady ... the lady ... she slapped me and knocked me over.'

Seeing no sign of anyone in the woodland, Hamish ran to the main road.

Here, there was no-one walking, but in the distance a woman was getting onto a bus. He now returned quickly to the boy and, picking him up, he hurried back to the house and into the kitchen where Mrs A. was handing Nyrene a cup of tea which almost fell from both their hands as they turned to look at the sobbing child in Hamish's arms.

'What is it? What's happened?' Nyrene was easing her son onto the floor, and the child repeated, 'The lady . . . slapped me.'

The three adults exchanged glances; then Nyrene, drawing the boy to a chair, took him on her knee and examined his deeply reddened cheek. Quietly she asked him, 'What kind of a lady was she, dear?'

'She wasn't nice, Mummy. She looked angry.'

'How was she dressed?'

The boy thought a moment, then said, 'She had a hat on and a long coat. They weren't pretty; just brown.'

They weren't pretty; just brown. A brown hat and coat.

'Not many women wear hats these days, ma'am,' put in Hamish.

No, thought Nyrene. That means a middle-aged or oldish woman. Someone who would want to hit my son. That points to only one person—Peter's mother. But up here! No, she dismissed the idea the brown hat and coat had brought to her mind . . .

The incident had put a damper on the day and caused the three of them to agree that in some way both the drive and the by-road would have to be put out of bounds to the child. When Mrs A. suggested that this might be hard to do, Hamish said, 'Not so; the boy himself now will likely shun the by-road and that particular piece of woodland anyway.'

*　　*　　*

316

It was Tuesday morning and Hamish was driving Nyrene back from Miss White's funeral. They had both been amazed at the numbers attending it, proving that she'd had many friends, and they were still discussing it when he turned the car onto the rough drive. It was Hamish who was speaking, but he stopped talking and drew the car almost to a stop. Ahead, the way seemed to be blocked by something.

'What on earth's happened?' Nyrene was straining towards the windscreen.

'We'll soon find out, ma'am, we'll soon find out. It's a lorry, and a big one at that. Now what on earth would he want here? He's lost his way, poor man.'

He pulled the car to a stop behind the huge wagon; and Mrs A. came running down the side of the vehicle, crying, 'Oh, am I glad to see you, ma'am! And you, Hamish. What a time I've had with this fellow. He's for tipping this stuff here. You've never ordered stone chippings, ma'am, have you?'

'Stone what?' and Nyrene was answered by the voice of a man now appearing from behind Mrs Atkins, and in a voice that was almost a yell he repeated, 'Stone chippings for your road. And it needs it; I'm telling you, it needs it. But it'll take more loads than this, and she won't let me tip.'

'Move back a way, ma'am; move back. Ye too, Mary, go back. Let's get into the daylight.'

They all moved along by the side of the hedge and the big lorry and when they were in the open Hamish demanded, 'Now tell me what all this is about,' and the answer he got was, 'You look here, mate. Don't you take that tone with me; I'm only

317

doing me job. There's me ticket.' He thrust a piece of paper towards Hamish, and he, after reading it, looked towards Nyrene and said, 'It's an order, ma'am, in your name.'

Nyrene now looked at the lorry driver and said, 'This is some joke, or they've got the wrong address. I have never ordered any,' she was going to say gravel, but changed it to, 'stone chips.'

In a somewhat calmer voice now, the man said, 'Well, ma'am, all I can say is you need them. Whether you ordered them or not, you need them. That drive from the road is a death trap with those tree roots sticking out a mile.'

'We prefer it like that.' Nyrene inclined her head towards him. 'And so you had better take your load back to the depot, and I will get on to your boss.'

'Clarke, it's Clarke's of Aberdeen. Charlie Clarke.'

The man now looked from one to the other and said, 'There'll be hell to pay for this; there's five tons back there.' He thumbed towards the lorry.

Nyrene's voice was conciliatory now as she said, 'I'm terribly sorry, but someone who doesn't like our road any more than you is playing a joke on us, a very, very bad joke. Our friends grumble about the road, but I don't think any of them would do such a thing.'

The man's tone had altered now as he said, 'No, missis, it'd be a poor friend who would land you with this lot; though, as I see it, I still maintain you could do with it.'

'Yes, perhaps; but on another occasion; if we should decide later on to have the road done, and it'll take more than five tons I should imagine, then we shall consult your firm.'

318

'Would . . . would you like a cup of tea?' put in Mrs Atkins.

Not only did the man look at Mrs Atkins, but so did Hamish and Nyrene, and all were quiet for a few seconds; then Hamish, putting out his hand and patting her on the shoulder, said, 'Sensible idea, Mary. Sensible idea,' then turned to the man, saying, 'You wouldn't say no to a mug of tea?'

'No, I wouldn't. No, I wouldn't.'

'Well, come on up to the kitchen. That right, ma'am?'

'Yes. Yes, of course, Hamish,' and Nyrene immediately turned to Mrs Atkins, saying, 'The child, where is he?'

'I had to lock him in the barn, ma'am. He was very excited about . . . well all this, so I had to take him up and . . .'

And now the man put in, on a laugh, 'Aye, and she threatened what she would do to me if I tipped before she came back again.'

So it could be said that the incident in part ended on a laugh and a crinkled note pushed into the man's hand before he finally drove away.

But the manager at Charles Clarke's establishment wasn't so affable. A Mrs Riley had ordered five tons of stone chippings and five tons he had sent out to the house. There had been time spent and the workmen's time was workmen's time, besides the loading and unloading of the stuff, in answer to which Nyrene retorted sharply over the phone, 'Then it's up to you to check on your customers before sending out such precious loads,' and she banged down the receiver.

Upstairs in the nursery the child was sitting quietly on a low stool to the side of the fire. When, earlier, Nyrene had run up the yard and unlocked the barn door, it was to see her boy sitting as he was now, quite quiet, just waiting. He hadn't jumped about or cried or battered on the door as would have been normal, a word she replaced in her mind with 'as another child might'.

She gathered him to her now, saying, 'Everything's going to be all right: the man made a mistake and, you understand, Mrs A. was so afraid he might tip all that awful stuff on to you, because, you know, you do run and jump so very quickly.'

He looked at her quite solemnly now, and his words were precise as he said, 'No, he wouldn't, he wouldn't have hurt me, he was a nice man.'

She nodded but said nothing, because, yes, at bottom, the man was a nice fellow; he was just doing his job. And yet that had not been her first impression of him; the child, as always, had seen much further than she or any of them. She pressed him still further to her.

Less than fifteen minutes later the phone rang again. Mrs Atkins was crossing the hall and she answered it. She always talked very loudly into the phone and her voice came to Nyrene, saying, 'What! Confectionery? What're you talking about? You've got the wrong address. Yes; yes, this is The Little Grange. Aye, yes, and the name is Riley. And yes, yes, I know Mrs Riley calls in to your shop . . . but you say this time she phoned the order?'

Mrs A. now walked to the foot of the stairs and shouted, 'You'd better come down here and deal with this.'

Nyrene took up the phone, saying, 'This is Mrs Riley here.' Then she listened to the voice from the other end before exclaiming loudly, 'What!'

'Well, we wanted to check up on your order.'

'I haven't given you any order; at least, not to my knowledge. I generally call in for my cakes.'

'Yes, yes, that's what the boss said, so we had to check up.'

'Would you mind explaining?'

There was a pause; then the voice said, 'Well, you are having a party for the child and you've ordered four dozen fancy smalls, a dozen of them to be cream horns; a five-pound fruit loaf; two dozen currant buns—'

Holding the receiver away from her ear, Nyrene yelled 'I have never given such an order! And I am not having a party for my child. Who gave in this order?'

'Well, it was supposed to be you, Mrs Riley. The caller said the name was Mrs Riley. It was Alice who took the order, and she said that it didn't sound like you. And yet the person described the house and how to get there so what were we to think? But we thought we'd better verify it; you were only in at the weekend.'

'Well,' said Nyrene, 'I might tell you this is the second hoax today. We've just had to send away five tons of stone chippings.'

'Never!'

'Yes, and I feel I must get on to the police now.'

'Oh, I should, Mrs Riley. Oh I should. Somebody's playing you up, somebody with a nasty mind.'

'Yes, I think so too. But thank you very much for phoning me.'

As she replaced the receiver, Nyrene turned to Mrs A. who shook her head and said, 'Who would do such a thing?'

'Yes, Mrs A., who would do such a thing? But I don't have to think twice; the same one who slapped Charles.'

'Yes, ma'am?'

'Yes, Mrs A., yes.'

'You mean?'

'Yes, I mean his grandmother. I've got to be sure; but I know who'll find out.' She turned to the phone again and rang Nurse Fawcett's house. A man's voice said, 'Alex Riley here,' and Nyrene said, 'Oh, hello, Alex. This is Nyrene.'

'Nyrene? Oh, it's lovely to hear you. How are you?'

'Very troubled, Alex. I think you can help me.'

'Well, you know I'll do anything in the world for you and him, you know that. You've just got to ask, and if it's within my power. So what is it?'

'Tell me, Alex, does your wife, dear Mona, does she wear a brown coat and hat about this time of the year? Or has she many changes?'

'Oh, to my knowledge she has only two changes. One is a light brown coat and a straw hat she had dyed to match it, and in the winter it's a dark brown coat with a felt hat. What has it got to do with her?'

And so she told him about the hitting of the child, and then about the morning's business.

For a time he seemed speechless; then he muttered, 'Oh my God! That woman! That woman! What she won't do. In the end she'll be the death of somebody, if somebody doesn't do for her first.'

'She's not on the phone, is she? You see, it seems that both these orders were through a private phone not a call box. So where would she get a private phone, Alex, except at Mrs Charlton's? She is a Justice of the Peace, isn't she?'

322

'Aye, she is that. Look, Nyrene, this has got to be checked straightaway. God knows where she'll go from here. Now leave it to me.'

'Alex, don't do anything rash, please; I don't want you to get into trouble.'

'Don't you worry, lass; I won't get into trouble.'

'By the way, how are you feeling?'

'Never better.'

'Well, as I've told you before, any time you feel like it you're more than welcome to come and stay and for as long as you like. As you know, I do miss Peter so much, so very much.'

'I know you do, lass; but no more than he misses you. Anyway, let me think about this business, and I'll phone you back after seeing my ... my beloved wife. Now don't worry, lass; I'll put a stop to her gallop if it's the last thing I do. Bye-bye now.'

'Bye-bye, Alex.'

Her next call was made to her solicitor in Fellburn, and his first words to her were, 'Oh, she's at it again? That woman is a menace. I think the police should be informed; and yet you have to have proof.'

She told him that she had rung her father-in-law and that he had said he knew what to do, which prompted the solicitor to say, 'Well, why not wait and see results from that quarter? He might have more power than either the police or myself with my pen.'

*   *   *

It was half-past nine the following morning, a bright sunny morning with a light sprinkling of frost. Alex Riley was sitting on the iron-backed seat

323

in what was called Cayman Gardens. This was a narrow strip of flower beds and greenery fronting Claremont Terrace, which was made up of semi-detached red-brick houses, and the Charlton family was resident in the end one: people did not live in Claremont Terrace, they resided.

Alex knew the daily routine of Mr and Mrs Charlton as if he had lived with them for, over the years, his wife would give him a rundown on their daily actions: he knew when Mrs Charlton had been appointed secretary of this, that or the other club; he knew the exact date and the year when Mr Charlton had been made a director of his firm; he was aware that Mr Charlton left the house every morning at half-past eight, which caused Mona always to make the point that he wasn't one of the lucky ones who could lie in bed scrounging. As for Mrs Charlton, once she became a magistrate she was out most days.

Alex had got here that morning in time to see Mr Charlton depart for the city in his BMW. He did not work in Fellburn; oh no, his destination was the city of Newcastle. As for Mrs Charlton, her time of leaving was an hour later, and there she was now. She didn't drive a BMW; hers was a Honda. A very nice little car, he thought.

Following this, he gave his wife ten minutes to get settled into her routine. Perhaps she would be looking up more telephone numbers into which to get her evil teeth.

He didn't go to the back door, but rang the front doorbell; and when it was opened and she saw him standing there, her hand went involuntarily to her throat, and her gasp was audible; and he remarked on it, saying, 'Yes, Mona, yes, you can gasp, but you'll be gasping a bit more before I'm finished talking.'

She swallowed deeply before she growled at him, 'Get yourself away from here! How dare you come here!'

'I dare because I've got a lot to say to you, and if you don't listen quietly then I am going to stand out here and I'll shout it out. That will bring the police. Quite candidly that's who I should've gone to first, but then my daughter-in-law's seeing to that part of it. She's waiting to inform both the police and her solicitor.' He watched her eyes which seemed to get rounder with each blink of her lids, and he said, 'It's a criminal offence, you know, to have goods served up to people who haven't ordered them, such as piles of confectionery fancies and tons of gravel dumped where it isn't wanted. But that isn't all. It can be proved that you were on private land one day last week and you struck the son of the house, knocking him to the ground. And that child happened to be your grandson. He's a very intelligent little fellow, and he described you, brown coat, brown hat and bad face. Oh yes, he described your bad face; and he would recognise you again, he could point you out to the police.'

Her hand sought the stanchion of the door for support and the knuckles turned white.

'Moreover, your phone calls were not made from telephone booths. Oh no, they were made from a private phone, and those calls can be traced, that much I know. Well, you haven't got a phone, have you, Mona?' His voice, which had remained even, now dropped to a deep growl as he said, 'You do your phoning from here, don't you, Mona? And

325

how pleased Mrs Charlton would be to know that. She would be able to recall the long-distance phone calls she made last week; in any case, BT would be able to tell her. Now I don't know how many orders you've put out since the stone chippings and the confectionery, but those you have, I advise you to get back on your mistress's phone and cancel, because, just one more order, dear Mona, and Nyrene will contact the police. She is holding her hand simply because I asked her to. Not that I don't want to see you up in court—oh my, that would be a pleasure—but to tell you the truth I am merely thinking of the effect it would have on my son.' He now thrust his hand out and wagged his finger almost in her face as he said, 'But even so, just one more evil move out of you against him and Nyrene and you're for it. And we haven't forgotten your trying to set fire to Nurse's house when we were both in it, and, on top of that, the filthy letters you wrote to Nurse. I'm telling you, woman, I'd open my mouth to the police if it's the last thing I did, and give them the link.'

His arm dropped to his side now and they stood staring at each other, the hate rising like steam between them, and it seemed that she was about to choke when, jumping back, she gripped the door and clashed it closed.

It did not cause him to turn away, but as he stood there he saw out of the corner of his eye the side window of the semi-detached house being closed, and it struck him that the neighbour would have had an earful.

CHAPTER TEN

Riley managed to get on the train at King's Cross just a few seconds before it moved off, and he was making his way through the second carriage when a voice stopped him in his tracks, saying, 'Hello, Peter!'

He turned to see Yvette, and inwardly he groaned even as he smiled. He did not, however, take the seat beside her but chose the one opposite. It was eleven o'clock and a slack time of the morning and there were a number of empty seats.

'Where're you off to?'

'Now where would I be off to on this train but Newcastle? You too, I surmise?'

'Yes. I'm meeting Mother at Uncle's and you, I hear, are back in the old homestead, where you started.'

'Yes, for a while; until The New Palace is ready.'

'I understand you're already living in one of the sumptuous flats, with the family and entourage.'

'Your informant has been exaggerating, as Fred often does. Nyrene has been coming down to see to the furnishings et cetera, and we've had the family, as you call them, twice I think. Yes twice, and at the weekend.' He asked now, 'How are things with you? Is Felix still on the scene, or is it Howard?'

'Oh.' She laughed outright now, saying, 'Oh, Felix kept on walking, as the old song says, shortly after I saw you in London, and Howard faded away . . . oh, about two months ago. You know you have a bad effect upon me, Peter. All my beaux seem to melt away after I meet you. And I maintain that our meeting in London was accidental: how was I to know you were going to the Barbican and that you have a love of Shakespeare? We haven't got that far in our, what shall we call it, acquaintance to discuss the arts that take our fancy, and it would seem that fate always brings you across my path when I'm alone and lonely and fed up.'

'I could never imagine you being lonely. As for being fed up, why don't you take a job of some kind?'

'Don't be silly, Peter. What job could I do, apart from modelling? And I haven't the patience to stand for hours and be moulded into clothes by somebody's impersonal hands. In any case, I thought you would know me a little, enough to realise that I can be lonely at times. Women of my type are always lonely. Men want to fuss, fondle and possess us, and other women would like to strangle us. We are an unhappy breed, you know, and I'm serious when I say that people with my exterior and personality have a raw deal.'

He smiled widely now, and his voice had a mocking note in it when he said, 'Oh, I'm very sorry for you, and all your kind. Oh yes, all your kind: poor, loveless creatures.'

'You can mock, Peter, but I'm right, and you know I'm right. The awful thing is being aware that people are afraid of one, especially women.' And Yvette now leaned forward and nodded to him as she said, 'You were afraid of me when we first met alone. Oh,'—she wagged a hand impatiently at him—'don't deny it. Don't deny it. You were petrified of me, so much so that you wrote home and told your wife straightaway.'

He knew his skin was turning that irritating pink again, and his voice was stiff as he said, 'How d'you make that out? Who told you that?'

'My dear mother. She got it from her dear brother. Her dear brother got it from his dear wife, and dear Louise got it from your darling Nyrene.'

He sighed now, but did not speak, and she said, 'Yes, we're very tiring, aren't we? May I ask if you've told her about our . . . chance meeting?'

'Yes. Yes, of course I have,' he lied firmly.

'Oh, that's all right then because I told dear Mama about it.'

He sat back looking at her. The sunlight was flickering across her face; her eyes were looking straight into his and they were giving off that . . . he shook his head against the words fascinating charm. He could imagine her driving fellows to the very end and then leaving them suspended. She had once said that Felix had been ready to throttle her, and he could well understand it.

Sometimes, just sometimes, he felt a spark of pity in him for her, but it never remained long: it would always be obliterated by her attitude and the tone of her voice, a tone that had the power to convey condescension while her smile remained pleasant. No wonder women hated her. Nyrene hated her.

His feet moved uneasily; he felt his shoulders hunching.

After a moment she said on a laugh, 'You want to watch that.'

'Watch what?'

'The hunching of your shoulders. Sure sign of nerves.'

Of a sudden he felt angry. Yes, it was a sure sign of nerves. Over the past weeks it had almost become a habit. It had started when they had seen the child sitting on the edge of the stage. He now pulled himself to the end of the seat and, leaning his forearms on the table between them, he leant towards her, saying, 'You know, Yvette, you're not only cruel to almost everyone you come into contact with, you're tactless, and unfortunately you will never know love. You haven't it in you to love anyone, and in that line you only get what you give, and I'm not now going to say I'm sorry for speaking frankly; but you only go after what you find hard to get, and when you've got it you drop it like a hot coal. And that's working to a lonely old age, let me tell you.'

He rose from his seat, and walked quickly down the compartment and into the toilet; and there he leant his head against the rail that ran below the opaque window. What in the name of God made him go for her like that! It was because she had mentioned his nerves, and his nerves had brought back the guilt feeling that had begun that day some weeks ago when Nyrene had brought the child and Hamish and Mrs Atkins to the flat for the weekend.

The theatre itself was nearing completion. The child had been running around wildly when suddenly he appeared on the stage and both he himself, and Nyrene were brought to a staring halt when they saw him sit down near the end of the footlights and assume a position exactly as he himself had done when playing the part of the handicapped boy in 'The Golden Mind'. His feet were tucked under him and his hands were resting

330

on his thighs, palms upwards, and his expressionless gaze was directed straight towards them.

They had taken a few quick steps forward, only to stop abruptly again, and the look that was exchanged between them was almost fearful; and when Peter said, 'Oh my God!' Nyrene muttered, 'It's nothing, just . . . just coincidence.'

'L-L-look!' he remembered stammering. 'Look at his face. Look at it! It is mine, and he's seven and he's Larry. Oh my God!'

He recalled how he had sprung forward and grabbed the boy from the platform, causing a cry of alarm to escape from the child. Nyrene pulled the boy from his embrace, saying, 'There now. There now. It's all right. Daddy was only playing.'

'I nearly fell asleep, Mummy.'

'Yes, yes, I know you did, dear; but come along, we'll go into the flat and then you can lie down.'

Peter now straightened up, brought his head from the bar and looked into the small mirror. He could see Nyrene and himself in the sitting-room of the flat. He was saying, 'I . . . I must have picked it up from Larry. I became lost in him and I never got rid of him. He's there in me yet. And oh, dear God! In some way I must have passed it on to the child: that was Larry sitting there, as real as when I portrayed him. And you know it. I could see it in your face.'

He remembered she had bowed her head as she said, 'Our son isn't mental,' and he hadn't come back at her, saying, 'Of course he isn't! Of course he isn't!' And it was then that she practically screamed at him, 'Peter, our son isn't mental! He's a highly intelligent boy. He's artistic and he is highly strung. The doctors themselves say that, every one of them. He is not mental; he's an intelligent child way beyond his years. The things he comes out with are way beyond his years. 'At this he had answered her, saying, 'Yes, yes, way beyond his years. Like Larry. Larry was way beyond his years, too.'

They had not loved that night, nor found any comfort even as they lay side by side.

He now turned on the tap and sluiced his face. There were no paper towels in the rack, so he used his handkerchief.

Again he stood looking into the mirror, asking himself how he was going to go back there and apologise, for apologise he must.

Apologise he did, and with much more fervour than he had intended, for when he saw her face, which was no longer pert, he had the desire to sit by her side and put his arm around her and say, 'I didn't mean all that, I really didn't.' She did not look beautiful at this moment: her eyes were deep and bright and sad. She could have been crying.

He slowly sat down in his seat again. She didn't look at him, but it was she who spoke first. Her eyes cast down, she said, 'You needn't say you're sorry, Peter, for you meant every word; and . . . and I know you're right. At least, up to a point, because, and I repeat what I said earlier, I am not inside as I appear outside. We all have facades and my beauty and dulcet tongue are mine. Now I can forget what you said and I would like you to forget it too. In a way I am glad that you came into the open with your thoughts about me, for it shows, as I have thought all along, that we could be friends.'

Oh no! No! Lord, friends with her! Nyrene

would go berserk at the mention of it. He could make no reply; and for the rest of the journey they exchanged few words, until, glancing out of the window, he said, 'We are running in now.'

He stood up and took his coat and hat and briefcase from the rack; and when she rose he had to force himself to help her into her coat, when he said, 'No hard feelings?'

'Of course not, Peter.' And there was the gentlest smile on her face as she said, 'Until we meet again then?' only to add quickly in her usual tone, holding a slightly sarcastic laugh, 'I'll be taking a taxi, but I won't offer you a lift.'

He decided not to take the bus, but to walk.

Her last look as he had helped her into the taxi remained with him. She was getting under his skin—if she wasn't already there. The thought hunched his shoulders and put a spurt into his step. He had to face Nyrene and tell her of his company on the train journey, for he knew that that disturbing sprite would tell her mother as soon as she got home, and her mother would definitely tell her brother. Of course, Louise would not pass such information on to Nyrene but Fred would. Oh yes, Fred had become a disturbing influence in the matter of his niece. At times he himself thought it was as if Fred were pointing out in his verbose way the difference in the ages of the woman and the girl.

The flat, unlike The Little Grange, was very modern, but comfortably so. It had two bedrooms, a small dining-room, an extra large sitting-room, all the latest in kitchen devices, and in the luxurious bathroom there was an exercise bicycle which was discreetly screened off.

The flat, being an end one on the ground floor, had its own side entrance situated up a short alleyway.

It was centrally heated, with an extra modern gas fire in the sitting room, and which looked so real it was always mistaken for a coal fire. Altogether, it was a splendid flat.

However, Nyrene could not see why Riley should not spend his weekends at home; it would give him a much needed break. But, as he had told her, he now had to prepare new plays and fetch the cast in often on a Sunday. He considered it to be much easier for her to come to the flat. But there was the child. Oh Lord! Yes, the child. Both knew this, but he had brought it into the open last week by saying pointedly to her, 'He's seven years old; you should be able to leave him with Mac and Mrs A. by now.'

She had kept a patient note in her voice as she replied, 'You know I have tried, and what happens? They both say the same thing: he just sits there waiting, hardly eats anything. And look what happened during the last two times I brought him here: he ran outside, and he's not used to traffic.'

This had brought the retort from him, 'Well, he's got to be taught to behave and to stay indoors when he's told. Something must be done with him; you can't let him rule our lives.'

Still quietly, but ominously, she had answered, 'Would you like me to put him into a home?'

They had stared at each other for a moment; then had fallen together and held each other close. They had both said they were sorry and that they understood the other's situation.

He was now inserting his latch key when the side

door was almost pulled out of his hand, and there she was. 'Hello!' Nyrene said. 'The train must have been on time. How did things go?'

Getting over his surprise, he said, 'Fine. I chose the less good-looking one, he could act; and two girls . . . well, young women, one very experienced. That completes the cast now.'

'Let me have your coat,' she said, 'I've got some broth on.'

'Do you mind if I kiss my wife first?'

A few minutes later, seated at the kitchen table, he said, as if making a casual remark, 'Guess who I bumped into on the train?'

'Now you know so many people whom I don't know, so how could I guess who?' She had stopped, the pan held over the basin that was set on a tray. Then she added, 'Well, we both know Louise and Fred, and his darling sister's daughter.'

The soup splashed into the basin; then she returned the pan to the stove, picked up a tea towel and dabbed at some splashes on the tray cloth, saying, 'Get started on that,' before adding tartly, 'Oh. I thought milady always travelled by high-powered car. It was she, wasn't it?'

He was thinking, Not always, because this was the second time he had met her in a train, but what he said was, 'Well, there she was. She was going to call at Fred's before going on home, I suppose, expecting him to give her a lift from there.'

She said now, 'She'd be travelling first class, but you rarely do.'

His spoon in mid-air, he said, 'That's odd. Yes, she does; she always travels first class. But there she was, second class, among the common lot. I wonder why.'

'Oh.' She sat down opposite him before saying, 'I think I can explain; or at least put two and two together. I understand from Louise, but I could hardly believe it, neither could she, that her dear mother was going to stop her allowance or make it almost negligible after Yvette had dropped yet another one of the swains who she had brought almost to the point of matrimony. And he wasn't all that old, but he was all that wealthy, and it should be remembered that dear Gwendoline has a keen eye for cash. Well, look where she's got.'

Riley shook his head, which she answered with a shake of her own, saying, 'Yes, yes, I know I'm being bitchy, but not half as much as Louise is, and with every reason. She's sick of the sound of dear Gwendoline and of Yvette. There's always talk about mother-in-laws bruising a marriage, but in this case a beloved sister is doing her best. Anyway, the second-class railway carriage proves that the rumour of a cut allowance has a firm foundation because, where is her car?'

Yes, Riley thought, where was her car?

He took a spoonful of soup, then another; then stared into the bowl for a moment as he saw a picture of himself leaning towards Yvette, telling her what he thought of her.

'Is it all right?' Nyrene was looking across at the bowl, and, as if slightly startled, he said, 'Yes. Yes. Of course it's all right. Beautiful. You've never made soup that could be anything else but good. I was just thinking though about that set-up; dear Gwendoline and her daughter both of the same type really, as far as one can judge, but living like cat and dog.'

Nyrene nodded at him now, saying, 'Yes, yes, it is

336

a queer set-up, and the cat and dog business is not far off the mark, so Louise says. By the way, I had a phone call from home just a while ago.'

'Oh yes? Is he all right?'

'Yes, he seemed so very bright. He asked to speak to you.'

'Oh dear! And I wasn't in. But I'll get on to him after I've finished this.'

'That would be nice.' Nyrene smiled at him.

Their compromise was holding.

CHAPTER ELEVEN

Riley had left David's office in The New Palace, where they had been discussing a suitable play for the Gala Night Opening.

When he passed through the doors to the canopied entrance, he was surprised to see Lily Poole sheltering there. Pulling his coat collar tight against the driving sleet, he said in surprise, 'What! You still here? I thought you had gone ages ago.'

'I missed the damn bus.'

'Well, look! I've left my car keys in my other coat in the flat. Come on! I'll give you a lift.' And with this, he grabbed her hand and ran her along to the end of the street and up the short alleyway to the door.

Inside she said, 'By, it's lovely and warm.' Then, looking at the pile of papers on the couch and the two empty coffee cups on the low table, she said 'How disgraceful! How untidy! Someone should have been in attendance here, shouldn't they, sir?'

'Yes, they should, cheeky face. Anyway I usually

have a Mrs Mop, but she didn't turn up.'

'I'll pop in tomorrow morning and do a bit of roughing. I'll bet your kitchen's in a muddle.'

'No, it isn't; you can go and see.' He was shouting from the bedroom now. 'A few dirty shirts, that's all.'

'Why don't you use your washing machine?'

'Too complicated, too many buttons. Anyway the shirts have to be ironed; I can only wear cotton. Nyrene will see to them when she comes.'

'Oh, that'll be a lovely welcome for her.'

He was in the hall now, pulling on his cap, and he said, 'Come on, you! Get going, and stop interfering in other people's lives.'

Their camaraderie could be explained by the fact that they were the only two remaining members of the cast from the time Riley had joined it. She was Lily Stewart then. He had been there only a few weeks when she came on the scene. She was then fifteen years old and acted as usherette, ticket office attendant, and relieved him of his tea-making; from the beginning she had addressed him as Mr Riley and confided in him that she wanted to be an actress.

Like his own at that time, her accent had been rather broad, and during her early efforts at acting she caused many a laugh with such lines as 'The polis is outside, ma'am,' for 'There's a policeman at the door.'

He understood it had surprised everyone when, two years before, she married a long-distance lorry driver, all of six feet two inches tall, and broad with it.

In the car, she said, 'If this is widespread Johnny'll stay in some lay-by the night.'

'Tonight, Lily.'

'Oh you!'

He laughed as he started up the car, saying, 'Those long distance lorries have enormous tyres; they can grip the ice, I understand.'

'He hates slippery roads. He doesn't mind it when it's coming down but when it becomes skid stuff, as he calls it, he never risks his lorry, because it isn't his.'

'Wise man.'

'What did you think of him when you saw him the other night in the bar?'

'Well, I thought he'd make a good boxer.'

'Funny, that's what he intended to be, but he was wise enough to know that it takes more than a good punch to get you to the top in that business, and he's too much of his own man to be bossed about.'

'He seemed a quiet fellow, with not much to say.'

'Yes, he is; but not all the time. He can do a lot of talking when he thinks it's necessary.' She gave a little huh! of a laugh here before she said, 'He's very jealous, you know.'

'Well, I can understand that. You're a bonny lass.'

'Oh, Mr Riley,'—her voice was mocking now—'you do say the most awfully nice things; but please don't say them in front of my Johnny or you'll likely get your nose punched.'

'Thanks for the warning, Lily.'

'Won't it be lovely when we get into The New Palace? Everything seems too good to be true: I have to pinch myself at times, and when I look back I say to myself, "If it wasn't for Mr Riley I'd still be running round with the tea urn." '

'Not you,' he said, 'you would've got there.

Anyway, here you are!' he said, stopping the car. 'Now run for it. Good-night.'

'Good-night. Ta . . . thanks.'

As he started the car, he thought to himself that it was funny how she was haunting The New Palace these days. The only reason she had been there tonight was to pass on a letter to David that had been delivered to the old Palace. Yes, she would've made it on her own. She had spirit, but, as he himself knew, it was always good to have a friend at court. What really would he have done without Fred and Louise?

Fred had a stinker of a cold. He was in bed, Louise told him, not with hot lemon but under the influence of a couple of double whiskies in hot water and brown sugar, and had been snoring now for the past hour, but she was so pleased to see Peter and hear all the latest news.

In the sitting-room, where they were drinking coffee, she said, 'His cold's been a blessing in disguise. He's had it for more than a week, with his eyes and nose streaming, but it's kept his dear Gwendoline at long distance. She's petrified of catching his cold, but she's very distressed, so she told me on the phone just a while ago, that she can't see him before she leaves for Italy tomorrow.'

'Are they going on another tour?' he asked.

'No. Apparently she's going alone.'

'Never!'

'Oh yes. Her dear daughter disappointed her deeply over her last love affair: she had felt sure she had manoeuvred it to a head and made that girl see sense; but apparently,'—Louise said now on a laugh—'the maid isn't for marrying and'—she now nodded to him—'I never thought I'd find anything to say in her defence, but rather than marry against her will she has suffered what must be to her penury. The latest I heard, she's got a part-time job in a boutique in London, and she's being allowed to stay in Gwendoline's flat and has been given back her car. Can't believe it, can you? But on the other hand, seeing this is the third fellow she's turned down it looks to me as if Gwendoline has washed her hands of her and so darling Yvette has to work for her petrol and her bite to eat.'

This imparted knowledge from Louise only made him regret that he had gone for the girl in such a way at their last meeting.

He stayed a little longer listening to Louise's description of her son's progress at school. Jason was way ahead of his class, but at present he was upstairs, like his father, in bed with sniffles. Lastly she talked about Nyrene, and what a pity it was she couldn't come and stay in the flat more often. But of course there was the child, and they were situated so close to a main road . . .

He was glad to get back into the flat. Tonight he was feeling lost somehow, and the place did look untidy. He gathered together the papers from the couch; then he switched on the gas fire before he sat down and stretched out his legs over the sheepskin rug. His hands behind his head, he relaxed, and like this his mind began to review his life. He had been lucky, very lucky. It was a pity though that his mother didn't share that feeling. It would have been marvellous if she had been like an ordinary mother, proud of him and his achievements. That would have capped everything. But it hurt him to know that his success had not only made her vindictive but viciously malicious.

341

Look at what she did to the child that time; and then those orders; and now from Betty he understood that she apparently had got the sack from Mrs Charlton's, for she was at home all day. But not in the evenings, so it seemed. To get away from home, Sue had gone into service as a nursemaid, which left only Florrie; and now she was turning up more and more often at either Betty's or Nurse's house. Apparently sometimes her mother didn't get in until late and she was frightened to stay on her own. It worried his father to think what she might be up to because he was sure she was out of her mind. And then, the morning he had confronted her, the neighbouring eavesdropper must have heard enough to pass it on to Mrs Charlton, resulting in Mona getting the sack.

The thought of his mother remained with him as a deep inner worry, which he aimed to put to one side and, in the words of the book, thank God for his blessings; and his blessings were, first and foremost Nyrene; then his work. At this stage, there would always be a pause in his thoughts: where did the boy come in? Well, if it hadn't been for the boy, where would he have been now? Certainly not married to her; he was sure of that, because before the child came, she had given him over to his career.

Why must he always come back to the boy? He loved the boy. His feeling for the child, in a way, now went beyond love, because in his mind the child was firmly linked with Larry, and his feeling for Larry was that of compassion.

He pulled himself up with a slightly guilty feeling as he thought he should have phoned her as soon

342

as he came in. What time was it now? Ten to eleven. She'd likely be in bed, and what would the sound of her voice do to him again? Set his urges working. Funny about that: he had only to hear her voice and it brought on the desire to touch her, to hold her, to love her. Oh, to love her. No, he wouldn't phone her now, he'd do it first thing in the morning; he'd feel different after a night's sleep.

He was pulling himself up from the couch when his head swung round towards the glass door that led from the sitting-room into the small lobby. The front doorbell was ringing. Who was it at this time, and on a night like this?

For a moment he thought of his mother, then he threw the idea out of his mind; more likely Betty, Harry with her because something had happened.

He pulled open the screen door, switched on the front light, then opened the door and gasped as the wet, bedraggled figure almost fell past him into the lobby and stood leaning against the wall.

'Good heavens! You? What's the matter?' Yvette said nothing because she too was gasping. 'I've ... I've walked from the station,' she blurted out. 'You were nearer than Fred's.'

Taking her by the shoulders, he pushed her into the room. She was wearing a long coat with a fur collar, which reached up to the back of her head and, tucked into it, was a plastic hood from which the water was still running down onto her face.

She was shivering visibly when he took the coat from her and spread it over a chair; and as she pulled the hood from her head she stumbled towards the couch. But having dropped on to it, she did not lean back: her body well forward, she thrust out her hands towards the flickering flames of the gas fire.

He stood by her side looking down at her, but when she did not raise her head, he said, 'I'll get you a hot drink.'

He almost ran into the kitchen, thankful in a way that he had washed the pans. He grabbed one, filled it half-full of milk and thrust it onto the lighted stove. From the kitchen door, he could see her still sitting; but she had taken off her high-heeled openwork sandals and was holding her feet out towards the flames, and steam was rising from them.

'Take your stockings off,' he called to her, then returned to the stove and the milk.

When, some minutes later, he went to hand her the steaming mug, he said, 'Now it's hot milk. I can either put coffee into yours or a drop of whisky. Which do you prefer?'

'Whisky, please.'

He poured a good measure of whisky into the milk, and when he handed it to her she straight away began to drink from it, and the mug was half-empty when she sat it down on the side table.

She now leant back, saying, 'I . . . I've never felt so cold in my life.'

'Well, it's come as a surprise. There were hail stones earlier on, and now it's turned to sleet.'

'Turned to sleet.' She shook her head as she repeated his words, then added, 'I don't know how you exist up here.'

He smiled down at her as he said, 'Oh, you'd be surprised. Newcastle is often warmer than Hastings, and that's on the south coast, mind, the holiday Mecca. What's brought you up here so late?'

344

He now took a drink from his own mug to which he had also added a little whisky; then he sat on the other end of the couch and looked at her as he waited for an answer to his question.

When it came it surprised him, for she said, 'I was on my way to Mother's to throw in the towel. She's off to Italy tomorrow and I'll promise her anything to be able to go with her, because I cannot stand the racket any more. It's been hell these past months.' She looked fully towards him now, saying, 'I wasn't brought up to it, Peter. I've tried and I've done my best to stick it out; served women in the boutique, women whom I wanted to spit on, dripping with money and as common as dirt, what you would describe as muck and dear Freddy as clarts. Well some of them were clarts.'

Her head was slowly shaking now as she added, 'It's my mother who is to blame: she let me be brought up with a silver spoon in my mouth, and then, when she had to take over, she found me too much, so she tried to marry me off. Her choice was the pot-bellied type, aiming to cover it up by dangling diamond bracelets in front of it.'

He was forced to laugh at the picture she presented of the diamonds being dangled in front of the pot bellies, but she didn't smile.

'She would even have bought a title for me, as she did with the count, but all his type are brainless, else they wouldn't be running round the watering places. When she came to Pious Percy she changed her tactics. I kept telling her that I have no desire to marry. From what I've seen of marriage, even with my delightful foster parents who supposedly loved each other, at times skull and hair would fly in private. He could have his mistresses—

345

it was supposedly natural for a Frenchman, but she hadn't the same liberty with lovers. Funny, but he would have had her in a chastity belt.' She was nodding at him now. 'That's what men do in happy marriages, they put the women into chastity belts.'

Again he was laughing outright, saying, 'Oh, Yvette! You know, you are a card.'

His laughter died away as she looked at him and, her lip trembling, she said, 'I'm . . . I'm not aiming to be a card, Peter. And I know what it means.'

'Oh my dear.' He automatically shuffled along the couch towards her and, taking her hand, said, 'Don't upset yourself; it'll all come right, you're so—'

Quickly she interrupted him: 'Don't say it, Peter, I'm not young, I'm as old as the hills inside and you're just talking like the rest of them. I came here tonight because I felt that you of all people would understand. Yes, I knew I was coming here, so there!'

She turned her head away from him, and again held out her hands towards the fire. Presently, in a very low voice, she said, 'You're the only one who's really ever gone for me and told me the truth about myself, at least the truth as you see it. But I am not the person you think I am, Peter. Fred and Louise and Mother, they all think alike. They want to see me tied to someone whom they imagine will keep me in order. They all seem old and it's as if they'd never been young. I'm young, and you're young, Peter.' When her body jerked upwards, her head fell on his shoulder and her arm went round his neck, and his arms were automatically drawn round her to save them from falling sideways on the couch. He said, 'Oh now, Yvette! Come on. Come

346

on,' and she whimpered, 'Let me lie here, just like this, just for a moment. I'm hurting no-one and you're hurting no-one. Please, please, Peter. And hold me, hold me close. Just for a moment, Peter, hold me close.'

'Yvette, listen. Now listen.'

'I'm listening, Peter. I've been listening to you ever since I first saw you in Louise's sitting-room. I . . . I can't help it, I'll have to tell you. I wanted you then, and the want has never eased. Don't . . . please don't move away, just hold me . . . just hold me. As I said, we are hurting no-one.'

'We are, dear, we are, we're hurting ourselves because—'

'Don't say it please, Peter.' She was begging now. 'Don't talk, just hold me and listen. I'm going to confess to you now. We've met only half a dozen times and four of those times I've manoeuvred. The car incident in York was manoeuvred too. I just wanted to see you. I can't help it.' Then she emphasised slowly, 'I . . . can't . . . help . . . it. I've tried, for, believe me, Peter, I don't want to do anything drastic to your life. Don't worry, I don't want to marry you. I'll never marry; I know I won't. I'll be like Mother in the end; but that's the end, now I'm just at the beginning. She started much younger than I shall do, but before I start a career of being a mistress, Peter, oh before that, be . . . be kind to me please, because I . . . I could have married you when we first met had you been free. Such were my feelings for you. But there, I suppose that wouldn't have lasted; you, too, are the kind of man who would have wanted to put a chastity belt on me. Oh, Peter!' Her lips now were moving around his neck. Earlier, he had taken off his coat and tie and now her lips were moving over the V made by his open shirt, and he remained still under their touch. It was a weird feeling, as if he were being massaged into sleep. He knew her voice was murmuring his name when her lips came up behind his ear, and so he went to pull himself away from her, but her grip was tight on him.

He heard his voice almost croaking, 'Give over, Yvette! Now stop it! Give over. This is ridiculous. You know it is.'

Now her voice came to him as if from a distance, murmuring, 'I only know, Peter, I've dreamed of this. I have. I have. We're doing no harm to anyone, I've told you, and we're young . . . young,' at which word he made a firm attempt to press himself away from her; but this action only brought her lying half-across him, and when her mouth fell on his he could hesitate only a moment before answering to her unrestrained pent-up passion.

They did not fall to the side on the couch but onto the floor . . .

She had come into the house at about ten to eleven. From where he lay prone on the floor he could just see the hands of the clock which now pointed to a quarter to twelve. She hadn't been here an hour, yet she had caused such an upheaval in his life. What had happened could never now be blotted out.

When her hand came onto his bare ribs he jerked himself into a sitting position, half-turned and looked down at her. She looked soft, all soft like a very young girl; but she wasn't a very young girl. Her arm now stretched up and her hand touched his chin, and, her words still slurred, she said, 'Wasn't it wonderful!'

348

He was thinking, wonderful. Yes, he supposed in a way it had been wonderful and had even surpassed his own introduction into manhood; yes, even that, because she was youth, all youth.

Like a blow, this thought was struck from his mind with her next words: 'It was for me like never before.'

The words brought him slowly upwards to his feet. Why was he such an idiot? He had imagined her so young she could never have had such an experience. Of all the blasted fools on this earth, he was the best of them. As he gathered up his clothes he said abruptly, 'Get into your things.'

She turned onto her knees and resting her elbows on the seat of the couch she looked over the back of it and watched him making for the bathroom, and she called to him, 'Oh, Peter! Peter, don't be like that. It's all right. It's all right. It will remain our secret; you needn't worry.' Her voice was cut off by his slamming the bathroom door; then he leaned back against it, his lips drawn tightly between his teeth and his eyes so screwed up that it felt as if he were pushing them back out of their sockets . . .

It took him only five minutes to take a quick shower and get into clean clothes, and when he returned to the sitting-room she was standing with her back to the fire and her dress across one arm, and although her voice was still soft it was accusing as she said, 'You never considered that I might need the bathroom too, did you, Peter?'

He moved towards the kitchen as he said, 'It's there for you now.'

He made more coffee, but drank his own before taking a cup into the sitting-room.

He did not go near the fire for he did not want to look at the couch or the floor. Instead, he began pacing the room.

When, twenty minutes later, she came out of the bathroom fully dressed, he did not look at her as he said, 'I'm phoning for a taxi.'

'Oh no. Oh no, Peter. Look, Mother won't expect me at this late hour.'

'It'll only be an hour later than if you had gone straight there. Do you expect to go to Fred's, then?'

In answer she put a hand on his shoulder, only to have it thrust aside as he said, 'No more of it now. No more. It was a mistake. I'm sorry. It was my fault, I'm sorry.'

'Don't be silly, Peter.' She was smiling tenderly at him as if at a naughty child. 'It wasn't your fault, it was nobody's fault. Well, perhaps it was mine. I intended that it should happen at some time. Oh, don't look like that, dear. But you don't understand.' Now her voice was changing. 'I care for you, in fact I'm in love with you.'

'Shut up! Now, look here, Yvette, once and for all, this is the beginning and the end. It was a mistake, and I'll carry the guilt of it for some time.'

'Guilt of it? Oh, you're thinking of your loving Nyrene. Dear, dear!'

'Yes. Yes, perhaps I am.'

'Oh my goodness! Peter, be your age, as she is hers. She's bound to know that you've made sidetracks before now, her at—'

'Shut up! Once and for all shut up. I'm sorry, Yvette, I am, but I must say it, I don't want to hear or see any more of you. I'm phoning for a taxi to take you home.'

'But you loved me at the time, all the time, I
350

know you did.'

'You know nothing of the sort,' he almost yelled, but then clapped his hand over his lips before adding, 'that wasn't love; that isn't love.' But when she bowed her head and her shoulders drooped, he said, 'I'm sorry. I'm sorry. Yvette. Just let us forget it happened. Do you think we can?' He put his hand out towards her, but she pushed it aside, saying, 'Phone for the taxi, Peter,' and turned from him and went towards the fire.

The receptionist said, 'Palace Buildings, ground floor flat. Oh, there's one in that vicinity now, sir. Perhaps five minutes. Right?'

And he answered, 'Right,' then picked up her coat from where it lay, still spreadeagled across the back of the chair, but when he held it for her to get into, she almost grabbed it from his hands and shrugged it on before staring him full in the face and saying, 'Don't look so contrite, and don't feel guilty; we've only done what millions of people are doing every day of the week.' She hunched her shoulders slightly. 'And I'm not sorry it's happened, Peter. I'll always remember it; but don't worry that I shall ever speak of it, please. And I'm going to say something to you, Peter, that you won't believe and will likely annoy you, but you are going to need me again before I need you because, say what you like, your life is not complete. You need love, you need loving like I've given you tonight, but your wife, unfortunately, has put you second, her son comes first. Everyone knows that. Oh, don't look like that, please; you spoke the truth to me once, surely you can stand it, too. Of course, Fred and Louise would never say such a thing; how they do put it is, it's such a pity that the child won't settle here and that

351

you can't be together. Yes, Peter, you'll need me before I need you. And yet that too is a lie on my part, for if I am to speak the truth, I might as well do it now: I'll go on needing you.'

When the doorbell rang she held up her hand, saying, 'That'll be the taxi. Don't come with me, please, I can let myself out.'

She made for the door; then turning swiftly about, she went back to him and, her face close to his, she muttered, 'Remember this, Peter, you've loved me tonight as you've never loved in your life before and never will again.'

He remained standing where he was, even after he heard the taxi move away. Her words were filling his head because he knew they were true. He must have been mad for a time. No! No! The contradiction came sharply. Don't let him excuse himself, he had known what he was doing: he had tasted youth and it had taken him back into that period of his years in which his maturing manhood had wrought fantasies beyond belief.

Yet what had transpired on this spot just a short while ago was past any fantasy that he might have had. He had no name for it: it wasn't love. Oh no, no, not love; yet there had been feeling there for her. Lust? No, no, he denied this too. He closed his eyes and recalled her face and all of her. She had been the personification of youth, yet he had been fully aware that youth was but the outer case of her, inside she was as old as the hills. He could say she had the knowledge of life and of men garnered from her mother's experience. In fact, she was her mother over again. How many men had she been with already?

Turning, he dropped onto the couch and there

bent forward and dropped his head into his hands. Odd, but that last was an unbearable thought, not only that he was one in a chain, but that that elusive semblance she had of youth had not only been sipped at but gobbled by such men as she had described, those with fat bellies and diamond-dripping bracelets. One thing was evident, she was no girl, she never had been; like her mother, she had been born a woman. He sat up and leant back against the couch. It was impossible to think that a life could be turned topsy-turvy in less than an hour. He'd had the happiest association any man could hope for with his wife.

Oh Lord in heaven! It was as if he had been brought back into his present existence by the thought of Nyrene, and he groaned out her name: 'Oh, Nyrene. Nyrene.' She didn't deserve this, for she had been so wonderful to him. But what was he yarping on about? She need never know, for he believed that Yvette, in this instance, wouldn't blab. No, because she hoped to repeat it. No, by God! Never! It must never happen again. Nyrene had made him; in all ways she had made him: she had taken the boy that he was and moulded him into a man. But what had Yvette done with the man? She had turned him into a boy again. Well, not exactly a boy, but a youth, a callow youth.

But no more of her, no more.

He now sprang up from the couch, went to the front door, turned the night key in the lock, then switched off the gas fire and the lights, all except the bedside light, and ten minutes later, undressed and sitting on the side of his bed, he voiced aloud a train of thoughts as out loud he said, 'Well, she'll just have to come and stay more often; he'll just have to get used to being without her. He's not a baby any more, there's no real reason for it, there's no real reason that she should be at his beck and call all the time. And I'll tell her. Yes, I will, I'll tell her.'

CHAPTER TWELVE

Riley found the Christmas holiday period to be more trying than he had imagined, although he joined in the merry arrangements being made for Hamish's and Mrs A.'s forthcoming wedding. He also showed a keen interest in the now established classes Nyrene was holding in drama, elocution and deportment, and romped and played with his son. However, he could not bring himself to provide his share of the entertainment by using his gift for mimicry. At the time no-one seemed to notice this, apart from Ivy who later remarked to Nyrene on the phone, 'Peter wasn't himself the other night; but we understood, because he must have a lot on his mind with the big day ahead. We're all looking forward to that; there'll be eleven of us coming.'

It wasn't until the night before his return to Fellburn that Nyrene said to him, 'Is there something worrying you, darling?'

'Worrying me? Now what would be worrying me?'

'Well, of course there's Barnum and Bailey's opening ahead.'

He laughed, 'And you know, it will be something like that, too,' he said. 'Miss Connie's got her friend Lord Very to do the honours. The mayor of

354

course will be there and the full corporation because we mustn't forget that the stage itself has held mayoral meetings from the beginning of the century.'

To this she remarked, 'It'll be a wonderful stage to work on.'

'It is, it is,' he said. 'The whole atmosphere of the place is marvellous, and the cast seem to feel it. The excitement is electric. I only hope it gets over to the audience.'

'Oh, of course it will. The play is very funny; even just reading it you have to laugh.' Then drawing him closer, she said, 'But you're very tired, aren't you?'

He wanted to deny this by saying, No, no, I'm certainly not tired, but it promised to be a good way out and so he said, 'Well, not *very* tired but . . . but a little anxious as to how things will turn out, because so much depends on it for all of us.'

He laid his head on her breast and pulled her close to him as he murmured, 'Oh, Nyrene. Nyrene.'

She said anxiously, 'What is it, dear? What is it? I feel that something's troubling you.'

And to this he answered, 'There's nothing, nothing; only I want to lie like this for ever; just like this.'

As he was making no attempt to love her, which surprised her on this particular night, she held him gently and stroked his hair; and like this he drifted off to sleep, leaving her staring into the darkness, puzzled: not for a moment did she really think that the forthcoming opening was having an effect on him, he revelled in such work. No, there was something on his mind, and she had felt it since he had first come home. The first night in this bed his love-making had been tender. There had been no feverish demand about it as was usual after an absence of one or two weeks, and she could recall his words as he lay in her arms, strange words for him to utter: 'Hold me close, Nyrene. Don't let me go. Never let me go.'

*   *   *

It was five days before the opening and the atmosphere in the theatre was indeed electric, as apparently it was in the town. Posters were everywhere; people were coming from far and wide to book seats, although not for the opening night, for those had been filled weeks ago; and there was a great interest in The New Palace and its restaurant and adjacent buildings.

It was half-past four in the afternoon and Peter was in the bedroom of the flat changing his shirt when the phone rang. When he heard Nyrene's voice he said, 'Oh, hello, darling,' and she answered, 'I tried to get you at the theatre, but they said you had gone home.' She gave a little laugh here as she added, 'The word home seemed strange.'

'You wouldn't consider it very home-like at the moment, dear. As Lily says, it's like Paddy's market.'

'What? Who?'

'Lily Poole.'

'Oh! Lily.'

'Yes, Lily. She's called round to collect my washing. She says you should buy me nylon shirts not cotton. She's been very good. But I'm just saying that because here she is, at my elbow, as nosy as ever. She wants a word with you.'

'Hello, Mrs Riley.'

'Oh, hello, Lily.' Nyrene's voice was quite cheerful; she knew Lily as well as Peter did, in fact more so for she had helped to train her. And she liked her. She had no fear of Lily. She said now, 'Is the place a mess, Lily?'

'Well, just untidy. He has a go at it every now and again, and he pushes his washing in the machine; but that's as far as it goes. He can't iron, and I've told him it's about time he learned. Anyway, he's all right and looking forward to you coming. Oh, I wish you were here, Mrs Riley, the excitement's great. Well, I'll hand it back as he's itching to get it. Bye-bye.'

'Bye-bye, Lily.' And her voice was low now as she spoke to Riley, saying, 'Her real accent never changes, does it?'

'Oh yes it does. Yes it does.' His voice was low too. 'You should hear her when she once gets up on those boards, the county isn't in it.'

A voice from the kitchen yelled, 'I heard what you said there; that's slanderous!'

'Could you hear that? She's been listening. She's a good sort, and she's doing splendidly. Larry's very pleased with her and so is David. As for me,'—his voice rose—'I just put up with her and that's all; just. I'm the one who has to carry her along on that stage.'

The voice came from the kitchen again, yelling, 'Oh, I like that! I like that!' Then it was almost at his side as she said, 'I'm off,' and almost on a shout, she said, 'Bye-bye, Mrs Riley!'

After the door had banged, he said, 'She's gone.
357

She's a real spirit-booster. Anyway, darling, how's the boy?'

It was a second or so before she answered, 'I'm worried, Peter. Since he had that fall into the ditch he has been coughing quite a lot. I got the doctor to him.' Then she added bitterly, 'Oh, doctors! All he said then was, "Don't worry. Don't worry; a ducking won't hurt him, nor clean mud." But it was ice-cold, and we didn't find him for ten minutes and he was struggling to get out of that muddy ditch. Something'll have to be done with that field; it will have to be drained. I had to call the doctor again yesterday—I had been up two nights with him. Anyway, he's putting him on antibiotics. He should have done that before, I think. Now, darling, there's something I must say to you, and I'm finding it terribly hard, but I'll be unable to get there tomorrow. I ... I just can't leave him like this; he's really ill.'

There was a pause before Riley said, 'Of course you can't leave him at the moment, dear, but do you think you'll make it for the night?'

'Oh yes, I must. I'll do my utmost. Oh yes, even if I have to come by the early train and leave later, I must be there. Oh yes, Peter. And I'm so sorry. But these things happen and I can't help but be afraid. One obstacle after another seems to be keeping us apart.'

He stared at the phone for a moment, not answering her as he thought: It wasn't one obstacle after another keeping them apart, it was just their son. But what did he expect her to do, leave the child in that condition? When he did speak, it was to say, 'Look here, dear, try not to worry. I know you'll get here for the opening through hail, snow, or rain, because as David said yesterday, you're as much a part of this place as he is, much more than Miss Connie; she's merely a newcomer ... although providing the money, of course.' He laughed gently here, 'Has the doctor been today?'

'Not yet, I'm waiting for him. I must say he's been very good since the first time. I was angry with him when he seemed to take it so lightly. In a way I should have understood that he was treating Charles as if he were an ordinary boy.'

Riley came back firmly now saying, 'But that's what you're always stressing, dear, isn't it, that he is an ordinary boy?'

'Mentally, yes, but not physically. He has a delicate physique, and you know it.'

In the ensuing silence, Riley thought: He has not only a delicate physique, his mind is delicate, too, if you would only face up to it.

'Are you there, Peter?'

'Yes, darling. Yes I am, but I'm so concerned for you; I should be there with you.'

Her voice was soft as she said, 'No, I should be there with you, and I know it. Every fibre in me tells me this. Mrs A. and Mac are wonderful and he loves them, but they both agree they're very poor substitutes for us.'

'For you, dear, for you.'

'No, not only for me, because yesterday, on three occasions between his croaking, he asked, "When is Daddy coming?" '

'Oh Lord! Nyrene, that makes me feel terrible.'

'Oh, don't, darling. I think it's wonderful that he wants you.'

She could have added, because he sees so little of you, but what she said was, 'Look, don't you worry. Carry on to the great night, and I'll be there. If it's at all possible, darling, you know I'll be there, because I've looked forward to it as much as you have. I must go now, but don't worry about this end. Nobody could be more attentive than Mac and Mrs A. and Ivy and Ken have been wonderful too. I suppose you are rehearsing madly all the time?'

'Larry had them on the boards at half-past seven this morning, and, apart from a break for a bite at twelve, we've just finished.'

'Oh, my goodness!'

'Well, as you only too well know, dear, that's the pattern before a first night. Look, I'll phone later this evening and if things are no better I'll try to get away in the morning and return here tomorrow night.'

'No, you mustn't, not now; you of all people are needed there. If there's any real danger I'll let you know immediately. Now try not to worry, darling. I hope to see you on the night . . . on the day of the night. Oh yes, I want to be there so much. Bye-bye, darling.'

'Bye-bye, my love.'

*   *   *

The town was agog. The headlines in the local newspaper proclaimed it to be the most exciting event in the town for years to take place. If the dress rehearsal was anything to go by the audience would have an uproarious time. There had been no rehearsal today for Larry believed in a free day before a first night.

Larry Fieldman and Riley sat in the circle

viewing the scene before them, and exclaiming yet again on the magnificence of the painted ceiling and the gold cornice surrounding it with its colourful stucco garlands hanging from it.

'I'd imagine there's not another place like it in the country.' Riley was saying, and Larry answered, 'Well there are one or two fine theatres left, but I agree with you this will take some beating. The beautiful mahogany panelling alone is magnificent, as is the entrance and the stairs.'

'Mr Riley.' The voice came up from the stalls, and Riley shouted down, 'Yes? What is it?'

'You're wanted on the phone.'

'Thanks, I'll take it up here.' He turned quickly and ran up the steps of the circle and into David's office, and there, taking up the phone, he said, 'Yes? Peter Riley here. Oh, hello, darling.'

'Oh, Peter.'

'What is it? What is it?'

'It's ... it's Charles; he has pneumonia.' It was clear that she was crying: she had to swallow a number of times before he heard her say, 'The doctor's been twice today. I ... I can't leave him, Peter.'

'Of course not, my dear. Of course not.' His voice was so low he could hardly hear himself speak; then he said, 'When did all this happen?'

'He's ... he's been getting worse. The doctor didn't say it was pneumonia right away. He ... he can hardly breathe, dear. I won't be able to leave him.'

'Oh, Nyrene!' There was a short silence before he added, 'But don't distress yourself. If you can't make it, you can't. I should be there with you. I know I should. I feel torn in two.'

361

Brokenly now, she said, 'Please don't feel like that. Your place is there ... I'll have to go now, sweetheart.'

'Yes, yes, of course. But phone me later and let me know how things are.'

'Yes, yes, I will, darling.'

'Goodbye, my love.'

He put the receiver down, then dropped into a low-backed chair, and swung around in it towards the desk, and there, his forearms resting on it, he clenched his fists and thumped it. What was happening to them? Through no fault of his own, the child was cleaving them apart. Once upon a time at night he could lie alone and visualise Nyrene's face on the pillow beside his and go over their love-making. Very often now, a different face would be looking at him, and his body would become hot with the recollection of Yvette's knowledgeable loving.

But now his son was ill with pneumonia, and he felt that this, in causing the absence of Nyrene, would create another opening in his already weak defence. He groaned. Whatever was to happen, much of the responsibility for the opening night was on his shoulders: it lay with him to carry the cast, for once again he would play the clown, the drunk, the simpleton, in fact, go back to where he started ...

He went downstairs and sought out David, and for a man who rarely swore, David said, 'Oh, hell's bells! Quite candidly, she would have been one of the main attractions. She was so well known and liked at The Little Palace they would have hooted for her.'

'I'm sorry.'

'Don't be silly; don't talk about being sorry. I'm thinking of her and the child, of course, and I know what you're thinking, you should be there. Well, you can't be, can you? So come on, make the best of it. So much depends upon you. Especially tomorrow night. Yet don't worry about it. If you have to go on Thursday, Tom is pretty well primed in your part, although he won't be you and the audience will be disappointed. But still, that's life, and they'll understand. So come on.' His voice changing, he added, 'Connie's just come in. She's like a teenager looking forward to her first party. D'you know what she said to me yesterday? She said that this venture had taken ten years off her; in fact it has given her the youth she never had. You know, Riley, she may be very rich but she's never been very happy so far as I can gather. Anyway, she wants to see you. Come on.'

As he walked through the broad, carpeted foyer, he was asking himself if anyone was really ever happy. One thought one was, then life produced one of its tangents and brought you to your knees. With him, it was Yvette, and now he wasn't only carrying a load of guilt but a fear of meeting up with her again, for she had opened a door in him that he couldn't close.

CHAPTER THIRTEEN

'You must get some rest, woman.'

Nyrene turned her face up to the doctor, but she didn't answer him, and he went on, 'McIntyre and your woman are quite capable of seeing to him;

363

they'll let you know whether there is any change.'

'How long do you think?'

'I couldn't say . . . a few hours. He's in God's hands now; I've done all I can, and you more than enough. You've contacted your husband?'

'Yes.'

'Well, I think he should be here.'

She turned her face up to him again, saying, 'It's the opening night of the theatre; he couldn't possibly leave. I . . . I really should be there.'

'You shouldn't be there; you should be here with your son, and so should he.'

He turned from the bed, and picked up his bag, then said, 'It's four o'clock now. I have a surgery at five. If you need me after that, give me a ring at home.'

She stood up and said, 'Thank you, thank you very much.'

He was making for the door when in his abrupt fashion, he said, 'Don't thank me until he's out of the wood.'

She made no reply, but when the door closed on him she sat down again and looked at her child. The bedclothes were heaving on his small chest, his face was bloated, the eyelids half-closed. She stroked the damp hair back from his brow, then put a moist pad on it.

The boy now had a bout of coughing, and when he brought up some dark phlegm she said, 'That's right. That's right, darling. Get rid of that nasty stuff and . . . and you'll soon be better. Yes, you will, yes, you will, darling.'

The door opened quietly and Mrs A. entered, carrying a tray, which she placed on a side table before tiptoeing to the bed, where Nyrene turned to her and said in a whisper, 'You should be in bed, woman, you should be asleep.'

، 'I've had three hours, ma'am. I went off straight away, so I'm perfectly all right. You're the one who should get some sleep; it'll be you who'll be in bed next, I'm telling you. Thirty-six hours and you've hardly moved out of this room. It can't go on. Look, have this cup of tea,'—she motioned to the tray—'then go and have a couple of hours.'

'No. No, I'll be all right. But I'll tell you what I'll do. I'll have the tea and then I'll have a shower.'

'A shower's not going to keep you awake.'

There was a pause before Nyrene said, 'It'll keep me awake as long as possible, Mrs A. He ... he can't go on much longer like this. I think the doctor might be back later.'

'I must say this, ma'am,'—it was a lower whisper still—'I had never had much room for him, but I've had to change my opinion these last few days.'

Nyrene nodded then she again stroked her son's hair back from his forehead and stared at him for a moment before she rose from the chair, saying, 'I'll take the tea next door.' Then she picked up the tray and went into her room. Presently, seated in an armchair, she looked towards the ceiling and said aloud, 'Spare my child. Please spare my child. If I am to lose one, I ... I will understand; but spare my child, please. Please.'

*　　　*　　　*

She was sitting by the child again. She glanced at the clock. Just after seven.

They'd all be on stage now. She could see them, the whole row of them, with Lord Very standing

365

out in front. The place would be crowded. People would be standing at the back of the stalls; they would be sitting on the circle stairway, and the gallery would be choc-a-bloc. She could hear the applause; it was thunderous. She saw the curtain go down; she heard the orchestra strike up; she saw the play begin. Adam and Eve in their fishnet tights and the serpent hanging from the tree. She knew that the first scene would bring a great peal of laughter, especially when the serpent, which was actually hanging upside down from a branch, a very strong painted cable, shook his pointed fanged head, then took a handkerchief from beneath his scales, wiped his eyes and blew his nose, while Adam and Eve below, oblivious of him, continued their chase amid the trees, strongly constructed posts but truly representing trees, at least from a distance. She had read the script and discussed it with Peter, and even without the fishnet figures and the serpent she had been brought to laughter. Peter always excelled in a comedy part and, as Eve, Lily herself had turned out to be a real comedienne.

She hadn't heard Hamish come into the room and when his voice came at her shoulder, whispering, 'He looks at boiling point, ma'am; the crisis won't be long,' she couldn't say again to him, I'm told that with the antibiotics they don't have a crisis; well, not as they used to, because once Hamish got anything into his head, it was as hard to move it as it was to make him believe that 103° to 104° Fahrenheit was much the same as 39° Centigrade: they were all new-fangled ideas and not to be trusted . . .

For the next two hours the child took her whole attention: he coughed until it would seem his small lungs would burst, but at least with each bout he brought up the darkish phlegm from his chest.

It must have been about eleven o'clock when Mrs A. woke her. Nyrene realised that she must have been dozing. The last time she had looked at the clock it was just on ten, at which time she had thought the play would have finished and the congratulations would have begun.

She blinked and looked down on the child, and Mrs A. said, 'I think he's easier.' And when he croaked, 'Mummy,' Nyrene said eagerly, 'Yes, darling? Would you like a drink?' and with this she held a feeding cup to his lips. But when he tried to swallow he choked and coughed again; but it wasn't so harsh as before.

After handing the cup to Mrs A. she took a soft towel and wiped the sweat from Charles's body; then, again stroking the tangled blond hair from his brow, she leaned her head against the high padded back of the chair and looked across the narrow bed to where Mrs A. was now seated, busily folding handkerchiefs into strips prior to their being moistened with witch hazel. In the pink-shaded nightlight, Nyrene could make out only the ends of Mrs A.'s fingers as they moved backwards and forwards over the bedside table, and it was their continuous motion that caused her eyelids to droop and her head to drop to the side and deep and much needed sleep to overtake her . . .

She was conscious of someone saying, 'God be praised! God be praised!' And when she tried to stretch out her legs she groaned and Hamish's voice came clearly to her, saying, 'Now, now, don't try to get up for a minute. You must be in a cramp. Sit where you are till you have a cup of tea. The child doesn't need you; he's fast asleep, natural-like.'

With an effort, she turned her head and looked towards the bed, and when she saw her son was sleeping peacefully, the relief caused her to slump inwardly. 'What time is it?' she said.

'Ten minutes to five, ma'am.'

'What!' She had spoken so loudly that she put her hand over her mouth; then eased herself to the edge of the chair and repeated, 'Ten minutes to five. I can't . . . I can't have slept all that time.'

'Yes, you did, ma'am. Yes you did, as sound as a bell'—it was Hamish again—'and the further you went over the more I knew you'd have a devil of a cramp when you woke up; and I was right, wasn't I?'

The only answer she could make was, 'Oh, Hamish.'

When Mrs Atkins said softly, 'Go down and fetch a tray up,' he said, 'Gladly. Gladly,' only to be stopped by Nyrene saying, 'Not yet, Hamish, thank you. First, I'll have a bath and change.'

Pulling herself up from the chair, she stood for a moment gazing down on the sleeping child. The little chest was still heaving but without that awful dragging effort. She put out a hand and gently touched his hair; then, her walk almost like that of someone drunk, she stumbled out of the nursery and into her own room, where, dropping into a chair, she again looked ceiling-wards, saying, 'Thank you. Thank you.' But the wave of relief was now threaded with a feeling she could not put a name to: it was as if she had made a bargain, for which the price had still to be paid.

CHAPTER FOURTEEN

As if they were returning from a party where the drinks had flowed, they stormed out of the small station bus to be met by Hamish's admonishing tone: 'Will you whisht a while, please. The child is still poorly up above.' He thumbed towards the upper windows of the house, and it was Ken who said, 'Sorry, Mac. But we're all still living last night. It was a wonderful time. Where's Mrs Riley?'

'If you turn your head, sir, you'll see her at the front door awaiting you,' said Hamish tersely.

Like softly buzzing bees, they swarmed towards Nyrene.

'Oh! my dear, my dear, how are you?'

'Oh, we did miss you.'

'It's been wonderful! Wonderful! You'd have been so proud of him, proud of them all.'

'There could never have been such a night in that town. This morning's local paper was full of it. We have one with us.'

They were in the sitting-room now and no-one, Nyrene remarked to herself, had asked after the child. Mick Brown was saying, 'I've never laughed so much in my life, Nyrene, never. That first scene was a wow. How they did it I'll never know.'

Angus Clarke said, 'And the opening was really excellent. He's a good speaker, that Lord Very. And they mentioned you, yes they did, Nyrene. The owner, he said there was one person missing tonight who really should be there. He said you had been the bulwark of The Little Palace Theatre for years and everyone in the town knew you. You

369

were Miss Mason then, but now you were Mrs Riley, and you know, they applauded. Yes, they did, didn't they?' He nodded towards the others.

Nyrene made no answer to all this; she was helping Mrs A. to hand round cups of tea.

Claire Brown now put in, 'There was a wonderful do afterwards. Of course, you couldn't get stirred, and they must have had barrels of champagne, the way it flowed. And then there were the photographers.'

At this Ivy cried, 'And Ken and I were taken with your friends, you know Fred and Louise. There was a group of us; Fred's sister was there with her daughter. By, she was something! All the men were oohing and aahing at her. Her dress was nobody's business; it fitted where it touched.'

'Well, who wouldn't gape?' put in Ken now, 'when you could almost see her backside at the top of those legs?' which created loud laughter, only for this to be hushed by Ivy's warning finger and her saying to Nyrene, 'How is he?'

'He's better than he was, thanks, Ivy.' Nyrene's reply was flat.

The quiet member of the party, Arthur Maine, put in, 'You've got a nice flat there, Nyrene,' only to be almost shouted down by Ken, saying, 'I don't know how you could see it, Arthur, it was so crowded. But by that time, you were probably seeing double, we were all seeing double.' He looked at Nyrene now. 'I don't know how we all got in there. There were Peter's people and his friends and the boss David and his partner, Miss Connie. She's a dainty piece, isn't she? and full of fun. And they were all still there at two o'clock when we left. By, it's been a night to remember! The only thing'—his voice dropped now and the expression on his face changed and he looked around the company as he said—'we all say the same, Nyrene; you were missed, definitely you were missed and, I can tell you, mostly by Peter. He kept asking after you and the boy, and the last words he said to Ivy, here, were, "Tell her I'll soon be home." '

'Yes, I was going to tell you, Nyrene, yes, that's what he said to me, "Tell her I'll soon be home." '

There was a great lump in her throat. She had been disliking this crowd of merrymakers as thoughtless individuals, but now the feeling had gone, they were her friends. She wanted to go to Ivy and lay her head on her shoulder and cry; but that certainly would put a damper on things, and so she forced herself to say, 'Last night, sitting by the boy's bed, I followed the performance right through from seven o'clock,' but her tone changed into one of jocular censure when she added, 'but then I wasn't invited back into the flat to join the ceilidh.'

They were all laughing again until Mike Brown, getting up, said, 'You know something? Here's one for home and bed. I shall fall straight into it without taking my boots off.'

One after the other now they rose to their feet, and their goodbyes were warm and thoughtful, but the last couple had not moved far down the drive before Hamish was into the kitchen and, addressing his future wife, he said, 'Friends, they say, friends. Thoughtless lot of tykes! Child ill upstairs and laughing their heads off, and she not able to be there. They could have kept their merriment until they got home.'

'Oh,' said Mrs A. 'They wanted her to know how

371

it went.'

'Fiddlesticks! Thoughtless, and to my mind, I'm telling you, some of them looked still half-cobbled. I know what people are like when they go to parties and the drinks are free; I've seen men of whom I wouldn't believe it, guzzling like pigs.'

'But they're always jolly, Hamish. You know they are.'

'Yes, Mary, but there is a time and place for jollification, and that child upstairs is still ill.'

'He's slept through it. I've just been up. Now you go on up and sit by him for a time; I'll be with you shortly.'

As Hamish passed through the hall, he saw Nyrene sitting on the edge of the couch reading at the newspaper spread out on the coffee table before her. She did not raise her head, and so he did not speak.

In fact, Nyrene had not noticed him, for her attention was riveted on a photo in the paper showing her husband standing with his arm around Lily and hers around him, both in the fishnet tights. It must have been taken during the early scene. Somehow, it no longer looked funny, but merely crude. There were other photographs, and the glowing report ended with, 'When Adam and Eve stepped before the last curtain, they really did bring the house down.'

She slowly folded the paper; then sat back on the couch and glanced at the clock on the mantelpiece. It was almost twenty hours since he had last phoned her. That had been around six o'clock last night. All morning she had made excuses for him: he would be dead-beat after such a play, followed by all that entertainment. And yet, no matter what time they had finished he could have rung her; he would know she would be waiting, if only to know how things had gone. In any case, he should have rung to enquire after the child.

There was something wrong somewhere. Things were changing. She couldn't actually put her finger on it, but she was aware of the change inside her. Why otherwise had she made that bargain with God?

CHAPTER FIFTEEN

He kept turning his head towards the phone table. He'd have to ring her; nothing had happened, not really, yet he was feeling so awful about it. He should have phoned her this morning when the house was finally clear, but instead, what had happened? Immediately after closing the door on the last of them, he had rushed to the sink and vomited his heart up. No, not his heart, just the overload of drink he had consumed. He should have eaten at the same time, he knew. And yet it wasn't the lack of food, or even the drink, that had made him vomit; it was the feeling that had flooded him, the desire that had filled him only a short while before. He had gone out to move his car, to allow Nurse to get her car out and take his still-laughing family home, for his father, Betty and Harry had had the time of their lives. He had just moved his car back into the yard and was making for the kitchen door when the arms came about him. He was for digging his elbows into the owner when her voice came in his ears, whispering, 'Peter.

Peter, you know something? You're wonderful.'

He had pressed her from him, but when he turned to face her, he found himself again in her arms, and now she murmured, 'No-one can see, no-one can hear, they're all sozzled back there. I've never seen so many tight people all together in my life.' Her lips now were on his cheek and he had managed to mutter, 'Yvette, give over; stop it! You've had a lot, and I've had a lot.'

'I rarely drink, Peter. Have you not noticed that? I rarely drink. I sip at a glass; I can keep it going for hours just sipping. I keep my wits about me. Oh, Peter.' Her body pressed him against the wall and her mouth was on his, and almost instantly he found himself responding.

The kiss seemed to bury deep into them both, until with a jerk, he thrust her around, and now she was standing with her back to the wall; and their bodies seemed to be about to merge when he gave a start as if someone had prodded him in the ribs. Then he was free from her, muttering, 'God! Yvette, you're awful; you're the very devil. Why me? There are dozens who would give their,'—he searched for the word—'eye-teeth to have you.'

Her whisper came to him now as thick as his, saying, 'I know that, I know that, but I don't want others. Strangely, Peter, I only want you. What a confession to make! But it's true; I only want you. But don't worry, I just wanted to kiss you; tonight at any rate. Come on, let's go in.'

She took his hand as if to lead him like a child back into the kitchen, but he pulled away from her, saying, 'You go in. Go on, get yourself away from me.' His voice was rough now, and she laughed gently as she went from him, leaving him yet again amazed at the coolness of her and her strength of purpose. She was dangerous. And his head was ringing with the words, It could've happened again. Within another minute it could have happened again. If something untoward didn't soon take place she'd be the means of wrecking his life, his well-ordered, successful life. What had come over him? He must get home to Nyrene.

But how would he be able to take her after what he was feeling for that one? Oh, she was a devil, a real devil. No—his thoughts changed—not a devil, a siren, a beautiful young siren. It . . . it was her ardent youth and that exotic body of hers.

He heard cars drawing up in the street, and he thought, Oh, thank God . . .

But he did not have an empty flat until ten minutes past four when Lily left, saying, 'Thank you, Peter, for the most wonderful night in my life. I only wish Johnny had been here to witness it.'

'Thank you, Lily,' he said, taking her hand, 'for being the best partner any actor could have. You yourself made that show tonight.'

'Nonsense.'

They were on the pavement now, and as he bent to kiss her cheek she took his face between her hands and shook his head, saying, 'You're a canny lad, and if I didn't love my man I would love you.'

After the cab had driven away, it was then he had gone into the kitchen and vomited, and realised he couldn't phone Nyrene, not yet anyway. He must sleep . . .

He would have slept on, but the continual ringing of the doorbell at twelve o'clock got him out of bed.

At the door, Larry said, 'Come on, me boy, come

on, you're wanted.'

'Who wants me?'

'Lord Very, my dear boy, and our dear Miss Connie. You're invited to lunch, and they are waiting. They both came in as bright as buttons, and I've had to get David up too. I seem to be the only one to have survived the night with a clear head. You can't take it, laddie, you can't take it. Have a shower and get yourself dressed pronto! I'll hold them for fifteen minutes. I think it's going to be a conclave of some kind. So put a move on.'

'Oh, my God!'

'That's what I said. That's what I said. But don't forget he's got a title and she's got the money, and we are but pawns in the game. So get going.'

'Are you invited?'

'Strangely, yes.'

When he was dressed he said, 'Look, I should make a phone call,' and at this Larry, glancing at his wristwatch, said in a hoarse whisper, 'They've been waiting all told more than half an hour. It doesn't do to keep backers waiting, I've learned that, so come on.'

*　　　*　　　*

He didn't get back to the flat until four o'clock and during this time he had learned that payment can be extracted in many ways for kindnesses rendered. He was the producer in this theatre because of the benevolence of Miss Connie Pickman-Blyth and if Miss Connie wanted a favour done for a friend, who is a lord, who was he to refuse to comply? And so, of course, he would see the writer of this book with which they had presented him and do his best

376

to turn it into a drama. One consolation was that he wasn't the only one who had to pay: Larry had been given a copy too; and after glancing at the first page or so, his judgement could be gauged by his exclamation, 'Oh, my God!'

Anyway, what did it matter about the book? he had to phone. He just had to phone. What was stopping him? She wouldn't see his face, she wouldn't detect his feelings; no, but she would do when he got home. Well he mustn't go home for a day or two; he just must not go home yet. He almost jumped up from the couch and picked up the phone . . .

'Hello, darling. Now listen to what I've got to say. First, how's the child?'

'Much better.'

He drew his head back from the mouthpiece . . . just two words, much better.

'Look, dear. By now you will have heard of the uproarious do here last night. It went on till early morning, and I'd had nothing to eat from the previous lunch time. I was dropping on my feet. I don't remember going to bed, and I only came to when Larry knocked me up at noon to tell me that Miss Connie and Lord Very were waiting for me to go to lunch . . . it was about a new play. When I saw the time I knew I must phone you; but he harassed me, for the others were waiting. "Those who pay the piper," Larry said, "must call the tune." I've just got back; and what d'you think the lunch was about? One of Lord Very's friends is a writer, and his novel, they imagine, would make a first-rate play. Larry's private opinion, after he had scanned through a few pages, was, "Oh my God!" And we've got to pay the piper again because Very wants us to meet the author tomorrow. This will stop me from getting home, as promised. I'm so sorry, darling. But how are you, dear?'

'Oh, I'm very well.'

'And is he really better?'

'Yes, he seemed to get over the worst just about the time you'd be going on stage last night.'

'That's odd, isn't it?'

'Yes. Yes, I thought so too.'

'And he's really out of danger?'

'Yes, the doctor says so; but I'm afraid it's going to leave him with a very weak chest. And it'll be some time before he fully recovers.' She did not add, if ever.

'Can . . . can he talk?'

'Yes, although it's more of a croak as yet, but he asked for you.'

The feeling of guilt whirled up in him, and he said, 'That . . . that makes me feel awful. I know I should have been there; and it makes me feel worse knowing I'll have to stick it out here until the weekend.'

There was a pause before she said, 'Oh that's all right, that's all right. It'll be Sunday, then, before you get back?'

'I don't know. There might be a late train, but you know what it's like on a Saturday night: the audience seem to hang around. Anyway, I'll try my best. It would mean my getting there early on Sunday morning.'

'Don't hurry, it's all right.'

From her first words he realised that her tone represented her real feelings; and that she had not once used any term of endearment.

His voice rising, he said, 'I can't help it, Nyrene.

378

If I was my own boss, well—'

'Oh, I understand. Who should know better than me about the claims of the stage? But don't worry; I am aware of the situation. Let me just say I'm glad everything went so well. The crowd brought a newspaper with them. It was a glowing report, and it seems Lily did a marvellous job.'

'Yes, she did; quite candidly, she stole the show. Our leading lady, Miss Petula Pratt—believe me that's her name, Petula Pratt—was slightly peeved, just slightly, but she hid it well and she, too, got a good reception.'

'How does David feel about things?'

'Oh, you can't imagine; he's over the moon. He's like a king ruling a country, and it *is* his country. But he's very fair with everyone, as always; and he's very good to me.'

'What are you going to do now?'

'Well, my darling, look at the clock. I must be on my way to the dressing-room, but to tell you the truth I would rather go to bed,' but he did not add, as he might have done, with you beside me. 'If I can ring you later, I will, darling.'

'Don't worry; tomorrow will do. Good-night, dear.'

She had said good-night, dear, not good-night, my love, or good-night, darling, just good-night, dear. He put down the phone, and remained staring at it. She was angry . . .

About to leave the flat, he switched on the outside light, then opened the door, only to step backwards, exclaiming, 'No!' and for any further protest to be cut off by her saying, 'It's all right, dear. Don't look so apprehensive. Put your head out of the door and you'll see mother is in the car.'

He did as she bade him, and he could see the Jaguar at the end of his short drive.

Yvette was saying, 'We're off to Greece via London.'

'What? Oh.' And then his next words sounded foolish even to himself: 'You're driving in the dark . . . I mean, through the night?'

'Yes, I'm driving in the dark. I like night-driving but it won't be through the night. We'll be at the flat by midnight, and the plane doesn't leave till about ten tomorrow.' She put her hand out and touched his arm, saying quietly, 'Come and say goodbye to Mother. She so enjoyed last night, as did everyone else.' Then her voice sinking, she said, 'And as for us, we nearly did, didn't we, Peter?'

'Yvette, for God's sake!'

And now almost grabbing his hand, she pulled him over the step, saying facetiously, 'No, not for his sake for mine.'

At the car, Gwendoline wound down the window and, putting out her hand, she took his as she said, 'Thank you again, Peter, for the most wonderful evening. From beginning to end it was what they would call a –' she glanced up at her daughter, then said, 'a cracker. I suppose you're feeling tired now?'

'Yes, I am a bit.'

'And you'll be on stage again very shortly?'

'Yes. Yes.'

'Well, we won't keep you. We're off to Greece, you know, for three weeks. I have to get warmed up every so often so as to tolerate this climate.'

He nodded down at her but made no response. Then he straightened and watched the window move up into place before he turned to Yvette and said, 'Have a safe journey.'

'Oh, I will.' She was laughing at him. 'The gods are on my side, and tonight I'll ask them to look after you until we meet again . . . shortly.'

The car did not just move away, but sprang from its standing point and sped away into the darkness. He stood on the pavement staring in the direction it had gone. She was the strangest creature; there was no-one like her. She had something. In a way, she was like a female Jekyll and Hyde, possessed of both good and evil.

No, no, not evil. With a toss of his head he dismissed the latter; it was simply an innate sort of magnetism.

On his way back to close the door, he thought, Three weeks. Thank God! It would give him time to pull himself together. He would get himself home as often as possible. He hadn't been with Nyrene when she most needed him. She must have had an awful time with the child being so ill. He would make it up to her. Yes, he would. And when the other one came back, he'd feel strong enough then to put her in her place.

CHAPTER SIXTEEN

Riley arrived home on the Sunday shortly after lunch, having taken a taxi from the station. His stepping into the hall brought a loud exclamation of 'Oh, Mr Riley!' from Mrs A., who had been attending to the fire.

'How wonderful to see you, sir. Oh my goodness! Here, give me your coat.' She had actually run towards him. 'You look frozen. I'll have a hot drink ready for you in a minute. Ma'am's upstairs.'

As she took his coat he said, 'Thanks, Mrs A. It's good to be back; I feel I've been away for years.'

'Feels like that to us, too, sir.'

When he reached the landing he saw Nyrene coming towards him, but she didn't run to him, nor he to her. When they met they clasped each other and he pressed her head into his shoulder as he murmured, 'Oh, darling, darling! 'Tis good to see you.'

She said nothing, and when she raised her head they looked deeply into each other's eyes for a moment before they kissed. Then he asked softly, 'How is he?'

'Oh, much better. Much better. He's been waiting for you to come.'

As though he were a stranger, she now led him into the nursery; and there was the child propped up in bed, and on the sight of his father he cried, 'Daddy! Daddy!' and when the child's thin arms went around Riley's neck he was unable to speak: his throat was full, his eyes burning.

After a moment he laid the boy back on to his pillows, and, as if he were addressing an older person, asked, 'How are you feeling?'

'Oh, better. I . . . I can talk now.'

What Riley noticed, however, was that the words came out hesitantly as if each one had to have a breath to assist it.

Nyrene was standing at the other side of the bed when she said, 'Have you had anything to eat?'

'No, but Mrs A. is getting me a drink.'

'Oh, you must have something to eat; I'll go down and see to it.'

He wanted to say, No, no, it's all right. Stay, I'm not hungry. The sight of the child was affecting him. The eyes that were staring at him had shrunken into their sockets, revealing a depth that was disturbing; it was the gaze of an older person, and a knowledgeable one, aware of the duplicity of his father.

He told himself not to be stupid, for what could the child be aware of? What could anyone in this house, she in particular, or any of his friends, know about him except that which he himself wished them to know? There wasn't a soul who knew about Yvette, so why all this inward turmoil and self-recrimination?

Conscience? Yes, that was what was troubling him, his conscience. He'd had no reason to think that he possessed one until these last few months, and now it was playing hell with him.

The boy now said, 'Are you . . . on holiday, Daddy?'

'No, dear, I must go back in the morning, but I'll have a holiday soon and then we'll have some fun together.'

He smiled at his son, but there was no answering smile from the boy and the words, 'Wish it was now . . . Daddy,' made Riley reply quickly, 'Well, you know, dear, I'm on the stage and if I stopped for a holiday someone would have to take my place. It's very difficult to arrange.'

The child was staring deep into his face. He began to stroke the small thin hand that lay on his palm, but when the child suddenly said, 'Mummy is tired,' Riley's fingers involuntarily gripped the hand within his for a moment. There was that look again, that look of knowledge that was beyond his age.

With the opening of the door, he turned eagerly towards it, and when he saw Hamish he gently released his hold on his son's hand and stood up, saying, 'Hello Hamish.'

'Hello, Mr Peter, sir. Am I glad to see you. And . . . and what d'you think of our linty now?' He pointed to the bed. 'Don't you think he's a clever fellow?'

'Yes indeed, Mac.'

'Hello there, big fellow.' Hamish was bending over the bed now, and the child's face was bright as he smiled up at him, saying, 'Hello, you yourself,' at which they both laughed, and Hamish, glancing towards Riley, said, 'I'm going to have a medal struck for him—a Scottish one, of course, and not a wee one, but a big one because, to my mind, he's the bravest and toughest linty at this end of the globe.'

The child was laughing as at a joke, and Riley knew a moment of envy of this brawny Scot because of the empathy there surely was between him and his son.

He said to Hamish, 'Will you be staying for a minute?'

'For a minute! Oh, I'm here for the rest of the day. Go on downstairs with you; they're getting a meal for you. I understand it was a splendid do the other night.'

'Yes, it went off very well, Mac, but it was tiring.'

'Oh, undoubtedly. All hard work is tiring. But go on now and have your meal, and I'll be second best with this young man here until you come back.'

It was a tactful way of putting it, second best, when the man knew that he himself had more

384

knowledge of the boy than he'd ever have.

Second best. So many people had to put up with second best. But it must not happen to Nyrene. No, no, it just must not happen to Nyrene. What on earth had made him think that! He'd have to pull himself together, he really would; he must make it up to her during the short time he would be here.

She was standing by the dining table, arranging dishes, and when she said, 'It's only cold beef and salad; I'm sorry,' he brought her round to him and held her by the shoulders, but the words that he should say just would not come.

Of a sudden, he pulled her towards him and, holding her tightly, he managed to say, 'Oh, I've missed you, darling, I *have*, I've missed you.'

As Nyrene leant against him she thought it was odd the funny things that entered one's mind. If he had just said, Oh, I've missed you, darling, but no, he had to emphasise it with, 'I *have*, I've missed you.' An old saying came back to her: the truth needs no emphasis. Then she told herself she must not be like this. What had happened hadn't been his fault. He had a job to do and the stage was an exacting mistress to any man, and a hard master to a woman. It was expressed in that threadworn saying, the show must go on. Yet most of these trite sayings stemmed from a core of truth. Such as the other day, when she had seen the photos in the paper and a thought had infiltrated her mind with another cliché: there was no smoke without fire. She had chided herself for it, associating the fire with that girl, but according to Louise she was now in Greece and likely to remain there for some time. Of course, there was Lily. But oh dear, that thought was ridiculous.

385

He held her from him again, saying softly 'You look so tired, you must be worn out. Look, I'll tell you what I'll do. This show has two more weeks to run; I'll let Tom take over the next one.'

She looked at him steadily for a moment or so; then quietly, she said, 'That would be nice. I'll look forward to it. Sit down and have something to eat, dear.'

Instead of doing as she bade him, he lowered his head to one side, saying, 'You know something? You've haven't kissed me.'

And she answered in like fashion, 'And do *you* know something? You haven't kissed *me.*'

He laughed. 'Well, I'm about to rectify that omission,' he said, and kissed her with an ardour he certainly wasn't feeling.

When she withdrew from him, she said gently, 'Sit down and have your meal, and . . . and then I have to talk to you.'

'Talk to me?' He looked up at her now. 'What do you mean, talk to me? What's wrong?'

'Oh, Peter!'

He tossed his head, saying, 'Oh, I know everything's wrong upstairs, but it was the way you said it.'

'I'm sorry. I'm sorry. But go on, eat something; I'll go and make some coffee.'

But it was a full minute before he started on his meal. There was something wrong. Talk to me. What did she mean? Had she . . . ? Oh, don't be such a damn fool, man. Who could know about that? Only the pair of them. You're letting your conscience get the better of you. In any case, just think: it's happening every day with other blokes, and they don't want to go and jump off a bridge because of it. Pull yourself together, man . . .

Nyrene had said to Mrs Atkins, 'Will you slip up, Mary, and tell Charles that I'll be up in a minute or so?' and Mrs A. had replied, 'You stay where you are for a time, ma'am; he'll be all right with Hamish.'

They had been sitting on the couch drinking their coffee for less than ten minutes. It wasn't half an hour since she had come downstairs, and so his voice now held a note of irritation as he spoke his thoughts aloud, saying, 'You've hardly been downstairs more than a few minutes. Is it always like this?'

She did not look at him as she answered, 'More or less, Peter. You see we nearly lost him. He was near death's door, and since he's come round he doesn't seem to be able to bear me being out of his sight. It's strange, but as Hamish put it, if the child doesn't see me he has the idea he might slip back into wherever he was going. You know how Hamish puts things, but there's something in that.'

He had hold of her hands now, shaking them as he said, 'But, my dear, you can't go on like this. He's not a baby, he's seven years old, and you know they take advantage. In fact, looking back, he's always taken advantage of you. Oh yes, he has.' His head was nodding, and when she just stared at him, he put in quickly, 'I know I'm not here all the time, but he hasn't only you; he has marvellous friends in Hamish and Mrs A. I say friends, but he must consider them as part of his family.'

'Yes, yes, he does.' The reply was flat-sounding; and he let go of her hands in order to lie back on the couch, and there was silence between them for some minutes before he said, 'What are you trying to tell me, Nyrene?'

She turned to him hastily now, saying, 'That . . . that I can't be with you as much as I want to. Don't you understand? And . . . and that it's got to be left to you now to try to get home more often. That's if you want to.'

He brought his body forward, put his elbows on his knees and held his head in his hands as he muttered, 'What's happened to us, Nyrene? Are you accusing me of staying away when I could be with you?'

'No. No,'—again her voice was flat—'but I do think you could get Tom to stand in for you now and again on a Saturday night, so you could get away and have the Sunday and Monday here.'

He lifted his head but did not lie back on the couch. She had it all worked out.

He didn't mind Tom standing in for him now and again during the week, but he liked the Saturday night audience. There was always a very warm feeling on a Saturday night. She should be aware of this. And anyway, he was tired. He, too, was tired.

When her arms came around him and she pulled him into her embrace, saying softly, 'I'm sorry, Peter. Oh, I'm sorry. But I miss you so,' she was immediately recognisable to him, not as the mother of his son but as the woman who had taught him to love and be loved. Yet, with this thought, there flashed across his mind another session of love he had experienced, and when he shuddered within her hold she raised herself from him, saying, 'What is it?'

'Nothing, dear, nothing. I just felt—' How could he truthfully say how he felt? So he said, 'You don't

388

miss me any more than I miss you, my love. And yes, don't worry, I'll try to arrange something.' He smiled now as he said, 'If Mahomet won't come to the mountain, the mountain must go to Mahomet.'

As they laughed she sprang up from the couch and pulled him to his feet, saying, even merrily now, 'Let's go up and talk to him, and we'll tell him Easter isn't very far off when you'll be home for two full weeks.'

As they were going up the stairs, he said, 'By the way, how's the drama school progressing? You haven't mentioned it.'

'Oh, there hangs a tale, a long tale. You must read the letters. And I've had a visit from two men, one of them from Aberdeen. Oh my, you wouldn't believe it! The talent that this country is missing. He has never been on the stage although he has always hankered after it: he wishes to change seats in mid-stream; and he wanted just a few hints. From what I could gather from his ego, the film directors will be flying in from all corners of the earth.'

'No!'

They were laughing now as they crossed the landing, and she said, 'Oh, yes, yes. But the business is growing. I already have a regular pianist. He's marvellous. He came out of forced retirement. And my assistant is a tap dancer.'

'Really?'

'Yes, really.'

At the nursery door, she stopped and leaning towards him, said, 'How would you like to come and work for me, Mr Riley? I really need a managing director,' and he, taking her cue, said, 'Any time. I always wanted to be a comedian.' They fell against each other, laughing silently.

She was to recall this moment and what it portended.

CHAPTER SEVENTEEN

He had managed only one long weekend in three. There had been an invitation from Lord Very to Sunday lunch through Miss Connie; and it was more like a royal command, which David had pointed out to him. Last weekend had, perforce, been spent in bed with a severe cold. It was still hanging about him.

On the phone, Nyrene had been very understanding, assuring him not to worry about her end. But not so Fred who had gone so far as to chastise him for not making more of an effort to carry out his duties. This had not been put in so many words; nevertheless, the implication had been there. He had almost retaliated with, Why don't you mind your own business? This is a family matter. But then, weren't Fred and Louise part of his family, even more so than his father and Betty? for it had been Fred alone who had guided his life.

He threw down the last of the Sunday papers; he was sick of reading. He had not seen a live face today; and he had spoken only to Fred and Nyrene on the phone.

The thought came to him to wrap up well and go over to Fred's. But that would mean getting the car out, and he just couldn't be bothered.

It was eight o'clock when he soaked himself in a bath for half an hour, after which he poured himself a good measure of whisky and took it to bed, where he lay listening to Alan Keith and his *Hundred Best Tunes*. There were always good records on this programme, and this man had a wonderful voice. His diction was perfect. He must have been an actor once, or perhaps he had been a lecturer.

He did not know at what time he turned off the radio, but he must have been asleep by eleven o'clock . . .

When did he first feel the presence in the room? He wasn't a light sleeper but, turning from his back onto his side, he slowly put his hand out to switch on the bedside light. The sight that met his eyes brought him almost springing out of the bed; but in any case he was sitting up and as stiff as a ramrod as he stared at what, for the moment, he hoped was an apparition, because there she was. And what was she doing? She was removing her clothes as a snake might its skin. And indeed she could have been a snake, because her voice came as a hiss, saying, 'Don't look so scared, darling; I'm very much in the flesh.'

'God. God.' He brought out the words on a gasp, and she said, 'Now there you go again, giving me a bunk-up: I am not God; just Yvette, dear.'

'What are you doing?'

'Well, open your eyes wider, darling, and then you will see. I'm getting out of my clothes; in fact I'm out of them.'

As he gazed up at her he experienced a feeling as might a virgin about to be raped: fear was predominant, mostly of himself, because he suddenly pulled the bedclothes under his chin, a reaction which brought a giggle from her.

391

He said, 'Don't! Go away. You're mad.'

'I will get mad, darling, if I stand here much longer. It's cold outside.' And she giggled again.

He screwed up his eyes tight and his voice was deep as he said, 'Oh! Yvette, please go away. I beg you, please!'

Her voice cool and steady now, she said, 'I won't go away because I know something about you that you know too. And it is that you want me. And so,' she added in a lighter vein now, 'if you don't let me in at the top, then I'll just get in at the bottom.' She moved to the foot of the bed.

Almost as he flopped back onto the pillows she was lying by his side, and her long body shivered as she pressed against him, saying, 'I'd never do this for anyone else; you should feel honoured, Peter, you should.'

He heard his own voice muttering faintly, 'How on earth did you get in?'

'By your back door. I had a duplicate key made. It can be done within a half-hour, you know. You should never leave spare keys hanging on hooks near the back door. I just happened to glimpse them the other night, and it gave me an idea. Don't you think it was a good one? Well, if you don't now, you will do shortly.'

Such audacity amazed him. She was talking like a practised whore. Well, wasn't that what she was? And the daughter of one, too. He now made the effort to distance his body from hers, which made her say impatiently, 'I've only got an hour; I'm on my way home ... Peter, Peter,'—she spoke his name as a plea—'don't let us waste it; we're hurting no-one. As Mother says in her pious moments, what the eye doesn't see, the heart doesn't grieve over.'

'Is your car outside?'

'I am not stupid, Peter. No, I have not left the car outside your front door, or round the corner; I have left it behind the theatre. There's a piece of waste ground there. Let's hope the hooligans don't spot it, because, you see, Mother has me timed.'

'Timed?'

'Yes, darling, timed. I phoned her from the flat and said I wouldn't be leaving for another hour or more as I had company. I didn't say who the company was, but I can always infer through the tone of my voice. I'm a very clever girl, Peter. You don't seem to realise that.'

'I realise it all right, Yvette; and I know you're a devil and what they call a starter, for wherever you alight there's trouble.'

'That's unkind of you, Peter.' Her tone held a hurt note in it, and she said now, 'I can't get you out of my mind. I've told you that before. I knew we would come together. I'm not asking you to divorce her or anything.'

'I would never divorce Nyrene,' he said vehemently.

'I know that, darling; and believe me, I never want to be married. But that's another thing; I'm going to have to get married.'

'What! Again?'

'Yes, again. And she's chosen him. I must say he's quite nice.'

He did pull away from her now as he said, 'And you mean you're going to marry this man and you're still here?'

'Look, Peter. Nothing has been settled: he doesn't know I'm going to marry him; only mother

393

and I are aware of it. He has money, he is kind, he is twice my age but he is handsome, and rich, and as yet he hasn't got a pot belly, so he has things going for him . . . but not love.'

He didn't know whether or not to laugh. This was a farce. He was acting in a real farce.

'Peter,'—her voice again held a plea—'we haven't much time. Love me; I need you.' She grabbed at him now and held him close, and when her mouth fell on his he became lost . . .

Yet it was he who, when she went to rise from the bed, held her back, which caused her to laugh so loudly he had to push her head under the bedclothes to stifle the sound.

Then he was watching her slip into her clothes in the same smooth way she had slipped them off, and listening to her voice murmuring at him, 'Now you are not to worry, darling: we are not going abroad for some time; anyway not so long as Ray remains in London. So don't worry. I'll keep a calendar on you. I have done so far: I know your comings and goings through dear Louise, through dear Uncle Fred and through dear Mother, but mostly through dear Uncle Fred. I sometimes wonder if he knows more than is good for him; yet no, for if he did he would surely put a spoke in my wheel. He's not very fond of me, you know . . . Uncle Fred. Anyway, darling—' she was now bending over him, whispering, 'don't ever think I'll embarrass you, I'll always be very circumspect; but I need you and you need me. Oh yes, you need me, don't you? Say you do.'

When he made no response, she said, 'Well, it doesn't matter; everything about you speaks for itself.'

Suddenly the room was empty; he didn't hear a door close, near or far.

He rolled over onto his back and covered his eyes with his hands. Something had begun which he had no power to stop.

CHAPTER EIGHTEEN

It was the first week in June and the month hadn't belied its flaming description.

Fred and Louise were sitting on the loggia at the back of the house: he was wearing a pair of striped shorts and Louise a scanty two-piece bathing costume.

She took a sip from a tall glass of iced orange juice, then pushed the hair back from her forehead before she said, 'We should have gone with Jason to the baths.'

'Yes, I know we should; but it would have meant getting there and, if you've noticed, woman, I am slightly older than my son. He's jumped on a bus; I couldn't jump on a bus, nor could I take that car out again tonight, at least I don't want to. The only consolation I have of being roasted alive is that I'm not the only one. I think it's the first time we've had a heatwave like this in years, but it's not going to last much longer, so it's forecast. Anyway, there's something I want to talk to you about.'

'Yes,'—she turned to look at him—'you're going to retire.'

'Don't be silly, woman. It's about Gwendoline.'

He pulled himself up from the deckchair and, wagging his finger across the bamboo table towards her, he said, 'Now don't sigh like that. I'm not going over there, I've told you and I've told her. I'm fed up with the whole business. Quite candidly I wish she would go back to where she came from in France or wherever.'

'Gwendoline or Yvette?'

'Both of them, to tell you the truth.'

'Oh my! This must be serious.'

'It is serious, Louise; not for us but for two people we're very fond of.'

He had her whole attention now, and she pulled herself to the edge of the chair and, looking towards him, asked anxiously, 'Now what's happened?'

'Nothing yet. Although I say nothing, I don't really know. It could have been happening for some time, for there's something wrong, I know those two . . . Peter and Nyrene. I can feel it.'

'And it's to do with that slinky bitch? Gwendoline's told you something?'

'Not exactly; but you know this Ray Zussman she's got lined up for her . . . in fact, they're all going away to Menorca next weekend when it will likely be settled. At least, that's what Gwendoline had thought, but it seems that Yvette is now stalling, as if she's got something up her sleeve.'

'She's said all that?'

'No. No, she didn't; but I'm just telling you what I surmise from what she did say. I can't repeat the conversation word for word, but what she did say, and right out, was that it was a pity about Nyrene's boy being so delicate that it was preventing her from being with her husband. Men get lonely, she said.'

'No!'

'Yes, she actually said that, and I think the same. It is a great pity that she doesn't come through more often. Do you remember she was expecting him home on two weekends last month, and on each occasion something happened to stop him? What I do know is that that girl has changed in the last few months.'

Louise sat back in her chair now and it was some time before she said, 'There lies the crux of the matter, Fred; she isn't a girl and the other one is.'

'You think it could be?'

'I wouldn't put anything past her or past anyone of her type.'

'Well, I'm with you there. But what can we do?'

'It's that blooming boy. I shouldn't say it like that'—Louise shook her head now—'because he's a lovable little fellow, but it's unnatural that he can't bear her out of his sight. She should've put her foot down in the first place and left him with Hamish and Mrs A. He would have got used to it.'

'You can't put your foot down, Louise, with what might be an autistic child, and one with a high-powered nervous system like his. I know, I have a similar type in the third form. He'd be a brilliant scholar if he could sit down long enough. There have been complaints from other parents that he should be sent to a special school. He'll likely end up there. Anyway, back to the business in question, have you anything on your mind?'

'Yes, I have; but it's up to you, of course. What about me telling her I would like a break and ask if I could go up for a weekend? I could take Jason; he would love to see Charles again. It would give her the opportunity to go and see Peter.'

'Very good. Very good.'

'And you wouldn't mind?'

'Of course I'd mind being left alone here in the wilderness; but at the same time you do need a break and it's a while till term ends. By all means go ahead.'

'Well, I could go up on Thursday night and she could come down on Friday morning; and I could stay until she comes back on the Tuesday. Too long?'

'Yes, of course it's too long.' He now leant across the table and caught her hand, saying, 'I'm going into my dotage, you know, and I need you more and more.' But then, his voice changing, he said, 'Go ahead. If it checks whatever we think needs checking then my sacrifice will not be in vain.'

She patted his hand now, saying, 'You're a nice old thing, Mr Beardsley . . . at times. But only at times.' And her tone changing again, she said, 'There's one thing we'd have to do, we'd have to tell him she'd be coming. I'd hate her to walk in on anything.'

'So you do think . . . ?'

'I don't know. I really don't know, but with one thing and another I think we shall soon find out.'

*　　　*　　　*

Nyrene put down the phone, then stood back and stared at it before walking to the open door. She went out onto the terrace and sat down in a low chair opposite the side drive they had made to the new gate, from where, across a broad expanse of green, could be seen the silver streak of the river and the hills on the far side. Presently Hamish came and stood by her side, and said, 'Well, I'll be

398

off, ma'am. You needn't go up for a time, he'll be asleep by now. After a day like this, I say, give me the snow any time. And to think this is what people go abroad to lie in. They must be mad, paying good money to get burnt and have the strength sucked out of them, and then having to come back for a rest. Mad. Mad. People are, you know, ma'am. Quite mad.'

'Hamish.'

The tone in which she spoke his name made him alert, and he stepped from the side of the chair to the front and, staring down at her, he waited. She looked up at him and slowly she said, 'Would it put you out if you didn't go for half an hour?'

'Put me out, ma'am? For half an hour? If you want me to stay the night you've only to say the word. You should know that by now. But the boy . . . he's fine.'

'For once I'm not thinking of the boy, Hamish.' She was staring up at him. 'I've got a decision to make. Mrs Beardsley has suggested my going down for a long weekend. In order to let me go and join,'—she paused before saying—'my husband,' she usually used the term Mr Peter when speaking of him to Hamish. 'Now if I decide to go at all I won't wait till Friday, when they will be expecting me, but I will go tomorrow.'

They stared at each other in the soft twilight, and she didn't find it strange that she could talk to this man in a way such as she could not to Mary or even to Louise.

'I shall go unannounced. You understand, Hamish?'

She saw him pull in a deep breath before he said, 'Aye, ma'am, I understand well enough, and have done for a long time, and my heart is sore for both of you. But I will say this: whatever is wrong he's greatly troubled by it.'

She was thinking, Yes, she supposed he was greatly troubled by it, and he hadn't been able to hide it.

'I'd like to arrive there about five o'clock tomorrow, and I've no need to say one word about the boy because you, Hamish, have been a father to him as his own father never has.'

'Oh, my dear ma'am, don't say that, no. 'Tis circumstance. It is always circumstances that set up situations like this. If Mr Peter could have been here he would have, except again for circumstance, and who is there at the time of the circumstance? Oh yes, who is there at the time of the circumstance? But there's one thing I'd like to swear on, ma'am, and that is, whatever else he has let go astray you'll always have his heart and his deep love.'

She thought she was going to cry. No, no, she mustn't cry. Out of the corner of her eye she could see Mary coming from the yard, and when she was near enough she said, 'There's a storm in the offing, ma'am, and it'll be a whopper.'

'Yes, I think you're right, Mary.' Nyrene looked up at the older woman. 'I've asked Hamish to stay on for half an hour. I've got to do a bit of thinking. It's because of the phone call I've just had. I would have told you straightaway, but you didn't happen to be on the spot and Hamish did, and so I'll leave him to tell you what I may do tomorrow.'

Mary stared at her for a moment, then said, 'Well, ma'am, whatever line you decide to take, we are with you. As me dad would say, if it's to hell,

400

it's to be rough, but far better rough it than be left behind.'

Rather than laugh, she still wanted to cry as she watched them walking away, the tall gaunt man and the woman not half his height, but ten years older. Yet the difference in their ages was in no way noticeable, not like that of a boy of nineteen and a woman bordering on thirty-nine. Yet their love had been more passionate than if they had both been youngsters. He had brought youth into his loving and she had brought experience into hers, and the combination had been dynamic.

But now, what was she to do? Let the present situation develop until there was nothing left of him for her? There was little enough now. Their positions in age could be reversed, for he could be the settled middle-aged man, loving still—oh yes, loving still—but gently, tenderly, considerate, aiming not to hurt, yet crucifying her mind with the knowledge that this man was not the Peter Riley who adored her and even, like his son, could not bear her to be out of his sight for very long. While he was 'on the road' his absence had tried him so much that it had brought him to the point of giving up his career. But now all that had changed. His work was swallowing him up, at least so he said, for was he not a producer, an actor and also a small partner in the business which meant he had to accept invitations to lunch and be present at meetings?

She pulled herself up in her chair. Well, there was one thing certain, her good friend Louise hadn't offered to leave her darling husband for a long weekend unless they had previously talked it over and thought it serious enough for a parting; to her knowledge they had hardly ever been separated since they married. There was a strong love tie between them that even Gwendoline, with her persistence in claiming her sibling relationship, couldn't fray in any way.

She got to her feet and began to walk slowly towards the gate. From here, the view was wide, and as her eyes scanned it through the gathering twilight she did not really see it, for she was arranging her arrival for tomorrow. The only free time he allowed himself during the day was that between four and six. Well, she would arrive during that period, and so there would be no excuse that he was too busy to talk about anything private. She would enforce upon him the reason she had chosen that time to arrive, to give him the opportunity to come out with the truth and tell her what was wrong, for something definitely was wrong. It hadn't needed Louise's tactful suggestion to make her realise this.

As she walked back towards the house it came to her that for the first time she could remember she wasn't worrying about leaving her son for a day.

CHAPTER NINETEEN

Outside Fellburn station the rain was stotting off the pavement like marbles and there wasn't a taxi in sight. When a flash of lightning made her jump back into the doorway, she remained crouched there until she realised a taxi was arriving at the far end of the rank, and with head lowered she dashed towards it, and as she pulled open the door she gasped, 'Flat one, Palace Buildings,' and the driver repeated, 'Right, ma'am; flat one, Palace Buildings. It's a corker, isn't it? There's a tree down in Grove Crescent.'

'Has it been like this for long?'

'Oh, it's been rumbling on and off since dinner time; but the last two hours it's certainly played up. There's flooding all over the place.'

It seemed a very short journey until the taxi pulled up, and she remained inside until she had paid him and extracted her latch key from her bag. It was as the driver reached over and opened the door that there was a flash of lightning followed immediately by a crash of thunder that seemed to cleave the heavens, at the same time lifting her out and across the pavement and up the short passage to the front door.

She had inserted the key in the lock and turned it without knowing she had done so. She stumbled into the small lobby and thrust the door closed, then stood leaning against the panelled wall gasping for breath.

The thunder was still rumbling when she opened the glass door; then she became transfixed where she stood.

There were voices coming from the bedroom, and she recognised not only the one.

Automatically, her hand moved to her hat and she went to straighten it. Then her hand moved strands of her bedraggled hair to each side of her face. Finally, spread wide, she brought it down over her rain-drenched face. Some part of her was wondering why she bothered to do this for it mattered no more how she looked.

The rumbling of thunder had diminished and

her husband's voice came to her clearly now: 'I've told you from the beginning, haven't I?'

And the answer to this was, 'Yes, you have, but I've also told you from the beginning that I never intended to marry, but now you've helped me to change my mind. Don't you understand what I'm willing to give up for you? Ray is wealthy, but you are not; he's a man of the world and you definitely are not; he is also generous, and so far I have yet to be the recipient of your generosity; except of course in one way. Oh yes in one way, but it's that way that makes me sure we are one. Oh, Peter, be sensible. Look, she's had her day. She's coming tomorrow; put it to her that you want a divorce.'

'I'll do no such thing.'

'Then I shall.'

'By God, you won't!'

'You try me. Just you try me.'

'Yvette,'—there was pleading in the voice now— 'please don't do anything like that.'

'Give me a good reason why I shouldn't after what we've been to each other these past months; come on. Anyway, she's not a child, she's a woman and she must know there's something wrong. Your excuses about being invited out to lunch and meetings and so on wouldn't hoodwink an imbecile, and she's no imbecile. She's a crafty woman though, who inveigled a young boy into giving her a child in order that he should marry her. Look, Peter, I'll ask you this. If you weren't married to her and you had met me, would you have married me?'

When there was no answer her cry was triumphant. 'There you see! And I'll tell you something else. If you let me go now you'll never

404

get me from under your skin. You know what the song says, "I've got you under my skin," and I'm under yours, and I mean to stay there.'

He was the first to emerge from the bedroom. He was pulling a shirt over his head and the neck of it was halfway down onto his shoulders. Then Yvette came to his side and what she, too, saw brought her mouth agape for a moment. But only for a moment, for then, her voice light and high, she said, 'Last scene, enter wronged wife.'

'Shut up!'

Riley had turned on her so quickly that his voice caused her to step back from him and to stare at him blankly for a moment. But then, recovering her poise, she said, 'Well, if she's been standing there all this time there's nothing more to say, is there?'

Now he did actually shout, and his words rang through the room as he bawled, 'Get out! Get out!'

And to this her remark was strangely quiet: 'No I'm not going to get out; I have a life to live as well as she, or you.' She nodded from one to the other now. 'What decision she makes is going to direct it one way or the other. I either marry you, stay here and mix in with your motley crowd next door or I marry a wealthy man, travel the world and live a life of luxury. Now,—' her voice took on an angry tone and she marched up to Nyrene to stop only an arm's length from her and say—'I couldn't imagine you in your youth being faced with such a decision and hesitating. You'd have gone for the money and the world tour, I am sure of that. You see I know a lot about you and your early days, more than you think. Well, you think I'm a trollop. Oh yes, I know what you think, and dear Louise, yet ... all right, be what I am, and the daughter of a trollop, I am

405

willing at this moment to give it all up in order to marry the man who is your husband. I should have said, the young man who is your husband now, and someone you should never have married because you could have borne him and fed him at your breast.'

When the small table crashed against the wall, they both started, and Riley, pointing at Yvette, said, 'That's enough!' Then they both turned to look at Nyrene who said in a strained low voice, 'You are quite right in all you say. You, Peter, make your own arrangements; I shall contact my solicitor when I get home. Also I shall have your things packed and sent down.'

She was in the lobby before he cried, 'Nyrene! Please! Please listen. It isn't like that. I don't want—'

Then he was dragged back by Yvette's arms around his neck.

By the time he had thrust her off Nyrene had reached the end of the alley and she was hurrying along the street before he caught up with her and pulled her to a stop, gasping, 'Nyrene, it isn't like it seems.'

'Leave go of me, Peter!'

'No, no! I can explain it. You are my wife; you will always be my wife.'

'If you don't leave go of me I shall call for help.'

His hands dropped from her, and she was about to turn from him when she said, 'Don't try to get in touch with me in any way; what I've got to say to you and you to me can be said through our solicitors. You understand?' And with this she walked from him, her head lowered against the force of the rain and the gale, while he stood still and let the rain drench him to the skin.

He staggered back to the flat and when Yvette approached him and went to put her arms about him he brought his forearm across her chest in such a swift cut that it knocked her flying. It was only the back of the couch that saved her from sprawling to the floor. Then he was bending over her, his lips bared from his teeth and grinding out, 'You, you vicious bitch, you!'

She had pulled herself up straight; and now she was confronting him and crying back at him, 'Me, vicious? I haven't betrayed anyone; I haven't married anybody yet. You were a married man; you could have stopped me any time you liked.'

'Stopped you?' He was spluttering now, the spittle spraying from his lips. 'Nobody could stop you, because you're a snake, a selfish, greedy, sex-mad snake.'

She was backing from him as she said, 'Be careful what you're saying, for you'll be sorry for it tomorrow. Now you heard what she said; she's going to give you a divorce.'

'She's giving me no divorce; but if I were divorced ten times I'd never marry you.'

The look on her face told him that at last he had hit home. In some strange way he had hit at the depth of her, for now she came back at him, saying, 'Well, it's just as well, I suppose, because I'm waking up too. Definitely at this moment I'm waking up, and I'm wondering what on earth attracted me to you. But attracted to you I was. Oh yes, by the commonness, the cheapness, everything opposite to what I had been brought up to expect in a man. And what did all this amount to? A ham actor, a big fish in a tiny bowl. And you wouldn't

407

have reached even that eminence,' she spat the words out, 'if it hadn't been that you married an old woman. She was old then, but look at her now, kicking fifty and looking it. Oh yes, and looking it.'

His tone was quiet as he said, 'Shut up!'

'Don't tell me to shut up, but I will tell you to listen. Have you any idea in that narrow small-town mind of yours the lengths that I was willing to go to in order to be with you? When I compare you with Ray, I realise that I must have been stark staring mad, because you're a weakling.' She now thrust towards him as she hissed, 'Even in bed. You never knew what it was all about.'

'Get out! Go away before . . . before . . .' he said, when she came back quickly, 'Before what? Before you break down and cry? You do cry, don't you?'

She was glaring at him, waiting for a response, and it was some time in coming.

'I've never cried in my life before,' he said, 'but I'll likely cry tonight because you, you sex-maniac, have spoilt something beautiful.'

He watched her throw back her head now and laugh derisively as she said, ' "Beautiful", he says; more like something touching on incest, because she could have been your mother. Having given yourself to a woman who could be older than your mother has driven that poor woman almost mad, I understand. And then you talk about something beautiful. Huh! She can't even carry her age. My mother could give her fifteen years and she doesn't look as old as her.'

'Well, she wouldn't, would she, being a registered whore and never off her back.'

When the clenched fist came out and tore at his face, he thought he was being ripped by a razor

408

blade, but it was just the stone in her ring that was acting as a substitute. He reacted as if he were fighting a man, with his fists pummelling her face. Then he had her by the throat, screaming at her, 'I could kill you at this moment. I could kill you,' when an odd thing seemed to happen: the thumbs that were crossed over her windpipe sprang apart as if he'd had a blow on the head and as she fell into an armchair he staggered back, because the figure he was seeing was that of his son.

He was going mad; he was going back to Larry.

He was supporting himself by leaning over the side of the couch when the croaking voice came through to him, saying, 'I'll make you pay for this; I'll create such a scandal you'll not be able to live it down. I'll put an end to your so-called career; you see if I don't. You'll end up doing the pubs with your comic touch. She won't have you back, that's for sure!'

He watched her, one hand holding her throat the other tight against the side of her cheek as she made her way to the bedroom and when she returned wearing her macintosh coat she had to sidle past him to get to the door, where she turned and said, 'We haven't seen the last of each other, Mr Peter Riley. The next time we meet will be in a courtroom.'

He heard the door close with a bang but he still stood where he was, but now he was nodding to himself, saying, 'Oh yes, the next time we see each other will be across a courtroom, I've no doubt of that at all and by tomorrow your face will be in a mess. Oh yes, it will.' His head still went on bobbing. She would have a photographer to make a record of it. Oh they hadn't seen the last of each other.

As if coming out of a nightmare he blinked his eyes and saw that his light shirt was covered with blood. His shirt had been sopping wet from his diving outside after Nyrene and he had taken no notice of it, because it had cooled his sweating body, but now the sight of the blood brought him fully to himself.

When he looked in the bathroom he couldn't recognise his face for a moment, not because the lower part was covered in blood from what looked like a gash across the bottom of his jaw, but because his eyes seemed to be staring out of his head; the expression wild. They weren't his eyes at all.

He wetted a towel and wiped it round his jaw only to see the slit, all of two inches long, freely oozing blood.

He felt sick, even faint. He put his hand out against the mirror to steady himself, then, turning, he leant his back against the sink and pulled off the wet bloodstained shirt and trousers for they, too, had blood on the waist.

He now opened the medicine cabinet and, taking out a piece of lint he pressed it over the cut, only to see it immediately soaked with blood. He looked round helplessly; then taking up a hand towel he tore it into strips and wound it round the lower part of his face.

As he staggered across the room there came a banging on the front door. But he took no heed of it and made for the couch until he heard a muffled voice saying, 'Open the door, Mr Riley! It's me, Lily.'

He stopped, but it was some seconds before he

released the door catch and turned back into the room, Lily following him and exclaiming, 'What on earth's happened?'

Standing before him, she simply pointed dumbly at his face, then brought out, 'Oh, my goodness, man! Who did that? Her?'

When he did not answer, but dropped on to the couch, she went on rapidly, 'I bumped into her. She was running along the front, her hand to her face, making for her car, I suppose. Oh! You needn't look like that,' and she flapped her forearm wildly, 'they all know. They're not blind or daft ... just because she hides her car round there. But about the other thing. Anna and Jane were in the dressing-room talking, and Anna turned to me saying, "It was her, I saw, Mrs Riley. I know she wasn't supposed to come until tomorrow. But there she was, out on the front street. And she seemed to be arguing with him. Then she walked off and left him standing." Well now,'—Lily shook her head—'hearing that, I put two and two together. And when I bumped into the other one I knew I wasn't far out. But she did that to you?'

He moved the blood-stained pad on his jaw, and then had to spit out some blood onto it before he was able to mutter, 'Be quiet! Lily. Just ... just bring me a wet hand towel.'

Within seconds she had brought him the towel, but when she went to place it on his face she exclaimed, 'Oh no! Mr Riley, a wet towel's not going to stop this bleeding; you'll have to go to hospital.'

'No!'—he had pulled himself to the edge of the couch—'No hospital. Listen! Give me a hand and get me a coat. Dr Carter will be taking his surgery

411

about now.'

'Oh aye. Yes, he's good. But can you make it across the square?'

'Of course, yes, just give me a hand.'

He had said, 'Of course, yes, just give me a hand,' but his head was whirling, and not only with the knowledge that the whole cast must have known what was going on, even David. No, not David, David would have waylaid him. But for the rest, during all these past weeks, their attitudes towards him had never changed.

He thought he was going to pass out.

'Steady up! Lean against there till I lock the door.'

She pressed him against the wall; then, putting her arm around him, she said, 'Come on now!'

The rain pelting against his face seemed to revive him, until Lily opened the surgery door and the smell of damp humanity came at him like a wave.

After she had guided him to the one empty seat in the waiting-room, she went to the reception desk and said, 'My ... my friend has had an accident. His face is badly cut, and he's losing a lot of blood.'

The woman looked past her to where the young man was sitting. His head back against the wall, he was holding a large bloodstained pad to his face. Then peering at Lily she said, 'You're one of the actresses from The Palace aren't you? And that's Mr Riley across there, isn't it?'

'Yes it is, and he's in a very bad way.'

'Oh well, I'll see what I can do.'

When the surgery door opened she slipped from her seat and said to the patient who was about to enter, 'Would you mind?' and she pointed back to

412

Riley.

The man gave way gracefully, saying, 'No, OK.'

Lily helped Riley up from the seat and into the surgery. It was as if she were leading a child, and the doctor, rising from his chair behind his desk, greeted them with, 'Well, well! What's this?' It was evident that he too had recognised them both.

After only a cursory examination of Riley's face, he said, 'You should've gone straight to the hospital with this, but we'll see what we can do without wasting any more time,' and from a cabinet he took a bottle and some dressings and a narrow case. 'This is going to sting, mind,' he said to Riley.

As he continued to clean Riley's face and staunch the flow of blood, he said, 'If this was done with a knife, it was jagged.'

When Riley made no reply, both Lily and the doctor stared down at him.

'Well?' It was the doctor's query.

'It was a stone . . . in a ring.'

Riley closed his eyes, and as the doctor started to ply the needle he gritted his teeth.

Yes, it had been done with a stone in a ring, and she had known what it would do when she had clenched her fist. She had used it as a knuckle-duster.

However, the doctor refrained from further questioning: he had decided the matter was touching on something personal here. But what he said was, 'There! That's as much as I can do for you tonight. I've put ten of the best in, and they're small and neat so there shouldn't be much of a scar. My advice to you now is, put yourself to bed. And don't take off that padding for a couple of days, no matter what it feels like. Come back in a week's time and I'll take those stitches out.'

He now turned and said to Lily, 'You've been very good, although at one time you looked a bit green around the gills,' and she, laughing, said, 'I was green around the gills, and you nearly had another patient.'

He laughed as he led them to the door, saying, 'You'll do.'

The rain was still pouring down, the wind was still blowing, and Lily had to put her arm about his shoulders to steady him as they crossed the square.

She did not speak until she had him in the flat and seated on the couch. 'As the doctor said, the best thing to do is to get you to bed. I'll make a hot drink.'

'I can manage, Lily, thank you. I'm all right now.'

'Don't be silly! You don't think you're going on the stage like that, do you? I must phone Mr Bernice, and Larry too. They'll have some rearranging to do, and quick! So, get it into your head, Mr Riley, that you won't be treading the boards for a day or so.'

*   *   *

Louise and Fred were about to leave the house for Louise's monthly treat of a trip to a good restaurant—the baby-sitter for the ten-year-old Jason was already upstairs playing chess with him—when the phone rang.

Jerking his head back towards the stairs, Fred said, 'Let Nancy take it.'

'No, you see who it is.'

Reluctantly, Fred grabbed up the phone, saying, 'Beardsley here.'

414

'I'm ... I'm Lily, from the theatre, you know.'

'Oh yes, Miss Poole from the theatre.' He glanced towards Louise, then nodded at the phone, saying, 'What can I do for you, miss?'

'It's Mr Riley, he's in a bad way. There's been an accident.'

'An accident? What kind of an accident; car?'

'No, nothing like that; there's ... well you're a friend of his and so you know all about him and his wife. Well, his wife came here unexpectedly tonight.'

'What!'

And then the voice was a shout, saying, 'Perhaps it's because of the wind; can't you hear?'

'I can hear all right, woman! You said his wife came unexpectedly tonight; we weren't expecting her until tomorrow.'

'Well, she was here. She was seen talking to Mr Riley in the street. But Mr Riley had another visitor. I don't know all the ins and outs, the only thing I know is his face is slashed. It's just missed his lips. But I've taken him to the doctor's and he's had it stitched.'

There was a silence on the phone now, and Fred again looked at Louise before he bawled, 'His jaw slashed? Where is he now?'

'In bed. Mr Bernice and the others have been in and gone; and I must go now, because I'll be on soon. I'll leave the key behind the footscraper; it's at the right of the front door. Are you there?'

'Yes, yes, I'm here, and thank you.' His tone was quiet now. 'Thank you very much for taking all this trouble. It's very kind of you indeed.'

'Not at all, not at all; I'm very fond of him. He's done a lot for me; I mean in my career, helped me a lot; but I can't help saying he's a silly bugger, and Mrs Riley's such a lovely woman. People would say he deserves all he's got but ... but he's nice at bottom. Anyway, that's where the key is.'

When the line went dead Fred put down the receiver and turned to Louise and, slowly shaking his head, he said, 'Yes, as she says he is a silly bugger. That should make me laugh but it doesn't.'

'What is it? What is it then?'

'We'll soon find out. As far as I can gather, Nyrene came on the hop, and he's got a split jaw. How, I don't know, but we'll soon find out. So you can say goodbye to your posh dinner.'

Louise dropped onto a hall chair and, beating one hand on her lap, she said, 'She must have figured something out and my invitation clinched it. And if she found that one there, there was bound to be words, plain words, and that'll be the finish of him with her because she's so conscious of her age and of him needing youth. It must have been going on all these weeks. And he's hookwinked us, too.'

'Well, what did you expect him to do, take us into his confidence? Don't be silly, woman. Come on now! Let's get away and find out exactly what's wrong.'

As Louise rose from her seat, the phone rang again, and almost with a pout of exasperation, he snatched it up, to hear a voice cry, 'Fred!'

'Yes, Gwendoline.'

'Get yourself over here quick and see what that common low-class individual has done to my daughter.'

'Well, before I come and see it, can you explain what he's done?'

'Yes, I'll explain. He's not only blacked her eyes and battered her face, but he's tried to murder her. You should see the marks on her throat.'

Fred said nothing, but turned to Louise and shook his head.

At this Louise put her head to the side of the phone and heard Gwendoline say, 'Did you hear what I said, Fred? I said murder. He attempted to murder her. Her beautiful face is ruined. He'll go to prison for this. I'll see to it. I'll make such a scandal.'

'I think you'll find there are two sides to this, Gwendoline, and before I come to see you I'm going to see him, because from what I can gather he's been slashed across the face. So, ask your daughter to explain that away, will you? Until I get to the bottom of this, goodbye, Gwendoline.' And he banged down the phone; then stood looking glumly at Louise for a moment before he said, 'My God! What an outcome! Where is it going to end?'

CHAPTER TWENTY

Nyrene was seated at one end of the kitchen table and, at either side of her sat Mary and Hamish. Mary had her hand on top of Nyrene's, patting it as she said, 'Oh! ma'am, it's the saddest day of my life, it is really.'

Nyrene looked at her and said quietly, 'And mine too, Mary.'

Her face was devoid of tears. Strangely, she hadn't cried at all since she had run from Riley through the rain to her father-in-law's house.

There, she had stayed the night and had left early next morning. That was yesterday morning; but there had been last night when, alone in bed and going over every minute from the time she opened the glass door until she closed it behind her, she still hadn't cried.

Hamish now said, 'I cannot imagine, ma'am, Mr Peter striking a woman, no matter what for, then trying to throttle her, but I can well imagine that long-legged piece whom I've seen but once taking a knife to a man; and a rough cut diamond would be better than any knife. Yes, I can imagine her using that. The devil creates beautiful fiends, but what I cannot get over, ma'am, is why you won't speak to him, especially as he is in such a state.'

Nyrene's voice was very firm now as she said, 'Hamish, I am determined on this point; I do not wish to speak to my husband, and so, as I said, I want you or Mary, whoever answers his call, to make any excuse you like; that I am out or busy; or to just tell him the truth: that I have no wish to speak to him.'

'Pardon me saying so, ma'am, but I don't think I can do that, so if you don't mind, I'll leave the answering of the phone to Mary. She is looking at it from a woman's point of view and I, at the moment, am seeing his; not, mind,' his voice changed now, 'that I condone anything that he has done, not one wee thing; no, no, I don't condone; but I know something of the temptations a man is brought to, and therefore I understand his plight when separated from you week after week. A young sprite comes on the scene and throws herself at his head . . . at his whole body. Ma'am, there are those things that I call circumstances that we have

418

discussed before. It's the circumstances that make the tragedies and the environment or the place that provides the setting for them.'

Returning his intense stare, Nyrene said, 'Well, Hamish, there could be circumstances in environments in the future. He is still a young man and I am a middle-aged woman.'

'No, it's not a matter of your being a middle-aged woman,' Mary put in quickly as she wagged a hand towards Nyrene in protest against such denigration. 'Nobody looking at you would say you were almost forty, never mind fifty.'

Nyrene did not reply, but just looked kindly at Mary and shook her head. Then she said, 'What I really want to talk about is our business venture'— she was looking at Hamish now—'both in the barn and on the land. Now the land will be entirely your concern, Hamish. You can hire what help you like, and you need a cultivator as you've said. Well, see to that. Once that rough patch of land is cleared and drained and fenced, then we can talk about what's best to be done with it.' Smiling wanly at him now, she added, 'By that time you'll have it all cut and dried in your own mind, if I know you,' to which his answer was simply, 'Likely, ma'am. Likely.'

She looked from one to the other now as she said, 'My end of the business, I can see progressing faster than I can cope with on my own. My main asset in this will be Mr Rice. For his whole working life he has been an accompanist and he's so happy to be brought out of forced retirement, or redundancy; and you've both seen Miss Gray at work: she's very good; at least with her feet, although, unlike Miss Fuller, she'll never make an

419

elocutionist.'

'Well, that's something to be thankful for; that Fuller woman gives me a pain in the neck with her plum-in-her-mouth voice. She's worse than any Professor Higgins.'

'She's a very good teacher, Mary.'

'Yes, I suppose she is,' Mary said, then added, 'What I can't get over is the child taking to her; she'll soon have him speaking as she does.'

'Well, that wouldn't be a bad thing, would it, Mary?'

'Oh, I don't know so much. Anyway while we're talking of the child, I think that both sides of the business are going to be good for him because whenever he can he'll want to be out with you, Hamish, and who knows? in time he might get his strength back and even do some digging for you.' Nyrene smiled, then letting out a long sigh she seemed to think for a moment before she added, 'I think it's good for him, too, to meet people, all kinds of people, and that's what the barn will provide for him.'

There followed a short silence before Hamish said, 'What are you telling him, ma'am?'

There was no need to ask to whom he was referring, so Nyrene answered, 'I told him that his father's been engaged by a touring company that had been about to go abroad when the leading man took ill and . . . and his father took over his place.'

'Do you think he believed you, ma'am?'

Nyrene looked back into the rugged face and answered truthfully, 'I don't know, Hamish.'

'What did he say to it?'

'Nothing.'

'Then he didn't believe you, ma'am.'

'That might be true, Hamish. That might be true.' She rose abruptly from the table, saying, 'Well, that's our future taken care of: the two concerns will eventually run as one; or, at least will be booked as one, and we'll share the profits.'

Both Hamish and Mary were on their feet now, with Hamish saying, 'It's kind of you, indeed it is, ma'am. Such a proposition is not to be sneezed at; but neither of us want it or need it. We've talked it over, haven't we, Mary?'

'Yes, ma'am.' Mary was nodding at Nyrene. 'We're only too glad to be with you and work here, and you pay us very generously. And then you're seeing to the alterations being made to the rooms, and that addition at the end. We couldn't ask for more. Hamish isn't in need of any; neither am I.'

Nyrene looked from one to the other and said quietly, 'I'm very lucky to have you, but the contract, as it will be made out shortly, will stand,' and she turned and walked out of the kitchen. In her bedroom she dropped onto the side of the bed. What she wanted to do was to lay her head on the pillow and ... the word 'cry' brought her up from the bed and to the dressing-table, where she combed her hair back, then marched out of the room and into the nursery where her son was endeavouring to copy large coloured letters from a book.

Two days later Riley phoned. As she left the room she heard Mary answer him: 'In the morning.' How long Mary was on the phone she did not know, but in the evening she knew he had called again, and after some time Mary put the phone down and came to her, saying, 'Ma'am, I can't stand it; it's awful. Won't you just say a word?'

421

'No, Mary, I'm saying nothing.'

The pattern was repeated the following day. Then, on the day following that she received a letter. She knew it was from him and she held it between her fingers as if it were burning her. She went up to her room and to the writing desk in the corner and, sitting down, she stared at it and her hand almost took up the paper-knife lying against the blotting pad, but she checked it. Then she tore the envelope down the middle; and continued to tear it until it looked as if the letter had been through a shredding machine. With her forearm she swept the myriad pieces into the wastepaper basket, and it was then that the tears came into her eyes.

When she reached the bed they were flowing freely; then what seemed to be a great hard structure moved slowly up from her chest into her throat, leaving its pain behind: it was like a knife cutting her heart in two. When, through her wide-open mouth the bolt erupted, it caused a sound like a scream to escape her lips. Then she was on the bed beating her fists into the pillow, and such were her cries that they reached the kitchen and brought Mary up the stairs at a run.

When, an hour later, Dr Johnson stood by her side, she was still crying, but softly now, and he, looking at Mary while at the same time taking Nyrene's pulse, said, 'What's brought this on?' and Mary answered, 'It's private. She'll likely tell you, that's if she wants to, when she comes round.'

To this, he said, 'Well that's something to look forward to. But the state she's in, I should imagine it will be a couple of days before I have that privilege.'

422

Nyrene did not give him the privilege, and he had to discover from other sources the reason for her collapse.

CHAPTER TWENTY-ONE

During the next month, Hamish and Mary were married, and the only thing that marred the day was the absence of Mr Peter. They had their three days' honeymoon while Ivy and Ken kept Nyrene company.

The other significant event was that Gwendoline made, through Fred, an urgent plea to Nyrene to drop divorce proceedings against Riley because her daughter had agreed to marry Mr Ray Zussman.

The fact that Yvette had been involved in a car accident and couldn't, for the time being, join him on the yachting holiday as arranged had brought him to the flat in London, where Gwendoline had diplomatically established themselves soon after the incident so as to escape further gossip and probing from the local paper. She had been wise enough to know that were she to accuse Riley of assault, thereby making the matter public, it would put paid to any further attention from the rich suitor.

To the message Fred carried, Nyrene had responded, 'I want a divorce, and so does he,' which brought a sharp denial from Fred. 'He wants no divorce, Nyrene. He's nearly round the bend and he'll carry that scar to the grave, and it's done nothing for his good looks.' And when she had interrupted him with, 'Fred, please!' he had come back at her, crying, 'If you told the truth, Nyrene, you don't want a divorce.'

'Oh yes I do, Fred,' she had answered him. 'I want a divorce for many reasons: I want to be able to grow old without fear of the coming years; I want to rid myself completely of the fear of what has just happened and for which I seem to have been waiting ever since our marriage; I want a divorce because I can no longer stand covert censure, even ridicule, a woman of my age snapping up a comparative youngster. That isn't a figment of my imagination. I've heard it said. Moreover, you forget, Fred, that I have a son to see to, and that he'll have to be seen to for some time yet, and that I may not have him for all that long.'

It had been a long pause before Fred came back, saying quietly, 'What about your heart, Nyrene?'

And to this she had answered, 'Fred, please don't make matters more difficult for me.'

'That would be the last thing on my mind, Nyrene, and you know it,' he said. 'Anyway, what message should I take back to my demented sister?'

She thought for a moment, and then said, 'All right, tell her I'll waive it for the time being; but only for the time being. And so she had better get to work fast on this suitor,' she had added bitterly.

'Well, Nyrene, I'm going to say this, and it's my final word on the matter, there'll be plenty of others waiting for him when you do go through with it, and they won't be youngsters either. I really don't know what happened between them to cause her to mark him, but I'd like to bet he's had his fill of youngsters for the rest of his life.'

424

It was the summer break. With the exception of Riley and Lily, the company was scattered. It had been arranged well beforehand that David, Larry and Riley should each give up a month to see to the overall running of the theatre and restaurant during the time it was leased for various stage entertainments. But when Riley emphasised that all he wanted was a fortnight free from duty and that for the rest he would see to the running of the business, David and Larry, being well aware of Riley's present circumstances, felt the reason he wished to remain in Fellburn was to be near his close friends and family, because if anyone needed support at this time he did, and so they had readily fallen in with his suggestion. Although his work had not suffered, he was a changed man in many ways.

In Lily's case, her husband being on the long haulage runs to the Continent, she knew it would be unwise to pressure him to take a holiday, for in the present state of affairs there was always somebody waiting to jump into his job. She had been glad of the opportunity to assist Riley in the work and to see to his everyday needs.

Fred and Louise had always insisted that he spend Sunday with them. Also, during the last very trying months he had become closer still to his father. Alex would often pop in in the mid-afternoon, and he and Nurse had taken to visiting the performance on a Saturday night. And after the performance they would join him at the flat for a late coffee. And should Betty and Harry happen to be present there would be much discussion and some laughter, especially over Harry's opinion of ballet dancers.

But there was no laughter on Betty's face the day she hurried to her dad's place, as she called Nurse's house.

Alex was on the point of going out. 'What's up with you, something wrong?'

'It's Mam,' she said.

'What's she been up to now?'

'That's to be seen. You know Christy's, the all-night café, opposite the theatre?'

'Aye, who doesn't?'

'Well, Peggy Mear, one of our assistants, her mother works there at night, washing up. She said her mother told her that Mam goes there and sits for hours over a cup of tea. She says she's known her get up, go out, then within an hour or so come back again.'

'In Christy's, your mam?'

'Yes, Dad, me mam.'

'Well, what would she be doing in there at night time?'

'Dad, wake up and think.'

'I am awake, lass, and I am thinking, but what mischief could she be doing in Christy's, or from Christy's?'

'She can see right across the road to the theatre and she can see Peter's flat, and the comings and goings there. Even after dark, the street is lit up like Blackpool Tower until well after eleven o'clock. She's not there every night, apparently, but often enough for Mrs Mear to take notice of her sitting there and staring out of the window.' Betty's voice was low now as she said, 'She's up to no good, Dad. Why should she be sitting in an all-night café? And what's happening to Florrie? She always used

426

to tell me things, though not of late. Mam's likely threatened her.'

'Oh, I know what's happening to Florrie,' Alex nodded, 'she's getting scared. She came round here yesterday and said her mam has started to lock her in at nights, both back door and front door. The place could be set afire. She told me she asked her mam if she could go and stay with Uncle Frank during the holidays, but the answer was a definite no. Frank would have the girl tomorrow, and so I'm going to look into that.'

Betty said now, 'I've got to get back, Dad, but oh, she worries me to death, that woman. She really does. She's me mother and I shouldn't say this, but she's bad, she's wicked. By the way,'—she looked at him keenly now—'you haven't got that pain again have you?'

'No, no, of course not. What makes you think that?'

She smiled wanly now as she said, ''Cos I never know whether you're lying or not.'

'Go on, with you! And don't worry about this other business. I tell you what, I'll have a walk round there late one night and perhaps I shall get an idea of what she's up to.'

As she was leaving she said, 'Peter's going on a holiday. He told me yesterday that he's going to take a holiday during the last fortnight before they open again. But he wouldn't say where he's going. Do you know, Dad?'

'No, lass, no, I don't. I've got my own ideas about where, but I may be wrong, so I'll keep them to meself.'

'Oh, I see.' She nodded to him, then asked, 'Does he ever mention her?'

427

'Never. Nor do I.'

Betty put out her hand and patted her father's forearm, saying, 'I'm glad he's got you, Dad. The Beardsleys are nice people, but they're not family.' She found herself now pushed roughly into the street. Then, his voice low, he hissed, 'You forget, lass, that your mother is family. The Beardsleys have been kinder to him than anybody else in his life, and that includes his wife an' all. Don't talk to me about family. Go on, get yourself away.'

She moved two or three steps back from him now and laughed as she said, 'Yes, when I think about it, Dad, you're right. You nearly always were. Be seeing you.'

'Be seeing you, lass.'

*　　　*　　　*

It had been a warm September, yet now in the third week, the larches were showing the first tints of autumn. This part of the wood was always beautiful in the autumn.

His heart beating painfully against his ribs, he saw he was but a dozen or so steps from the path; and there, right in front of him, was the back gate.

What would she do on the sight of him, and what would she say? Well, it was his son's birthday and he was bringing him a present. Surely she would allow him to see his son. However she viewed it, he had a special love for the child despite, deep inside, blaming him for having kept them apart so much. But what he really wanted was a sight of her face, just to look into her eyes again, even if he were to see nothing there but scorn.

The wood thinned into the copse and he stepped

428

from it and onto the rough road in front of the gate.

Having heard the distant sound of the boy's voice he had expected to see him with Hamish, but there he was walking down the drive by her side. It must have been the boy who first saw him, because his high cry brought her to a sudden halt, and now the child was running towards him.

It wasn't the run he remembered interspersed with leaps like that of a young antelope, but more like a hurried shambling walk; and then the boy's arms were around his neck and he was on his hunkers before him, their faces close.

'Daddy! Oh, Daddy! You're back from abroad parts. Oh, Daddy!' The arms were tight around his neck, the cheek was pressed tight against his; then the fingers were tracing the scar that ran from near the lobe of his ear to the bottom of his chin. 'You've scratched yourself, Daddy.'

'Yes, son. Yes.' He could hardly make out the child's face now. He stood up and gazed up the drive. She hadn't moved, not a step. He stooped sideways now and pressed the parcel into the boy's arms, saying, 'For your birthday.'

'Oh, Daddy! Oh, thank you! Thank you. Mummy!' The boy turned and seemed surprised to see his mother was still standing where he had left her. For a moment, the bright smile disappeared from his face; then, grabbing his father's hand, he pulled him slowly towards her. 'Look! Mummy, a present from Daddy.'

Suddenly, they were standing but an arm's length from each other. The child to the side of them looked first at one face then the other. Then he seemed to throw his body round, and now he was walking, not running, towards the yard, calling, 'Mr Mac! Mr Mac! Daddy's home.'

'Hello, Nyrene.' Riley's voice was scarcely above a whisper. He had wanted to say 'dear', but had thought better of it. When she did not respond, but simply stared at him, he added hesitantly, 'I ... I wanted to see him and give him something for his birthday.'

'You had no need to make the journey; you could have sent it.' Her voice was cool.

But now his came back harshly and snapped, 'I ... I couldn't have posted it; I wanted to see him. That's my due if nothing else. You ... you can't stop me seeing him.'

'In the future a time can be arranged.' The words caused him to jerk round from her until his back was almost turned towards her, where he stood silent for a moment before turning to her again, muttering, 'Oh, Nyrene, if I live to be a hundred I shall never forgive myself for what I've done to you. Yet I must say, it had nothing like the importance you have put on it. But I'm not going to blame anyone but myself; I tried to explain to you in my letters. Couldn't you understand?'

'I never read your letters.'

His eyes widened, his head jerked, his lips fell apart, and then, his voice full of disbelief, he said, 'You didn't?'

'Yes, I do mean I didn't read them. Of the five you sent, one was shredded, the rest were burnt. Perhaps this will now convince you of the extent of my feelings about the matter. I withheld instigating divorce proceedings because of a plea from Fred, but now that the person in question is married they can be taken up at any time; and then you'll be free to carry on with your life as I will with mine.'

He stared at her.

'I don't want any life away from you, Nyrene, and in your heart you know that, and in my own defence I will say just this: what I did is happening every day between thousands of couples, but it doesn't break up their lives irrevocably. If you had deigned to read my letters—at least the first one— you would have understood that what happened had nothing to do with love, a love such as we had for each other, and that there wasn't a minute of my day, any day, that you weren't in my mind, and that I didn't long for you.' He paused and, his voice dropping to a quivering whisper, he ended, 'And still do. Oh, and still do.'

For a moment he imagined he saw a softening in her face: her eyelids blinked, her tongue moved over her lips as if searching for saliva which it must have been doing because when she spoke her voice was hoarse: 'What's done's done, Peter,' she pronounced, as a judge might a sentence. 'You can't erase the past. The greater the intensity of it the greater the break. All I want now is peace of mind, and that I could never have with you. The knowledge of life garnered during those extra twenty years told me so at the very beginning; but I wouldn't listen, so I've had to pay for my deafness.'

He stared into her now stiff face. He had never in his life felt really young, not gauche young, but at this moment he was being made to feel so for he was being confronted by a middle-aged woman. Her skin was still unlined, her figure was still slim, her hair showed no grey, yet the eyes had aged. She *was* middle-aged. He had noticed this, particularly with women: they could be in their sixties and their

431

figure could look spruce, their hair could be dyed to a natural tint, the face could hardly show a line, yet it was in the eyes that age was written. Never before had he looked upon Nyrene as a woman approaching fifty, which was definitely middle-aged, but the woman now standing before him seemed to be set in her years, and he realised that she was acting no part now, she was being herself, her true self. All she wanted, she had said, was peace of mind. She was talking like age, age beyond her own age. In his opinion, you didn't desire peace of mind until you recognised that death was imminent.

The well-remembered thick Scottish brogue, raised high now in excitement, broke the spell that was binding their glances, and Hamish's voice came at them, crying, 'Oh, Mr Peter, sir! Oh, am I glad to see you! Oh, this is a nice surprise!'

The tall Scot now grabbed Peter's hand and was wagging it vigorously as he continued to express his pleasure: 'Oh, it really is good to see you, Mr Peter, sir! And you remembered the linty's birthday. Well, well!'

When he could get a word in, Riley said, 'How are you, Hamish?'

'Me? I'm as fit as a fiddle, Mr Peter, sir. Now that I've got a wee wifie to knock about, my life is full.' His laugh was high, and it brought a smile to Riley's face; but there was no laughter in him, for he was now watching her walk quickly up the drive towards the yard.

Hamish too turned and looked after her, then turning back to Riley, he said, 'Come along, sir. Come along. And we'll have a cup of tea.'

'No, thank you, Hamish. I'd . . . I'd better be—'

The Scot now bawled at him: 'You're not going on your way, if that's what you were about to say, before you have a drink. And there's the child; look at him, dancing along with his mother now. He misses you. He's missed you more than some people would notice.' Hamish's head was bobbing now, his face straight. 'That child knows more than he gives away; he knows fine well things are not right.'

'I'll go into the barn, Hamish.'

'Oh, Mr Peter, sir; come into your own kitchen.'

Riley's voice was low now as he said, 'It's no longer my kitchen, Hamish, and you know it, so if you don't mind I'll have a cup of something in the barn. I'm sure Mary'll bring it across.'

Mary brought across a tray of tea and scones, and long before she neared him she was exclaiming, 'Oh, Mr Peter! Well, it has come to something, hasn't it? Dear, dear, dear!' She put the tray noisily down by his side; then taking one of his hands in hers, she patted it, saying, 'Oh, 'tis good to see you again. Oh, why has this come about? You know something?' She leant her head towards him. 'My heart's broken for you both. She's lost, she is. All this business of drama and dancing and that big fellow's'—she thumbed over her shoulder to where Hamish was now coming up the room—'allotment or market garden business, whatever he calls it, is just padding to suppress her feelings, like salve on a sore.'

Riley's throat was full, and he found it difficult to speak as he said, 'Thanks, Mary,' then added, 'It's good to see you again. I . . . I was sorry I couldn't get to the wedding.'

'So were we. Oh yes, so were we, Mr Peter.'

Hamish had now seated himself on the edge of the stage next to Riley and, addressing Mary, he said, 'Didn't you bring another cup, woman?' to which she answered pertly, 'No, I didn't! and yours is on the kitchen table, and in a mug as usual. And you drink that up when it's hot, Mr Peter.'

Hamish looked sadly at Riley as he said, 'It's a mistake I made late in life; I made the mistake, not in marrying ... no, because I had a number to choose from, but in picking an old body with a tongue.'

Mary reached out and brought her hand none too gently across the big head as she retaliated, 'And one that abuses me. You're a witness to that, Mr Peter.'

'I'll go now and get me mug meself.'

'Sit where you are! I'll fetch it.'

Hamish had half-risen but then he sat back with a smile on his face, saying, 'Do that woman. Do that.'

Mary let out a sigh before turning and hurrying down the studio, and Hamish spoke quietly to Riley, 'There mighn't be much time before she's back,' he said. 'Where are you staying, Mr Peter, sir?'

'Oh, I took a room in a hotel in Aberdeen. I'll be going back tomorrow.'

'You'll be still on holiday?'

'Yes, I've just started on a fortnight. I've stayed on during the summer break to see to things.'

'Oh, so your time's your own?'

'Yes. Yes, for the next few days, Hamish.'

'Well then why don't you stay on? Now, now!' He raised his hands as if to silence something that Riley was about to say. 'There's no reason why you

434

shouldn't have a holiday at this end? Wait!' Again his hand was up. 'There's my little but an' ben. There are only two rooms, but they're comfortable. Everything you need for living. Well, I lived in it for years. I keep it aired; I wouldn't part with it. You've seen it, at least from the outside. As for the linty, he knows the inside of it as well as me. And if you are fixed up there, well, I could bring him down. Now, how about that?'

Riley looked at this kind man, and his throat constricted again so that he had to swallow deeply before he said, 'As you say Hamish, it sounds a good suggestion. I would like it very much. Do you think she would let the boy—?'

'Oh, yes, yes. Anyway she can't stop you seeing your own son, even the bad ones get that privilege.' Then lowering his voice he went on, 'If there is anything I can do for you, Mr Peter, sir, let me know, because I consider it's a bloody shame—and that's swearing to it and I'm not a swearing man— that you should be forbidden your own house while my little woman and me are sitting cosy in those rooms up there; and what's more, deep in me I know I'll never feel really at home until you're back in your own place.'

It was really too much: this thoughtfulness, this kindness, this sincerity would break him down. Quickly now Riley turned to the tray and poured himself a cup of tea, and as he did so Mary entered the barn again, accompanied by the boy, and after handing Hamish his mug of tea she turned to Peter, saying, 'This young man'—she tousled the boy's hair—'is dying to show you his poultry, Mr Peter.'

'Oh, you have hens?'

'Yes, Daddy, ten hens and a cock. They call the

cock, Jock.' He laughed, a high boyish laugh, and they all smiled broadly at him; but, glancing towards the tray and the plate of scones which had not been touched, he said, 'May I have a scone, Mary?' Not Mrs A. now but Mary. She said sternly, 'Not to feed to the hens, Master Charles.'

'Half . . . and half, Mary. I promise.'

'Oh you!' She took the scone from the plate and thrust it into the boy's hand, and at this, Riley said, 'And may I have one too?' And as he took one from the plate he exchanged a look with his son, and the boy's eyes twinkled back at him.

Mary and Hamish watched the father and son walk down the barn together, and as the outer door closed on them Mary turned to her husband now and in a low voice said, 'She wants to see you; and I think it's to tell you to mind your own business.'

'Oh, very likely, my dear, very likely; I would expect nothing else.'

'What have you said to him?'

'Me, woman, said to him? Nothing, except I've offered him the cottage for a few days. He's weary. Can't you see he's weary? And what's more he's lost, a spent man. But she won't see it.'

'I know that as well as you, but you're not going to make her see it.'

'No, but God works in strange ways.'

'He might,' she came back at him quickly, 'but you're not a relation of His so don't expect Him to hand you a wee miracle.'

His head went back and his laughter filled the barn, and when his arm went about her and he pulled her tightly to him and, bending down to her, gave her a very wet kiss on the mouth, she pushed him, saying, 'Give over. Stop your antics. But go on

436

in and face the music. One thing I do know is that she won't take kindly to you letting him have the cottage.'

'You never know. You never know.'

Hamish's knock on the sitting-room door was tentative and when he entered the room Nyrene was standing near the fire. 'You wished for a word with me, ma'am?' he said.

She turned towards him and stared at him before saying quietly, 'What are you planning, Hamish?'

'Planning, ma'am?'

'That's what I said. We know each other, you and I, and you think I'm a very hard woman for taking my present stand, and knowing you I'm sure you are thinking of ways that could bring about a reconciliation, aren't you? But let me tell you, you're merely going to embarrass me.'

'Ma'am, ma'am, just wait a wee, please. As for planning, you're quite wrong. I never had a thought in my head that way; and as for embarrassing you, it's just because I don't want to embarrass you that I have done what I have. But I wouldn't call it planned; it was done on the spur of the moment. And I was thinking of you as I did it. There he is, walking with his son as if in a strange place, and I must say truthfully I can't help feeling very sorry for the man. However, that said and done, the rest is your business. But what I have done is to *save* you embarrassment. He has been working hard all the summer months in the theatre keeping things going in a managing capacity, probably because likely he had no place to go. And now he's taken a fortnight off, so I understand, so as to see his son. To my eye and ear he looks weary and sounds it, and even though you intend not to have anything to do with him, there still remains his son. I know that for some time now he hasn't seen him very often, but I also know he has a deep love for the child, and he wants to see him during the next few days of his leave, so would you rather have him come here every day, or let me take the boy to see him at the cottage? You know, ma'am, you can't stop him from seeing his son. Now am I causing you embarrassment, ma'am, or saving you embarrassment? If it be that you would rather have him up here so you can have the boy under your eye, it's quite easy for me to tell him that you have given permission for him to come. But one thing I do know, whichever way it goes, he means to see the boy a few times more because it may be a long, long time before he sees him again. Your tale to the boy of his daddy going abroad may have some truth in it; for I understand he's had a very good offer from America.'

Immediately, Hamish asked himself why on earth had he added that? Surely, it could only have been God or the Devil who had prompted him to stick in such a lie. One thing for sure, it had made her eyes widen. And now he ended, 'So, ma'am, there it is: what would you have me do? He'll be out of your hair, so to speak, if he goes to the cottage. It is at the back of beyond, so it's unlikely he'll be recognised anyway. And either way it'll only be a matter of days.'

She had turned from him, realising that with those knowledgeable eyes peering she could not give him a true answer, and so she muttered, 'It must be the cottage then.'

'Thank you, ma'am. And now, would it be

convenient for me to have an hour or so off to show him the ropes? Besides everything else, I think, ma'am, the rest will do him good. So, it'll be all right to take the boy now and again to see him?'

Again it was a moment before she was able to answer. 'Yes. I suppose so. You can get Mary to pack a basket with what is necessary for his meals for the next day or two.'

'Thank you, ma'am, that will indeed save a lot of trouble. And will it be all right on these occasions to take the car?'

This time she did not hesitate in answering, saying, 'Certainly.'

Half an hour later she stood looking out of the window of the spare bedroom from where, just visible, she had a view of the end of the drive and the car standing in the roadway. She could just see the tall figure of Hamish depositing something in the boot; then she saw her son put his arms around his father's neck. They held each other for a moment before Riley turned hastily and got into the car while Mary stood holding the boy close to her side. And when the car moved out of sight they remained standing, not looking down the road now, but at each other as if one or other was talking. It was when the boy leant against Mary and she stroked his hair that Nyrene turned away; she could take it no more.

What had happened to make her son do that? He must have been disturbed in some way. Hamish must have told him he would be going to see his father again tomorrow, and at the cottage, and he had always looked forward to going to Hamish's wee house; then there was the birthday present that Peter had brought him. Normally, he always brought his presents to her and they opened them together; but this time she had noted that he had gone straight upstairs to his bedroom. He no longer slept in the nursery, as that room had been turned into a schoolroom, part of which had been given over to the display of his train set, although it was now an area very much reduced from what it had been in the barn.

These were the actions of her son that were troubling her because they were the outcome of his thinking and his thinking was much older than his years.

When she went downstairs she found Mary in the kitchen on her own and, looking round, she said, 'Where is he?'

Mary was bending down to the oven—she was pushing an earthenware dish along the bottom shelf—and she said, 'He heard a hen cackling, so he's gone to see if it's laid.' She could have added, 'He's got one of his quiet turns coming on and he's trying to walk it off.'

Mary straightened up and dusted her hands one against the other; she then moved to the sink. Still with her back to Nyrene, she heard her say quietly, 'What happened at the gate, Mary? I mean, was Charles very upset?'

Mary did not turn round to her for some seconds, and when she did she drew her forefinger across the bottom of her nose: her cheeks were wet and her voice was thick as in a tone that she had never before used to her mistress, she said, 'Of course he was upset about something, ma'am! What did you expect? I could say the less he sees of him the more he misses him. And you want to know what happened? Well, the child looked up at me and came out with one of his strange sayings, and this broke me down. And what did he say, ma'am? He said "My mummy and daddy aren't glad any more, are they, Mary?" Did you ever hear anything like that, ma'am, "My mummy and daddy aren't glad any more, are they, Mary?" ' Then, grabbing a tea towel, she rolled it up into almost a tight ball and threw it onto the draining board, and with that she left the kitchen almost at a run, across the yard and up into her comfortable sitting-room; and sitting there on the couch, she cried as she hadn't done for years . . .

Back in the kitchen Nyrene remained standing, but now she was leaning against the kitchen table as if for support. And she was asking herself why it was that in circumstances such as she was now in, the sympathy and understanding always seemed to go to the perpetrator, with the victim being made to feel guilty, guilty of hardness, of lack of compassion and understanding.

Slowly now she went upstairs, and when she entered her room and made as to sit on the side of the bed she checked herself. No, a straight-backed chair was what she needed at the moment: bed created all the wrong feelings, feelings that weakened you, saddened you, frightened you and, yes, even made you feel guilty.

CHAPTER TWENTY-TWO

The first week's play of the season was over. Riley and Larry Fieldman were standing outside the theatre and Larry, drawing in a deep breath, said, 'Phew! I'm always glad when the first week's over, especially with a comedy.'

The doors behind them opened and they turned to see Lily Poole emerging, accompanied by one of the cast, and it was the young woman who on a laugh, said, 'Thank God that's over. Only thirty-six more to go before the next holiday.' Then, as they too laughed, she added, 'But it went down well, didn't it?' And she looked at Riley, adding, 'And by, your legs must be tired!'

'They are. You've said it, they are.'

'Are you coming for a drink, Riley?' Larry asked.

'No, not tonight, Larry, thanks; all I want to do is get my feet up.'

'Well, I'm going to have a short one. You coming Lucy? and you, Lily?'

'You bet,' said Lily; 'I want my one gin and tonic to build me up for tomorrow.' She giggled, then added, 'It's cleaning up and wash day. Which reminds me: I might as well slip along with you now, Mr Riley, and gather up your odds and sods. Be seeing you in five minutes, Mr Larry, and you, Lucy.'

'What about Mass tomorrow?' Larry said, and she answered pertly, 'I'll leave it up to you, Mr Larry, to do enough praying for us both.'

'You'll have Father Honeyset after you one of these days.'

'Oh,'—she waved her hand at him—'I've already had him. He called one Sunday afternoon. I was still in my dressing-gown and he never turned a hair, nor when he asked where Johnny was and I said he was still in bed. We sat and had a cup of tea together and he told me an Irish joke, he did, yes he did. But the climax came just as he was about to go. He went to the bedroom door and banged on it

442

with his fist and yelled, "Get out of that, Johnny Poole! I've come to take you to hell." '

They were all laughing loudly now, and Riley said, 'He didn't!'

'Yes, he did. He's a star, that fellow.'

She now turned to Riley, saying, 'You don't mind if I pick them up now, do you?'

'Mind? Why should I mind the washerwoman following her trade?'

'Watch it, or you'll get all your stuff back unironed! Anyway, be with you in a few minutes, Larry,' she added.

Good-nights were exchanged; then Riley and Lily walked along the pavement towards the flat.

'When are you expecting Johnny back?' Riley asked.

'Oh, any time now. It could be early morning. It's an awful job really, and I think he's getting fed up with it. I'm sure he must be because he's been very short-tempered these last few weeks, snappy like, and that's always a sure sign there's something wrong at the works. They're always changing drivers, you know, which you can understand, driving endlessly through the night. He hates going through France because of the farmers there. They're a crazy lot: they imagine every van has some sheep hidden in it. He's had his load pulled out onto the road before now, and when they found nothing they wouldn't put it back. He had to wait for another driver.'

They now turned into the alley. He took a key from his pocket and was saying, 'It must be a dreadful job. It isn't everybody that can do it.' As his hand went out to the door, he heard her scream and when he was dragged round he saw her fall on

443

her back; then his face was being pounded with blows; and his own fist, going out in retaliation, could make no contact. He could still hear Lily screaming as a knee drove into his stomach and he was almost lifted from the ground. Then he knew he was falling ... falling, falling, and he screamed out.

By the time his head touched the ground, he was aware of nothing. Not of the foot kicking him again and again in the side, nor of Lily's screams as her fist battered her husband, nor of the people now blocking the short alley, nor of the appearance of the police who pulled a now quiet man from against the wall, where he was supporting his drunken body, while his wife knelt on the ground holding the blood-stained head of her dear friend and benefactor, as she always thought of him.

When the ambulancemen gently lifted Riley onto the stretcher and into the ambulance, they took the young woman with them.

CHAPTER TWENTY-THREE

Although Nyrene had been sleeping fitfully for some nights past she refused to resort to sleeping tablets. This night she had read until half-past twelve; then she had lain thinking, and as usual her mind had gone round in circles until she was forced to turn on her side and bury her face in the pillow; like this she would go into a doze.

She had been asleep longer than usual when the phone rang. She picked it up, dazedly saying, 'Yes? Who is it?'

'Am I speaking to Mrs Riley, wife of Mr Peter Riley, the actor in Fellburn?'

She paused before answering softly, 'Yes.'

'I am Police Sergeant Smith, ma'am, and I have to tell you that your husband has been badly injured.'

For a moment she did not speak and a sudden coldness had come over her, then she said, 'In . . . in a car?'

'No, ma'am, he was the victim of a vicious attack.'

'An attack? Who would attack him?'

'A man who happens to be the husband of one of the actresses at The Palace. He's now in custody; the name of Poole.'

'Lily,' she whispered the name. 'Lily's husband.'

'So I understand, ma'am. Anyway, he was brought to the hospital in Fellburn, but such are his injuries, at least to the head, that he has been taken into the Royal Victoria Infirmary in Newcastle.'

She said something that sounded to him like, Oh dear God! then he said, 'I know you're a great distance away, ma'am, and it would take some time for you to get here. Have you any close friends I could contact for you?'

'There . . . there is his father.'

'Could you give me his address?'

She gave him Alex's address.

'I will get in touch with him right away, ma'am. I'm very sorry to have brought you this distressing news, ma'am.'

'Thank you.' Her voice was small.

What next? What next? She should go. She *must* go . . . Fred. She must phone Fred; he would find out the real state of affairs.

She dialled the number. Presently a voice came as a grunt: 'What? Who is it?'

'It's Nyrene here, Fred.'

'Nyrene?' There was a pause. 'It's ... it's half-past three in the morning, what's up?'

'It's ... it's Peter. He's been attacked. The police say he's been badly injured. He's been taken to the RVI in Newcastle.'

'Peter?'

'Yes. Yes, wake up.'

'I am awake, woman.'

'Oh, I'm sorry, Fred, but I'm in a state. It seems that he's been brutally attacked by Lily's husband.'

'Whose husband?'

'Lily's. You know, Lily Poole, the young actress. She does his washing and things.'

'Never!'

'The police are getting in touch with his father. Would you go and find out what's really happened to him?'

'I'll get there straightaway and let you know.'

'I'm so sorry to have troubled you, Fred.'

'Don't talk rot, woman. Look, here's Louise, I'm going to get my clothes on.'

Louise's voice was low and her tone unbelieving now as she said, 'What I've just heard I can't take in. Why would Lily's husband want to do anything to Peter? He's that big goof of a man, isn't he, a lorry driver?'

'Yes.' Nyrene was nodding towards the mouthpiece as she said, 'Yes, a big goof of a man; and Lily used to say he wouldn't hurt a fly.'

'He must have been drunk.'

'Very likely. Yes, very likely.' Nyrene said.

'Fred is almost ready, dear. I'll go downstairs
446

with him. We'll ring you as soon as we have news.'

'Thanks, Louise. Thanks.'

Later, when she looked back she could not remember what she did between the time she got out of bed and the phone ringing at six o'clock. By this time she wasn't alone, for Hamish and Mary were with her.

Fred's voice came to her saying, 'Listen. Now listen, Nyrene. I don't know exactly what's happened to him; he's still in the theatre. I only know that one of those fancy spikes that support the footscraper to the side of the flat door must have struck him somewhere in the neck. The Night Sister gave me a brief outline. I also went to the police station to find out if they could put any light on why this had happened. It appears that the man Poole was paralytic drunk, but then cried himself practically sober. From what I can gather, someone had been writing him letters about his wife carrying on with Riley. But he had to get bottled up before he could do anything about it, because, so I understand, he's normally a very quiet fellow.'

When he had stopped speaking, Nyrene murmured, 'Anonymous letters? That could only be his mother again!'

'Yes, I thought that, and so does his father. He'd been to the police station too. He's sitting now in the waiting-room here, with Betty and the fellow's wife, Lily. She's in an awful state. She can't stop talking. The Sister gave her something a little while ago, and it's calmed her down somewhat. She should go home to bed, but she won't move until she knows what's happened to him.'

There was a short silence before he said quietly, 'Nyrene?'

447

'Yes, Fred?'

'I . . . I think you should be here.'

'I'm all ready to come, Fred. Although it's Sunday I should be there by this afternoon. I'll go straight to the hospital, Fred.'

'Yes. Yes, of course. See you later then. Goodbye.'

*   *   *

She was standing in the small office facing a young man, much too young, she thought, to be a doctor. He was saying, 'You know he is in intensive care?'

'I didn't. I have just come off the train; I know nothing as yet about his condition.'

'Oh. Oh well.' He now picked up a clip of papers from the desk and, scanning the first page, he nodded as he said, 'He seems to have had a bad mauling. His assailant was a boxer, I understand, but apparently he's been very lucky in that the spike he fell upon didn't penetrate his skull. He has lost part of his ear, although plastic surgery will soon put that right. We've yet to find out if the spike has done any damage to his brain.' He fumbled again with his notes. 'Apparently he lost some teeth when his jaw was broken, but again that's of little consequence. But what can be ascertained at the moment is that the femur has been damaged. Then there will be the shock to consider.'

'May I see him?' The question was flat and he answered, 'Yes. Yes, of course, but he won't know you, not for some time.'

A few minutes later she was standing by Peter's bed looking down on a mummified head, for all she could see of his face were his closed lids, his nose and part of his mouth. There was a tube leading from his left wrist to a bag of blood attached to a stand near by.

Someone placed a chair to her side. She didn't thank them for it, but dropped on to it. Then she put her hand up to her mouth so that the moans that were filling her throat wouldn't escape. She thought, Oh, Peter, Peter. Oh, Peter, Peter. Oh, my dear, if I'd only ... if I'd only ... The words were racing each other in her head now and she was only dimly aware of a voice saying, 'Take deep breaths,' and then of being helped up from the chair, and it seemed to her that she took only three steps before she was once again in an office and the voice was saying, 'Shall I get her a cup of tea, Sister?' and the answer, 'Yes, yes.' Then 'There now. There now.' And it had a jocular tone as it went on. 'We nearly had another casualty on our hands, didn't we? It was a good job Nurse was passing.'

Oh, Peter. Peter.

'Ah, here it is! Now drink this up. Your friends tell me you've had a long journey all the way from Aberdeen, and Sunday travel can be very slow.'

Oh, Peter. Peter. Oh my dear, don't die. Don't die. Give me time to forgive myself; don't die.

'We'll take her straight home.' It was Louise's voice. She brought up her head and opened her eyes, and in a whimper now she muttered, 'Oh! Louise, he's—'

'Don't worry, dear, don't worry. He'll be all right, won't he, Sister?'

The Sister's voice did not come back immediately, but when it did it said, 'All he needs now is rest; then his constitution will take over.

449

And he's young and strong. It's all in his favour; and I'm sure he'll feel better tomorrow when he sees you.'

As Louise led her down the corridor it came to her mind that again she hadn't thanked either the Sister or the nurse for the tea. What had happened to her? Had she fainted? She had never before fainted in her life, that she could remember.

When they entered the waiting-room, Fred was quick to move towards them and to say, 'Let's get you home.'

She looked from him to where Alex and Betty were standing, and then some distance behind to Lily. Lily's husband had done this to Peter and all because of what he had imagined was happening between them. She was sure of that. It was that evil woman's mind and her hate that had brought this about.

She was aware that Alex now had hold of her hands, and as she was about to flop down into a chair again, Fred's voice came at her, almost barking in his old-fashioned way, saying, 'No you don't! You're getting home and to bed.' Then he repeated the Sister's words, 'Or we'll have another patient on our hands. It's sleep you want; the same as me. Everything will look better tomorrow, Peter included, you'll see.' And with this, he put his big arm around her, and with Louise at the other side they almost carried her to the car.

*　　　*　　　*

It had taken a sleeping pill finally to push her off and she didn't become fully awake until ten o'clock on the Monday morning; and then she had the

450

desire to stay where she was for she felt exhausted. That was until her mind gave her the reason she was in Louise's house.

Only an hour had elapsed from the time she came fully around until she was once again in the hospital and standing by Peter's bedside. His lids were half-open and it looked as if he was straining to see; and yet he wasn't aware of her presence until she murmured, 'Peter. Peter.'

He could not move his head, it was as if it was in a vice, but he turned his eyes in her direction, and then his lips moved. But no sound came from them, yet she knew he had mouthed her name.

'Oh, my dear.' She was bending over him, looking down into his face. 'I'm sorry. I'm sorry.'

The hand that had been lying limp on the coverlet moved slowly towards her, but it seemed it had no power to lift itself; and now she clutched at it and held it to her, saying in a broken mumble, 'As soon as you're able to be moved you must come home.'

When his lids closed she muttered again, 'Oh, Peter. Peter,' and at this, a nurse appearing at the far side of the bed said quietly, 'It's time for his injection; then he'll be asleep almost immediately.' And as if apologising for what she had to do, she said, 'It's better this way, otherwise he'd be in a great deal of pain; he's very bruised.'

Nyrene asked quietly, 'How long will it be before he will be . . . well, fully round?'

'Oh,'—the nurse gave a little shrug—'it all depends on his progress; it's early days yet.'

The eyes had closed now. She gave a lingering look at him before turning away and at the door she waited for the nurse to leave the bed, then asked her quietly, 'Is he in immediate danger?'

'Well, he wouldn't be in this ward if he wasn't. But I've seen worse than him, and they've gone out from here and finally from the wards on their two legs. So try not to worry.'

It was little comfort, but Nyrene nodded her thanks, and when the nurse opened the door to allow her to go out, she hesitated a moment to look back to the bed.

Only Louise was in the waiting room, and she didn't greet her by asking, Well, how is he? but, taking her arm, she turned her quickly about, saying, 'We're going to have some lunch. You've got to eat; we've all got to eat.' Then she added almost ominously, 'There might be some long nights before us.'

CHAPTER TWENTY-FOUR

The local newspaper had two field days: 'Jealous Husband Attacks Actor' followed by 'All Night Vigil At Hospital'.

The Monday evening paper went further: 'Ex-Boxer Gets Into Ring Again, Batters Actor'.

In each case there were descriptive paragraphs about Riley's injuries that had caused him to be taken from the local hospital to the RVI in Newcastle, where he was now in the intensive care unit with severe head injuries, as well as a broken leg, et cetera. The third day there was nothing, but on the fourth day another headline appeared: 'Actor Fighting For His Life, All Night Vigil By Wife And Father'. Then it went on: 'In a specially allowed interview with our reporter, Johnny Poole said he was sorry to the heart at what he had done, but that it had all been caused by anonymous letters. He'd had them for some weeks now. They would be awaiting him at the depot, telling him of his wife's visits to the actor's flat which, apparently, had been solely for the purpose of collecting the actor's washing and replenishing his freezer. The actor's wife was mainly taken up attending to their invalid son.' The reporter went on to say that Mr Poole hadn't mentioned the fact that he had lost his job and that his wife had left him and would sue for a divorce.

Nothing more appeared in the papers until five weeks later when the case came up.

However, between times, the question cropped up amongst the theatre people and others as to who could have written those letters.

Any member of the family and immediate friends could have enlightened them, but they all knew, because Riley had voiced this from the beginning, that he didn't want his mother's name to be mentioned, because if his mother were brought to court the situation would be made public and he would never be able to get her off his mind; it was bad enough having to carry it in the background of his life. Alex had warned them to keep their tongues quiet and leave her to him. He would see to her. Oh yes, he would see to her.

*   *   *

She had been home only four times within the last five weeks, but she phoned the boy every morning and every evening, and he was responding to her absence much better than she had imagined he would because there was the promise of his father coming home, after his leg was better.

She was on the phone now to Charles and was saying, 'Daddy was out of bed yesterday and could walk a little, so it won't be long, darling, before he's home.' But even as she said the words she wondered why she was so sure, because the man she was seeing every day now was nothing like the one who had stood in the driveway making the excuse that he had come to see his son. This man was quieter; he never spoke of going home, and rarely asked after his son.

The child's voice came again: 'Have you told Daddy I can write my name?'

'Yes, he was delighted to hear it, and he said if you will write down your address he will send you a letter.'

The boy's laugh came over the phone; then he said, 'Mr Mac wants to speak to you, Mummy.'

'Hello there, ma'am.'

'Hello, Hamish.'

'How're you finding him?'

'Oh, much the same as yesterday; but . . . but he can move the leg a little more.'

'He'll be here for Christmas then?'

When she did not answer straightaway his enquiring voice came again, saying, 'He will now, ma'am, he will, won't he? We can arrange something so he can be stretched out in the back of the car.'

'I . . . I don't know whether he'll be fit for it, Hamish.' She hadn't the heart to say, I don't know whether he wants to come, for that would have been nearer the truth.

'Oh well, we'll just have to go on thinking on the positive side, won't we, ma'am? And herself's got a list of cookies that she's going to make as long as your arm. She's upstairs at the moment. Will I call her?'

'No, I'll speak to her tonight, Hamish; I must get back. You know, it's the day of the trial.'

'Oh aye. Oh aye. He deserved two years; but I'd give him three.'

She made no comment on this for she knew who should go to prison for three years, and it wasn't the big gormless ex-boxer.

When she reached Riley's small private ward she found him sitting on the edge of the bed in his dressing-gown.

He smiled at her, as if she had only recently gone out of the room and had now come back, as he said, 'I'm for therapy, they tell me.'

She pulled up a chair and sat close to him, but she did not make any move to kiss him, or he her: except for the short intervals when she had gone home, she had seen him daily and their intimacy had never gone further than holding hands. She said to him, 'I've just been on the phone. Charles sounded very bright.' He did not answer this, but just nodded, and then said, 'What time is it?' She glanced at her wristwatch and said, 'A quarter to ten.'

'The case will have started.'

'Yes, yes.' She hadn't thought she would mention the case to him, and here he was openly speaking of it, so he must have been thinking about it; and it certainly proved that he had been when he said, 'I hope he gets off.'

Her voice was indignant as she said, 'He doesn't

455

deserve to get off! You could have died!'

'From the footscraper perhaps, but not from what he did.'

Her indignation now almost made her rise from the chair as she said, 'A split groin, a cracked hip bone, a broken jaw, and the loss of four teeth, and half your ear gone.'

'That was from the spike.'

'Well, if he hadn't beaten you up you wouldn't have fallen and he needn't have used his feet on you; and that spike, remember, could have entered your skull. The surgeon stressed you're very lucky.'

'Yes, I know, but even so you know as well as I do, Nyrene, that he's not really to blame.' He did not put a name to who was to blame, nor did she, and then he added, 'And he was mad drunk.'

There was silence between them before he spoke again, when he said quietly, 'He wrote to me, you know.'

'Never!'

'Yes, and he said he was sorry to the heart of him for what he had done. I've ... I've told Lily, she was in earlier this morning, that she mustn't divorce him; at least I didn't put it like that, I said she shouldn't leave him because he's going to need somebody, for if, as I understand, it'll be Judge D'Arcy on the bench he's more than likely to send him along the line.'

Her voice was soft as she said, 'Well, it's what he deserves, for he could have crippled you for life.'

He stared at her. He wanted to tell her that he had crippled him for life, not so much in the body as in the mind. He had done a lot of thinking whilst lying here during the past weeks. Pain was a clarifier, it sorted out your values. What did you

456

gain from being an actor except applause from an audience and the gratifying of your enlarged ego? But before you got the applause you had to please, and what did you give up in the pleasing? In his case he had given up time: time with his wife, time with his child, and what had that resulted in? The answer lay in the scar on his chin. And to continue to be an actor, you must hold on to verve, and verve meant enthusiasm and vigour. Well, there was no vigour left in him; as for enthusiasm, he knew that he would never step on to a stage again. The desire to express himself, to please, in fact to exhibit himself, had gone. All he wanted to do now was to find some place where he could be by himself for a time; not home, oh no, not home. She kept talking about home, about his coming home for Christmas; but most of her talk, he felt, was partly out of pity. As for the rest, she was trying to expunge her feeling of guilt for putting the child before him, because she knew if she were able to leave the child now she would have been able to leave him before and that had she done so none of this would have happened, and he certainly wouldn't have had the scar on his chin.

'Is your face hurting?'

He took his hand away from his cheek. He had unconsciously been feeling the scar, and he said, 'No. No, only my ear feels a bit odd at times. But they say they'll finish it this week and that I won't know any difference.' He now put his hand up to his padded ear.

He looked at her now as he said, 'You're not going to the court then?'

'No, Peter, I just couldn't.'

'Well, there's no need. Anyway, Dad'll be there,

457

and Betty and Lily. Poor Lily.'

He seemed very sorry for Lily, yet as she thought this she had no feeling of jealousy towards the girl. It wasn't her fault that this had happened; indeed it was her own, because if she had been at the flat to see to her husband's laundry there would have been no need for Lily to pop in. She gave a quick shake to her head. She mustn't let herself go into it again; this constant taking the blame for everything that had happened onto her own shoulders, would break her down.

The door was pushed open and a nurse said, 'Chariot's on its way, Rip Van Winkle. Get prepared!'

The door closed again and Nyrene, now smiling at him, said, 'Rip Van Winkle? That's what she calls you?'

'Yes, she's from the therapy room. She calls me that, I suppose, because it's from the story, you know where he slept for a hundred years, Rip Van Winkle.'

'Yes, yes, I know the story.'

'She said I slept for the first fortnight; but to tell you the truth, I've only vague memories of those first few days.'

The door opened again and a long wheelchair was pushed in, and, as Nyrene stood aside for Riley to be helped on to it, she said, 'I'll go to the flat; your father said he would call there.'

He turned his head to look up at her, saying, 'Yes, do that, dear. Do that. I'll see you this afternoon.'

'Yes, dear. Yes.' She kept nodding her head as he was wheeled away, attended by two laughing and joking nurses, a sight which somehow added to the

458

constant hurt. Again here was youth being represented, gay and unaffected. She did not stop to consider that those two nurses might just as likely have acted the same with a doddering old man. No, because, together with her husband, they formed a triangle of youth.

CHAPTER TWENTY-FIVE

In the small bleak room, Lily stood before the man who, since she had last seen him, seemed to have lost most of the flesh from his body. That had been the day after the incident, when he was allowed bail and she had told him that she was leaving him for good. She recalled that he had made no reply whatever to this, nor had he followed her home; but she understood he had been staying with his sister. And now she was looking up at him, her face twisted in pain and pity, and she was repeating to herself the judge's words: 'Although you committed an unprovoked crime the blame does not lie entirely with you, but also with the writer of the anonymous letters.' And he had gone on to voice his own opinion of such writers. He had said he would have them publicly horse-whipped if they could be found; and he suggested that the police should take the same trouble in discovering the culprits as they would in their search for a murderer: such letter-writers were evil, and they ruined lives, they ruined families. In this particular case they had brought a man near to being charged with murder. In any case, the career of a talented actor had been wrecked, such that it was doubtful if he would ever again return to the stage. However, what had transpired was a serious crime to which the prisoner had confessed, and although he had expressed his deep sorrow, nevertheless, what was done was done, and he must bear the punishment.

She now put her hand out and gripped Johnny's forearm, saying, 'It . . . it won't be all that long. I'll . . . I'll be waiting for you . . . at . . . at home.'

The muscles in the big bony face all seemed to move together as if being controlled by a tick; then in a sort of throaty whisper the words came, 'I'm sorry, Lily. I am. I am.'

'I know, but . . . but try not to worry any more.' She half-leant towards him now; then she looked to the side to where the policeman was standing, and when he made a motion with his head, an indication that time was nearly up, she suddenly put her hands onto the big shoulders and lifted her face, and when his arms came about her and held her close, she could feel the trembling of his whole body. It was as if he was afraid, and she could never imagine him being afraid.

Their lips parted as the policeman's voice came from behind them, saying, 'Time's up. Come along.' And now Johnny's words came in a muttered rush: 'You mean it, Lily? You'll wait?'

'Yes, yes.' Her bobbing head emphasised her words and he slowly let go of her and took two steps backwards before he turned about and went through the door that the policeman was holding open.

She did not move for some minutes. Her eyes were screwed tight, her throat was full; she was overwhelmed with a pity she had never imagined she could feel for him. He wasn't the kind of man that evoked pity; scorn yes, for at times she had been irritated by his ignorance which she believed was due to what she thought of as his inability to learn; yet there had been other times when he had surprised her by speaking with knowledge on certain subjects. She had, in a way, made excuses for him in her mind by telling herself he wasn't a talker.

When she reached the street she was touched to find Mr Riley's family waiting for her. There was his father, his sister, Nurse Fawcett, and his wife, Nyrene, and her friend, Mrs Beardsley.

It was Nyrene who said to her, 'We thought we'd go and have a coffee somewhere; will you have time?' She looked from one to the other before she stammered, 'Ye ... ye ... yes, I've got time. Thank you very much.'

In the restaurant the conversation had been general until, of a sudden, Alex looked towards Lily and said, 'He got off lightly; a year with six months suspended.' But at this, Betty put in quickly, 'Dad doesn't mean that he blames him entirely. He really doesn't, do you, Dad?'

And at this, Alex said, 'No, no. As the judge said, it was the letter-writer.' He had stressed the last two words, and Betty, her head nodding, looked from one to the other, saying, 'Yes, as Dad says, it was the letter-writer.' But when her gaze came to rest on Nurse, Betty almost vehemently cried, 'Yes, the letter-writer! And I've had some of them too. She should be—'

'You know who it was?' This came sharply from Lily, and there was almost a chorus of, 'No! No!' from the others, with an explanation from Nyrene of, 'It's usually a woman who takes to this form of
461

malice, Lily, and Nurse had similar letters some time ago.'

'Oh.' Lily looked at Betty again; and then her gaze turned on Alex as he said, 'It was because I had gone to live with Nurse, you see.'

'Oh. Oh.' The explanation seemed to satisfy Lily, at least for a moment, that is until she said, harshly, 'You know something? I'm going to make it my business to find out who was spying on me, and judging by those letters it must have been over a period. Yes, that's what I'm going to do.' Her head was bobbing now.

It was Alex who said quietly, 'If you did find out, what would you do about it?'

'Do about it, Mr Riley? I'd make them pay for it; I would take them to court. By, yes! I'd make sure they wouldn't write any more anonymous letters, he or she, whoever it was.'

He was nodding at her now as he said, 'You're right in your feelings, oh yes, because that's how we all feel. Every single one of us at this table feels like that, but we wouldn't do it.'

She looked puzzled for a moment; then she said, 'Why . . . why wouldn't you do it, expose them?'

'Because Peter wouldn't like it; he's not for it.'

'Peter? You mean if he knew who caused him to be beaten up like he is and my Johnny to do a prison stretch, he wouldn't?'

'No, he wouldn't.'

Alex looked from one to the other, and when his eyes came to rest on Lily again, he said, 'We all know who did it.'

'What! You do?'

'You can sound amazed; you see it was Peter's mother, my wife.'

462

Lily sat back in her chair and her eyes ranged around the group, and her voice was a mere whisper as she said, 'No!'

'Yes, lass, yes; and it's been going on for a long time.'

'Because of me.' Nyrene had all their attention now; and when Alex put in, 'No, lass, no; she was no good before that. I went through it for years,' Nyrene put in, 'Yes, but differently.' Then she turned to Lily and said, 'From when Peter married me, a woman nearly as old as herself, she set out to destroy him.'

'Eeh, my God! Poor Mr Riley. How . . . how has he managed to put up with it all this time?'

It was Alex who answered, 'Because she's his mother, and I did the same earlier because she is my wife. Anyway, now you know, and you wouldn't hurt him any more by bringing it into the open, would you?'

Lily answered by a slow shake of her head before she said, 'No, no, I wouldn't. But . . . but I can't take it in: a mother would do that?'

When no answer was forthcoming, she went on, 'But it doesn't seem fair.' She looked around them again. 'She . . . she should be punished in some way because if she can go as far as she has gone she won't stop now.'

'Yes, I agree with you, lass,'—Alex was nodding at her—'something should be done, and it will, lass. But let's leave it until Peter's really on his feet again. Yes, then we'll see.'

CHAPTER TWENTY-SIX

They had the day-room to themselves. Riley sat in a wheel-chair and Nyrene was by his side and holding his hand and shaking it up and down as she said, 'Oh no, no, Peter, you can't.'

'Look,' he patted her hand now quickly as he said, 'it's better this way.'

'You still need attention.'

'Well, what better than a nurse in the house? Maggie's a good nurse; she's on night duty, and if I should need help in the daytime she'll be there. And then there's Dad. I'd like to spend some time with Dad. He should go into hospital again, but he keeps putting it off, for I think he feels it will be his last visit. Maggie thinks so too: he's been in severe pain and his pills are not having much effect now.'

'Oh, I am sorry, I really am, Peter, but . . . but if you came home, your dad could come with you. He loves being there.'

He looked at her and shook his head tolerantly for a moment as he said, 'Aberdeen's a long way from the RVI, dear.'

'Oh, Peter!' Her voice had dropped almost to a whimper now. 'They're all expecting you for Christmas, and I'—her gaze dropped from his as she added—'I want you home.'

'Nyrene . . . look at me. Now, look at me.'

When she lifted her eyes to his he said, 'If this hadn't happened'—he touched his head and then his leg—'we would still have remained in the situation we were in, wouldn't we? You would never have had me home again, as I was then.'

'Oh. Oh, you don't know: I was warring inside myself all the time; I ... I wanted you, but I couldn't make the first move.'

'No, you couldn't, dear; nor would you ever have, being you. And now you are again playing a part, because circumstances have set a different scene.'

'Oh no! Peter. No.'

'Oh yes. You were playing a part so as to give me a career, you were playing another part to give me my freedom. This business of youth to youth was filling your mind again. Oh I know. I know you wouldn't let yourself understand that I didn't need youth; I was never young inside myself. There was no call in me for youth.' He now turned his head away and stared at the line of chairs flanking the wall to the side, and when he began to count them, he stopped himself—it was a habit that had come on him lately, of counting things—then he went on, 'The urge was sex, pure and simple, and sex by itself knows nothing about love. Painfully I've learned that.'

A silence ensued for some minutes; and then in a low murmur, he said, 'There's another thing: you are suffering with a feeling of guilt towards me and although I know that things could never return to what they were before, I couldn't tolerate ... I really couldn't tolerate being accepted back on your feelings that swing between pity and guilt.'

'Peter. Peter, believe me, you're wrong. Oh, you are very wrong in thinking along those lines. Yes, I *have* felt guilty, and yes, pity too. Who wouldn't in the state you were in? And any guilt I felt stemmed from that state, for we both know that, in the first place, I was the cause of it. Listen. Listen.' She had

465

hold of his hands again, gripping them now, but she found she couldn't utter the words that were filling her throat because they might not touch any reciprocating feeling in him. Yet she knew if she did not say them, she would never know, so, her eyes dropping from his, she murmured, 'I love you, Peter, as much as ever I did; if it's possible to say, more. And I want you; but much more I need you; I need you in my life to make it whole. My love over the years has been tainted with fear of what might happen, and it happened. Since then, all such feelings and fears have gone from me. No matter what you are likely to do in the future, with me or without me, I shall continue to love you.'

'Oh, Nyrene.' His head was bowed and both his hands were returning her grip when suddenly the opening of the door made them spring apart, then they both sighed as Alex entered the room.

'Hello, both! Nearly ready for the road?'

Alex pulled a chair round to face them both and, looking at Nyrene, he said, 'He's told you he's coming to us? It'll only be for a few days, just until he hobbles a bit better. It'll not be for long. You'll soon have him home. In any case I have to go back into hospital soon. But as I told them'—his head now moving in a cocky fashion—'I'll come in when I'm ready, and not afore. Well now, Nyrene, will you come along home with us?'

She could only nod: there was that lump in her throat again, the lump she dreaded. But Alex went on, 'And you know there's no need for you to stay on at Mr Beardsley's, there's another spare room upstairs.' Shrugging his shoulders, he added quickly, 'But of course it isn't as swanky as theirs. Still, the sheets are changed once a month.'

'Oh, Alex!' She found that she had to laugh, and it dissolved the lump, and when she said, 'I'll take you at your word, Alex,' Riley put in quickly, 'No, no, you'd better go home again; it's nearly a week since you were there.'

'I'll go when I'm ready,' she said sharply now; then, turning to Alex again, she muttered, 'Thanks, Alex, I'll stay for at least a couple of nights.' Then she looked at Riley and they held each other's gaze until he turned his head away . . . things were now out of his hands.

*   *   *

It had been five days since he was in the hospital listening to his father making arrangements for him to stay at Nurse's; and now here he was again making further arrangements as to where he was to go, for Alex was saying, 'It was a good idea at first, when I thought you'd have rest and peace and quiet and we'd have time for some cracks, but my heavens! Cracks? We've hardly had time to say hello. I wouldn't have believed it. I could see you being visited by our lot and by Mr and Mrs Beardsley, but I didn't count on the whole blooming company from The Palace dropping in.'

He punched his son softly in the shoulder now, saying, 'Remember when I was in hospital and you brought me those flowers and Sister said men never got flowers? Well, just look round here, it's like . . . it's like a chapel of rest.'

'Oh, Dad, shut up!'

'Shut up, you say! Well, I wouldn't mind shutting this place up, 'cos it's been like a blooming café: with all the cups of tea I think *I've* earned half the

467

boxes of chocolates and the wines. They'd certainly save me on Christmas boxes. And it's not going to get much better, for too many people know where you are now, and with kids coming to the front door wanting autographs. I bet you never guessed you were so popular.'

Popular. He could hear Yvette's voice saying, 'A big fish in a little pond,' and he had enjoyed being the big fish. Oh yes, he had. But now he knew he'd never be a fish of any kind again, the way he was looking now. But it wasn't only his looks that had carried him through before, but his body and the agility of it. But now that was gone, too.

It was as if his father had picked up his thoughts, because he was saying, 'And you're walking better, fine, but, as I said, you'll never get any real rest with all the people who know you're here.'

Alex stopped speaking and walked towards the fire, and stood staring down into it before he muttered to himself, 'Why the devil didn't I think about her before? Of all the people who would know he was here, she would; and God knows what she'll be up to next.'

Riley was saying, 'But, Dad, you broke your neck to get me to come here, and I'm happy here.'

'Happy here,' Riley had said; at times he longed to be back in hospital, in that quiet little room where there were set hours for visitors. People were kind, more than kind, so wonderfully so he would never have believed it; but nevertheless it was wearing, and he was tired, very tired, much more so than when he was in hospital. His father was saying, 'I know I did, and it was all for the best at the beginning; but I didn't think it would turn out to be like Newcastle Central. Yes, what you want now is peace and quiet and rest.' He came to Riley now and, gripping his wrist, he said quietly, 'Go home, Peter. I'm asking you this specially: I'm going to say to you, do this for me. I've never really asked anything of you, have I? But now I am. I want you to go home. She's been gone only two days and already you're missing her, and lost without her. You always will be, so swallow your pride.'

'Pride? Dad, I haven't any pride left.'

'Well, whatever it is, and I'm telling you this, I know that you want to be home, that you're longing to be home, and that that woman of yours is praying daily for you to come home. Lad,'—he shook his head slowly now—'don't waste any more days. Don't waste another minute of your life because, no matter how long it is, it's a very short trip. Oh yes, lad, it's a very short trip. And I know this: whatever's keeping you two apart, it's on your side; so, swallow it, lad, and go home. Will you . . . will you do this for me? because I'm also gonna tell you this: as long as you're in this house I'm not going into hospital.'

'Don't be silly, Dad. If you don't go next week you'll miss your place and you might have to wait weeks.'

'No,'—Alex tossed his head from side to side and his tone was bumptious now—'I won't have to wait weeks; I'm a special case: I go in when I want to.'

'Don't be silly, Dad.'

'All right, I won't be silly; but what about it?'

'I don't feel up to travelling, Dad.'

'I'll come with you.'

'No, you won't; if I'm going I'll go by myself.'

469

Alex stood up laughing now, saying, 'I'll go and tell Nurse and I'll go and pack your things.'

'Sit down!' It was almost a bawl from Riley and his father sat down. He was still smiling when Riley took his hand and in a low voice, said, 'I don't suppose we'll have time together again like this, so I'll say it now. I'm . . . I'm glad we've come to know each other, Dad.'

Riley waited for his father to say something, but Alex only stared at him. Then, almost springing up, he fell forward and when his arms went about his son's neck Riley held him and they clung together for a moment; then Alex pulled himself roughly away and hurried from the room. He hadn't spoken a word, but his action had expressed his feelings more eloquently than anything he could have brought himself to say.

CHAPTER TWENTY-SEVEN

Nyrene stood by the gate, her gaze fixed on the silver line of the river. There was no movement of the water; it looked still, frozen, and perhaps it was. When she shivered, she asked herself why she was standing here, there were all those letters to answer. It had been a strange day and she had been unable to settle. She had been home only two days and now she wanted to get back to him. But that little house was so crowded, and they were never alone for a minute; he wasn't improving, nor would he improve there. What he needed was rest, peace and quiet. Although he was walking better, his head and face wounds had healed and his body bruises must have eased, she felt he was still suffering inwardly from the shock of the attack.

It would soon be dark: the twilight was so short in the winter. As she turned away from the gate her gaze flickered to the rough road and she was brought to a halt. Someone was slowly making their way along there. It wasn't Hamish, for the figure wasn't tall enough, and anyway Hamish would have Charles with him. The last time she had seen them they were in the barn where Hamish had been painting some backcloth, helped, of course, by his assistant. This figure was walking very slowly. She leant over the gate; then her heart seemed to stop for a full beat and she suddenly recalled how uneasy she had been feeling all day; and now she knew that something had happened to him, and there was his image on the path. Oh dear God! She clutched at her throat.

When the figure moved nearer, its limping step quickening, she wrenched open the gate, then stood stock-still before running forward and crying, 'It's you, Peter! Peter, it's you!'

She had to support him and herself from falling by releasing one hand from him and clutching at a post that supported the fence.

'Oh, Peter! Where? Why? No-one with you?' She looked over his shoulder. 'Oh, darling, you should have let me know.'

He did not speak, but when he bent forward and gently kissed her they both rocked again as if they would fall, and now she cried. 'Oh, come on! Come on!' and at the top of her voice she yelled, 'Hamish! Hamish! Mary! Hamish!'

They were halfway up the path when Mary emerged from round the corner of the house and

Hamish from the yard, and they were both running, as was the boy. It was Charles who saw them first, and on a high squealing cry, he leapt over the ground, and then he was clinging to them both, crying, 'Oh, Daddy! Daddy, you're home. Oh, Daddy!'

Hamish was on one side of him now, his arm about him practically carrying him forward and exclaiming all the time, in part orders and in part comments, 'Dear God, how have you managed it? Open the front door, woman! You haven't a thing with you?'

At the house, Riley drew them all to a stop, and he was laughing as he gasped, 'The luggage, Hamish, is halfway down the road. The taxi man kindly put it there.'

'Dear God in heaven!'

'Never mind, dear God in heaven, woman! Get that kettle on; and no tea, mind; it's a hot toddy he needs.'

When they sat him in the big chair in front of the blazing fire, he lay back and closed his eyes, and they stood about him: Hamish, Mary, the child, and Nyrene, and no-one spoke for a moment until Hamish's bellow filled the room again, crying, 'The toddy, woman! The toddy!'

Mary now turned about, laughing, and ran towards the kitchen, while Hamish, nodding towards Nyrene, said, 'I'll away down and fetch the luggage.'

He was halfway across the room when, looking back, he said, 'You, linty, aren't you coming with me? You can't expect me to carry everything.'

The boy laughed, his mouth wide open, and he looked at his father; he flung his arms around his
472

neck, gave him a quick kiss, then turned and darted in his rocking gait towards Hamish.

Now they were alone and she dropped onto her knees by the side of the chair and, taking his hands, she pressed them tightly between her breasts saying softly, 'Oh, my darling. You have no idea: you gave me a shock, I thought you were your own ghost. How . . . how on earth did you manage it on your own?'

'I didn't, Dad arranged everything: tucked me up in a first-class compartment, and must surely have tipped the attendant well, judging by the attention he gave me all through the journey. It was just a piece of cake.'

He now pulled himself forward and put his arms about her, and they were holding tight when Mary entered the room; but they didn't disengage themselves straightaway, not until she cried, 'Break!' as if she were in a boxing ring.

After the first sip of the hot whisky, he looked up at Mary, saying, 'Three times a day, Mary. That's what the doctor said, three times a day,' and to this she answered in his own vein, 'Yes, sir, and I'll see to it, sir.'

After a dinner of casseroled lamb and dumplings, with fruit salad scooped out of a decorated half-melon, followed by a chocolate gateau and coffee, they gave an hour to the boy, watching his attempts at writing, and listening to his attempts at reading. Lastly, Nyrene read a story to him while he sat curled up on his father's knee, his head on his shoulder, his body pressed tight against him, until Mary came in calling loudly, 'What are you going to have? Take your choice: the top or the bottom of the bed?' To which Charles's

473

answer was a gurgling laugh, and, 'The middle, Mary.'

Then without raising his head from his father's shoulder he looked at his mother and said, 'Must I?'

'Yes please, darling.'

At this he reluctantly raised himself, kissed his father three times, once on either cheek and once on the mouth; then just before he let himself down from Riley's knee he turned to him again and said anxiously, 'You ... you'll be here in the morning, won't you, Daddy?'

'I hope so. And all the other mornings, son,' and the boy's immediate reply of, 'Well 'tis something to know, as Mr Mac himself would say. Ah, weel! Sure 'tis something to know,' brought forth from Riley a gale of free and hearty laughter.

Hamish was waiting for Charles at the bottom of the stairs, and the big Scot, frowning down on him, said, 'I won't be mocked, Master Charles, I won't be mocked.' Then the laughter in the room rose again as the reply came, still in Hamish's voice, ' 'Tis sorry I am. Aye, 'tis that,' followed by a scrambling up the stairs. Mary's face was wet with tears as Riley looked up at her, asking, 'How long has he been at that game?'

'Oh, quite a while. You wouldn't believe it how they tease each other; like two old men, they are.' She sighed now, a long happy sigh, and turning from them, she said, 'If anybody ever had a new lease of life, that child's got one tonight.'

Left alone, they gazed at each other; then Nyrene, with a sudden movement, was kneeling by his side, murmuring, 'He's not the only one.' And to this Riley answered fervently, 'No, he's not the

474

only one.' . . .

It was some time later before the house became quiet and they were in bed. Whereas downstairs they had talked freely, now, lying together, it seemed that embarrassment was flooding them both. Although he had his arms about her his body was not close to hers.

Frantically she searched in her mind for something to say, but what? What hadn't they spoken about downstairs? The Palace. And so, on a gulp, she said, 'Did you see David and Miss Connie before you came away?'

'No. No.' He was quick to answer. 'But . . . but I phoned him. They had been in yesterday, and were disappointed they didn't see you.'

'They'll be wanting to know how soon you'll be back, I suppose?'

He was silent for a moment; then he said, 'I'm not going back, Nyrene.'

'You mean you're not going back to The Palace?'

'Yes, that's what I mean; nor to anything else in that line.'

She sat up, resting on her elbow and, looking down on him through the pink glow from the bedside lamp. 'You . . . you can't mean it; it's . . . it's your life.'

'It's not my life, not any more. I don't think it ever has been; I seem to have been pushed into it. Perhaps if I'd remained the stand-up comic things might have been different; I'd have been my own man then.'

Her voice had a touch of anger in it now as she said, 'Don't be silly! You were never made to be a stand-up comic. You're an actor, a splendid actor.'

His voice was soft and even sad when he said,

475

'I'm what *you* made me Nyrene. Anyway, I ask you am I fit to go on a stage again?'

'This'll all pass; you'll be walking straight in no time. What was it they said, six months or a little more?'

'I know what they said, but it isn't only my leg and it isn't only my face; it's what's inside.'

'Oh.' She fell back onto his arm. 'You ... you can't do this, Peter, not give up altogether. You were made for that life. I know you were. You could direct and do it better than Larry. I know that because, to my mind, he is often slipshod.'

For a moment, he didn't speak, then he said, 'Would you really mind very much if I didn't go back to The Palace or on the road again?'

What could she say if she spoke the truth? No. She wouldn't mind in the least because whatever he took up she must be near him, whereas if he went back to The Palace, and more so, if he went on the road again, once more life would be divided between him and the child.

She pulled herself away from his arm and sat upright, and he, also pulling himself up, said, 'What is it? What's the matter?'

She twisted round and took his face tightly between her hands and said, 'Downstairs, on the writing desk, there are at least twenty out-of-work actors applying to an advert I put in for an assistant to manage the drama school, or words to that effect. I stipulated that he or she must have a wide knowledge of acting.' She took her hands from his face and now her arms were round his neck as she said, 'Do you hear?'

'Yes, I heard. But do you have enough pupils to call for an assistant?'

476

'Already I have twenty-five ranging from tap through voice to ordinary acting.'

'Twenty-five?'

'Yes, and more applying all the time.'

'How has this come about?'

'Word of mouth, dear, word of mouth; and I don't charge half what the so-called drama academies do. Also I stipulate that they can book up for just three months, not three years. I have a few on enforced rest but who want to keep in trim, and quite a few whose feet will never touch a legitimate theatre board. But they are all serious. I also stipulate that a pupil can have time off to attend auditions.'

'But if you don't charge much how can you make anything out of it? You've got to pay this—'

'Oh, I make enough. The main thing is, it's an occupation which keeps me in touch with life; and what's more, I feel I've got something to give back.'

'Oh yes, my dear, so much to give back; you always have had.'

She shook the hands within hers now, saying, 'But you see what I'm getting at? I'm advertising for an assistant. You heard what I said?'

He shook his head as the thought flooded his mind like water from a spring: it swept away the uncertain future wherein he had given up the stage with only a commercial job ahead, if he could find one.

'Oh, Nyrene,'—he was holding her close now— 'could . . . could it really be workable?'

Her words were slow and broken as she murmured, 'It really could be. It's all here, our future together; and that's not counting Hamish's promising market garden.'

They fell onto their sides now and although he was holding her tightly he made no effort to love her; but when his body began to tremble and his breath came in short gasps she said, 'Don't ... don't cry.' Her face, too, was wet as she pressed it against his, and she held it there until his paroxysm of weeping ceased. They lay quiet for a time; then he spoke her name softly, 'Nyrene?'

'Yes, darling, what is it?'

'Never leave me. Never let me go.'

'No, darling, never, never.' They held close now as she repeated, 'Never. Never.'

They did not make love: they were one and that oneness was love.

CHAPTER TWENTY-EIGHT

Mary took up the phone. 'Hello?' she said.

'Hello, Mrs A., I mean Mrs McIntyre. This is Betty, Peter's sister.'

'Oh, Peter's sister. Yes, hello, Betty. You'll be wanting Mr Peter?'

'Yes, if you don't mind.'

'He's upstairs with the boy; I'll get him.'

Mary went to the foot of the stairs and called, 'Mr Peter! you're wanted on the phone. It's your sister.'

Riley appeared at the top of the stairs, saying, 'Oh, I'll take it up here. Thanks.' He turned to Charles, saying, 'Now go and finish that exercise; I'm sure you can. I won't be a minute.'

'All right, Daddy.' The boy turned away obediently and Riley went into the bedroom.

'Hello, Betty.'

'Hello, Peter. How are you?'

'Oh, heaps better; I can't tell you.'

'Everything all right?'

'Everything. Everything.'

'I'm so glad. Peter?'

'Yes, dear?'

'I've something to tell you.'

There was a pause before Riley said apprehensively, 'Dad?'

'Oh no, although he's going into hospital at the weekend, you know. But he wants me to tell you about what's happened, and you are not to attempt to come here, because you can do nothing . . . you see, Mum's dead.'

'What!' He reached out and pulled a bedroom chair towards him and sat down heavily before speaking again: 'When?'

'We don't rightly know. Uncle Frank found her yesterday afternoon, but it could have happened the day before.'

'What d'you mean, found her?'

'Well, she had written to him to say that if he didn't bring Florrie back she would go over there to fetch her. Well, as Uncle Frank said, Florrie was terrified of going back, so he went over to reason with her. He knocked and knocked, he said, but couldn't get an answer. And all the curtains were drawn, even round the back. So he forced the kitchen window and got in there and went upstairs, and there she was. Now, Peter, what I'm going to tell you next Dad says mustn't worry you one jot, because it's not worrying him, and it's not worrying me; and as he said, a lot of people'll sleep easier in their beds now she's gone. Even so he's sorry that he has to say this. You see, Peter, she committed suicide.'

His mouth fell into a gape: it was as if he was actually seeing her lying there, the bottles or whatever all around her, and his voice was very faint as he said, 'Oh no, Betty.'

'She was up the pole, Peter, she really was; but I could never see her taking her own life, she was too selfish. Yet that's what she has done. I think she must have got drunk because there was an empty whisky bottle near.'

'She never drank.'

'We don't know what she did, Peter, we never knew what she did, for she was always secretive. Anyway, I can tell you this: I'm glad she's gone. No matter how she's gone I'm glad, because, besides everything else she had a filthy mind. You should have seen some of the letters she sent to Nurse. And then look how she tried to set the house on fire. And never forget there's a man doing time because of her letters; and then there's you; she's done her best to ruin you all right.'

'I'd better come.'

'No, no, Peter. That's what Dad emphasised. He said it's no use anyway. It was the day before yesterday she died, and she's going to be buried tomorrow. There won't be any funeral as such, and there'll be few mourners, I can tell you. Dad said he'll phone you tomorrow sometime and'—her voice dropping now she said—'he also said, well suggested, that you shouldn't tell Nyrene about it until after the holidays because, as he said, she sounded so marvellously happy on the phone last Saturday when he called her.'

'Oh yes. I think Dad's right, but, oh Betty, what a
480

sad way to go. And thinking back, she had no life really.'

'Don't be so soft, our Peter. She played hell with all of us, until . . . until we had to leave home, you know that. For certain you know that. And then her bitterness made her evil. I'm going to tell you something because I've never forgotten it. When she knew you had married Nyrene, do you know what she said? She said she would dance on your grave one day. It was from then that I began to fear her, really fear her, and I knew she was evil; and Uncle Frank said yesterday that he knew where she got her badness from, and that was from their own father: he did time for beating up their mother and for lashing Uncle Frank until he was almost insensible when he was eight years old. Their father got eighteen months for that. We didn't know about that, did we?'

Riley turned to see Nyrene coming towards him, and so, lightening his voice, he said, 'Oh, here's Nyrene, Betty. Have a word with her.' And smiling to Nyrene he said, 'It's Betty, finding out how I'm doing. Here, have a word with her,' handing her the phone.

'Hello, Nyrene. How are you getting on?'

'Oh, wonderfully, wonderfully. Did Peter tell you about our new enterprise in the studio? Nothing so common as the barn now.'

'No, what's that?'

'Well, he has become my manager. Would you believe that?'

'You mean for good?'

'Yes, Betty, for good: no more Palace and no more road work. Anyway, he wouldn't have been up to it for a long time, and he's very taken with the idea.'

'Oh yes, it'll be right up his street. Up both your streets.'

'How about you and Harry coming for Christmas?'

'Oh, we would have loved that, Nyrene, but we're going to Uncle Frank's. Sue's got Christmas off because her people are going abroad, and with Florrie being there already me Uncle Frank thought—'

'I understand, dear. I understand.'

'I've got to go now, Nyrene, but I just thought I'd like a word with Peter. He sounds marvellous and so much better. And you?'

'Oh, I'm fine; and so so glad to have him home, Betty.'

'I bet. I bet. Well, so long.'

'Bye-bye, dear.'

Nyrene put the receiver down and turning to where Riley was still standing at the end of the bed she said, 'She's a nice girl, Betty. I've always liked her; so thoughtful. What is it? Are you all right, dear? Come and sit down. You're losing your colour. What did she want, really? Has anything happened?'

'No, no, she just wanted to know how I was and were we all right, and I told her,' and he smiled at her now as he added, 'and you, too, told her.'

She took his arm now and said, 'Come on, let's go down and have a cup of tea. I'll make it; Mary's clearing up over there; the coach has gone. They're all full of the Christmas party on Friday. I've told them it'll be only tea and buns, but they all insist on turning it into a party and having a bit of a dance. It should be fun.'

When he was seated on the couch in front of the fire, she bent and kissed him before asking, 'Sure you are all right?'

'No, I'm feeling terribly ill. Go on and make that tea, woman.' He slapped her on the bottom as she walked away, and her light laugh as she left the room reminded him that knowing about the suicide would have wiped that away. His dad was right and Betty was right, too. He himself had no reason to feel any guilt. 'I'll dance on his grave.' Oh, how she must have hated him, and to the extent of wanting him killed; for a few more blows to the head from those fists would have done what the spike did not manage to do; or, at least his brain would have been damaged.

He drew in a long shuddering breath as it came to him, on a wave of release, that from now on he would be rid of the fear of her. In the depths of him there had always been a shivering fear of her. Yes, that's the name he could put to it, shivering, for, as a youngster, she had at times petrified him and made him wonder why she should go to Mr Beardsley and encourage him to beat the daylights out of him. He recalled, too, how she herself had brayed him one day—he would have been about fourteen at the time—and all because Cissie Morgan, from lower down, had come calling for him. For a time he had liked Cissie Morgan. One day after school she had let him touch her breast. He recalled that there wasn't much of it, but that it had excited him. And that day when she had come to the front door asking for him, his mother had sent her flying. Then she had taken him into the back room and laid about him, all the time using the word sex. It was the first time he had really heard the word; body attractions were always referred to as 'the other' or 'it' or 'a bit off'. There were other names, but they were coarser, and sex seemed to bundle the whole lot together.

The train of thought took him to his father. What a life he must have led with her all those years. Behaving as they did, how did they manage to breed the four of them? But why on earth was he asking such a question? If anybody should know that sex had little to do with love, it should be he.

At the sound of his son's hesitant walking down the stairs and his voice crying, 'I've done it, Daddy,' Riley got up from the couch and went to meet the boy. Then looking at the exercise book being held out to him, he exclaimed, 'My! Yes, that's splendid. Wonderful!'

With a quizzical smile at his father, the boy said, 'Daddy, you have a word for that.'

'For what, Charles? For what?'

'Saying things that are not really true; not lies, but not quite true. Exadge, you call it. My exercise was good, eh, Daddy? Not wonderful.'

Riley stared into the beautiful pale face, into the childish face which held the old eyes, and he could find nothing to say; he could only act his feelings. And so, in a quick movement he picked up his son and held him in his arms.

And this was how Nyrene found them when she entered the room bearing the tray of tea.

Quickly putting the tray down, she hurried towards them, crying, 'What's this? What's this exhibition all about?'

As Riley swung about, the boy still in his arms, he said, 'I'm celebrating the fact that I have an exceptionally intelligent son, Mrs Riley.'

Now throwing her arms around them both Nyrene exclaimed, 'And I have a very lovable and wonderful son, Mr Riley.'

When, rising above the laughter, the boy's voice cried, 'Exadge, Daddy, exadge,' Riley said, 'No, not this time, my dear, not this time.'

The kitchen door gently closed on Hamish and Mary who had been standing viewing the scene in the sitting-room. They exchanged a long and bright-eyed look; then Hamish, giving a soft hoot, picked Mary up and planted a smacking kiss on her lips, then shook her gently before putting her down again, saying, 'A Happy Christmas to you, Mrs McIntyre.' And to this she answered, 'And the same to you, Mr McIntyre. And did I ever tell you I love you?'

And Hamish, staring at his wee wifie, did not immediately reply; but presently, with deep sincerity in his voice, he said, 'Thank you, Mrs McIntyre, thank you. That's all I've wanted to hear.'

AFTERWORD

As Fred walked across the empty school yard he drew in deep breaths. He'd be glad of the Christmas break; he was tired; it had been a heavy term. He was finding the terms seemed to get heavier now. Louise was right, he should more than think about retiring at sixty, he should do it.

There were only two cars in the car-park, and, apart from a small man standing in the shelter of the wall that edged the playground, there was nobody about. He had already glanced towards him; but now he was looking harder, for the fellow was walking into the car-park.

He unlocked his car door and switched on the lights; then looking over the bonnet, he could see the man picked out in the headlights and he said, 'That you, Mr Riley?'

'Yes, sir, Mr Beardsley, it is me. I've ... I've been waiting for you; I mean I've been hoping that I could have a word with you.'

'Yes, of course. But ... but I thought you had gone into hospital.'

'The morrer.'

'Oh, not till tomorrow? Well, get in; we don't want to be found dead in the morning here, do we?'

Settled in the car, Fred stretched out his arm past Alex, saying, 'Let's have the heaters on full blast until we get home; I'm sure, like me, you could do with a cup of tea. How long have you been standing there?'

'Oh, not long, not long; but that doesn't matter.

And if you don't mind, Mr Beardsley, I would rather . . . well, I would rather talk to you outside.'

'Outside? What d'you mean?'

'Oh, I don't mean out in the open, I mean outside your house. If I could sort of . . . well, if you could give me five minutes or so I could tell you what I've got to say here.'

'Oh well, fire ahead.'

'You're sure I'm not taking up your time?'

'Oh, man, you've been standing there for how long? You don't say, and you expected me to listen to you, and now you're apologising and talking about taking up my time . . . well, you are, so get on with it.' Then his voice softening, he leant towards Alex, adding, 'What is it, Alex? Something on your mind? In trouble of some sort?'

'No. No, Mr Beardsley . . . well, not trouble any more; I've got rid of trouble, so to speak, and when I've gone into hospital I don't think trouble'll worry me very much after that.'

'Oh, come on, man! They do all kinds of things today: they perform miracles.'

'Aye. Yes, they've already performed two on me. That's why I'm still here. But anyway—' Alex stopped speaking; he looked downwards and his hands became locked on his knees as he said, 'I . . . I want to make a confession.'

'A confession? Oh, Alex, I think you've come to the wrong bloke; I mean, why come to me? Have you thought about a priest? Well no, you're not a Catholic, are you?'

'No.'

'Well, what about a parson?'

'I couldn't tell the parson: I never think about them being . . . well God-like.'

At this Fred gave a laugh and said, 'Well, I'm afraid I've had little truck with the deity these many years.'

Then the banter going out of his voice, he asked softly, 'You've been up to something that you're ashamed of, Alex?'

Alex looked fully at Fred now, and he said, 'Aye, I've been up to something, Mr Beardsley, but I'm not ashamed of it. Nor am I sorry I've done it, but . . . but I felt I had to tell somebody. I know the one I should have told is Peter, but he's just got settled in again and he wouldn't be up to taking this. You see, what I've done is because I wanted him to live in peace.'

'Well, I'm sure he will.' Fred's voice was gentle now. 'He's back with the woman he loves and who loves him. I was on the phone to them only last night: they sounded as happy as Larry, so to speak.'

'I know, and that's as it should be, so I didn't want to upset him; because he's not all that strong. Anyway, you know he's had such a bashing it's going to take him a year or two to get over it, mentally as well.'

'Oh, I'm with you there. Yes, I'm with you there. But you know, he's going back into his old business of acting; or, at least, being connected with the stage. Did you know that?'

'Oh yes, yes, he told me all about it. He's very, very pleased.'

'And there's another thing,' said Fred quietly. 'Now his mother's dead he won't have her on his mind for, as long as she lived, she would have been a worry to him. She was an unpredictable woman.'

'You said it, Mr Beardsley, an unpredictable woman. But that's what I want to talk about. You

489

see, she didn't die naturally; I killed her.'

Fred actually bounced on his seat, exclaiming, 'You what?'

'As I said, Mr Beardsley, I killed her; murdered her, I suppose. It was either her or him, because she had an obsession about him. She would have done for him in some way or another. She wasn't satisfied that he had been almost hammered to death. No, no, she would never have been satisfied. She once told her daughter that she would dance on his grave, and mine.'

'What?'

'Oh yes, she told Betty that one day she would dance on our graves. She wasn't right in her head where he was concerned, nor about others, too. She was bred on hate. She came from an odd family. It's a wonder her brother Frank's not like that, an' all.'

Fred had to swallow now before he said, 'But I thought they decided that she had—' He swallowed again and Alex put in, 'Yes, committed suicide. Well, I planned it all out, every detail; but at the same time I knew after she was gone Peter would have a guilty feeling about her, so, as I thought, you being his best friend, Mr Beardsley, I'd ask you to put him straight with regard to her by giving him this letter later on.' He now put his hand inside his coat and brought out an envelope, which he handed to Fred, saying, 'There's a confession in there; I'm no hand with a pen but I've given him the outline. I . . . I'll leave it to you, Mr Beardsley, to fill him in with what to tell him. There's also a letter in there that proves that she meant to go on. I didn't come across that until I was about to leave the room, but there, on the corner of the dressing-

490

table, lying on a blotting pad, was this letter. As you see, it's addressed to Nyrene, and it was sealed and ready to go off although it hadn't a stamp on. So I read it, Mr Beardsley. It was filthy; you wouldn't believe a woman could write such stuff. If that doesn't give Peter proof that she meant to dance on his grave eventually, well, nothing will. You read it, Mr Beardsley.'

Fred lifted his hand and switched on the interior light; then he took from the brown envelope the smaller white one, opened it and read the contents. But before his eyes had covered half the page his gaze lifted sharply towards Alex who, as if in answer to something he had said, nodded his head.

By the time Fred had finished the letter his teeth were pressing into his lower lip. Slowly now, he folded the page, returned it to the envelope and put it back where it had been; and then he said two words, 'Dear God!'

'Yes, Mr Beardsley, dear God! When a thing is bad they say it's rotten, but when it gets beyond rotten it's putrid; and wouldn't you say that letter is putrid?'

Fred looked at him for a moment before he replied, 'It's hard to believe, Alex, that any woman, especially a mother, is capable of thinking such things, never mind writing them; I think she must have been insane.'

'Yes, she was, in a way, but until I found that letter it would have been hard to prove it.'

Again there was silence between them before, with a quick movement, Alex leant forward and knocked on the glove box as if he were asking for admittance, and as he did so he said, 'After I did it I didn't ask God for forgiveness, oh no, because I knew I had set a number of folk free from worry and on to a comparatively happy life. Not only Peter and Nyrene; the girls suffered, too, especially poor Florrie.'

'Oh, I can vouch for that, Alex. I know the effect the letters and the fire business had on Nurse. And she's a strong woman.'

Alex was nodding in agreement as he said, 'As for me, since we were married I have had nothing from her but disdain and being made to feel smaller than I am in every way.'

Fred too was nodding; then he asked, 'You say, Alex, you killed her, but how did you do it? Didn't she fight or anything?'

'No, I didn't give her much chance. You see, I had everything worked out; it was really easy. I've always had a key, and I left it until after midnight and made sure there was nobody about in the street. Of course, I know the house like the back of me hand. There was no light on except in the bedroom. She was funny about that. She always had thick curtains that would pull over the lace ones so nobody could look in anywhere, upstairs or down, yet she was afraid to sleep in the dark.' His voice rose as he said, 'She wasn't afraid to go out in the dark or stay out in the dark, which she must have done until sometimes two in the morning, if Florrie's nervous prattling is anything to go by, but, as I knew over all the years, the little bedside light had to be left on. She was a heavy sleeper and, being troubled with her sinuses, she slept with her mouth open. She didn't snore, but she snorted every now and again; and there she was, sound asleep and she didn't stir a muscle or an eyelid when I took the items from me pocket and laid them out round the lamp: a medicine bottle full of whitish liquid; a half-flask of whisky about a third full, there were two pill bottles with those press down screw tops, you know, to prevent children opening them but which always make a clicking sound. I'd even prepared for that: they were half-open, and I scattered what was left of one bottle round the table and a few on the floor. Then I took from me pocket one of Sally's silk headscarves. It was already folded up, and very gently I tied one end around the wrist of her hand that was hanging over the edge of the bed. I next took a thick pad from me pocket and put it on the table. Following this, I lifted the hand that was tied with the scarf gently upwards towards the other one and I just slipped the silk loop under it. When she stirred I moved her further on to her back and quickly jerked the loop tight and bound the two wrists together. Her eyes then snapped open and she was staring up into my face, and when her mouth opened to scream I rammed the pad into it. Being unable to move her arms, she brought up her knees, but I got on the bed and knelt on them.' He paused now and began to tap again on the glove box door before he went on, 'I was holding her down by the throat and I said to her quite quietly, "Mona, if you make a sound when I take this gag out of your mouth I'll mark you." And at this I slipped my hand into my coat and brought out me cut-throat razor and when I flicked the blade her whole body jerked in the bed and I said, "Mind, I'm warning you, I'll follow in the places where your last effort has marked Peter, and then I'll leave you with the razor in your hand as if you had done it. Do you understand me?" You know, Mr

Beardsley'—he turned to Fred again—'even at this stage there wasn't so much fear in her face as hate, terrible black hate; and that's how I wanted it, for if she had shown fear or had whimpered in any way I don't know whether I'd have been able to carry on, even though I had primed meself before I left the house with a double dose of pain killers, the kind, you know, that calm the mind too; and I did feel calm. Anyway, I now took up a medicine bottle in which I had stuck a cork because it's easy to pull out a cork with your teeth. Then, whipping the gag from her mouth, I stuck the bottle in, and at the first impact of the mixture in her throat she struggled like a wild beast. But I held her nose and she had to gulp for breath, and it went down. After three or four gulps of it, she stopped struggling and lay panting, and do you know what she said?' He paused, then repeated, 'D'you know what she said then?' He did not wait for a statement of any kind from Fred but went straight on. 'She spluttered, "This won't stop me; I'll haunt you from the grave," and you know what I answered? I said to her, "There'll be no need, Mona, for you to come up and haunt me, for we'll both be in hell together shortly." But d'you know something, Mr Beardsley? I don't feel that I *will* go to hell. If there's a God and he's just, I won't go to hell; I'll get a good ribbing of sorts and have to do a penance perhaps, like the Catholics; purgatory they call it; but I won't go to hell.'

He was looking down at his joined hands on his knees as he said, 'After she had taken about three parts of the medicine bottle, I knew it was enough. The sleeping tablets and the whisky alone would have knocked her off; then there was nearly a